D1161998

WITHDRAWN

FOR INFAMOUS CONDUCT

Derek Lambert

Coward-McCann, Inc. New York

FOREWORD

STUDENTS of Indian history may note that in this novel liberties have been taken with chronology. This has been done in the interests of the narrative; nevertheless I apologise to anyone whose susceptibilities are offended by such manoeuvring of events. In fact the passage of time has little effect on Mankind's problems: in India at the beginning of this century—the period in which the book opens—two of the most dangerous threats to peace were considered to be student agitation and Russian expansionism.

With the exception of such historical notabilities as Lord Curzon, all the characters are fictitious.

THE HIPPOCRATIC OATH

I WILL look upon him who shall have taught me this Art even as one of my parents. I will share my substance with him, and I will supply his necessities, if he be in need. I will regard his offspring even as my own brethren, and I will teach them this art, if they would learn it, without fee or covenant. I will impart this Art by precept, by lecture, and by every mode of teaching, not only to my own sons but to the sons of him who has taught me, and to disciples bound by covenant and oath, according to the Law of Medicine.

The regimen I adopt shall be for the benefit of my patients according to my ability and judgement, and not for their hurt or for any wrong. I will give no deadly drug to any, though it be asked of me, nor will I counsel such, and especially I will not aid a woman to procure abortion. Whatsoever house I enter, there will I go for the benefit of the sick, refraining from all wrongdoing or corruption, and especially from any act of seduction, of male or female, of bond or free. Whatsoever things I see or hear concerning the life of men in my attendance on the sick or even apart therefrom, which ought not to be noised abroad, I will keep silence thereon, counting such things to be sacred secrets.

BOOK ONE

1

THE vultures flew down to the boulders beside the Tower of Silence and perched there waiting for their meal of human flesh. They waited as patiently as well-fed humans waiting for a turkey or chicken dinner.

On top of the tower the mourners placed the naked body of the young Parsee teacher on a grill. The sacred liquid had been burned on the eternal fire, the last rites performed in the presence of a dog whose gaze would expel the corpse demons; now the last act of the funeral ceremony awaited the beaks and talons of the big, bald-headed birds. They flew lazily in the hot sky, floating like flakes of charred paper.

'They must be well fed to take their time like this,' Spenser said.

'They are,' Couldridge said. 'This is Parsee country. There's a lot of plague and cholera around at the moment and they have a funeral every day.'

'It's all so bloody primitive, isn't it. It doesn't inspire you with much hope for the future of Imperial India.'

'It's no more primitive than putting a body in a box and leaving it to decay nine feet under the ground.'

'Sorry,' Spenser said. 'I didn't know you were so touchy on the subject of funerals.'

A vulture, weighted by gluttony, staggered into the air, reached the top of the stone tower and settled heavily on its dinner. The rest of the birds followed, and below the two men on horseback fancied they could hear the tearing and gobbling of flesh; although neither admitted revulsion or nausea because both were soldiers—and one was a doctor.

'Soon only the bones will be left,' Couldridge said. 'They will drop through the grill into the quicklime below and be destroyed. Bones to the earth, flesh to the heavens.'

'Very practical,' Spenser said.

'It's a very practical religion. No time wasting—you're expected to pray while you're washing, eating and relieving yourself.'

Spenser looked speculatively at the man mounted on the bored black stallion beside him. A man of contradictions: gentle eyes in a determined brown face, hard athlete's body, soft doctor's hands holding the reins. He sensed certainty of purpose and breeding—he always despised himself for discerning breeding in people—and envied both. 'You're very knowledgeable about religion,' he said.

'I should be—my father was a missionary.'

It was not the sort of breeding that Spenser had expected. A small flame of friendliness destroyed the envy. 'You were born out here?'

'In Bombay. But I was brought up and educated in England. St Mary's Hospital not Sandhurst. I suppose you went to Sandhurst?'

Spenser nodded, grateful that he could establish an acceptable upbringing even if he could not aspire to breeding.

'And you're joining the Gurkhas.'

The hostility returned. 'You know damned well I'm joining the Gurkhas. Is there any reason why I shouldn't?'

Couldridge looked surprised. 'No reason at all. I was just thinking aloud, stating a fact.'

'If you were wondering how they came to accept me, I would remind you that I got pretty high marks at Sandhurst.' Spenser knew that academy honours did not necessarily ensure acceptance by the Gurkhas.

Couldridge said, 'I wasn't wondering anything of the sort.'

'If you must know,' Spenser said, 'I have an aunt on my

9

mother's side married to an officer who put in a good word for me.'

'I see,' Couldridge said. The vultures rose laboriously from their meal and returned to the boulders, eyes glazed by over-indulgence, hungry carrion heads incongruous on their swollen bodies. Couldridge pointed at them and said: 'They don't know it but they're all loaded with cholera bacteria now. Or perhaps they've immunised themselves by now. I don't recall having seen a vulture suffering from cholera.'

Spenser accepted the diplomatic change in subject. 'Is the cholera particularly bad round here?'

'Not as bad as it is around Calcutta. Do you know why that teacher died? Probably because he drank water from a con-taminated well which should have been purified and tried to cure himself by squatting over a pan of lime or smouldering straw. He died of dehydration so I don't think the vultures had much of a meal this time.'

'These people will never learn,' Spenser said.

Couldridge turned on him, all the gentleness erased from his face. 'They'll never learn! Nor will we ever learn. Did you know that a man named Robert Koch found the cholera microbe in 1883 and it was years before his discovery really gained recogni-tion? Did you know that he injected himself with a tubercular vaccine to convince the world about his discoveries—and was criticised for not publishing his findings through the proper channels?'

'I didn't,' Spenser said, trying to stem the wrath. 'I certainly didn't. This Robert Koch—is he something of a hero to you?'

'I suppose so.' Couldridge smiled apologetically. 'Most of us have heroes. Who is yours?'

'Kitchener,' Spenser said. 'Horatio Herbert Kitchener.'

The mourners were gone, the body was gone, only the sated vultures remained. The two men turned their horses towards the dozing maze of Bombay's suburbs, towards the plague and the cholera and the blindness, towards starvation, corruption and indolence, towards belief in gods and beasts and trees and prophets that was balm for all doubt and fear; towards tableaux of human dignity in dark corners discernible only to those who bothered to look.

Both rode well: Couldridge had been born with saddle graces, Spenser had learned them. Although both were in mufti both were obviously soldiers, and when they cantered up to a village the inhabitants got out of the way.

'I gather there was trouble here,' Spenser said. 'The usual thing —Moslem and Hindu. We had to restoré order as usual.'

'We?'

'The infantry in this case. Duke of Cornwall's I believe. About a dozen Indians were killed.'

'Putting the natives down, I believe it's called.'

'Call it what you like. I call it restoring order. As you can see order *has* been restored.'

The sky was cooling above the pale green shisham trees and the village was fading into water-colours. Parrots and monkeys meditated over the day's quarrels, oxen and buffalo slept, white dhotis fluttered among the trees, the limbs and faces of their wearers dissolving in the dusk. Old men stirred from slumber or prayer to light oil lamps in home-made shops impregnated with the smell of their wares—honey and butter, maize and sugar, dates and roseleaf jam.

Couldridge peered into dark rooms where many due to die and many dying prematurely were expending their last pulses of life. Where invalids were being treated with cures that hastened death—or reincarnation. Where children suffering from glaucoma or trachoma were retiring into dusk and night that would never brighten because their eyes were rubbed with paraffin-wicks or berries. He said: 'I think one doctor would have done more good than two platoons of infantrymen.'

'You forget you're a soldier as well as a doctor,' Spenser said. 'And in any case a doctor wouldn't have stopped them killing each other. After they'd killed a suitable number of themselves they'd have started on any Europeans living near here.'

Couldridge didn't reply. Instead he spoke softly to his horse and it broke into a trot; Spenser had to use his spurs.

Couldridge and his horse were as one, Spenser thought. Breeding often showed in a man's ability to handle a horse. But Couldridge's father had only been a missionary. 'What was your mother?' Spenser asked.

'I beg your pardon?'

'Your mother. You said your father was a missionary.'

'Ah yes. My mother was a lady of leisure. Until she met my father that is. Her leisure ended the day she set sail from Liverpool with him.'

That was it, Spenser decided. The breeding was on his mother's side. You could always tell.

'She was the daughter of a Dublin innkeeper,' Couldridge said.

The envy was again destroyed. 'Do you know what my mother was?' Spenser said.

'No idea,' Couldridge said.

'A schoolteacher in Streatham. And my father was a bank clerk.' He felt that he had made a confession.

'Good combination,' Couldridge said. 'Brains and money. Why did you become a soldier?'

'To get away from Streatham. To get away from teaching and banking.' He glanced at Couldridge jogging up and down beside him, dark hair falling over his eyes. 'Mind you, this is only between the two of us.'

'Of course. But you haven't made any fearful revelations, have you?'

'No, but I know what it can be like in the mess and it's good to have one person you can confide in. What made you join the Indian Medical Service?'

'My father wanted me to. He had tried spreading the word of God in India without much success. I think he wanted me to continue the good work in a more practical way.' He urged his horse forward again and the trotting hooves swept into a canter. 'Anyway hurry up—it's our last night in Bombay. Let's make the most of it.'

The curried scents of the village faded and the moist dusk

air streamed past their faces. Together they shared one of those rare surges of exaltation that no drink or drug can ever simulate. A single star glittered in the darkening sky and the countryside accelerated past them with twilight speed. From canter to gallop they rode into their respective futures. On his horse Spenser stormed the shanty suburbs of Bombay at the head of a column of cavalry. Beside him Couldridge galloped to the aid of the wounded and the dying.

2

SURGEON Second Lieutenant John Couldridge, just twenty-three and uncomplicated by any doubts that he was destined to emulate Koch or Pasteur in the conquest of disease, sat on the verandah of the hotel in Bombay, sipped the whisky he had brought from England, watched the moths committing suicide in the oil lamp flame and wondered when Spenser would finally assemble the courage to ask him if it was all right to sleep with Indian women. He guessed another whisky would do it and refilled Spenser's glass.

The air smelled of rain but it was an olfactory mirage. The sky was smeared with stars and in the garden the leaves of the palm trees, as straight as ships' masts, rasped wistfully in the warm sea breeze.

Couldridge rested his long legs on the balustrade and regarded Spenser through the lacework of smoke drifting from his pipe. A shy man, he thought, in danger of brutalising himself to disguise his lack of confidence. In fact most people who noted the steady gaze of his grey eyes *would* have diagnosed an element of cruelty in his character; but not Doctor Couldridge who did not judge people by the pigment of their iris or the stability of the orbicularis oculi—or so he smugly told himself. A healthy man, Doctor Couldridge diagnosed, with a tendency to nervous tension and ancillary disorders—one leg hinged on the ball of the foot jogging up and down, fingers tugging at his moustache. And a handsome man, he supposed, with a strong face belied by the small boasts and vanities of insecurity.

Spenser drained his glass of whisky and, right leg bouncing up and down, began his preamble. 'How long did you live in India?'

'Most of my life. I went back to England when I was seventeen.'

Spenser lit a cheroot and nodded. 'I was very fortunate to meet you here before going up north. Normally, of course, I would spend a couple of years with the British Army before transferring to the Indian Army. But apparently there's an emergency on and they're very short of officers up there. You'll be able to tell me a lot of things I should know. I've done my best with books but you can still make a fool of yourself by quoting them.'

Couldridge, who had slept with an Indian girl the previous evening, smiled inside himself and waited. In the garden the frogs added bass to the tenor chorus of the cicadas.

Spenser said: 'I'm not really too sure about a lot of things. Just how friendly I should be with Indians, for instance.'

'You seemed pretty knowledgeable about Moslem and Hindu antagonism in the village this afternoon.'

'Not really. It was probably how I thought I was expected to speak. I'm hoping you'll be able to help me a bit. In confidence of course.'

'The best thing is to treat them like human beings.'

'Ah yes.' The knee bounced a little quicker. 'But what about the other officers? How do they view friendship with Indians?'

'I don't know,' Couldridge said. 'I've never been up to the North West Frontier.'

Spenser approached from another direction. 'I suppose being a son of a missionary you were pretty friendly with the Indians

14

when you lived here.'

'Naturally. But we lived in a village and there wasn't a great social life. Weddings, fairs, festivals and the occasional wrestling match. We were accepted because the people sensed my father's sincerity. But he didn't do any good. They wanted food and he gave them Bibles. I suppose it was witnessing the futility of what he was doing that made me a bit of a rebel. When I was seventeen I used to come into Bombay to enjoy myself.'

'You had girl friends here?'

Couldridge laughed. 'I can't stand it any longer,' he said. 'Come on. Yours is called Padma. It means lotus.'

The knee stopped bouncing. 'You're very quick to jump to conclusions.'

'I'm a doctor and I happen to know an available cure for frustration. And don't start fretting about whether it's right and proper or whether or not you'll catch the pox. They're both very discreet and quite clean. But promise me one thing— don't burden me with your shame afterwards.'

Spenser stood up and squashed his cheroot with a decisive gesture. 'It's strange but you can't really believe that a doctor of medicine has the same carnal desires as other men.'

'You should have been at St Mary's,' Couldridge said.

Doctor and soldier left the hotel together, friendship burgeoning in the common territory of healthy lust, and walked through the dark streets smelling of jasmine, spice and sewage. They saw no women, only men in phantom white haunting the shadows and sleeping in the gutters.

Couldridge said: 'Have you ever seen an Indian brothel?'

'No,' Spenser said. 'I haven't seen any brothels.'

'Want to go to one?'

'Not particularly.'

'Are you sure?'

'I don't mind seeing one.'

'I'll show you one if you like. But for God's sake don't sample the wares. The cure would be very painful.'

They turned off a side street where the jasmine and spice

15

conceded victory to the sewage and the rooftops leaned towards each other leaving a narrow canal of sky afloat with stars. Couldridge stopped outside a crouching building on which cracked plaster hung like scales. A man with no legs waddled up, his pocked face starting with sweat from the effort. 'You like girls?' he asked. 'All very pretty. All pink and clean inside like Queen Victoria.'

'You'd better watch your tongue,' Spenser said.

'I shouldn't let it worry you,' Couldridge said. 'After all he is paying the Queen a compliment and he is one of her subjects and in any case I don't think Her Majesty would object very much.'

Inside the girls sat in a dim hall flanked by a couple of morose potted palms. They were either very undernourished with flaccid breasts showing through grubby saris, or fat and sullen. Some had glass beads in their ears; only their hair was beautiful, polished and centre-parted above their resentful eyes. There were six cubicles behind them, each equipped with a mattress, a soiled towel and a bowl of water.

'What do you think?' Couldridge asked.

'I can't make out how any man ever goes with them,' Spenser said. He hesitated. 'Do white men come here?'

'I'm bloody sure they do, judging by the number of cases of syphilis and gonorrhoea among the white population.'

'They must be pretty desperate.'

'So must these girls,' Couldridge said. He surveyed the pitiful enticement to fornication but instead of disgust experienced once again the stirring of a desire to help the great tormented country hanging helplessly from the Asian continent, a desire bequeathed to him by his father—a desire to find some balm for its sores. Sores such as this where the bacteria of syphilis, gonorrhoea, typhoid, cholera and the plague gambolled among the spent organisms of bought love.

A girl of about fifteen came out from one of the cubicles and clutched at his arm. 'You come with me,' she said. 'I am going to make you very happy.' He disengaged her hand and looked into her eyes. The conjunctiva was inflamed and already dis-

16

figured with tiny nodules like grains of sago. He said to Spenser:
'She'll be blind soon.'

'Good God,' Spenser said. 'Why? What's the matter with
her?'

'Trachoma. Soon her eyes will be permanently scarred.'

'Can't you do anything?'

'What can I do? One girl. I can't treat her in one evening and
she won't go to a doctor even if I tell her to. In fact the establishment here probably likes a few blind whores—they aren't put off
by some of their more disgusting-looking customers.'

'Can't you give her anything for her eyes?'

Couldridge shrugged. 'I haven't anything with me.' He pointed
at the girl's eyes. 'Are you having those treated?' She shook her
head in astonishment. 'If I gave you some ointment for your
eyes would you use it?'

The man with no legs became agitated. 'Sahib,' he said. 'Please
if you are liking the girl take her to one of the cubicles. Do not
bother too very much about her eyes.'

'Shut up,' Couldridge said.

'Please, sahib. I am telling you she is a very good girl. Very
clean.'

The girl tried to lead him to a cubicle. He repeated the question. 'Would you use the ointment?'

She shook her head. 'I do not want medicine. I want you to
make the love. Jig-a-jig.'

Couldridge turned to Spenser. 'It's hopeless. In any case there
are probably a dozen people going blind in this street. Did you
know that there are more than two million blind people in
India? I don't want to cure one girl—I want to cure them all.
I want to educate them. There's one type of blindness in children, you know, that can be cured with a diet of fruit and fresh
vegetables. And I want to help stamp out the quackery that
sends many of them blind. I once went to the clinic of a medical
officer called Colonel Wright in Madras. He had a picture on his
wall of a father and his four children. All blind because some
fake healer had got at them.'

'And I suppose you also want to prevent cholera and typhoid and dysentry and smallpox and yellow fever.'

'That's the trouble,' Couldridge said. 'I want to do everything.'

As they left the brothel the man with no legs was shouting at the girl and she was gazing down at his head, which only came as high as her belly, and rubbing her pink eyes.

'I think I've lost my appetite a bit,' Spenser said.

'Nonsense,' Couldridge said, quickening his long stride. 'And even if you have it will return when you see the girls. I've known mine since I was seventeen. She was only about twelve then. Her name is Usha—it means dawn. She's very gentle and very loving.'

Perhaps a little too loving, he thought. A love that approached adoration, a love that was too easily wounded. He was fond of her, loved her a little perhaps, but he knew he would never marry her.

'Are they prostitutes?'

'That's an unpleasant word. But they would probably be agreeable to living with you for as long as you wanted them. You'd have to support them and then when you decided that the time had come to marry a decent white girl from Streatham you'd have to pay them off. It's an accepted system and the Army doesn't mind as long as it doesn't become involved. Even officers and gentlemen have lusts of the flesh. And these girls are also damn good cooks.'

Spenser pulled at his moustache. 'Do you propose to marry a decent white girl one day?'

'I couldn't give a damn whether she's white or brown or black. But I'd have to love her. And I don't love Usha enough to marry her.'

They were in a wider street now where beggars prayed and pleaded in the light from stalls selling samosas, betal nuts, spices and dried fish. Beggars without arms or legs or both, beggars with cloudy eyes or no eyes at all, beggars with sores and scars, beggars with nostrils but no noses.

'And you love India?' Spenser said.

'Difficult to explain, isn't it. But you've got to smell the smoke from the charcoal burners, listen to a thousand voices talking at once, look at the colours, feel the pulse of the place, sense its great ant-heap vastness. And it's all our bloody responsibility. Yours as much as mine. You're the soldier. One day you might even become a general and have the lives of hundreds of thousands of these people in your hands. If you don't think you can love India then you might as well leave on the next boat.' He felt his anger mounting and gave a rupee to a startled beggar sitting on atrophied legs. 'Go back to Streatham or wherever it was you came from. Marry the vicar's daughter and take the dog to do its business on the common every evening.'

'Steady on,' Spenser said. 'Give me a chance. I've only just got here.'

'All right,' Couldridge said. 'But don't mock it.' His temper faded. 'Do you know I didn't realise I was so attached to the place until just now.' He turned down an alley and knocked at a thick, studded door. 'We're here. I'll introduce you and leave you to get on with it.'

And when Spenser had left them to get on with it Couldridge felt his girl's cool skin and silken triangle of hair and wondered, as he had wondered before, how a doctor whose material was the human body, who saw female nudity every day, could find pleasure in the body of a naked woman. But, unlike many other men, Couldridge had to have affection or tenderness for a woman before he could make love to her; otherwise his physician's mind appraised her body and quenched passion.

They had finished making love and she lay in his arms searching his face by the light of a candle. His mind had left their love-making: hers, he knew, still dwelled there, wondering how much it had meant to him, how much longer it would continue. 'My John,' she said. 'Do you love me?'

It was the moment he feared because he was ashamed. 'Yes,' he said because you could not say no or even qualify the answer. But soon he would have to tell her and pay her money and depart. Sometimes he told himself that he could marry her and that she would make him a better wife than any memsahib; but he knew that he lied. And after he had admitted the lie he always told himself that it was not because she was Indian—and wondered if he was lying to himself again.

'Because I love you, my John. I always will.'

Guilt made him restless. He kissed her mouth to make her stop. Stroked her breasts, the nipples soft after the passion. And while he kissed her he continued to lie to himself: her words had no depth, she slept with other men, when he was gone she would recover swiftly.

A breeze sneaked through the half-open window, ruffled the mosquito net and sent the light from the candle leaping round the walls. His surgeon's fingers wandered across belly and thigh, not clinically but with the wonderment he always felt when he touched the human body. 'You know I have to go tomorrow,' he said.

'I know.' He could feel her trust and acceptance. He sometimes wished that she would show anger. She smelled of lemon and cinnamon and her body was clean and fragile. 'But you will come back.'

'I'll come back,' he said. 'But not for some time.'

'I will wait,' she said.

A part of him hoped that when he returned he would find that she had been unfaithful to him because the affair could then be ended brusquely and commercially. He held her close, feeling the resurgence of the affection that he sometimes mistook for love. He made love to her again and she accepted him eagerly and passionately. A mosquito whined viciously outside the white muslin and a wandering moth scorched its wings in the candle flame and fell to the ground.

'I wish you would say that you loved me,' she said.

'I just did.'

'But not the words. Say the words, my John.'

Perhaps this was the moment to tell the truth. But John

20

Couldridge, soldier, doctor and crusader, knew that he lacked the courage. 'I love you,' he said.

'Thank you,' she said. 'They are beautiful words to hear.' Her voice was sad.

'You don't believe them?'

'No,' she said. 'I don't believe them. But I believe that you are fond of me. Perhaps that is enough.'

'I'll come back,' he said.

'I know you will,' she said.

The smell of lemon and cinnamon lingered with him as he walked back to the hotel with Spenser. Spenser said: 'You're very quiet.'

He wants to tell me how he got on, Couldridge thought. He said: 'How did you get on?'

'A beautiful girl,' Spenser said. 'I'm very grateful to you.'

'Did she say she loved you?'

'No. Why? I was only with her for a couple of hours.'

'They often say it without meaning it.'

Spenser looked at him shrewdly. 'But not in your case?'

'Not in my case.'

'You sound as if you're in a bit of a fix. Surely you can get out of it easily enough. After all she's only . . .'

'Only an Indian, Spenser?'

Spenser shrugged. 'I'm not going to have a fight with you.'

'You're probably right,' Couldridge said. 'She's only an Indian. Poor little bitch.' They passed the sentry-straight palms, their footsteps quietening the chorus of frogs and cicadas. 'It's a funny thing, Spenser, I feel I should dislike you. But I don't— I rather like you. Perhaps it's because you're so bloody vulnerable.'

Spenser said, 'We seem to have been thrown together. We'll see who's vulnerable.'

3

THE first thing Couldridge saw when he awoke at Jinjabad was the range of mountains crystallised on the horizon, white and crumpled and remote. The next thing he saw was the expressionless face of his Gurkha batman, Bhawansing Rai.

Bhawansing Rai was a man of fifty-five who had seen much service. He had killed many Pathans in his time and bore the scars on his stubby body of the many attempts the Pathans had made to kill him. Now he was in semi-retirement.

Couldridge had once read that Gurkhas were merry people: in his servant he had found the exception. Bhawansing was not sulky or hostile, nor was he insubordinate or impudent: Couldridge found it difficult to label his character but settled for enigmatic—or stupid when he was sufficiently angered by his incompetence. The incompetence, too, was an elusive phenomenon, neither deliberate nor the result of misunderstanding: it just happened.

In most aspects Bhawansing was a true Gurkha. He was loyal but he wasn't servile, he didn't steal but he liked to gamble and drink rum. He was just over five feet high with slanting brown eyes, a mandarin moustache and a forehead that barely managed to separate his hair from his eyebrows. He only had nine fingers and with a lot of grunting and gesticulating tried to show Couldridge how he had lost the tenth. Couldridge was left with the impression that he had eaten it, but it was later explained to him by another officer that the finger had been partially severed during a hand-to-hand fight with a Pathan. Bhawansing had strangled the Pathan, bitten through the hanging finger and brought it back to base to be replaced by the medical officer. But he had overestimated modern surgery.

While Bhawansing Rai filled the zinc tub with boiling water Couldridge inspected his new home. It was brown and bare and it smelled of sandalwood. He opened the window. The mountain air prickled in his nose and he heard the distant bellow of a havildar drilling his men. Excitement expanded inside him.

His quarters were two rooms—the bedroom and a bathroom fitted with a thunderbox. On the wall above the bed hung a picture of Queen Victoria and Prince Albert in their youth, on a bookshelf above a mahogany chest of drawers the Collected Works of William Shakespeare and Queen's Regulations leaned against each other forming a small tent.

Bhawansing Rai grunted and pointed at the steaming water. Couldridge tried to indicate that his skin was not made of asbestos; Bhawansing grunted monotonously and uncomprehendingly. Finally Couldridge dismissed him with a gesture that not even Bhawansing Rai could fail to understand.

After the bath which withered his skin Couldridge shaved with the bone-handled razor that his father had given him and thought about his parents. Every day in their cottage beside the Thames at Sonning they would, he knew, pray for him. And his father would pray, that his son would succeed in helping India where he had failed; that perhaps medicine would clear the way for the word of God among the turmoil of India's conflicting beliefs.

Couldridge, staring at his own face as the razor scythed his bristles on his chin, had no doubt that he would be able to help heal India's sores. But he didn't see himself as a medical missionary. India had changed little in the past hundred years and was unlikely to change much in the ensuing century. Political agitation was mounting, particularly in Bengal; but political reform, even ultimate self-determination, would hardly change the way of life of India's millions. Their existence was rooted in religion not politics and he saw no reason why they should substitute Christianity for religions just as devout and demanding. If the Parsee was committed to helping the good and fighting the wicked why should the missionary try to convert him to similar beliefs? Was the Hindu, seeking salvation from the vale of tears and revering a cow or a monkey or a squirrel, any different from a Christian hoping to be admitted through the gates of heaven and revering bread and wine? Could the prayers of Christianity be more studiously and devoutly uttered than the incantations of the Moslems praying towards Mecca five times a day? Couldridge believed in the philosophy of the Hindu God Krishna, 'Whatever God a man worships, it is I who answer the prayer.' That, he thought, should be the philosophy of all religions. He imagined his father's reactions and nicked his chin with the razor.

But his thoughts raced on, stimulated by the mountain air, by the excitement of arrival. He stared into his eyes in the shaving mirror and saw the healthy cornea, the blue fibres of the iris. He would concentrate on trying to prevent blindness, he decided. Then he remembered the latest plague figures he had heard—in one month 451,892 had died of the disease that had once been called The Black Death; and he remembered how fourteen people had died from tetanus after being treated with the newly-discovered vaccine for the plague. There were ample opportunities there for research. And in combatting the comma-shaped cholera bacteria discovered by Robert Koch.

Still heady with the triumphs that lay ahead of him Surgeon Second Lieutenant John Couldridge put on his uniform and walked across the balding grass to meet a man who could deflate youthful ebullience as savagely as he lanced carbuncles.

Captain Randolph Buckingham was an indifferent doctor astute enough to realise that, although he would find it difficult to survive professionally in civilian life, he could prosper in the Army. He deserted Gray's Anatomy for the Queen's Regulations, cultivated sycophancy in the presence of his medical superiors and arrogance among laymen below the rank of major. When, on the orders of the colonel, a Pathan tribesman had been kicked in the testicles until he died in retaliation for atrocities perpetrated on Gurkha soldiers, Captain Buckingham readily agreed that the Pathan had died from injuries sustained resisting capture. He patiently treated the colonel's wife for a dozen non-existent maladies when he knew, even with his limited knowledge, that she was merely suffering from frustration accompanying the menopause.

In the surgery in the sick quarters he listened with distaste to Couldridge's theories on opthalmology, sterilisation, water purification and vaccination.

Finally he said: 'That's all very well, Couldridge, but do you know how to operate on piles?'

Couldridge looked at the sharp sandy face with surprise. 'I should have thought anyone could do that.'

'The chaps up here seem to suffer from them a lot. I can't think why. They get enough exercise and God knows they drink enough. It must be the food, I suppose. Too many lentils.' He poured himself a glass of water. 'I shouldn't worry too much about following in Koch's footsteps up here. The main vaccines you'll need are quinine, castor oil and aspirin. You'll have to treat quite a lot of bad feet, too.'

'Don't you treat many wounds?'

'Oh wounds, certainly. The occasional amputation, too. But they're not often very successful. In fact I took a leg off a few weeks ago but the poor chap died from gangrene.'

Couldridge said: 'The best thing is to plug the flaps with gauze soaked in one in four thousand perchloride of mercury and sew the flaps over the plug. If that doesn't work properly then irrigate the wound continuously with sodium hypochlorite. You can make that by adding carbonate of soda to a saturated solution of bleaching powder.'

'Is that so? How very interesting.' Buckingham picked up the swagger stick lying beside his stethoscope. 'How very, very interesting.'

Couldridge smiled uncertainly, aware that he had exceeded the bounds of communication permitted between captain and subaltern. 'That's the way I would do it, anyway. I expect you have a better method.'

'I have some advice for you,' Buckingham said. 'First of all I would remind you that you are in the I.M.S. not at Edinburgh University experimenting with cadavers. In this context I would remind you that I am your superior officer and that shortly I shall be transferred with the rank of major to Calcutta. From there I shall follow your career with interest.' He tossed back the water as if it were an unpleasant medicine.

'I'm sorry,' Couldridge said.

'And I should be grateful if you would recognise my rank by calling me sir. We may be doctors but we must recognise military etiquette.'

'I'm sorry, sir,' Couldridge said.

'Secondly a word of advice about your medical aspirations. You can't try and embrace every specialised subject. That's what the word specialised means—you concentrate on one aspect of medicine, no more.'

'You mean I shouldn't treat both a middle ear disorder and say interstitial keratitis?'

Buckingham looked momentarily vague and intuitively Couldridge knew that he was having difficulty identifying the condition of the eye caused by hereditary syphilis. 'Just do your job up here,' Buckingham said. 'If it's something too big for you or something you don't understand send it down to a specialist.'

Couldridge said maliciously: 'Then if it were a case of interstitial keratitis I should dispatch the patient to a specialist?'

Buckingham's freckled hands tightened around the swagger stick. 'Don't argue with me,' he said. 'I'm just warning you for your own good. Don't meddle in too many fields. It just isn't done.' The last four words emerged almost as a hiss.

Couldridge considered the information with alarm. It had never occurred to him that the medical profession might not approve of one man undertaking too many responsibilities. But if that man succeeded in more than one line of research then surely there could be no reproach?

'I believe you had a pretty good record at St Mary's,' Buckingham said.

'Not bad.'

'Not bad what?'

'Not bad, sir.'

Buckingham took some papers from his drawer. 'I see that at St Mary's you won the annual prize as a demonstrator of physiology among other things.'

Couldridge nodded.

'Then now is the time to forget everything you've learned,' Buckingham said, converting all the awareness of his own mediocrity into venom.

'Forget all I've learned?'

'You've got to understand men here. You've got to be able to spot the malingerer and the coward. You've got to be able to practice medicine at its most basic level because there's nothing more basic than a soldier's complaints. If he's malingering give him enough Number Nine to keep him on the thunder-box for a week, if he's caught a dose of clap give him the treatment he'll never forget.'

Couldridge's contempt for Buckingham began to harden into hatred because there was no person he detested more than the doctor who belittled or vulgarised his own profession. 'Surely none of this precludes research?'

'You're an Army doctor. You're here to look after the health of soldiers. You stick to that. And to put you on the right footing you can take sick parade tomorrow. I'll see you in the mess later.' He stood up and extended his hand. 'Don't forget what I've told you. I wouldn't like to see you making a fool of yourself.'

For the rest of the day Couldridge pondered on Buckingham's advice. While he arranged his books, while he wandered around the brown buildings half way up the mountains returning the salutes of small muscular men in cardboard-stiff shorts, while he tried out his primitive Gurkhali on Bhawansing Rai who declined to understand a single word, while he gazed at the aloof white crests of the peaks separating India from Central Asia.

In the mess after dinner Couldridge stood awkwardly against the mantelpiece beside the spitting fire waiting for someone to talk to him. He was alone in a forest of dark green mess jackets, light green trousers and stiff white shirts; he was glad when Spenser came up to him holding a glass of whisky and soda.

Spenser said: 'How did the first day go?' His cheeks were slightly flushed from the food and the whisky and the heat from the flaming logs.

'Not too bad,' Couldridge said. 'I had to endure some unsolicited advice though.'

'I suspect you regard any advice as unsolicited.'

'You suspect wrongly.' Couldridge mustered the courage to send a steward for a whisky.

'I can't wait to get away from all this,' Spenser said.

'What the devil are you talking about? We've only just arrived.'

'I want to get up there—' Spenser pointed vaguely through the thin silk curtains—'and see a bit of action.'

'Then so you shall.' The man who spoke was six foot four inches tall with a lean face, faded eyes, a small tough moustache, hair surprisingly long, and a mouth that could be described as cruel or sensitive—it depended on how you had been treated by Colonel Richard Hatherley. Certainly the Pathan who had been kicked in the testicles until he died on Colonel Hatherley's orders would not have noted the sensitivity.

Spenser and Couldridge stiffened to attention.

'Relax,' Colonel Hatherley said. 'Steward—three more whiskies with soda.' The faded eyes appraised the two new members of the mess. 'So you want to see some action.'

Spenser took the initiative. 'Yes sir, if it's possible.'

'It's possible all right. The question is whether you are ready for it.'

Couldridge noted the broken capillaries beneath the tanned

skin on his cheeks and diagnosed too much alcohol.

The colonel said: 'And you Couldridge. Do you want to see some action? Tend the wounds, perhaps, of some poor Pathans captured in the act of disembowelling some of our troops?'

'I don't mind going, sir. As a doctor I would treat any wounded man.'

'Quite right, Couldridge. Very commendable. You have heard, I suppose, of the fate of one of the Pathans we captured?'

'Yes, sir.'

'Then I think you should see some action with Spenser here. I think it would do you good to see how the Pathans treat some of our men.' His voice was thin and dreamy. 'Do you know for instance how their women kill prisoners?'

Couldridge shook his head.

'They peg them down and then urinate into their mouths until they drown.'

Couldridge sucked at his whisky: it seemed the best thing to do in the circumstances.

Spenser said: 'How bloody disgusting.'

'It is disgusting. People living their cloistered lives in Britain will never know just how disgusting it is.' He took another whisky and soda from a silver tray held by a steward with a peeled-banana grin on his face. 'But although you might find it difficult to believe I have a lot of respect for the Pathans. They're very brave men. Not brave perhaps—they just don't understand fear.'

'Can we have a shot at them?' Spenser said.

The faded eyes surveyed Spenser and placed him in a file from which he would find it hard to escape. 'Certainly you can have a shot at them. Our help is needed up near the Khyber. I'm sending a detachment to Peshawar in the morning. You can go along with them if you like.'

Spenser said: 'That would be wonderful, sir.'

The colonel turned to Couldridge, filed him away and said: 'And you, Couldridge?'

'Of course, sir. But Captain Buckingham has asked me to take sick parade in the morning.'

'Plenty of time for that. You won't be leaving until eight. And when you get to Peshawar you can visit the Mission Hospital there. Plenty of evidence there of our friend the Pathan. A few women with their noses cut off by jealous husbands, a few men with their arms hacked off in blood feuds. They tell the story there of a young Pathan who qualified for a reward for killing an old brigand. He informed the authorities that he didn't deserve the reward because the job was too easy because he knew the brigand's ways. The brigand, it turned out, was his father.'

Firelight flitted among the silver trophies in the glass showcase, a tiger's head on the wall snarled at them with impotent, glassy-eyed rage. The colonel discussed the endless warfare of the hills and the fears in Whitehall of Russian incursion into Afghanistan; he talked bitterly of the ignorance of the British people about their most populous possession; he talked about Kitchener's plans for reorganising the Army.

He drank more whisky and said to Couldridge: 'I suppose you as a doctor think I am a bloodthirsty man.'

'I hadn't really thought about it, sir,' Couldridge lied.

'I don't like killing, Couldridge. I only like fighting for what I think is right.' He stared into the fire as if searching for some lost idea among the white crumbling ashes. Couldridge and Spenser seemed to have been dismissed.

'I think I'll turn in now if you don't mind, sir,' Couldridge said.

The colonel waved them away and continued gazing into the fire, head slightly bowed, back parade-ground stiff.

'So tomorrow we die,' Spenser said as they walked back to their quarters beneath the thick stars.

'Thanks to you,' Couldridge said.

'Don't you want to go?'

'Don't worry—I'll be there to dress your wounds.'

'And I'll be there to shoot your attackers when you get ambushed.'

'It's a deal,' Couldridge said.

4

DURING the next three days John Couldridge learned about the essences of the life of an Army doctor in the hill country: he saw fighting and he treated boils.

The first case he treated was a boil swelling tautly in a thick brown neck. 'The knife please, doctor,' said the boil's owner.

Couldridge shook his head. 'It's not ready yet.'

'Captain Buckingham always uses the knife, sir.'

'I'm not Captain Buckingham.'

The smile narrowed a little. 'But I want it cut away, sir. If you are not cutting it out, sir, I would like to leave.'

'If in doubt cut it out?'

'Sir?'

'I'm not cutting it and you're not leaving without having it treated. And I don't give a damn what Captain Buckingham would have done.'

Couldridge dispatched his first case to the treatment room next door with a prescription for a kaolin poultice.

The boil was followed by a sore throat, a mild dysentery, an ingrowing toenail, an ear full of wax and a bullet wound rapidly healing in a muscular thigh.

Couldridge's interest was aroused by a rifleman with inflamed eyes complaining of head pains and vomiting. Couldridge immediately thought of glaucoma. The pain was supposed to be the most agonising known to man; the rifleman was not whimpering with agony—but Gurkhas were famed for their courage. He recalled that, with an early diagnosis, the fluid pressure within the eye could sometimes be relieved. And there were the symptoms—inflamed conjunctiva, pupils semi-dilated, acute pain in the early morning. Although it was true that the cornea was not steamy.

'Where exactly is the pain?' he asked.

The rifleman pointed vaguely at his forehead. Couldridge recalled a phrase from his text books—'so ill the patient cannot localise the pain.'

Buckingham entered without knocking. 'How's it going?' he asked.

'Fine,' Couldridge said. 'This may be an interesting case.'

Buckingham looked at the rifleman sitting mournfully on a chair. 'Not you again,' he said.

The patient nodded like an old lag trying to humour a judge.

'What the devil's interesting about this man?' Buckingham asked.

Couldridge sensed humiliation. 'Nothing in particular,' he said.

'Come now. I find the most persistent malingerer in the battalion sitting in my surgery being treated like a general.'

'I thought he might be suffering from an eye disease.'

'Not interstitial keratitis again?'

'No, sir.' Couldridge wondered if he had looked it up since the previous day. 'I thought it just might be glaucoma.'

'You mean you think this man's going blind?'

'I thought it possible, sir.'

'I suggest you smell his breath,' Buckingham said.

Couldridge leaned near enough to smell the sickly staleness on the Gurkha's breath.

Buckingham said: 'That's rum. This man isn't going blind. But he was blind. Last night. Blind drunk. Headache, vomiting, bloodshot eyes. It might mean glaucoma to you but it means a hangover to me.' His freckles danced with triumph and he gripped his swagger stick with both hands. 'How are you going to treat him? Send him off to see a specialist?'

Couldridge looked at the patient, now philosophically awaiting the judge's verdict. 'I think I may have made a mistake,
sir.'

'You're too bloody right you've made a mistake. Here, give
me that pad.' He scrawled a prescription on it with cultivated
illegibility. 'That's what he needs. A damn great dose of it.'
Buckingham waited for Couldridge to ask him what it was but
Couldridge didn't oblige. 'Don't you want to know what it was?'

'Castor oil I expect, sir.'

Buckingham looked annoyed. 'As a matter of fact it is. How
did you know?'

'I guessed, sir,' Couldridge said. A small glow of pleasure
warmed his dejection.

The first officer to enter the surgery was Colonel Hatherley.
'Two doctors today,' he said. 'I think I can dispense with one.
I only want some pills.'

Buckingham said: 'You'd better wait in the treatment room,
Couldridge.'

Colonel Hatherley sat down, crisp and polished and martial
except for his long hair which gave him the air of a retired
pirate. 'No, you stay, Couldridge. It's you I shall be coming to
in the future. I might as well start now.' He waved his hand at
Buckingham. 'You may go, Buckingham.'

The pleasure swelled and obliterated Couldridge's humiliation. He sat and waited for the colonel to confide in him.

'How old are you?' Colonel Hatherley asked.

'Twenty-three, sir.'

'I'm fifty-five. It's a strange position when a commanding
officer has to consult a doctor who is also a young whipper-
snapper of a subaltern serving under him. I'm not sure that
I like it very much.'

'No, sir. I see what you mean.'

'An odd aspect of discipline. How can you issue an order to
a man who is treating you for varicose veins?'

Couldridge looked speculatively at Hatherley and dismissed

33

the possibility of varicose veins. Spinal trouble, perhaps, disguised by the stiffness of his posture, a touch of arthritis proudly concealed, an old wound or a pellet of lead trying to work its way to the surface. Or even a hangover.

Colonel Hatherley said: 'My complaint is not a physical one.'

Panic fluttered inside Couldridge. 'I see, sir,' he said.

'You will appreciate how repugnant it is for me to have to confide in you. You will also remember that you are my doctor and as such are bound by the Hippocratic Oath. "I will keep silence thereon" I believe it says.'

'I am aware of the wording of the Hippocratic Oath,' Couldridge said—doctor now instead of junior officer.

'If I find that you have broken the confidence of doctor and patient in any way then by God you'll pay for it.'

'What can I do for you, Colonel Hatherley?' Couldridge said.

'Just give me my sedatives. You'll see the ones that Buckingham used to give me if you look in my file. If I've been melodramatic I apologise. But you will read my medical file and I had to emphasise the need for discretion.'

Couldridge glanced at the file. '. . . occasional irrational outbursts which have a tendency to culminate in violence.'

Couldridge looked into the faded eyes of his commanding officer whom he now knew should not be commanding anyone.

Hatherley said: 'If you are wondering why Buckingham never took this any further I will remind you of what I have just said. He was my doctor just as you are. Now perhaps you personally will get the tablets—I don't wish to have the orderly involved in this.'

Couldridge handed him the pills.

5

THE map described the area as 'stony waste'. Spenser loved maps. But sometimes, he thought, as he sipped the grey tea that tasted of wood-smoke and buffalo milk, the cartographers were completely devoid of imagination.

Ahead lay the entrance to the Khyber Pass. Behind lay Jamrud Fort built by the Sikhs in 1835-49: the Sikhs whose cruelty had shocked even the Pathans. There were the grey peaks of Tartara, the Bazar and Bara hills, and beyond the snows of Safed Koh, the White Mountain. Beyond the entrance to the Pass, along a stretch of road built by a Colonel Mackeson who was murdered for his pains, stood the fort of Shagai. At Shagai, from the time of Alexander the Great, invading armies had paused for their first glimpse of the great breast of land they had come to rule or plunder.

Spenser sipped, without tasting, the greasy liquid cooling in his mug and stared in what he imagined was the direction of the Pass. There, before the British had hacked a road during the second Afghan War, a single camel track had joined India to the trade route from the East so that jewels and spices and carpets joined the flow of silks and porcelains to Mediterranean ports and Byzantium markets. There a stream, reputed to contain fish, issued from hidden springs and vanished after a few hundred yards.

Further along the Pass, just before the Pathan village of Zintara, stood a Buddhist stupa where the art forms of Buddha were thought to have originated. Spenser's mind wandered along the Pass to Landi Kotal and stopped because he remembered that they had called the streets there by London names—Pall Mall, Whitehall, the Strand, Piccadilly. His thoughts vaulted continents and alighted in Streatham.

Potted plants and piano lessons. His mother smelling of Eau de Cologne, telling him to say 'Good Day' and never 'Hallo', and showing him letters from his aunt in India who had married so well. The stamps and the postmarks on the letters, and the stories of tiger-hunts and duck-shoots penned incongruously in prim mauve script. Always, it seemed, his mother talking while his father earned money and played bowls. Then the scholarships, the lack of money and clothes, the humiliating letter to the husband of the aunt who had married so well.

Spenser looked warily around him and wondered if any of them knew. Couldridge knew but he felt that he could trust Couldridge. You had to trust doctors.

Beside him two Gurkhas supervised by a naik were pegging down the tent which he was to share with Couldridge. Sparks like red maggots from the fire chased each other into the darkening sky, the White Mountain retired and black ink filled the other crests of the range. The air smelled of smoke, the damp of dusk, canvas and roasting meat. In Streatham you could always hear a piano tinkling and smell beef broth simmering at mealtimes.

John Couldridge, grandson of a Dublin innkeeper, joined him. Spenser put away his map and said: 'Do you know it dismissed all this as "a stony waste"?'

'It doesn't seem quite adequate.'

'It's completely inadequate.' He began to recite his knowledge of geography and military conquest.

Couldridge stretched out his legs and rested his head on a pack. 'I don't give a damn about how many times we've beaten up the natives. I'm just wondering how they've purified this water we're drinking.'

'Boiled it, of course. That seems pretty elementary.'

'Provided it was really brought to boiling point. If not we all stand a good chance of catching cholera or typhoid.'

'Let's hope it's been properly boiled then. It's the only way, isn't it?'

'Not really. I was reading a paper in the *Journal of Public*

Health the other day by a young doctor called Nesfield. He seems to have found a way of sterilising water with chlorine. He reckoned that he could kill all typhoid bacilli in one minute flat.'

'I wouldn't fancy drinking water that tasted of chlorine.'

'You wouldn't have to. After the bacteria have been killed the water can be dechlorinated and made tastless with sodium thiosulphate.'

'You could be talking in Gurkhali as far as I'm concerned.'

Couldridge lit his pipe. 'It's not the discovery, right or wrong, that intrigues me. It's the drive and ingenuity of the man who's made it. And a young man, too. Do you know what my first sick parade consisted of?'

Spenser, who wasn't very interested, shook his head.

'A couple of boils, a clogged-up ear and a hangover.' And, he nearly added, a paranoic colonel. 'I didn't expect to find much medical equipment up here. But I did think I'd find the diseases for research.'

'If the diseases aren't here then you can't be expected to cure them,' Spenser said.

'That's not the point.'

'After all it was only your first sick parade. God knows what lovely cases of leprosy and blackwater fever are lying in wait for you.'

'If they ever did I should imagine Buckingham's killed them off by now.' He added: 'No, I shouldn't have said that.'

'It's all in confidence,' Spenser said. 'Remember?'

'Everything anyone says seems to be in confidence.'

They ate meat from wooden skewers and drank more grey tea. The air chilled. The naik sitting on the other side of the fire with his men poured rum into his tea and produced a set of dice as yellow as old teeth.

'Come on,' Couldridge said. 'Let's get in the tent or I'll be treating myself for frostbite.'

They lay on their stomachs staring into the red caverns of the fire.

37

After a while Couldridge said: 'We seem to be stuck with each other.'

Spenser said softly: 'Do you mind?'

'I don't mind. I suppose it was written. I'm here to equate the number of people you kill with the number I cure.'

'I'm not a professional killer. I've never killed anyone in my life.'

'You're a professional soldier. And a good one I should imagine. Doesn't the thought of the number of men you are going to kill or order to be killed frighten you?'

Spenser paused before answering. He had thought about killing before. He wasn't sure. He tried to delegate responsibility to the Army as a whole; but then there hadn't really been any need for him to join the Army. 'I'll kill when necessary,' he said. 'When it's a case of saving my own men's lives.'

'Never just for the hell of it? Never to teach the natives a lesson? Give them a good hiding and all that?'

'Never for the hell of it,' Spenser said. 'And only to teach them a lesson, as you put it, if I'm ordered to. If teaching them a lesson means stopping a mutiny in which thousands will die then the lesson must be justified.'

'I don't believe killing is ever justified.'

'Then you shouldn't have joined the Army.'

Couldridge knocked out his pipe. 'Perhaps you're right. But you must admit it's pretty ironic the two of us teamed up like this. One killing and one curing.'

'Perhaps we'll both fluff it.'

'Well at least I will have dealt with a couple of boils, softened a plug of ear-wax and given a hung-over rifleman diaorrhea for a week.'

'Goodnight,' Spenser said. 'See you in the morning.'

'They're calling us at dawn,' Couldridge said. 'Then I think we'll be after teaching the natives a lesson.'

But it was the natives who roused *them* at dawn and gave them a lesson with a volley of shots from the hillside in the first milky light. One bullet killed a guard; the bullet ripped through his skull and knocked him backwards into the fire where he lay, flames cautiously feeling their way over his clothes. Another lodged in a rifleman's abdomen and a third holed the tent where Couldridge and Spenser were sleeping.

An officer, young and fluffy-jowled, whom Spenser had earlier designated as Haileybury or Harrow, tripped and fell outside the tent. 'The bastards,' he said. 'We didn't think they were anywhere near that bloody hill.

Rifle shots barked on the hillside again. Spenser heard the bullet hit the young officer's chest—a gentle ripping noise. 'The bastards,' said the officer. Couldridge crawled to his side but the officer was already dead, a boyish look of surprise on his face as if he had been hit below the belt in a boxing match.

The rest of the Gurkhas had taken cover behind a natural barrier of rocks on the stony waste and the officer in charge, a bristling pugnacious major who was also the champion pig-sticker in the battalion, was shouting orders.

'Come on.' Spenser scurried for the rocks. Couldridge followed carrying his heavy tin case of medical equipment.

The wounded rifleman lay with his head resting on a smooth stone, one hand clutching the wound in his belly, the other still holding his rifle. His face was greasy with sweat from the shock and pain, but there was no fear in his expression. His slanting eyes watched Couldridge placidly as if he were pleased that an officer should take so much trouble over him.

Couldridge cut away the coarse material and looked at the huge wound baring the white coils of the intestine. He said to Spenser: 'This man's going to die.' He pressed his fist into the abdomen above the wound to try and stem the blood pumping from the artery, plunged his hand into the ruptured tissues and tried to grasp the artery.

Spenser, who had studied his Indian religions, said: 'He's not worried—he knows he'll be reborn.' He was squatting behind a boulder, revolver in one hand. He was pleased to find that he was not frightened; not yet anyway. Nor was he particularly concerned about the Gurkha dying beside him.

39

A bullet smacked into the barrier of rocks and whined off in a vicious ricochet looking for prey. Major Prendegast shouted some more orders in Gurkhali and a dozen riflemen shuffled into line behind him. Major Prendegast turned to Spenser and said: 'I'm going to try and get behind them. Otherwise we'll be hemmed up here all bloody day. Do you want to come?'

'Of course, sir,' Spenser said.

'It's bloody dangerous.'

Spenser sensed the patronage of the old school. 'I said I'd come, sir.'

'You'd better come as well, Couldridge. All the men here have got good cover. They won't be needing you.' He glanced at the wounded rifleman. 'What about him?'

'He's dead, sir.'

Major Prendegast nodded. 'That's three dead. That means we must get at least nine Pathans.' He spoke with the authority of a champion pig-sticker.

The sky above the mountains was blushing and the White Mountain had returned for the day. Mist hovered in hollows in the 'stony waste' waiting for the sun to ferret it out.

They moved to the right seeking the cover of a spine of rock that would enable them to climb above the Pathans. The Gurkhas moved easily, breathing as regularly as if they were out strolling in a village on the Deccan. Spenser's lungs pumped faster seeking oxygen for his blood.

Finally Major Prendegast stopped them, put his finger at his lips and pointed down at the nest of Pathans sniping at the rest of the Gurkhas. He smiled the smile of a master tactician and deployed his men along a hundred yards of natural battlements. But they were not pigs he was dealing with.

The new outburst of shooting came from higher up the hill-side. But the firing was thin—two men perhaps.

'It's the bloody look-outs,' Major Prendegast said. 'We'll have to shoot it out with them.'

Below the Pathans were re-adjusting themselves to the menace from above. They looked small and unreal, their rifles like steel pins.

Major Prendegast said: 'I hope Jamieson has got the sense to attack now while they're confused.' He let out a growl of pain, dropped his pistol and clutched his wrist. Blood from the bullet wound flowed down over his knuckles. Couldridge examined the wrist: there was no sign of the bullet. He applied a tourniquet, a field dressing and a splint. 'To hell with it,' Major Prendegast said. 'There go my chances of the Kadir Cup this year.'

Far below Lieutenant Jamieson, an officer whom Spenser admired, attacked. Spenser watched the pigmy figures with fascination, a spectator high up in a vast natural stadium. The Pathans turned again and levelled their steel pins at the attackers. One of the attackers fell, the rest took cover.

Major Prendegast gave the order to open fire. Cordite and smoke and a faint pain in the ears: the unreality vanished and Spenser found that he was scared: in a way it was a relief. But although he was scared he knew that he would always be able to fight. The union of schoolteacher and bank clerk had not failed him.

Two hundred yards away a vulture settled on a crag to await its meal. Spenser killed it with one shot. Below the Pathans' fire was becoming more sporadic and Lieutenant Jamieson's men were moving in closer.

Major Prendegast held his wounded arm as if it were a parcel. 'I think we've got them where we want them,' he said. He ducked as a bullet from one of the look-outs buried itself in the shale beside him.

Spenser fired his revolver at a movement behind the small mushroom of smoke from the look-out's rifle but the bullet didn't carry. Beside him a rifleman took aim and fired and one of the look-outs stood up and fell lazily over a small cliff. The Gurkha allowed a grin to join his ears; his ears moved in acknowledgement.

Below, the Pathans were fleeing before Lieutenant Jamieson.

Spenser saw one Gurkha fall and lie still, and two Pathans stop, arms outstretched above them, toy figures in classical mould, as lead tore into them from behind. Then the rest of the Pathans were gone, over the crest of the hill, away to regroup and wonder if they would ever again have the fortune to find a detachment of troops as exposed as Major Prendegast's men had been.

Three hundred yards away the Pathan look-out who had been shot stood up and stumbled towards them, hands raised above his head, blood congealing on his long matted hair.

Spenser took aim methodically, resting his pistol on his left forearm, as if he were on a range. He felt no emotion, no doubt: it was what was expected of him.

Couldridge struck his balancing arm and his shooting arm dropped. Spenser rounded on him. 'What the hell do you think you're doing?' Broad, brown faces watched with interest.

Couldridge said: 'Stopping you commit murder.'

'Mind your own bloody business.' Spenser aimed the revolver again, but Major Prendegast, marksman as well as champion pig-sticker, fired first, potting the wounded Pathan at a hundred yards. 'Sorry, Spenser,' he said. 'But you had your chance.'

Couldridge scrambled up the shale to the body of the Pathan. Spenser joined him. The wild brown face of the tribesman with kohl around the eyes was set in a snarl of death.

Couldridge said: 'Aren't you glad you didn't do that?'

Spenser found that his body was trembling. He didn't know whether it was the reaction from fear or awareness that he had almost made his first killing. Or frustration that he had been prevented from making it. 'You shouldn't have stopped me,' he said.

'I think I did right. The man was helpless, trying to give himself up. He needn't have died.'

'They say the Pathans are reckless of life.'

'No one is reckless of life when they're peering at death.'

Major Prendegast joined them. 'Not bad from a hundred yards with my left arm,' he said.

'We seem to have done pretty well, sir,' Spenser said.

'Not too bad,' Major Prendegast said. 'Not too bad at all. A good recovery I should say.'

A few weeks later Major Prendegast was court martialled for endangering the lives of his men by striking camp in a position which unnecessarily exposed them to enemy fire.

6

THEY took the wounded to the mission hospital at Peshawar and there, for the first time since his return to India, John Couldridge came across the sort of cases that he wanted to treat and investigate.

They lay placidly on simple iron beds dying from cholera, typhoid, amoebic dysentry and tuberculosis; dreaming in the haunted limbo of tertiary syphilis; sweating out malaria, and pneumonia encouraged by undernourishment. The young and the senile, the delirious and the insane, the sick, the dying and occasionally the dead were laid out beside each other.

Couldridge mourned briefly for those who could not be cured, but the sadness was swiftly replaced by hunger for knowledge; a hunger that sometimes made him wonder about his motives. Were any humanitarian instincts involved or was the hunger merely a primitive urge to conquer? To conquer and be praised and to hope for immortality in medical history. He often worried about his motives when he went to bed, but the worry was soon thrust aside by an onslaught of queries and theories. And soon his hunger for knowledge became incurable.

He toured the primitive wards with an apologetic Indian doctor who tried to hurry him past the cases that he had been unable to diagnose and past the patients preparing for death. In one corner of the ward Couldridge saw a male orderly hastily putting up screens around a patient. 'What's he suffering from?' he asked.

'Nothing for you to worry yourself about,' said the doctor gripping his arm. The doctor was very thin and moved suddenly and rapidly like a bird looking for worms.

'I'd like to see him,' said Couldridge. 'I'd like to see everything if you don't mind. I may even be able to help.'

'You should not bother yourself,' the doctor said. He made a run for another ward, pulling Couldridge with him. In the corridor two Indians crouched in a pile of rags.

'What's wrong with them?' Couldridge asked.

The doctor tugged frantically at his arm. 'We think they have leprosy,' he said. 'That is why we are keeping them away from the other patients.'

In the next ward he saw a small boy sitting up in bed rubbing at his eyes which were discharging pus. Couldridge knocked his hands away from his eyes. 'Stop it,' he said. 'Do you want to go blind?'

The boy looked at him incomprehendingly.

Couldridge said: 'How did his eyes get like that?'

'His mother suffered from gonorrhoea, poor woman,' the doctor said.

'Do you mind if I have a look?'

'No, please, you are to help yourself.'

Couldridge washed his hands and examined the boy's eyes, remembering his humiliation in front of Buckingham. He straightened up and said: 'I think you're wrong. Are you sure his mother suffered from gonorrhoea?'

The doctor made a dart for the next bed but Couldridge remained by the boy. 'Are you sure?'

'Not absolutely. But whenever we get children with running eyes their parents are usually suffering from gonorrhoea.'

'This boy's suffering from xerophthalmia,' Couldridge said.

'Ah,' said the doctor.

'The discharge has been caused by the boy continually rubbing his eyes. Do you know the cure? It's one of the most common

44

causes of blindness in children in these parts.'

'Eyebaths?' said the doctor hopefully.

'Plenty of fruit and vegetables.'

'Just fruit and vegetables?'

'That's all. And try to stop the boy rubbing his eyes. Is he a Moslem or a Hindu?'

'A Hindu, I'm afraid. We are trying to teach the patients the word of God.'

'Forget the word of God for the time being, and tell him that if he doesn't stop rubbing his eyes he'll have to answer to Siva the Destroyer.'

Pale sunlight slanted in through the open windows and a warm breeze circulated the germs. Couldridge examined the floor and the bedclothes and discovered to his surprise that they were clean: it was only the poverty and overcrowding that gave the impression of dirt.

The doctor said: 'You are, perhaps, particularly interested in illnesses of the eye?'

'I'm interested in them certainly. But I'm interested in all other illness.' Except, he thought, boils and piles and hangovers.

'I sometimes think that the answer lies in that most wonderful book, The Bible.'

'The Bible? How do you come to that conclusion?'

'Tobias,' said the doctor.

'Tobias?'

'If you remember,' said the doctor patiently, 'Tobias restored his father's sight annointing his eyes with the gall of a fish. After half of one hour a white film came away from the eyes and his father could see.' He looked puzzled. 'Do you mean to say you have not read about that most Christian of cures for blindness?'

'Good grief,' Couldridge said.

'What seems to be troubling you?'

'Just promise me one thing. Promise me that you'll never try anything like that?'

The doctor hopped from one foot to the other. 'But it's in the good book.'

45

'To hell with the good book.'

The doctor began to bob up and down in agitation. 'That is a most unhappy remark to make about the good book.'

'Just promise me. You are not supposed to take the Bible literally, good book though it is.'

'Very well,' said the doctor. 'But it is most puzzling.'

Before leaving the hospital Couldridge returned to the first ward he had visited and went up to the bed with the screens around it. Behind them sat a Pathan, both arms severed at the elbow. Colonel Hatherley had not been exaggerating. The Pathan smiled at him hesitantly and wagged a stump.

Couldridge smiled back but he was depressed. What point was there in making any discovery in the face of such barbarism and vast communal disease? If he helped to find a cure for say tuberculosis then nature would find a substitute killer. What, in fact, was the point of any cure if God allowed men to maim and kill each other?

When he left there was one woman in charge of the entire hospital. She told him not to worry—all the patients had been taught to take their own medicines.

That night, over a bottle of Eagle whisky, he learned that the Pathans had been punished for ambushing the Gurkhas: a village had been burned and all its crops destroyed. Some white men, he thought, needed help more than the Indians. But they were beyond his powers of healing.

7

In the ensuing months at Jinjabad John Couldridge found a deep affection for the Gurkhas rooting itself inside him. He was moved by the honesty and loyalty of the little mahogany men from

Nepal who had refused to take part in the Indian Mutiny, but as a doctor he was constantly reminded of their two principal frailties—rum and women. Often the two weaknesses blended and a rifleman reporting sick with a soldier's oldest complaint would confess, 'It was the rum, sah.' But he would endure the painful treatment with the same stoicism that he endured the pain of his wounds. He also found that he need not worry about them fracturing their skulls: the story was told of a Gurkha who was kicked full on the forehead by a mule—and complained of a slight headache for the rest of the day.

In his own quarters Bhawansing Rai consistently declined to understand almost any order either in English or faltering Gurkhali. Every morning he filled the tub with boiling water that took half an hour to cool, laid out the wrong uniform for Couldridge and swept the dust under the bed with a few rebellious flourishes of the broom. He had one English phrase—'It just happened, sah.' Couldridge discovered that Bhawansing Rai had been the handicap of many a newcomer to the battalion.

But he didn't complain too much about Bhawansing Rai because grumbling about servants was the prerogative of the memsahibs. They complained endlessly about the slothful water carrier, the promiscuous children's nurse, the temperamental cook and the disgruntled washerman whom they paid 25s. a month. In fact the women had a great deal of time to complain about the servants because the servants did almost all their work for them. When they were not discussing their ayah or their bhisti or their khansamah they were playing bridge or plotting to depose the current 'senior lady' of the community or coming to him with maladies that were mostly slight, often imagined and very occasionally serious. They came to him with sunstroke, vapours, false pregnancies and headaches which he attributed to excessive indolence. They were coy about their bowels and surprisingly frank about their reproductive organs. Of such frankness and readiness to be examined Couldridge had been warned. 'Always have another woman present,' they had told him at St Mary's. He had never quite believed that the warning was necessary until he returned to India. And he was still astonished by the speed with which one particular young woman could take off her long silk dresses, and the candid nature of her conversation.

'But you are my doctor,' she said. 'I always thought I could confide in my doctor.' She had a pretty, pouting face and her dress and bodice and petticoats failed to conceal the plump outlines of her breasts.

'Your husband is a brother officer,' Couldridge said. 'I would rather not hear anything derogatory about him.' Her husband was a good officer who excelled in the field and detested life on the base at Jinjabad. He began to understand why.

'I don't see why that should matter,' she pouted her lips. 'If we were in London you might both belong to the same club. But that shouldn't stop me telling you about my troubles.'

'I would rather you didn't. I don't mind treating you for your ailments but your physical relationship with your husband is not my concern.'

'You're a bit starchy, aren't you,' she said. 'I shouldn't have thought you were starchy. You must have had a lot of girls after you in your time with that handsome face of yours and those lovely hands.' She gave a theatrical smile. 'Don't you find me attractive?'

Couldridge wondered how her husband, a fierce and sombre man, had come to marry a tart. To his annoyance he found that her flattery pleased him. 'Mrs King,' he said. 'I don't think there is a great deal the matter with you and I do have a lot more patients to see.'

'How do you know? You haven't examined me.'

Panic fluttered inside him. 'If you really think you need examining, Mrs King, I would be obliged if you would come back tomorrow with another woman.'

'Oh, don't be so prim,' she said. 'And in any case when the other woman saw you she would probably want examining as well.' She sensed that she might have gone too far and added: 'But I really do think I'm pregnant, doctor.'

'Even if you are it's far too early to confirm a pregnancy so I see no point in examining you.'

'But I do have this other trouble. Don't worry—I won't compromise you.' She jumped to her feet and darted behind the screen in the corner of the surgery. He sprung after her but her dress was off by the time he reached the screen. He saw the tops of her fat little breasts thrust up and balanced by bone and experienced a pulse of feeling that would do nothing to further medical research.

'Mrs King,' he said, 'please put your dress on again.' She began to remove her bodice. Couldridge, who had only associated promiscuity with chorus girls, tarts and some nurses, ran for the door. But there was no one in the waiting room. He ran down the corridor and stopped a grey-haired woman passing by: it was the adjutant's wife. 'I would be most obliged if you would come and assist me,' he said. She looked surprised but followed him down the corridor.

By the time they reached the surgery Mrs King had removed all her clothing and was lying on the examination table with her thighs apart. She leapt to her feet when the adjutant's wife came in and disappeared behind the screen.

'I rather hoped you would agree to be present while I examined Mrs King,' Couldridge said.

The adjutant's wife smiled. 'I rather think it won't be necessary.'

A minute later Mrs King reappeared fully clothed. 'Thank you, doctor,' she said. 'Good morning, Mrs Fulton.' She hurried out, flushed face held high, plump breasts resentfully in captivity once more.

Couldridge said: 'I hope you don't think ...'

'Of course I don't,' Mrs Fulton said. 'You wouldn't have called me if you had. But you mustn't think too badly of her. Of any of us for that matter. It's not a life for a woman in this part of the world. And all our men are married to the Army. It affects us in different ways. Some of us become very petty. Others, like Mrs King perhaps, try and find other outlets for their frustrations. You are a pretty vulnerable target, I'm afraid. You're young and you're attractive. And even worse you're both a bachelor and a doctor. You will have to be very strong-willed indeed, Doctor Couldridge. Either that or you will have to find yourself a wife.'

'Preferably the latter,' Couldridge said.

Mrs Fulton smiled. 'You must come and have drinks with us. I think you and my husband will get on very well together.'

Couldridge was not so sure: he had not noticed any common meeting ground during his few conversations with the adjutant.

'Don't worry,' she said. 'He's quite different away from the office. He puts his tin of metal polish away and brings out a bottle of gin.'

And with the Fultons Couldridge found companionship and discovered for the first time that there were many officers whom he could admire. Lean, fighting men whose characters were tempered by the humility that accompanied awareness of the grandeur and vast, inchoate suffering of the land they ruled. Not sensitive men but honest men; men who condoned the brutal treatment of the Pathans and were also confused by the compassion which the suffering of the tribesmen aroused in them. Men who subjugated any doubts about their actions by obeying orders. Men whose kind had won an empire and would fight to keep it despite the first glimmering doubts that all was not perfection within its red, white and blue boundaries.

With their wives they sat on the Fultons' verandah smoking their pipes, drinking whiskies and soda, watching the bats slashing the scented dusk and listening to the first insect sounds of night. Owls hooted, small animals awoke in the avenue of poinsettia bushes, large predatory animals patrolled the perimeter of the base—or so Couldridge believed when he fancied that he could see yellow eyes glaring at him from the darkness.

They talked about the Pathans, their courage and their atrocities; and Couldridge found that they admired the tribesmen and harboured no hatred, even though a brother officer might that week have been found dead, blinded and emasculated. They talked about the mounting anti-British agitation, particularly in Bengal where students were organising robberies and a boycott of foreign goods. They talked about Moslem and Hindu riots; about child marriage and suttee; about the discovery of an anarchists' bomb factory in Calcutta; about jackals with rabies; about the Viceroy, Lord Curzon, whose marriage to Mary Leiter, the daughter of an American millionaire, had brought him wealth and happiness and softened his character; about the new C-in-C, Kitchener, whose brutality in South Africa had crushed the Boers; about duck-shooting and pig-sticking and polo; about the latest plague figures and the agitators' claims that the British had deliberately spread it. Occasionally and guardedly they talked about Colonel Hatherley, frequently and without reserve they talked to Couldridge about their ailments.

Couldridge was grateful for their company. In particular to Captain Fulton, a punctilious man by day who took nightly leave from the Army when he took off his uniform, and his wife who understood men in her mature way. But he wanted other pastimes and interests; in particular he wanted the company of an attractive woman who would love and flatter him without involvement. Such a commodity was rare in the North West Frontier.

Six months after his arrival an American girl called Joanne Pinkerton came to stay with the Hatherleys. She was related to Lord Curzon's wife and engaged to one of Colonel Hatherley's Lieutenants, a precise, handsome and fiercely-moustached young man, a keen hunter of sandgrouse, wildfowl, bears and Pathans. She had a pretty, pointed face with smoke-coloured eyes, a ready temper and an aggressive contempt for almost all masculine achievement. She was said in the mess to be spirited and desirable. And her fiancé—for no good reason that Couldridge could fathom —was considered to be a lucky fellow.

Couldridge met her one evening at the Hatherleys for drinks. Her fiancé, Lieutenant Anthony Sykes, was there; so were other young officers and their wives. Mrs Hatherley, a vague, wasted woman awaiting retirement and the last fatal symptoms of one of her imaginary diseases, wandered around the big, faded room introducing people with well-remembered lines, and getting most of their names wrong. Colonel Hatherley removed glasses of whisky from the bearer's tray with a conjuror's flourish and re-fought old campaigns with a captive audience.

Mrs Hatherley said: 'My dear, I want you to meet Lieutenant Sykes. He's our doctor and he'll look after us in the morning if we drink too much tonight.' She had made her small joke many times before.

Joanne Pinkerton giggled. 'I don't think you are Lieutenant Sykes,' she said. 'I'm supposed to be marrying him. You've never bought me a ring, have you?'

Couldridge, who disliked flirtatious women noted for their sense of fun, said: 'No I haven't.' And stared deeply into her eyes.

Joanne Pinkerton was momentarily confused. Men had told her before that she had beautiful eyes but this sort of dumb flattery was unnerving. 'What's the matter?' she said.

'Nothing much. Nothing to be worried about. It's just that you're myopic.'

Her cheeks flushed and she prepared to defend herself and her sex. 'You're very rude,' she said.

'Rude? There's nothing rude about telling you that you're myopic. Millions of people are.'

'They are?'

Couldridge helped himself to a whisky and soda. 'Do you know what it means?'

'Not really. Something to do with the eyes?'

'It means that you're short-sighted and in all probability you should be wearing spectacles. But of course you never will, because of your feminine vanity.'

'If I'm short-sighted then I shall wear spectacles.'

'You'd better ask Tony Sykes first. He might not approve of a bespectacled wife.'

'It's none of his damned business. If I want to wear spectacles then wear them I darn well will.'

Couldridge peered closer. 'And a touch of astigmatism I shouldn't wonder.'

'Great suffering catfish,' Joanne Pinkerton said. 'Just what is that when it's at home?'

'Nothing to worry about. A defect of the curvature of the re-fracted surface of the eye causing a distorted image. Most people have it to a degree.'

'You pay a pretty compliment. Mr ...'

'John Couldridge. Can I get you a drink?'

'Sure,' she said. 'I'll have a whisky. Most of the ladies here drink lemon squash, I see.'

'When they're on show. I've treated a few ladies suffering from an excessive intake of alcohol since I've been here.'

She sipped the whisky and shuddered because he had given her one without soda in it. 'I'll give you one thing, Mr Could-ridge, you have an original line of party chat.'

Couldridge shrugged. 'These sort of parties bore me.'

'Perhaps it's because you're not a very good conversationalist.'

'Perhaps.' He didn't care.

'Doesn't that bother you?'

'It seems to me,' he said, 'that you're the one who's desperately trying to make small talk.' He paused. 'Here, I'll make my contribution. How's Lord Curzon?'

'He's very well. Snowed under with paper-work as always. Not hitting it off with Kitchener I hear.'

'You hear that do you. How extraordinarily interesting.' He found the information extraordinarily uninteresting. 'How is his back these days?'

'How did you know there was anything wrong with it?'

'It stands out a mile. A curvature of the spine. He wears a steel corset and that accounts for his posture. No man—not even Colonel Hatherley—would perpetually sit as straight as that with-out a surgical appliance of some kind.'

Couldridge did not add that the steel corset did not account for the unbending nature of the mind of Lord Curzon of Kedle-ston, scholastic prodigy at Eton, Tory member of Parliament, Viceroy of India at 39, the man who had created the North West Frontier Province. Nor did he add that he had been told

53

about the corset by a friend of Lord Curzon's physician.

'That's very clever of you. And very lacking in respect. Doesn't it worry you that I'm related to his wife?'

Couldridge laughed aloud. 'You're not serious.'

Joanne Pinkerton was not a girl who stamped her foot; nor did she on this occasion: she would have preferred to slap his face. 'Don't laugh at me.'

Couldridge tried to stop and choked on his whisky. 'Doesn't it worry you that one day soon I may be your doctor?'

'How do you work that out for pity's sake?'

'When you marry Tony Sykes you'll live here, I presume. Then I'll be your doctor.' Except, he thought, that he had no intention of staying.

'I'd rather go to a witch doctor.'

'There are plenty of those around here.' The laughter lines at the corners of his eyes vanished. 'Or murderers. It's just a question of terminology.'

'Your voice changed suddenly then.'

'It's nothing you'd understand or even be interested in.'

'You're very sure of what I feel about things.'

'I don't think you feel too deeply.'

'Is that a crime? I'm only eighteen, Dr Couldridge, it's a trifle early to become intense about things, don't you think?'

'A lot of Indian women have been married, borne children and died by the age of eighteen. Some have even died on the nuptial bed. Do you want the details, Miss Pinkerton?'

'No,' she said, 'I don't.'

'Never mind,' he said. 'None of it need concern you. You'll soon have five servants and a life of leisure.' He paused. 'But I suppose you already have that. I'm told you are very rich.' His antagonism was out of character and it surprised him.

'For a young doctor,' she said, 'you seem to have a pretty comfortable life.'

It hurt because it was true. 'I don't intend to stay here for very long.'

'Does Colonel Hatherley know about that? Does the head of

54

the I.M.S. know about it? And in any case where do you aim to go?'

'I'll get a posting all right. Then I'm off to Calcutta because that's where all the disease starts. That's where the world's cholera comes from—from the lower basin of the Ganges. In Calcutta I should think you could find every disease known to man.' His antagonism had vanished as his words flowed like green sap. 'I'd like to set up my own clinic and laboratory. To follow in the footsteps of Robert Koch. Have you heard of him, Miss Pinkerton? He was the first man to discover that each disease is caused by one particular microbe. It seems pretty obvious to us now but it was only a few years ago that he made the discovery.'

She seemed to be quelled by the short barrage of words. 'No,' she said, 'I haven't heard of him.'

'I didn't really think you would have done.'

'Is there any reason why I should? I doubt if there is one other person in this room who has heard of him.'

Mrs Hatherley drifted up and said: 'I see you two have met. He's our doctor, you know, Joanne.'

Joanne Pinkerton nodded. 'Do you know who Robert Koch is?'

'No my dear,' Mrs Hatherley said. 'Is he here tonight?' She wandered on, wondering if the pain caused by a restrictive corset was the onset of an attack of pleurisy.

'You see,' Joanne Pinkerton said.

'You picked your subject with care.

Lieutenant Anthony Sykes materialised beside them, fierce face alert above his white shirt and green jacket.

Joanne said, 'You know each other, I presume.'

'We do,' said Couldridge, who had that morning treated Sykes for a septic bee sting on his left buttock· 'You might say intimately.'

Sykes, a man of few words, laughed unhappily.

Joanne said: 'Is this some secret joke?'

'No joke,' Couldridge said. 'Ask Tony.'

Sykes said: 'I was stung by a bee.'

'Where?'

'It doesn't matter,' Sykes said. 'Can I get either of you a drink?'
'No thank you,' Couldridge said.
'No thank you,' Joanne Pinkerton said.

Conversation faltered and died. Couldridge looked around him and saw above the green shoulders, above the decolletage, mouths opening and shutting, jabbering and drinking; each mouth waited impatiently for another to stop so that it could open and shut in reply. Alcohol opening the floodgates of trivia. He was very bored.

Joanne Pinkerton tried to ignite the conversation again. 'Tony darling,' she said, 'when are you going to take me up in the hills?'

'Any time you like,' he said.

'I don't mean just around here. I mean far away. Where you go when you stay away for weeks on end.'

'I'm afraid that's impossible,' Sykes said. 'It's against orders.'

'I want to go,' she said.

Sykes grinned proudly at the spirit of his girl. 'Absolutely impossible,' he said, and put his arm around her shoulders.

'Why is it impossible?'

'Because the Army says so. And you're in the Army now.'

'Not yet I'm not.'

Couldridge said: 'If you'll excuse me, I have some studying to do. Goodnight, Miss Pinkerton. Goodnight Tony.'

As he turned to leave Colonel Hatherley marched up, patches of red burning on his pirate face. With him was Buckingham who was visiting Jinjabad from Calcutta.

Buckingham said: 'How's it going, Couldridge? Diagnosed any more cases of glaucoma lately?'

'Not lately,' Couldridge said.

Joanne Pinkerton said: 'What's glaucoma?'

'It's a very serious eye condition,' Couldridge said.

Colonel Hatherley said: 'I didn't know Couldridge had diagnosed any such disease up here.'

Couldridge waited fatalistically for Buckingham to explain. He did so with controlled relish, addressing Joanne Pinkerton, Hatherley and Sykes in turn.

56

When Sykes had finished laughing he said: 'What a wonderful story for the mess.'

On the perimeter of their group one or two officers smiled as if they had overheard Buckingham telling the story. Couldridge tried to smile but his facial muscles didn't co-operate. He felt himself flushing with anger and embarrassment and was ashamed. Only Joanne Pinkerton didn't laugh.

Couldridge excused himself again and walked away. Behind him he heard Sykes telling the anecdote to two other officers and heard them laughing. He wished that he, too, had been able to laugh at his own mistake. He thought that perhaps he might have managed it if the girl Joanne Pinkerton had not been present.

8

Joanne Pinkerton was accustomed to meeting young men who conformed. The young men who worked for her stockbroker father in New York and conformed to his imperious wishes; the young men at the court of Lord Curzon in Calcutta and Simla who conformed to the style set by their master, who revelled in luxurious living and official inquiries; the young men in the officers' mess who conformed to British military traditions with disciplined dedication. Thus her meeting with the non-conformist John Couldridge worried her; and the worry annoyed her because it was spoiling the pleasure of her escapade.

The escapade, she believed, would soon be the talk of the conformist society circles of New York, London and Calcutta and might even be recorded in the history books of India. After all, it would be the first time that a white woman had crossed the line into the forbidden part of the North West Frontier.

She had planned the escapade in Calcutta; now she put it into operation in Jinjabad where she had found a Pathan who spoke a little English. He appeared to have no occupation and probably earned his living from spying on the British. But he could be bought for a few rupees; and for the sort of money that Joanne Pinkerton offered he could be purchased and retained for the rest of his life. He considered her to be quite mad; but if Allah in his wisdom had sent him a rich white lunatic who was he to reject her money? And as his money belt grew heavier around his lean belly he obtained for her the commodities she required—brown stain, ragged tribesman's clothing, food, three mules and the services of two other 'tame' Pathans. He refrained from telling her that there was no such person as a tame Pathan.

'She wants to reach a village fifty miles over this line which the British have drawn,' he told his two friends.

'Then she is mad,' said one.

'But we would be mad not to take her money,' said the other.

They made Joanne Pinkerton write out a statement swearing that she had asked them to take her up into forbidden territory in case anything happened to her and British wrath was aroused. Because they liked her they told her of the dangers, and were relieved when she disregarded them.

She set out from the town at dawn on the back of a mule with the two Pathans. Her face was stained brown and she wore Pathan dress.

For two days they climbed, stopping every three hours, sleeping in two tents, searching the hillsides for Pathans and mountain leopards. The greenery thinned and waned to grey, at night the air was iced; by day showers of rain came racing across the crags soaking their clothes and stinging their faces. Joanne Pinkerton had not expected rain: it seemed an unfair phenomenon.

Nor had she expected British troops, Gurkhas in fact, to open fire on her. The first bullets smacked into a boulder beside her and cracked it in half.

'Holy Moses,' she said, 'what was that?'

Her two companions didn't bother to try and translate. They

abandoned the fighting instincts of their brother tribesmen and ran for the cover of a crop of rocks. The mules followed, placid eyes starting with fear. Joanne Pinkerton's mule followed with Joanne Pinkerton sitting side-saddle.

Behind the rocks she dismounted and peered down at the Gurkhas far below. There were only a few of them. It would be ironic, she thought, if Sykes were in charge of them. A few more bullets whined past them but even she could tell that they had spent their force. She imagined Sykes' face if he took her captive; and she imagined Couldridge's reaction if she were wheeled into his surgery, brown-faced and bleeding from a bullet wound; he would, she thought, be phlegmatic, anxious to dress a mundane flesh wound as soon as possible and get on with his research.

She turned to the two Pathans squatting beside the mules. 'Will they follow us?' She pointed towards the Gurkhas.

The Pathans were not frightened but they did not intend to make a fight of it. 'Sport,' one of them said. 'British like to make sport.'

'You mean they just shoot at you for sport?'

The Pathan nodded. 'They like good sport.'

She wasn't sure if they had understood properly. But the soldiers were moving away in search of other prey. She and the Pathans waited for twenty minutes before resuming their journey.

'Are we over the forbidden line?' she asked slowly. 'The line which no memsahib has crossed?'

'Yes,' they said. 'You are over it.'

Next morning she awoke in her tent to the sound of excited voices. She crawled out and found herself surrounded by Pathans. They looked at her in astonishment. She smiled and tried to look gay.

One of her companions said : 'These men fighters.'

For the first time she began to regret the escapade. She tried to appear excessively friendly. But her appearance did not help— rain-soaked rags clinging to the curves of her body, stained face streaked with white. On the other hand her appearance might help because she was plainly crazy. If she escaped with her life,

59

she vowed, she would never post the letters she had planned to send to her society friends.

A Pathan with polished brass cartridge cases gleaming in his bandolier came up to her. She noticed with surprise that he had blue eyes above his beak of a nose. 'You are a foolish woman,' he said in laboured English.

She nodded: she was. A foolish woman who desperately wanted to stay alive.

'We could kill you,' he said. 'Some of my men are in favour of it. We have a special way of killing women. It is not pleasant.'

Her body began to tremble uncontrollably.

'But these men'—he pointed at her companions—'tell me that you are playing some sort of trick on the British.' His beak twitched beneath the startling blue eyes. 'We ourselves like playing tricks on the British.'

'You will let me go then?'

The nose and the eyes smiled in the hawkish face. 'Provided you play the trick.'

'I will,' she said. 'I will.'

He made a gesture with his long-barrelled rifle and his men ran off behind the cover of the rocks. 'We will be watching,' he said.

'But you don't know what the trick is.'

'I think it will be a big enough trick on the British just for you to reach one of their outposts. You a woman.' He peered closely at her as if to make sure that she was a woman.

'You very lucky woman,' said one of her guides when he had gone. 'We were lucky too. At first they thought you a spy. They wanted to kill you and us.'

'Come on,' she said. 'Let's go.' But the escapade had lost its savour. Another shower bowled along a ravine, chased them and caught them. She shivered and began to cough.

Half a mile from the outpost they raised white flags and entered the mud-walled fortress—reinforced with concrete—followed by the barrels of half a dozen rifles.

It took a long time to explain the joke to the officer in charge, even after he had agreed that she was apparently a woman and, unless her rain-streaked complexion was some freak of pigmentation, was not a Pathan.

'I tell you I'm an American citizen,' she said. This was not how she had imagined the escapade ending; she began to cough again. 'It's all supposed to be a joke.'

'I see.' He was very young and usually waited for other people to laugh before acknowledging a joke. 'You say you are engaged to be married to an officer in the Gurkhas?'

She nodded.

'And he let you come up here like this with these two fellows?'

'No, no one let me come up. They'll all be very angry.'

At last he saw the joke. 'I bet they will,' he said, tears of mirth forming at the corners of his eyes. 'I just bet they will.'

'They? Aren't you one of them?'

'No,' he said. 'Another regiment altogether. But we're delighted to have a fugitive from the Gurkhas in our midst.'

Joanne Pinkerton knew then that the retribution awaiting her fifty miles away would be far worse than she had imagined. But, she thought, she might as well see the thing through. 'Have you any concrete?' she said. 'Wet concrete?'

'Loads of it. I think I can anticipate your wishes. You wish to leave a footprint here for posterity.'

'Yes,' said Joanne Pinkerton. But none of it seemed very humorous any more.

'And I suppose I'd better let those two fellows go who came with you.'

'Please,' she said.

Next day the young officer gave her an escort of three to take her back to her retribution. But Colonel Hatherley and his subordinates had to contain their anger, because by the time she returned she was running a temperature of 104 degrees and had to be carried to the sick quarters.

9

WHEN she surfaced from her delirium two days later John Couldridge was standing beside her. It was perfectly natural, she
thought, that he should be there. She started to speak and the
pain clutched at her chest.

'Don't try and talk,' he said. He took her pulse and stuck a
thermometer under her tongue. She wanted to tell him that his
bedside manner was just as she had imagined it would be—
non-existent.

He took the thermometer from her mouth and said: 'You're
getting better.'

She searched for the truth from the wild disorder of her dreams;
from the peaks of elation and the chasms of fear and the footsteps taking her with the regularity of heartbeats towards death.
But the footsteps had stopped on the brink and the heartbeats
had gained strength. He saw the puzzlement on her face.

'You can't remember what happened? Just shake your head if
you can't.'

She shook her head.

'Perhaps this will bring it all back to you.' He held a mirror
in front of her eyes and she saw her face still mottled with brown
stain. She remembered and croaked with alarm.

'You might well croak,' he said. 'Do you want to know if they
were very annoyed?'

She nodded.

'They were,' he said. 'But it's worn off a bit now. They thought
you were going to die.'

She wanted to say, 'But you don't seem very worried.' But she
only managed another croak.

He grinned at her.

She began to cough and he handed her a piece of lint. She noticed that she was spattering the lint with blood.

'You were pretty bad,' he said. 'Bronchial pneumonia. Everyone was very worried. But you're all right now.'

She returned to sleep and dreamed that the blue-eyed Pathan was taking her pulse and kissing her at the same time. She awoke and found Couldridge beside her bed once more. 'It's nice to know you never leave my bedside,' she said; and smiled because she could talk again.

'It's twenty-four hours since I was here,' he said. 'You've been asleep.'

'You might have pretended that you'd been here all the time. Aren't you ever gallant?'

He stuck the thermometer under her tongue. 'You're much better,' he said. 'You can see visitors now.'

'I don't want to see visitors.'

'They want to see you.'

'That's what I'm afraid of. What do I look like?'

'You look as if you've had bronchial pneumonia and some strange skin disease unknown to medical science that only affects the face.'

'Why only the face?'

'Because it's not on the rest of your body.'

'You mean you've looked at the rest of my body?' She knew it was a fatuous remark because he was a doctor. But it was embarrassing to think that a man she had met at a cocktail party should have looked at her naked body while she was asleep.

'For God's sake,' he said. 'For your information you have two breasts and the rest of the equipment just like any other woman. Don't be coy—it doesn't suit you.' He replaced the thermometer in a tumbler of disinfectant and stood up. 'Now prepare yourself for your first visitor.'

Lieutenant Anthony Sykes sat down elaborately beside her bed and said: 'Hallo, how are you?' He couldn't have looked more awkward, she thought, if he had been wearing sword and spurs.

63

'I'm all right,' she said. 'Am I in disgrace?'

He shifted from buttock to buttock. 'You're not terribly popular,' he said.

'I suppose not.'

'It wouldn't have been so bad if you had picked an outpost that we were manning.' He remembered the bunch of Peshawar roses he was holding and put them on the table beside her. 'They're for you,' he said unnecessarily.

'I guess the whole thing was pretty silly. Have I embarrassed you professionally, Tony?'

He examined a Peshawar rose with the interest of a professional gardener. 'You haven't made it easy for me,' he said. 'I realise what spirit the whole enterprise showed. But not everyone is quite so enthusiastic.'

'Is Colonel Hatherley mad?'

'He isn't very pleased.'

She put her hand, white and patterned with fragile mauve veins, on his arm. 'Will it affect your career?'

'It shouldn't,' he said. 'The trouble is people don't seem to realise what initiative you showed.' He pinched an invisible green fly on the petal of a rose.

'Do you still want to marry me?'

'Of course I do,' he said without conviction.

'Are you sure?'

'You've made it very awkward for me,' he said. 'It might be just a jape to you but it's my career.'

'Then you don't want to marry me any more?'

'I thought perhaps we could put it off for a while.' He tried to hold her pale hand but she pulled it beneath the bedclothes. 'Then, when all the fuss has died down perhaps we could take some leave in England and get married there.'

Joanne Pinkerton laughed and the pain clutched at her chest again. 'You're not trying to spare me the whole truth because of my illness, are you?'

'I don't think you should be upset. Couldridge told me not to upset you.'

64

The laughter expanded painfully in her lungs. 'Tell me,' she said. 'For God's sake tell me the truth. Are you calling it off?'

He nodded.

'Thank God,' she said. The laughter made a strident, painful escape. 'It's the best tonic I've had so far. Thank God.'

'Then you're not upset?'

'I'm delighted. If you hadn't called it off then I would have.'

He finished shredding the petal of a rose. 'Then it's all over?'

'It's all over.'

'I hope you won't hold it against me.'

She looked puzzled and then remembered that she had influence at the court of Lord Curzon. 'No,' she said, 'I won't hold it against you.' She began to laugh again. 'Now for heaven's sake leave me alone or I'll have a relapse.'

She relaxed happily in her pillows and waited for John Couldridge to return. But he didn't visit her again that day, nor the next.

10

IN a village at the foot of the hills a small Moslem boy gazed up through the dark leaves of a mango tree and noticed that, although it was only just after noon, the sunlight seemed to be fading. He told his parents; but they told him not to be foolish—it was as bright as ever and it was time for him to pray towards Mecca.

Thirty miles away in another village set among sharp grey peaks a young Pathan tribesman who had been industriously helping to torture a captured British officer fell wounded, his kneecap shattered by a bullet, as an avenging party of Ghurkas stormed the only street.

65

Surgeon Second Lieutenant John Couldridge of the Indian Medical Service went to the aid of the boy; Second Lieutenant Neville Spenser of the Indian Army attended to the Pathan.

The Pathan lay in the dust clutching his ruined knee and looking at Spenser, who was in charge of retaliation that day. Bright red blood flowed over his fingers covering the congealed blood of the officer he had been helping to torture in the hut. The torture had not been skilful because Lieutenant Jamieson had died within the hour.

Spenser went into the hut and looked at the mangled dead flesh. He turned away from the rest of the platoon gathered at the doorway so that they could not see him trying to swallow back the vomit. Then he said: 'The eyes. Why couldn't the bastards leave his eyes?'

They shook their heads. He went out into the street and drew his revolver on the young Pathan trying to stop the blood flowing from the wreckage of his knee. 'You bastard,' he said.

The Pathan waited patiently to be killed. No one in the village stirred except a child who peered from a hut and aimed a stick at the Gurkhas as if it were a rifle.

A lance-naik said, 'Excuse me, sah, but the colonel always likes to question prisoners.'

Spenser shivered because he had never killed a man and because he knew what would happen to the Pathan if he didn't kill him. The Pathan began to whimper as the first shock passed and the pain stabbed him; but he continued to stare at Spenser without fear.

Spenser leaned closer, gun pointing between the Pathan's eyes. The Pathan, knife in hand, lunged at him. The point of the knife opened the flesh from cheekbone to mouth and Spenser thought irrelevantly that he would always wear the scar. Spenser's hand went to his face; the Pathan lunged again but the lance-naik kicked the knife high into the air.

Spenser was conscious that he had both learned a lesson and made himself look foolish. 'Put him on a mule,' he said. When they returned to the base three hours later the Pathan was still sitting upright, his blood congealed on the flank of the mule.

Colonel Hatherley said: 'What did they do to Jamieson?'

They showed him.

Spenser said: 'What do you propose to do with the prisoner, sir?'

'Do to him?' The faded eyes were vacant. 'Do to him? Why the same as he did to Jamieson, of course. But slower.' Muscles danced along his jaw-line.

Neville Spenser, son of a bank clerk and a schoolteacher, born and bred in Streatham, said: 'Isn't that rather bringing us down to their level, sir?'

The faded eyes examined Spenser. His fingers combed the long hair which brigadiers and generals disliked but never criticised. 'Take another look at Jamieson,' he said.

'I've already seen his body, sir.'

'Take another look.' It was not even a body: it was a carcase.

'That man did that to him.' He pointed to the Pathan sitting on the ground. 'You think he should be spared?'

'Not spared, sir. I just didn't think he should be tortured.'

Colonel Hatherley fingered the flesh, just beginning to sag, under his chin. 'And if I did torture him I wonder what you would do, Spenser. Retire to your quarters and write a letter to the Viceroy or Kitchener dictated by your conscience?' He walked around Spenser like a farmer appraising a horse up for sale. 'No, I don't think so. You're not the type.' He seemed to imply that Spenser wouldn't have the courage. He let the implication linger for a moment and then said: 'You're a born soldier, Spenser. You're not a sneak or a mutineer. You obey orders because that's the way of life you've chosen. For the rest of your life you'll give orders and obey orders. None of them will ever be questioned, just carried out.' He paused. 'But I'm not sure about your friend Surgeon Second Lieutenant Couldridge. He's not a soldier, he's a doctor. Buckingham was more of a soldier than a doctor.'

Spenser waited. The Pathan's head began to slump towards his chest. The Gurkhas watched impassively, smiling occasionally at rum-sweet gambling thoughts.

The colonel said: 'In fact I've decided to give this man a chance.'

'A chance, sir?'

Colonel Hatherley smiled without humour, the muscles still flickering along his jaw-bone. 'Just to show you what a humane man I can be. Just to show you how I can forgive and forget what this bastard did to Jamieson.'

He spoke rapidly to the Pathan. The Pathan's head jerked up and there was fear there for the first time, fear of the unexpected. The colonel snapped at him again and he raised himself on to his good knee. Colonel Hatherley said: 'I'm going to give him a chance to escape. See what sort of stuff he's made of.' The snarl had gone and his voice was dreamy again. 'Give him more of a chance than he gave young Jamieson.'

The Pathan was trying to hobble away over the starved grass. Colonel Hatherley said: 'Give him a stick to help him on his way.'

Even with the stick it took the Pathan five minutes to cover a hundred yards. He kept looking back over his shoulder, like a dog wondering why its master wasn't following it.

Colonel Hatherley said: 'You know what he's thinking, don't you?'

'No, sir,' Spenser said.

'He's thinking that if he ever gets back with his own chums they'll accuse him of collaborating with the British. They might give him a hard time.'

'I suppose it's possible, sir.'

'We wouldn't want that to happen to the poor fellow, would we, Spenser?'

'I don't know, sir.'

Colonel Hatherley took out his pistol and held it at thigh level, arm swinging like a pendulum. He waited until the Pathan was about to hobble behind a wooden hut, raised the revolver and fired one shot. The Pathan lurched forward, twitched and lay still.

'Shot while attempting to escape,' Colonel Hatherley said. 'Don't forget that, Spenser. And don't forget to tell your friend Couldridge that he was shot trying to escape.'

'No, sir.' He walked back to his quarters to finish the letter he had been writing to the girl in London whom he was supposed to love. But the words wouldn't flow. He read what he had already written.

'Dear Charlotte, I think you will like it out here. It won't be long now. I miss you terribly ...'

But he knew she wouldn't like it; that she was only coming because they were engaged and she had promised. He wanted her comfort and understanding now after the act of military brutality that he had just witnessed. Very briefly he wanted all that he had left behind.

Church on Sundays and gentle evening skies plumed with pink cloud. Charlotte and the three children that they would have cosily preserved behind decent red brick and windows patterned with blue and red glass. A nanny—when he became branch manager of the bank—wheeling the bassinet across the common. Punts on the river, straw hats on the promenade, kites in the sky.

That's what she had wanted; it was her birthright, too. And it would have been hers if he hadn't rebelled, hadn't peered into the ordered years ahead and rejected them because they seemed such a waste of the world and the experience that was there for the taking.

The decision had been taken. Astonishingly, he was now writing to Streatham from a reckless outpost of the British Empire probably uncharted on any school maps. He thought of the wounded Pathan glancing behind him, of the gun swinging in Colonel Hatherley's hand. And he wondered: is there still a chance for me to escape?

He stood up and looked into the mirror on the bare wood wall. It was a face that should have been peering out from behind the grill at the bank on the corner. Except that the moustache was clipped with military precision and the grey eyes would never have revealed sympathy for the overdrawn customer. Deliberately he pictured again the mutilated body of Jamieson; deliberately he set about persuading himself that Colonel Hatherley had been right in shooting the Pathan in the back; that justice had been carried out swiftly and cleanly; that the method of execution had been more humane than a firing squad. He summoned admiration for Colonel Hatherley and found that it presented itself at the double.

He stared hard into the mirror and, seeing the cashier's face for the last time, experienced momentary sorrow for Charlotte. The soldier's face replaced the clerical face; military conformity for clerical conformity. Gazing deep into the mottled glass Spenser almost saluted.

Half an hour later, when he had finished the letter and sealed the envelope, Couldridge came into his room. 'I've got a dead Pathan in the mortuary,' he said. 'What happened to him?'

Spenser said: 'He was shot trying to escape.'

11

John Couldridge pondered on his relationship with Spenser as he rode towards the other village to stitch and splint the casualties from a banyan tree riot. He looked too big, too long in the leg, for the small black horse; but he rode well and the horse appreciated the way in which he spread his weight.

Spenser, he knew, would make a good soldier; but he doubted if he would ever be a happy one. In the beginning there would be snubs and small humiliations from the other officers as, instinctively, they nosed out his background, his unfamiliarity with the polo field, his earnest intent to succeed. And he would succeed because the Army rewarded good soldiers whatever their background. He would advance and harden until he believed that every decision he took was right. At the moment Spenser was still vulnerable; and it was this vulnerability that held them together;

the relationship almost of doctor and patient. Would the relationship continue, he wondered, when the patient was cured?

The village appeared like a mirage. Behind him, behind the hot tongue of the plateau, stood the white teeth of the mountains. He urged the sweating horse forward and patted its neck. First a few matchstick huts, a couple of dogs laughing at the heat, then the district officer's dak bungalow resting beneath the green lace of an acacia, fringed with cosmos and lupins. Further on the banyan tree.

The district officer, whose name was Markham, was tall and serious and worried; incongruously he wore a monacle. He had a peeling, muddled face and his shorts almost covered his sharp knees. He poured tea beneath a lazy fan in the living room and told Couldridge about the riot.

'The usual thing,' he said. 'A Moslem procession and a Hindu banyan tree. It was Moharrum yesterday—the Moslem day of mourning. The Moslems wanted the Hindus to lop the lower branches of the tree to allow a replica of the tomb of Mohammed's grandson, Imam Husain, to pass underneath. The Hindus refused. Then they started fighting each other. It doesn't matter so much when they're equally divided. But this is a predominantly Moslem village like most of them round here and I was scared that the Hindus—there's only a handful of them—would get murdered.' He sipped tea from a cup that looked as if it had been taken from a dolls' set in his big-knuckled hand.

'So what did you do?'

'I managed to arrange a truce and then got my spade out.'

'Your spade? What were you going to do? Trying to clobber a few Moslems yourself?'

'Good Lord no.' His monocle dropped to his chest and his face looked very honest. A once-pretty woman with a tired face came in. 'Lucy, I want you to meet Dr Couldridge. The Army has kindly loaned him to us to patch up our wounded zealots. I was just telling him about the spade.'

She said in a tired, Scottish voice: 'My husband had a hollow dug under the tree so that the Moslems could walk underneath

71

without touching the branches with the replica of the tomb.'

Couldridge said: 'That was very ingenious. How did you come to think of that?'

'It's pretty obvious when you think about it,' Markham said. 'It was the only way really.'

Mrs Markham nibbled at a melting chocolate biscuit. 'We've lost all our respect now,' she said hopelessly. 'We might as well leave and start all over again somewhere.' There was no expression in the neglected face above the high collar of the silk striped dress.

Markham put his hand on her knee and she let it rest there. 'Don't say that, Lucy. It's not as bad as all that. They know I only did it to stop them getting hurt.'

'Now all your authority's gone,' she said, as if there had never been much. 'What do you think, Dr Couldridge?'

'I'm the last person to ask. I've only just got out here.'

'But you've lived in India a long time.'

'How can you tell that?'

'From your skin.' Her hand strayed to her own cheeks.

'You should have been a dermatologist,' he said. But neither of them laughed.

Markham said: 'I think I'll take Dr Couldridge to see the casualties now. There aren't very many. But I think one or two of them need a few stitches and there are a few broken heads.'

'It's a bit late for stitching,' Couldridge said. 'But I'll see what I can do.'

Outside the bungalow Markham said: 'Don't take too much notice of her, doctor. You know how women are sometimes. Especially you being a doctor.'

Couldridge did know how women were sometimes; but he suspected Mrs Markham's attacks of cynicism occurred more than once a month.

The wounded were in two different houses, Moslem and Hindu. Couldridge went first to the Hindus because he was British and they were in the minority. He stitched a few wounds and hoped they would heal, and put dressings on them. He also cut hair away from two head wounds, decided there were no fractures, and

72

went to the Moslems where he did much the same.

He told Markham that he would return in a couple of days to see how the wounds were healing. They sauntered back through the village, the warm sloth of the place thick around them. A dog urinated half-heartedly against the wheel of a leaning ox cart, an old man slept in the thick dusk of his shop.

As they neared the bungalow a small boy came running from a wooden house. They stopped expecting him to run around them; instead he ran straight into them.

'Hey,' Markham said, catching his swinging monacle. 'Watch where you're going.'

The boy clutched at their legs, peered around him and tried to run back into the house again. Couldridge caught him by the arm and held on while the boy kicked and threw himself on to the ground.

The boy's father, middle-aged and bow-legged, appeared at the dark mouth of the house and shouted at Markham.

'I should let him go,' Markham said. 'Apparently he has been naughty and was trying to escape punishment.' He looked at Couldridge with surprise. 'He didn't hurt you, did he?'

'No, he didn't hurt me.' Couldridge tried talking to the boy in Urdu, but he didn't understand. 'Can you tell him to lie still a moment? Tell him I won't hurt him.'

'I think you'd better leave him alone,' Markham said. 'His father is getting pretty upset. He's one of the big noises in the village. A Moslem and a trouble-maker.'

'I don't give a damn if he's a dancing dervish,' Couldridge said. 'I think that boy's going blind.'

'Blind? What makes you think that?'

'I saw his eyes just now. Take a look at them. They're almost red. Trachoma. If he isn't treated now he'll be blind in a few months.'

'It's not uncommon around here,' Markham said.

Couldridge turned on him. 'I don't give a damn how common or uncommon it is. The sight of that boy can be saved if he's treated in time. Now tell the father.' The boy lay still in the dust,

73

face averted from Couldridge.

Markham talked to the father. 'He says leave his son alone,' he said. 'He says go back to the hills and carry on killing Pathans.'

'Did you tell him I'm a doctor?'

'I did. He knew that anyway because you have been treating the wounds of the Hindus.'

'And the Moslems, damn it.'

'He seemed more concerned that you treated the Hindus first.'

'Did you tell him I think his son is going blind?'

'I told him you thought he had eye trouble'

'Tell him I think he's going blind.'

Reluctance showed on Markham's face. 'I don't think it will make any difference. They don't like us interfering with their families.'

'Tell him.'

Markham spoke again to the Moslem, with deference approaching servility.

'What did he say?'

'He said leave his son alone or he will report you to me.'

'To hell with him. Tell him I'm taking his son to your bungalow. Tell him he'll be quite safe and that he can come along as well if he wishes. But tell him I'm taking the boy whatever happens.'

'I must tell you I don't like it,' Markham said. He adjusted his monocle but it gave him no authority. 'It will only cause trouble and we've had enough of that already.'

But Couldridge was on his way back to the bungalow pulling the boy behind him. After a few moments Markham followed, and the boy's father followed Markham.

In the bungalow Mrs Markham said: 'What's going on?'

Couldridge said: 'I think this boy is going blind. I want to examine his eyes here because I think I may be able to save his sight. His father isn't very keen.'

The boy's father stood at the open door of the bungalow. He had been joined by two other men. Soon, Couldridge thought, there would be others.

Markham said: 'We'll have another riot on our hands in a minute.'

'Don't worry,' Couldridge said. 'I'll stitch their wounds up for them again.'

'And perhaps your own,' Markham said.

Mrs Markham said: 'Is there anything I can get you, doctor?' The weariness had lifted from her face and she stood behind the frightened boy like an anxious mother. 'Don't worry about the father. He's only capable of inciting a riot when he's backed by religion.' She turned to her husband. 'If Dr Couldridge thinks he can do some good for the boy, for God's sake let him get on with it. Stand up to them for a change.'

Markham's muddled face was starting with sweat. 'You don't understand,' he said. 'You don't understand.'

Couldridge washed his hands in a rust-stained wash-basin and bent over the boy. The boy shrank back, red eyes staring with fear, as if he expected Couldridge to torture him.

'Tell him not to be frightened,' Couldridge said. 'Tell him I want to make his eyes better. I can't examine them properly because I haven't got my instruments with me. But I can probably get an idea how bad it is.'

He lifted the eyelid and saw the tiny eruptions on the conjunctiva. The cornea didn't appear to be damaged; but it was difficult to tell from such a superficial examination. But if the trachoma wasn't treated immediately there would soon be scarring and vascularisation of the cornea caused by secondary infections.

Couldridge straightened up and said: 'I want to take him back to my surgery to treat him.'

Markham's monocle fell out of his eye with theatrical surprise. 'Absolutely out of the question,' he said. 'His father would accuse you of kidnapping.'

'You can explain the situation to his father.'

'He wouldn't understand. And I must say, Couldridge, that I see his point. You, a perfect stranger, cantering into the village one day and expecting to be able to take a small boy away back to an Army camp.'

75

Couldridge cracked his fist down on the flimsy table. 'For God's sake, I only want to try and save the boy's sight. Even now it may be too late.'

Mrs Markham said: 'I'll try and explain it. You go and wash your hands again or you'll be catching trachoma.'

'You sound as if you know a bit about medicine, Mrs Markham.'

'I was a nurse once,' she said. 'A long time ago.'

She talked to the father who was now surrounded by a dozen excited Moslems. Even if he had wanted to, the father could not now make any concessions in front of the audience.

Mrs Markham shook her head sadly, the weariness beginning to descend upon her again. 'I'm sorry, doctor,' she said. 'But it's hopeless. Short of kidnapping the boy there's nothing you can do'.

Couldridge marched around the room, stopping only to pull the boy's hand away from his red eyes. Finally he said: 'Then I'll come back tomorrow. Tell the father that. Tell him that I'll come back with medicine and ointments and that if they are used properly the boy may keep his sight.' A thought occurred to him. 'Ask the boy how much he can see.'

The boy spoke in a soft scared voice.

'He's too frightened to talk,' Mrs Markham said. 'He just keeps saying that the sun is fading.'

Couldridge nodded. 'It doesn't sound too good. Tell him to try and leave his eyes alone. Tell him not to be frightened and that I'll be back tomorrow with something to make his eyes better. And tell the father to keep him in a dark room. Can you keep an eye on the boy?'

'We can try,' Markham said. 'But it won't be easy.'

'We'll do our best,' Mrs Markham said.

'Tell the boy he can go.'

The boy darted to his feet and ran into a chair. His father took him by the arm and the crowd dispersed.

As he rode back to camp Couldridge thought about the prostitute with trachoma in the Bombay brothel. Why had he not been

76

so eager to try and cure her? Because, he decided, he had been on his way to the Punjab next day and she was so immersed in squalor and disease that a cure was impossible. He hoped the fact that she was a prostitute had not subconsciously influenced him.

When he arrived back an orderly told him that there was a corpse in the mortuary. He noted the knee smashed at the front and the bullet wound at the back of the head. He wondered vaguely about the disparity—and about the presence of a Pathan near to the base, because bodies were never brought back from the hills. But he was too concerned with the boy with trachoma to worry too much.

After sick parade next day, after two boils, one chronic catarrh, one sprained wrist, one rupture and one female hypochondriac, Couldridge obtained permission from Colonel Hatherley to return to the village for a few hours.

Markham was standing on the verandah drinking gin. His monocle hung around his chest and his peeling face was blotchy: it was not his first gin that day. His wife was sitting in a wicker rocking chair; she had been crying.

'Well?' Couldridge said.

Markham tossed back the gin. He poured himself another and said: 'Bad news, I'm afraid. You'd better have a drink.'

'No thanks. For God's sake, what's happened?'

'We couldn't help it,' Markham said.

Couldridge turned to Mrs Markham. 'What happened?'

Mrs Markham's voice was devoid of emotion. 'The father called in the local medicine man, witch doctor, quack—call him what you like.

Couldridge sat down, hope replaced by defeat, because already he knew. 'What happened?'

'The medicine man treated the boy's eyes with a lamp wick. He can't see at all now.'

'Oh God,' Couldridge said.

Markham said: 'I'm dreadfully sorry.' His words were fused together with gin. 'It must have happened immediately after you

77

left. We went round in the evening. I'm dreadfully sorry. Dreadfully sorry.' He poured himself some more gin.

'Give me one,' Couldridge said. He swallowed it neat and clenched his teeth as the scented alcohol reached his stomach. 'I'll go round and see him.'

'You'll find them praying,' Mrs Markham said. 'It's about their time.'

But they weren't praying. The father tried to stop him entering the house but he pushed past. The boy lay on a mattress on the floor, his eyes covered with two pieces of dirty white cloth. His mother sat on the floor beside the mattress, her face covered.

Couldridge removed the pieces of cloth from the boy's eyes. They were swollen and bloodied and unseeing. The cornea and sclera were burned, the lids damaged so that he could not blink. Couldridge held the boy's hand and said: 'I'm sorry boy.' He realised he didn't know his name. The boy stared at him and through him.

Couldridge turned to the father. 'You know you've blinded him,' he said. 'He'll never see again.' The man shrugged.

Couldridge grabbed him by the shoulders and shook him. 'You've blinded him. Do you understand.' He was shouting and the boy on the mattress turned and directed his eyes in the direction of the noise. Couldridge let the man go; he stood there calmly, hatred settling on his face.

Couldridge walked out into the noon heat. He untethered his horse and mounted. Markham stumbled down from the verandah and said: 'I'm dreadfully sorry, Couldridge. Most dreadfully sorry.'

Couldridge said: 'You'd better go and see the boy's father. He'll probably take out an action for assault against me. But you won't get the boy as a witness against me—he couldn't see anything.'

When he got back to his quarters he wrote a letter applying for a posting to Calcutta. Away from futile fighting, away from isolated suffering and ignorance. To the capital of disease, the fount of research.

BOOK TWO

1

In Calcutta the scale of suffering—and the unquestioning acceptance of it—appalled and infuriated John Couldridge. He hungered to cure some of the disease around him; to cultivate bacilli shaped like commas or queries or tadpoles and to stalk their bodies wriggling in beef broth or blood serum jelly until they led him to discoveries that would electrify medical opinion. But the starved, sleepy air of resignation of the sick mocked such naïve aspirations. If they were to be reborn into another life, the placid faces implied, what was the point of prolonging this one? Their fatalism was as infectious as their diseases. It wasn't the tenets of Hinduism that worried and angered Couldridge: it was the suspicion of ultimate futility that they imparted. What was the point of delaying death? If he discovered a cure of tuberculosis then nature would surely appoint another executioner.

But Couldridge's occasional moods of defeatism were always overtaken by his pioneering instincts, his contribution to the processes of evolution. Cholera, typhoid, dysentry, plague, smallpox, malaria, scrofula—all around him the bacteria prospered as ebulliently as the shopkeepers in the bazaars. All around him he saw eyes dead or dying from smallpox, keratomalalia, trachoma, glaucoma, ophthalmia neonatorum, congenital syphilis. All around him he saw children with pot-bellies dying of starvation and old men with collapsed faces dying of neglect. He saw women dying of burns when they had failed completely to destroy themselves after their husband's deaths, he saw a twelve-year-old girl dying from a haemorrhage sustained on the nuptial bed. He was overwhelmed by the pain and misery around him and exhilarated by its potential for research.

He was working in a military hospital on the banks of the River Hooghly. It might have been argued that the position of the hospital exposed the patients to further risks from water-born infections; but wherever a hospital had been built in Calcutta it would have exposed patients to some sort of contamination. And at least the warm wet breezes flowing with the river gave the impression that they were washing all the infection towards the saline antiseptic of the sea eighty-two navigational miles away.

The hospital was wooden and rambling, with long verandahs caged to keep out mosquitos, slow fans that hypnotised the ever-susceptible Indian orderlies into excesses of lethargy and floors so highly polished that the lethargy was frequently overthrown. Some efforts were made at isolation; but trying to isolate disease in Calcutta was like trying to isolate a dandelion in an English meadow.

Couldridge spent a lot of his time in the hospital laboratory; but the authorities did not encourage private research. And the medical officer in charge told Couldridge that urine tests were more important than the pursuit of plague and cholera bacilli and the chlorination of water. At night when officialdom had retired to the mess Couldridge continued with his experiments.

Couldridge was sometimes joined by a young Indian doctor called Bose. Bose was a Bengali, strong and quiet, powered by a hunger for medical knowledge and a dour determination never to be servile to the British, like so many of his people. His hair was blue-black and as bright as metal; on one side, just above the ear, it grew in a white patch the size of a penny—the texture of this patch was coarser than the rest of his hair and he wore it like a badge above his watchful face. Couldridge was aware of the sensitive desire for knowledge behind the muscles of Bose's personality, and together they tracked the bacilli that others had trailed and tried to control. But he never paid much attention

81

to the contained pride of Bose's character. At night in the warm, acid-smelling laboratory Dr Bose was his assistant, nothing more.

First Couldridge copied the experiments of Dr Nesfield in the purification of water. He nursed some typhoid bacilli and infected a litre of sterile tap water with them; then he made a solution of chlorine and added potassium iodide and starch, and titrated it with sodium thiosulphate to estimate the quantity of chlorine. Then he added some of the chlorine solution to the infected water. After one minute he put a sample on a peptone agar slope and turned triumphantly to Bose as if he had just made the discovery. 'There you are,' he said. 'What did I tell you? All dead.'

'You're very clever,' Bose said.

'In fact if chlorine in water kills typhoid bacilli then it must kill all bacteria borne by water.'

Bose nodded.

'Do you believe me?'

'Yes, I believe you. I was wondering about the taste. I don't think many people will enjoy the taste of chlorine or any of the other ingredients in their drinking water.'

'You're absolutely right. They won't.' Couldridge was in full showman's stride. 'But the water can be dechlorinated and made absolutely tasteless by adding Sodium Thiosulphate. Do you want to taste some?'

'If you like.' He smiled briefly. 'I suppose you're sure that the bacilli are all dead?'

'Absolutely. If we don't have the courage of our convictions then no one else will. You must always remember that. If we don't drink some purified water now there is no point in continuing our research. We must have courage.'

'All right,' Bose said. 'Let's prove that we have the courage of Dr Nesfield's convictions.'

'I have. I've just tested them and proved them. Come, are you going to drink or not?'

'I have said I will.'

'Good man. Now let's go down to the river and get some water.'

'Water from the Hooghly?' Bose's hand strayed to the patch

of tough white hair. 'It's got every possible type of infection in it. Sewage, dead rats, even human corpses.'

'Wonderful,' Couldridge said. 'Then we'll be able to kill every possible kind of infection.'

They walked through the hospital garden to the riverbank. There was the smell of paint and mud and garbage, and in the moonlight the water was molten silver.

'There are probably a few snakes around,' Bose said.

'Nothing to worry about,' Couldridge said. 'After all we're doctors. Heal thyself. . . .'

Couldridge filled a jug with water, then took it back to the laboratory. 'There,' he said. 'What do you think of that?'

'It looks a bit murky.'

'So what do we do about that?' Couldridge talked with the confidence of a man with the answers in front of him.

Bose said: 'I suppose the particles of solid matter will interfere with the action of the chlorine.'

'Exactly,' Couldridge said. 'So what do we do about it?'

'Filter it?'

'Absolutely right. Or we can precipitate the particles with alum. That's what Nesfield did when he took water from the Thames.'

'Perhaps we should do both.'

Couldridge did both because after he had filtered the water through a cotton bag it was still discoloured. He said knowledgeably: 'Actually Nesfield found that water from the Shat-el-Arab at Basra could be sterilised without filtration.'

'Did he,' Bose said. 'Quite remarkable.'

'Now we must drink,' Couldridge said. 'A toast, Bose, to the conquest of disease.'

Bose gazed speculatively into his cup of water as if he thought disease might score an immediate victory. 'Very well,' he said, 'to the conquest of disease.'

They clinked cups, hesitated for a moment and then tossed back the drinks like confirmed chlorinated water addicts.

'One thing bothers me,' Bose said.

'What's that?'

'If Nesfield's method of sterilising water is so successful why is it not used all over the world? Why, for instance, is it not used in the Army? Isn't it practical?'

'It's practical all right. You can transport liquified chlorine in steel cylinders. Or on a small military camp you can use sodium hypochlorite. You make that by dissolving bleaching powder and adding sodium carbonate. Nesfield called his sodium hypochlorite solution Chlorogen. Twenty drops purify a kerosine oil tin of water.'

'Then why are we not using it in this hospital?'

'Because Nesfield's methods have not yet been completely accepted.'

'Why not?'

'It's difficult to explain,' said Couldridge, who did not understand himself.

'But surely in the Army hundreds of soldiers are dying from typhoid and cholera. Why is this still allowed to happen?'

Couldridge's enthusiasm to contribute to medical progress—an enthusiasm amounting almost to lust—shrivelled a little as he explored the possibilities. Premature publication of evidence, bad theory? But neither were so: the proof was there on the peptone agar slope. He was left with the only alternatives—resentment towards experiment and discovery, or simple jealousy of youthful achievement. Couldridge did not normally examine such possibilities. But now he had been forced to by Bose. And having met Randolph Buckingham, he had to accept that prejudice and jealousy in his profession were realities. The knowledge chilled him and he began to put away the apparatus.

Bose said: 'You don't seem to have answered my question.'

'I know.' Couldridge peered into the future and shivered. 'I hadn't really thought about it before.' But he had often wondered about the reluctance of the recognised experts to accept the discoveries of men such as Koch. Couldridge had made a study of Koch: how he had established that every disease is caused by one particular microbe; that cholera flourishes in wet places in Calcutta such as Hindu drinking wells; that disinfectants like

84

mercuric chloride and carbolic acid can control its spread. But Koch had found that the battle to overcome dogma was as tough as the battle against disease.

Couldridge had not worried himself too much about the antipathy of the elders towards progress. He had presumed that the answer lay in the arrogance of Dr Robert Koch, or perhaps in scepticism generated by all the false discoveries at the end of the nineteenth century. And he had hoped that caution was necessary to ensure that no false cures were put on the market, that no false hopes were aroused. Now he was not so sure.

Anger suffused him as he considered the possibility that progress could be retarded by envy, malice or reactionary stupidity. He saw himself standing on a platform—as Nesfield had stood—before an audience of experts triumphantly proving his theories with a tank of Thames water. He saw himself triumphantly routing the bacilli of consumption on a stage before a massed audience of elderly specialists in London: he saw himself performing a masterly corneal graft before a group of cynical ophthalmologists. On each occasion it was the victory over the practitioners of conservatism rather than the alleviation of suffering that made him exhilarated.

Through the mosquito mesh covering the laboratory window he could see fireflies flirting in the sweating night. And beyond them the river, its cargo of germs and dirt lacquered by the moonlight.

Bose said: 'You're very quiet.'

'I was thinking about your question.'

'About the reluctance of the learned men of medicine to accept the theories of the young? We in India are equally puzzled by the unwillingness of those in political and military authority to allow progress. Almost everything we ask for is refused by the British. Then there are riots and boycotts and bomb outrages and the British wonder why.'

Couldridge washed out the test tubes and flasks, replaced the pipettes, erased all evidence of activities that would be regarded with as much condemnation as the performing of an abortion.

'Good heavens,' he said, 'you're not an agitator, are you Bose?'

'No,' Bose said. 'But I see the point of view of the young people. The British can no longer go on treating them like children. They must have a say in their government, in their future.'

'I didn't know you felt so strongly about such matters.'

'You're the only sahib'—he pronounced the word with heavy sarcasm—'who does.'

'Well, don't get involved in any trouble. You're too valuable a doctor.'

'Do not worry,' Bose said.

Couldridge patted him on the back and immediately felt that the gesture was patronising, like patting a faithful dog or a child that has performed a service. 'Together we'll wage war on bacteria —and stuffy doctors who try and stop us.'

'Together,' Bose said. They clasped hands, and Couldridge wondered whether he or Bose should release the grip first. Bose relaxed his hand and said: 'Tell me, John'—he uttered the Christian name almost shyly—'what will give you most satisfaction when one of your experiments is successful? The fact that it is a personal triumph or the knowledge that you have made a contribution towards the easing of Mankind's suffering?'

Couldridge said: 'Does it matter? Surely the fact that an experiment has been successful is sufficient.' He paused. 'The fact is that I don't really know the answer to your question. It's one of those questions you avoid asking yourself because you don't want to hear the answer.'

'Just as famous doctors don't want to hear the answers of those younger and less experienced than themselves?'

'Yes,' Couldridge said. 'Something like that, I suppose.'

Bose explored his abdomen with his fingers. 'I've got the stomach ache,' he said. 'I hope your faith in this Dr Nesfield is justified.'

'Absolutely. But if you feel ill in the morning report sick to me.'

'But what if you're sick?' Bose said.

'Then I'll report sick at your surgery and we'll meet half way.'

But instead Couldridge was summoned to the principal of the hospital, a precise little colonel who had long ago accepted his own lack of personality and relied on the mystique of his profession to impress laymen, and snappy authority to cower subordinates. Colonel Little, whom no one called Tich, abided by two unbreakable rules: never tell a patient what's wrong with him and never commend a junior officer if he's done well. He was in his forties and although he had spent thirty years in India the sun had never tanned his face. He spoke abruptly and confused conversation by irrelevancy and answering questions with questions.

'Sit down,' he said to Couldridge, pointing to a chair lower than his own, a method of asserting authority which he had once read about in a novel. 'I've been hearing reports about you.' He waited for a reply.

Coulridge said: 'I see.'

'Midnight experiments in the lab and all that sort of thing.'

'That's right, sir,' Couldridge said.

'What sort of experiments?'

'Not experiments exactly. I've been following the research into the purification of water carried out by Dr Nesfield in London.'

'Filtration and boiling,' Little said. 'Notter and Firth field watercart filters. Nothing to beat them.'

'I beg your pardon?' Couldridge said.

'What was that?' Little said.

Couldridge plunged on. 'Dr Nesfield has discovered a way to purify water with chlorine. It's quick, simple and the water stays tasteless after sodium thiosulphate has been added. I can't understand why the Army hasn't adopted his ideas.'

'Because the Army knows better,' Little said. 'There's nothing wrong with filtration and boiling.'

'But hundreds of troops die from cholera and typhoid and dysentry.'

'And thousands die from wounds suffered on the field of battle,' Little said.

87

'I don't quite see what that's got to do with it, sir.' He emphasised the sir.

'What about the Rideal Walker Method?'

Couldridge paused confounded; then realised that Little must have been told what he had been doing in the laboratory and had done some homework. 'What about it, sir?'

'What's that?' Little said.

'I said what about the Rideal Walker method?'

'Ah yes,' Little said. 'The Rideal Walker method. It proved that the germicidal value of chlorine was only 1 in 1,000, did it not?'

Couldridge was glad that he, too, had done his homework. 'Only because the peptone and meat broth used neutralised the chlorine. The Rideal Walker method might be effective for some antiseptics—carbolic acid for instance—but not those that have been neutralised by peptone broth.'

Little drank theatrically from a glass of water on his desk. The fan was rotating quickly and the morning sun was still weak, but already his face was sweating and his pale skin looked spongy. 'Nesfield's methods are too risky, Couldridge,' he said. 'Too damn risky.' He didn't pursue Rideal Walker.

'I don't see that, sir.'

'It's not your place to see it. You're a very junior officer.'

'It's not my experiments I'm defending, sir. It's Dr Nesfield's work.'

'Second Lieutenant Nesfield I think you mean. A very junior officer like yourself.'

'Sir, I don't see that seniority or otherwise enters into it if the experiments have been proved to be successful.'

Colonel Little drained his boiled water. 'Some Frenchman thought he had isolated the cholera microbe. In fact he had found nothing of the kind. What happened? He subsequently died of cholera.'

'But Koch has isolated the microbe,' Couldridge said, happy to pursue one of Little's irrelevancies.

'All this sort of thing is too hurried. What do you young fellows

88

know about the effect of chlorine on a man's system if he keeps on drinking it?'

'He wouldn't,' Couldridge said. 'The water is dechlorinated after purification.'

'Nothing like a good boiling,' Little said.

'Quite impracticable on the field of battle, if you don't mind me saying so, sir. The whole method is unwieldy and almost impossible to carry out effectively when troops are on the move.'

'I expect young Nesfield's ideas are being studied,' said Little, implying that they were being filed away in a Whitehall vault. 'Much too premature for action. I have had Buckingham's views.'

Couldridge, who had forgotten that Buckingham had been promoted to an administrative job in Calcutta, said: 'Buckingham's views on what?'

'Exactly,' Colonel Little said.

'You have Buckingham's views on Doctor—sorry, Second Lieutenant—Nesfield's experiments?'

'I've got his views on you,' Little said. He took a sheet of paper from a tray. 'Much the same as mine.'

'Sir?'

'I said Buckingham's views are much the same as mine.'

Couldridge waited but Little didn't enlighten him.

Little said: 'It's got to stop.'

'Got to stop, sir?'

'This experimenting. You're in the Army now, Couldridge. And another thing—I'm told that you're interested in several specialised subjects.'

'I don't want to confine myself to boils and piles, if that's what you mean, sir. I have many interests in medicine. Surely every doctor should. I'm particularly interested in ophthalmology.'

'Very unwise,' Little said. 'Doesn't go down well. If a doctor is going to specialise then he must stick to his subject. You can't attend to eyes and ears at the same time.'

Couldridge guessed that Little was memorising Buckingham's report. He said rather pompously: 'I think doctors should specialise in alleviating human suffering.'

89

'It's got to stop,' Little said. 'Understand?'

Couldridge said: 'Understood, sir.'

Little looked mildly surprised. Then relaxed and poured himself another glass of boiled and filtrated water.

That night under his mosquito net Couldridge listened to the whining of a frustrated mosquito and tried to decide how he could set up his own laboratory. But his thoughts were interrupted by a mild attack of dysentery. He preferred to think that it was reaction to his conversation with Little rather than an infection picked up from the water of the Hooghly sliding silkily past his window.

2

DR BOSE had a surgery in a lane behind the bazaar. Often his tiny waiting room was so crowded that patients jostled against each other swopping germs and ensuring that Bose continued in business. At night in the lane outside, beside an open sewer, as many Indians died in the moonlight as Bose had cured in the day.

At Bose's request Couldridge set up a primitive laboratory in a small hot room at the rear of the surgery. There, after the last patient had departed with a prescription for impotence or gonorrhoea or chicken pox, Couldridge and the quiet, intense young doctor tried to follow, catch up and overtake the pioneering professors of the world.

It was, Couldridge knew, quite hopeless; almost farcical. Any school laboratory in Britain had better equipment than they possessed. And any progress in one direction was thwarted by his unbridled curiosity in all fields of medicine. He wanted to emulate Walter Reed's work on yellow fever and the German Emil von Behring's research on tetanus and diphtheria; even to investigate the open-air sanatorium treatment of tuberculosis practised by Edward Trudeau at Saranac Lake in the U.S.A. And always he wanted to extend his knowledge of eye defects; but for this he had no equipment at all. Soon, he knew, he would have to curb his appetite for knowledge.

But in the hospital there was so much material for research that it was difficult to impose discipline. Occasionally, when the hunger was temporarily assuaged, Couldridge lay on his bed beneath the fan and worried that he was sacrificing the humanitarian urge for the clinical. If this were so then he was no longer a doctor: he was a scientist.

Most of the patients in the hospital were soldiers suffering from dysentery, cholera, typhoid and pneumonia. Once or twice he persuaded his seniors to allow him to carry out an autopsy and, as he had won a certificate of honour for dissection at St Mary's, they reluctantly agreed. In the intestines of one cholera victim he saw the micro-organisms that Robert Koch had found before him—and rushed round to Bose with the news. But all the time he was aware that he was a disciple rather than an apostle of research; and that he would remain so until he could work in a fully-equipped laboratory.

Bose, he knew, feared the time when he found such a laboratory because he thought that it would be the end of their relationship. The two of them, one white and one brown, on equal terms: it was still hardly credible in a community where the British treated an Indian doctor with little more respect than a Brahmin would show to an Untouchable. Bose suffered many humiliations from the British and always looked as if he were filing them away for future reference.

And, while they worked together in their stuffy little laboratory, India pursued the same chaotic, suicidal policies that had stultified its progress since the Aryan invasion in 1,500 B.C. and probably before. But in Calcutta there was a new intensity to the hatred—hatred of the British and hatred of each other. To Couldridge the chaos seemed to be the negation of all that he aspired to.

Students led the agitation. They formed gangs and robbed

banks and stores for money for their funds, they accused the British of deliberately spreading plague, they tried to assassinate prominent British civil servants, they ordered a boycott of all foreign goods and they made bombs.

In one bomb factory police found all the equipment for the manufacture of anarchist-type bombs. Dry batteries, picric acid, gunpowder, dynamite, cartridges, detonators, moulds, thermometers, test tubes. The fear of anarchy was contagious and even in the U.S.A. there were reports of a conspiracy to reorganise rebellion in India. Only in Britain was the situation reviewed with a calm approaching indifference.

In India there was talk of another Mutiny and sahibs and memsahibs who had been contemplating hesitant friendship with Indians firmly pulled the lace curtains across the windows of enlightenment once more.

And still, despite such distractions, the Indians pursued their own remorseless blood feuds. Hindu versus Moslem. Banyan trees versus procession. Cow versus pig. All over the subcontinent Indians continued to put aside festive days of the year for the slaughter of each other.

'Will it never end?' Couldridge asked Bose.

Bose, who was travelling to the Holy city of Benares the following day to immerse himself in the waters of the Ganges, said: 'I see no end to it. Not in our lifetime anyway.'

'But why? Doesn't it worry you that while we are standing here trying to find ways of saving life your countrymen are busy killing each other off?'

'It does not worry me. Why should it? I am assured of another life. If I uphold my religion then I am doing no wrong. It is they who pray to Mecca who should be worried.'

'Bose,' Couldridge said, 'sometimes you and India defeat me.' He looked at their primitive equipment and considered their lack of achievement. Frustration exploded into anger. 'Everything defeats me. You, India, the Army, my profession.'

Bose said: 'You and I have only just started. There are many useful years ahead of us.'

Couldridge ignored him. 'I might just as well have stayed in the Punjab treating athlete's foot and dandruff. Or stayed in London for that matter.'

'You don't mean that.'

'I bloody well do mean it.' He turned sweeping half a dozen test-tubes into the sink; all but one broke. He wasn't sure whether the gesture had been deliberate or accidental.

Bose said nothing.

'For God's sake stop looking so bloody holy.'

Bose shrugged.

Then Couldridge apologised. 'It's just that it all seems so futile,' he said.

'It is just something that you will have to overcome. All great men have difficulties put before them.'

'I'm not a great man, Bose.'

'Perhaps one day. When you have overcome these difficulties.'

Couldridge grinned. 'Then you'll be great with me, Bose.'

'Not I,' Bose said. 'I am an Indian.'

'Perhaps we should both stop feeling sorry for ourselves,' Couldridge said. 'Come on, help me pick up the broken glass.'

After he had cleared up Couldridge left Bose's three small rooms with their black and white painted nameplate outside and walked back to the hospital. Past crouching buildings, past sleeping bodies like balls of soiled cottonwool, past scavenging dogs and restless shadows. He felt that eyes were watching him from the darkness, that the shadows were peopled with bodies, oiled and sinuous and sulky with hatred. He smelled the squalor and, he fancied, the hatred.

When he reached his quarters he found a letter awaiting him. It said that he had been appointed as one of the medical officers on the train taking the official party from Calcutta to Delhi for the Great Durbar to commemorate the coronation of Edward VII. It would be, he had been told, the most majestic and spectacular event in the history of Imperial India.

93

3

THE first to alight from the train was Neville Spenser. Authority, Couldridge thought, had grown upon him since they had last been together two years before. His face was deeply tanned, his moustache neatly clipped: it was no longer the face through the cashier's grille: it was the face of a professional soldier, already promoted to lieutenant. Except, perhaps, to those in whom he confided: those who realised that he had assumed his character as an actor assumes a character in the dressing room.

With Spenser came his wife, a tall girl in a grey and pink dress, ordinary brown hair centre-parted, a parasol on her arm. She had a pale face, full of uncertainties, lips that quivered slightly as she spoke; a girl with the same background as Spenser who had not been born with his talent to adapt character to environment.

'Neville,' he said.

'Hallo, John. It's been a long time.'

They clasped hands. The pleasure at their reunion was sharp and genuine.

Next came the Fultons. The best type of British officer and the best type of wife, Couldridge thought. Fair-minded, uncomplaining, resilient. While there were such people in the Service there was hope. His old buoyancy returned and the images of Little and his colleagues receded.

They shook hands and Mrs Fulton said: 'Have you had many young women demanding to be examined in Calcutta since we last saw you?'

Couldridge shook his head. 'Not all that many.' Then he looked up and saw Joanne Pinkerton standing on the steps of the carriage, the argumentative girl who had made a fool of herself in the hills.

'Hallo,' she said.

'Hallo,' he said. 'How's the eyesight?'

'Then you remember me?'

'Of course I remember you. I treated you for bronchial pneumonia.'

'And I made a fool of myself.'

Couldridge didn't comment.

Mrs Fulton said: 'All has been forgiven and forgotten.'

'Except,' her husband said, 'that she's left her footprint to posterity in cement. The story will be talked about for decades to come.'

Couldridge said: 'I didn't know you were coming. I somehow thought you had returned to New York.'

'Or hoped I had.'

'No,' he said. 'I didn't hope one way or the other.'

Her dress was also grey, but scattered with tiny pink roses like wallpaper in an old lady's bedroom. She wore a pink Easter bonnet; contrasted with such gentle colours her face was sharply pretty. But not as assertive or as emancipated as it had been two years before; or so it seemed to John Couldridge.

They stood on the platform assessing each other after two years. Steam from the train hissed into white cumulus that billowed among the colours alighting from the carriages—bright silk saris beside drawing-room fawns and greys; martial hues beside off-white dhotis; brown beside white. Then they walked past the exhausted engine into the courtyard outside, alive with rickshaw coolies and box wallahs and clutching blind beggars.

'I wish I could say I was glad to be back,' Joanne Pinkerton said.

Couldridge said: 'You didn't have to come back—it's not your home.'

She, Spenser and Couldridge took one carriage, the Fultons

another. The horses trotted prettily and precisely through the chaotic streets.

Joanne Pinkerton was shedding her unnatural reticence. 'I know I didn't have to come here. Nor is it any of your business. It just so happens that I do not particularly like Calcutta. It's not my India.'

'What is your India, Miss Pinkerton? Pathan country?'

'Very funny,' Joanne Pinkerton said.

Neville Spenser said: 'Perhaps we'll be able to get together for a drink this evening, John.'

'Don't worry,' Joanne Pinkerton said. 'I shan't embarrass you with my presence.'

Couldridge bought them lunch at the faded hotel where the Fultons were staying. Curried chicken with chapattis and popadoms, mangoes and desiccated coconut served by waiters in white turbans, white jackets and trousers with blue sashes across their chests, and plimsoles.

'How is it up in the hills these days?' Couldridge asked.

'Much the same,' Fulton said. 'Much the same as it has been for the past hundred years and much the same as it will be for the next hundred. Gurkhas killing Pathans, Pathans killing Gurkhas. The colonel had one of his turns again the other day and had a Pathan bayoneted to death after two of our lads had been pretty badly done up.'

Couldridge gazed out of the window at the oasis tranquility of the hotel garden. Hibiscus bushes with blossoms daubed on them, a sprinkler showering diamonds on the shaved lawn, a tall palm surveying it all. And he recalled John Laurence's remark in the 1860s—'India is quiet. As quiet as gunpowder.' He turned to Spenser. 'Yours is a very different India to this,' he said.

Spenser said: 'I prefer ours.'

'Yours is so futile. Beautiful and futile. And deceptive. You're killing, torturing and treating it all as if it were an episode from G. H. Henty. Or trying to. What's the point of it all?'

Spenser crumpled a chapatti. 'You seem to forget that the Pathans are killing British soldiers.'

96

'I said, what's the point of it? If you didn't send out patrols all the time they wouldn't kill British soldiers. Even if you argue that dissident tribesmen—as the Government likes to call them—must be controlled, none of it seems to be real soldiering to me.'

'Mutinous talk,' Fulton said goodnaturedly. 'Supposing the Russians did get ideas about pushing through Afghanistan into India. It wouldn't be very healthy for us if they found the hill country in the hands of anti-British tribesmen.'

Joanne Pinkerton sipped her iced water and said: 'You don't really believe all this talk about a Russian invasion, do you?'

Fulton shrugged. 'A lot of people didn't believe that the Boers would ever turn on the British.'

Couldridge said: 'The point I'm making is that none of it seems to be real soldiering. Keeping the natives down. A minor adventure story involving a lot of senseless killing and suffering.'

Spenser said: 'The Pathans don't give a damn about loss of life.'

'And do you?'

Spenser's face was devoid of emotion, almost placid. And ruthless because of its deliberate lack of feeling. 'I'm a soldier,' he said.

'That doesn't answer my question.'

'I think it does.'

Mrs Fulton mounted one of her rescue operations. 'Isn't it amazing,' she said, 'that both you and Neville have been chosen to go on this Durbar. I mean out of all the officers in India . . .'

Couldridge nodded. 'I can't imagine how it happened. I'm sure Little would never have recommended me. All the other doctors are very envious. It's a bit embarrassing really.'

'I'm sure it is,' Spenser said.

'What do you mean?'

'Well it's hardly real doctoring, is it?'

Couldridge grinned. 'Point taken,' he said. 'What exactly are your duties?'

'An assistant security officer. Strange, isn't it, that we're together again.'

'Yes,' Couldridge said. 'Quite a coincidence.' But Spenser was right, he thought. Perhaps he should refuse to go. Refuse to leave his research however elementary and futile it was, refuse to leave the noble slum of Calcutta, the biggest natural source of bacteria in the world. Or perhaps he could treat the trip as a holiday in which the greatest emergency he would have to cope with would be the vapours or a septic mosquito bite.

Spenser's wife, Charlotte, said: 'Perhaps Dr Couldridge doesn't want to go.' They were the first words she had spoken since they sat down for lunch. Even this one sentence, Couldridge suspected, had been an effort of will; such was her shyness.

He said kindly: 'You are very observant, Mrs Spenser. In fact I don't know whether I want to go or not.'

She smiled down at her curry and Couldridge sensed her desolation, her longing for dusty London gardens with their predictable beds of antirrhinum and stock, for familiar shops, and ferns in brass bowls in the hall. Spenser would have to be very kind to her.

Mrs Fulton said: 'I'm sure John will decide to go. It will be a wonderful experience. I only wish we had been invited. But still a fortnight's leave in Calcutta makes a pleasant change from the Punjab.'

Fulton said: 'John must have been selected for grooming for some important post.'

'I don't think so,' Couldridge said. 'Nor would you if you spoke to Little. Or Buckingham for that matter. They regard me more as a criminal than a doctor.'

'Why is that?' Joanne Pinkerton asked.

'Because I have the temerity to try and seek cures for all illnesses. Because I'm concerned with causes and not just cures.'

'Perhaps they have a point.'

'Point? What possible point can they have?' Couldridge stirred his weak sweet coffee with vigour.

'I don't see how you can tackle research into more than one

98

disease at a time. If you have any talent in that direction then you have a duty to mankind to concentrate on one subject.'

Couldridge said: 'Then you're as stuffy as Little and Buckingham and all the rest of them. When you go to University you don't stick to one subject, do you?'

'That's just learning, I guess. You're going beyond the boundaries of learning.'

'Perhaps,' Couldridge said deliberately, 'you do not have the mental capacity or the vision to conceive that research need not be limited.'

'There's no need to get upset,' she said. 'I was only wondering if perhaps these two officers you keep harping on about did have a point. After all they do have much more experience than you.'

Couldridge resisted the temptation to argue with her because he knew that she was trying to provoke him.

Again Mrs Fulton stepped in. She was, Couldridge thought, the sort of wife every officer should have. Uncomplicated by social aspirations, happy with whatever her husband sought from military life even when it did not involve ambition for promotion. Fulton would never rise higher than captain; both of them knew it and both accepted it. 'Don't forget to write to us from Delhi,' she said. 'I'm told all sorts of exciting people are going to be there as well as Lord and Lady Curzon. Lord Kitchener, the Duke of Marlborough. Why you might even have to treat Lord or Lady Curzon themselves for sunstroke.'

'Mary never gets ill,' Joanne Pinkerton said.

And then Couldridge realised why he had been invited to the Durbar. He said: 'You arranged this, didn't you?'

Joanne Pinkerton filled her mouth with vanilla ice-cream. 'Arranged what?'

'My selection for the Durbar.'

'Don't be silly,' she said through the ice-cream. 'And egotistical too.'

'But you did, didn't you?'

The smokey eyes avoided his accusation and stared at the

butterflies, as big as hands, flirting and tasting the hibiscus blooms in the garden.

'Didn't you?'

Even Mrs Fulton seemed to know that she was powerless to divert the conversation.

Joanne Pinkerton said: 'I didn't arrange anything. The subject of a suitable doctor did come up at Simla. I just happened to mention that I knew of a good Army doctor in Calcutta. You are a good doctor, aren't you Lieutenant?'

'Yes,' he said, 'I am. Too good to waste my time treating ladies like yourself for hot flushes and heart flutters.'

'Gosh,' she said, 'you're the touchiest man I've ever met.'

Fulton said: 'I shouldn't let the fact that Joanne mentioned your name put you off. I shouldn't imagine—with due respect —that whatever she said to the Viceroy would have all that much affect on him.'

'Don't you? You may be right. But I'm bloody sure that whatever his wife said to him would have some effect.'

Charlotte Spenser gazed deeply into her coffee.

Couldridge realised that he had sworn and said: 'I'm sorry.'

'For what?' Joanne Pinkerton said.

'Nothing that you would have even noticed. I swore. But don't worry—my language won't be assaulting your ears on the train to Delhi.'

'Oh for crying out loud,' Joanne Pinkerton said.

Mrs Fulton said: 'I shouldn't make any rash decisions, John.'

And Spenser said: 'You know it's a court martial offence to disobey an order.'

'Not when it's been issued by an interfering lady from the United States of America.'

Spenser said: 'It was presumably issued by Kitchener.'

Fulton said: 'In that case there's still hope for Couldridge. I should imagine that any order issued by Kitchener is immediately over-ruled by the Viceroy.'

Couldridge called for the bill from an agitated waiter who did not like to see his masters arguing among themselves. 'I'm not concerned about the feeling between Curzon and Kitchener. All I'm concerned about is that I'm a doctor and not a lackey either of British aristocracy or New York society.' He paid the bill. 'Now I must be off. If you will excuse me. I'll see you later this evening, Neville.'

Spenser said: 'So you're definitely not going?'

'That's right,' Couldridge said. 'I'm definitely not going.' He turned to Joanne Pinkerton. 'And by the way, if you fall sick at all while you're in Calcutta I can recommend you to a very good doctor.'

'Really,' she said. 'Who's that?'

'A Doctor Bose. But I don't really think you'd take to him.'

'And why's that, pray?'

'Because he's Indian,' Couldridge said.

He walked rapidly out of the hotel restaurant, gaining a little comfort from the knowledge that if they had been alone together Joanne Pinkerton would have thrown her coffee at him.

4

CHARLOTTE SPENSER lay on her bed beneath the mosquito net watching the gentle scything of the fan and trying to contain her unhappiness. But the feel of India around her and the knowledge that she wouldn't see England again for years, filled her with a grief that could sometimes be subdued but never obliterated. If, she thought, Neville would understand then there was a chance that the unhappiness would be dispelled.

The night sounds and smells of Calcutta breathed in through the mesh covering the window. The lonely call of a steamer on the Hooghly, the monotonous chant of a man singing—or was he praying?—the scents of jasmine, river-water and putrescence.

She closed her eyes and remembered horses hooves trotting and garden gates clicking and smelled lilac after rain and a side of mutton roasting.

She heard the squeak of the teacher's chalk on the blackboard and saw the pink dewlap of India on the political map, as inaccessible and remote as Canada, Australia and Manchuria. Bombay, Delhi, Madras, Calcutta. She had never thought: I want to go there—the possibility had never occurred to her. Thankfully she had closed her books and run on to the common where, in the spent sunshine of autumn, children bowled hoops along the paths and flew kites in the pale sky. She had been happy in her suburb.

Outside the mosquito net her husband read the newspaper with absorption, concentrating on the political and military news so that he would always be able to participate in a conversation in the mess, or with Joanne Pinkerton's friends from the Vice-regal Lodge. These were the people that Charlotte dreaded meeting; in their company all her words seemed to be synthesised into naïvety and every statement she made floated in the air to be examined and ridiculed.

Her husband turned a page of the newspaper. From agitation for the appointment of an Indian on the Viceroy's council to the latest famine figures—32.59 deaths per thousand people— to Kitchener's reorganisation of the Army. Nothing, she thought, ever happened on a small scale in India. Except the snobberies and jealousies of the other wives.

When she and Neville had become engaged her friends had said: 'Aren't you lucky. Getting married to an officer and going to live in India.' No one knew much about India, but marrying an officer stationed there ranked hazily with becoming the wife of a doctor or a chartered accountant. And after two years she had gone through with it because she had given her word. The affection, she had thought, would follow the mutual respect.

She looked at his face, intent on the results of the Kadir Cup. A handsome face, she supposed, strong and soldierly. But, as he had once said in an unguarded moment after she had submitted to him on their honeymoon, a face that lacked breeding.

If only he would put down the paper and appreciate her unhappiness. 'Neville,' she said.

'Yes?' He didn't put down the paper.

'What's the time?'

He looked at his watch. 'Seven thirty. I'm going over to John's quarters at nine for a drink. You'll be all right here, won't you?'

'I'll be lonely.'

'No more lonely than you've been when I've been up in the hills.'

'No,' she said, 'I suppose not. But it's different here in this great rambling city. It makes me feel lonely.'

'Don't worry,' he said, 'you won't come to any harm. I shan't be out late.'

'It's very hot in here.' She unbuttoned the top few buttons of her blouse.

He folded up the paper and speeded up the fan. 'Don't worry about the city,' he said. 'You'll soon get used to it. In a fortnight's time we'll be off to Delhi and you'll be just as homesick for Calcutta as you are now for the hills.'

With startling clarity Charlotte Spenser realised that her husband had never sensed her misery. 'Neville,' she said, 'when do you think we'll go back to England on leave?'

'Back to the wilds of Streatham? Never I hope.' But she knew that part of him lied. 'I suppose we'll have to go back and see our people sometime. In two or three years' time, perhaps.'

'Not before?'

'Certainly not before. I can't afford it for one thing. And in any case you know how you hate the sea. You don't want to go back, do you?'

'I just thought it would be nice for a little while. I know it's impossible of course.'

'Don't worry,' he said, 'the Durbar will be a wonderful experience for you. And after that we'll be back in the hills.'

Back with the servants whom she didn't want, who laughed

at her and stole the sugar and flour. Back to the wives and the incessant disagreement about which of them was the senior lady, back to bridge which she played badly, back to vegetables washed in potassium permanganate, back to the careless brutality which was their reason for being there.

'I suppose so,' she said. A cockroach darted across the floor, antennae waving wildly. 'Neville,' she said, 'kill it.'

'It's only an old roach,' he said. 'Did you know there are something like sixty different varieties?'

'Kill it,' she said. 'Please kill it.'

He crushed the cockroach with his shoe. 'You're in a funny mood this evening. Anything up?'

Nothing except that he regarded home as India and the only home she knew was thousands of miles away.

'I'll be all right,' she said. 'It's just the strangeness. But I do like your friend, John.'

'Marvellous chap,' her husband said. 'My only real friend. I confided in him a lot when I first arrived in India.'

'I wonder why,' she said. 'Because you never confided in me.'

He came over to the bed, drew back the mosquito net and sat down on the edge of the bed. 'What's the matter, Charlotte?' he said. 'What's the matter?'

She managed to smile. 'Nothing, Neville. Nothing at all.'

'That's better,' he said. And, encouraged by her smile, put his strong hands on her breasts.

Oh God, she thought, not that. But she smiled again. And tried again to recall the smell of lilac blossom and a roast joint cooking in the kitchen.

5

AFTER Neville Spenser had made quick energetic love to his
wife he lay back on the bed and guiltily thought of the responses
of the Indian girl in Bombay, and the girl who had seduced
him, two months before Charlotte's arrival, on the cushions of
a gondola on a lotus lake at Srinagar. Of their musky scents, of
silken hair between brown thighs, of thrusting bellies and frantic
limbs, and warm juices. But such abandonment would be incongruous on the matrimonial bed. He tried to imagine Charlotte's
lips pouting with passion and smiled at the ceiling. Dear Charlotte.

He dressed in a fawn linen suit, white shirt, regimental cravat,
kissed his wife on the forehead, walked out into the soupy
Calcutta night and headed in the direction of the hospital.

'What happened to that girl of yours in Bombay?' he said
as Couldridge poured him a whisky and water in his room.

'I wrote to her,' Couldridge said.

'The coward's way.'

'I'm afraid so. I sent her some money. Quite a lot by my
standards. I feel pretty badly about it. But she'll find someone
else. And you—what have you been doing with yourself?'

Spenser drank some of his whisky. 'Nothing very much. Some
boozey nights in the mess. A trip to the fleshpots of Srinagar in
Kashmir before Charlotte came out.'

'A lovely girl, your wife,' Couldridge said.

'She's a great girl,' Spenser said. He felt vaguely surprised
that anyone should find her lovely.

'And what else?'

'A spot of fighting,' he said with studied nonchalance.

'Kill many Pathans?'

'A few. They've been pretty bloody lately. They captured a lance naik and castrated him, poor bastard. They kept his body and sent back the parts they had cut off with his uniform.'

Couldridge poured more whisky. 'So I suppose you went and burned a few fields of crops while the good colonel set about capturing a couple of prisoners so that he could have them ceremonially booted to death in the testicles.'

'Certainly we burned some crops. What did you expect us to do—grant all Pathans in the area a free amnesty if they promised not to castrate any more of our men?'

Couldridge tossed back his whisky. 'You're learning,' he said.

Spenser decided that Couldridge was a little drunk. 'What's wrong with you? Not still upset that you're only going to the Durbar through the grace and favour of Joanne Pinkerton, are you?'

'You forget—I'm not going.'

'Then you're crazy. It's the opportunity of a lifetime.'

'I've got the opportunity of a lifetime here in Calcutta.'

'You don't seem to be enjoying it,' Spenser said.

'The hell I'm not. Come on, finish up your whisky. I'm going to take you to see Calcutta by night. It might not be Srinagar but it has a charm all of its own. First we'll go to a little place I know of where you can get a nice glass of soapy beer and whisky that hasn't been watered.'

But the whisky had been watered, Spenser decided. And the morose Bengalis slumped in wicker chairs by the bar would be only too happy to argue the point. 'Where the hell are we?' he said.

'Near the docks. This is a place used by seamen. But British seaman are a bit unpopular here at the moment. There was a big fire in one of the wharfs. It spread to a ship laden with kerosene. The ship blew up and a hell of a lot of coolies were hurt—about a dozen were killed. They reckon that ship should have been unloaded as soon as it berthed. The explosion capsized a tug and they claim that the British were none too keen to fish the Indian crew out of the water.'

'And were they?'

Couldridge shrugged. 'The water was covered with blazing kerosene. What could they do? They tried to rescue as many as they could. But the Indians around here don't see anything reasonably any more.'

'Did they ever? Did they see things reasonably in 1756?'

Couldridge said: 'What happened in 1756?'

'The Black Hole of Calcutta.'

'I think that's what this bar is called.' He turned and snapped his fingers at the Bengalis.

'Sahib?' The voice of the waiter in a once-white jacket that looked as if it had recently been fished from the Hooghly was edged with contempt.

'Two more whiskies.'

'Very well, sahib.' He wandered away to find the worst watered whisky in the bar.

Spencer said: 'You're an unconventional sort of doctor, John.'

'And you're a conventional sort of British officer.'

'Is that meant to be a compliment or an insult?'

'Take it whatever way you like.'

'I wonder why we remain friends. We don't seem to have anything in common.'

'I suppose that's why. The difference is that I love the bloody place and you hate it.'

'Hate it? You must be crazy.'

Couldridge drank the dregs of his pale liquid, cloudy with specks of solid matter. 'It's quite true—you hate it. Only you'll never admit it to yourself. If you did you'd be finished because there would be no point in killing Pathans.'

'You're quite wrong,' Spenser said. He pondered for a moment and decided that Couldridge was wrong. He said: 'I want to help India.'

'Don't make me laugh,' Couldridge said.

'I seem to be happier here than you are.'

'What the hell's that got to do with it?'

The waiter put two glasses in front of them. 'We'll pay later,' Couldridge said.

'Pay now, sahib.'

'Bugger off,' Couldridge said. He picked up the glass and swallowed half the whisky.

'Pay now, sahib.'

'You heard me,' Couldridge said. 'Bugger off. We'll pay when we leave.'

The waiter smiled malevolently. 'Very well, sahib.'

Spenser said: 'You don't talk to them like a man who loves India.'

Three British seamen, chunky and drunk and aggressive, rolled in. Spenser looked around the bar at the watchful Bengalis, at the low ceiling scrawled with obscenities by customers standing on the tables, at the crippled chairs and leaning tables. He took off his military cravat and stuffed it in his trousers pocket.

'I don't love it tonight,' Couldridge said.

'Are you like this just because of that girl Joanne Pinkerton?'

'It's not just her. It's everything.' He gestured flamboyantly and knocked over his glass of whisky. The seamen pointed and laughed. 'You haven't seen my lab, have you? It's beautiful. A room about the size of the lavatory here—if they've got one that is—and enough equipment to keep a classroom of schoolboys engrossed for one lesson. And in the hospital they've got all the equipment I need. But can I use it? Can I hell. It's not India or Indians I hate. It's officialdom, arrogant, bloody-minded officialdom—as corrupt in its own way as any village money-lender. And somehow its arrogance, its stupid, unseeing, patronising arrogance is all summed up by Miss Joanne Pinkerton.'

Spenser shrugged. 'She means well. She only got you on this trip to help you.'

'I don't need her help.'

'You need someone's help. We all do.'

'You might,' Couldridge said. 'I don't.'

'And you talk about arrogance.'

Two Indian whores came in and sat down at a table near them. They wore grubby saris and their black hair centre-parted and braided, was dull and tired. They smiled professionally and winked grotesquely.

Spenser said: 'I think we ought to get out of here. We'll be court-martialled if anything happens.'

Couldridge put his elbow in a puddle of watered whisky. 'We're staying,' he said. 'Some of these people are my best patients.' He winked laboriously back at the two whores who consulted each other earnestly because Couldridge and Spenser were not their usual type of customers. 'More whisky,' Couldridge said, snapping his fingers at the waiter again.

'You're determined to get drunk, aren't you.'

'Absolutely determined. But I shall get drunk decently like an officer and a bloody gentleman. I shall get drunk the way they do at the Court of Lord Curzon or at a Durbar.'

'An officer and a gentleman wouldn't be here in the first place.'

'Correct. I only said I'd get drunk *like* one.' He held the sleeve of the theatrically-polite waiter. 'Give these two ladies here a drink.' He pointed at the two puzzled whores

The waiter said: 'You would like them perhaps to join you at your table, sahib. We have some very good rooms at the rear of these premises. Very clean.'

Couldridge said: 'Just give them some drinks. Orange or whatever they want.'

Spenser said: 'You're crazy if you don't go on the Durbar.'

'Back on that old track, are we? Trying to distract my attention from these good ladies.'

'Trying to stop you making a bloody fool of yourself. Joanne Pinkerton would be delighted if she knew how she had made you behave.'

'To hell with Joanne Pinkerton.' He drank more whisky and spilled some of it down his shirtfront.

One of the seamen said in loud Cockney voice: 'I see we've got some toffs with us tonight lads.'

Another swallowed a broad Glaswegian accent and said in parody of Oxford English: 'So we have chaps. How spiffing. Do you think they would buy us poor seamen a jolly old drink, what?'

The seamen were drinking Eagle brandy and shamshu Chinese spirit. One of them belched with vigour and feeling. The Bengalis, slight and sinewy, stood up and leaned against the bar. The barman held a bottle by the neck: like Spenser he knew there was going to be a fight.

Spenser said: 'This is our last chance. Do you want to get out?'

'Why should I want to get out? We're having fun. You can get out if you want to.'

The whores sipped quickly at their warm orange squash, yellowing eyes flitting from seamen to gentlemen.

'If you're staying then I'll have to stay.' Spenser found with pleasure that he was not scared. He was merely astonished at the incongruity of the situation. He thought briefly about Charlotte asleep beneath the mosquito net, a dew of sweat on her upper lip.

The third seaman shouted across the bar in a North Country accent: 'Hey, colonel, buy us a fucking drink.'

Couldridge stood up and walked across to the seamen's table. He had taken off his jacket and Spenser noted the hard-muscled forearms. He looked very tall standing over the seamen. His long dark hair had fallen across his forehead and the sensitivity in his Irish face had been erased by controlled anger.

'You,' Couldridge said pointing to the North Countryman. 'Would you mind apologising to the ladies? They don't like bad language.'

'What ladies?' said the North Countryman.

Couldridge bent and pulled him up by the ear. 'Those ladies,' he said and pointed at the excited whores who had never been called ladies, let alone fought over, in their lives. 'Now apologise.'

Spenser found that his body was trembling. Not fear—excitement. The palms of his hands were greased with sweat. He was glad he had met Couldridge. Already they had been through a lot together. He jumped to his feet and joined Couldridge.

'You fucking bastard,' said the North Countryman. He brought his knee up towards Couldridge's crutch; but the tap-room brawling instincts from his mother's side stirred within Couldridge; as the knee came up he let go of the ear, stepped aside and helped the knee on its journey with both hands. The seaman crashed backwards on to the table; the table legs snapped with a satisfactory crunch and the seaman cracked his skull on the floor.

The Bengalis stayed beside the bar hoping that all the antagonists would knock each other out so that they could rob them and slit their throats if necessary. The whores sipped away at their empty tumblers.

The Cockney brought the inside of his boot down Spenser's shin and, as Spenser bent involuntarily, punched him low in the belly. Spenser gasped and cried out with pain and thought: I've failed. He saw a knee coming up to his face, but it never reached him. Instead he heard the thud as Couldridge's knuckles smashed into the seaman's face. The seaman's nose split down one side, like a split plum, and blood poured over Spenser's clothes.

The third seaman hit Couldridge from behind, a chopping rabbit punch on the back of the neck. Couldridge fell forward and Spenser knew that now was his moment. As the seaman tried to kick Couldridge in the groin Spenser picked up a chair by the seat and rammed the back of it into the seaman's big, beer belly. He sat down swearing and groaning. Then, as the North Countryman started to get up, Spenser kicked him neatly on the jaw. 'You bastard,' said the North Countryman. 'Oh you fucking bastard.' He shook his head and a tooth with shreds of flesh around the root fell out of his mouth.

That left the seaman with the split nose still operative. And he was going for Couldridge who was still on the ground. But Couldridge's legs were bent and as the seaman marched into him with his boots Couldridge unsprung both legs in a double-loaded kick. Then they were both wrestling on the floor, slipping on the blood, grunting and trying to get in body punches. Spenser stood back gripping a bottle. All the brandy fight had gone out of the other two: one was winded and the other was sitting on the floor feeling his broken mouth.

Then Spenser noticed a flash of light like a silver fish between the two men struggling on the floor and shouted to Couldridge, 'Look out, John—he's got a knife.' The knife flashed again and Spenser saw it slice through the muscle on Couldridge's forearm.

Spenser kicked at the blade and sent it skimming across the floor. Couldridge got in a punch just below the ear and it was all over.

Then the Bengalis moved in. Deliberately, venomously, with ballet-dancers' tread.

Couldridge and Spenser turned and waited for them. 'I reckon this is it,' Couldridge said. 'Thanks anyway.'

It's not over yet,' Spenser said. He spoke rapidly and angrily. The Bengalis faltered and stopped.

After a moment the waiter said: 'You are paying now?'   .

Couldridge threw some rupees at them. 'That was Gurkhali, wasn't it?'

Spenser nodded, wiping blood from his face. 'I've learned quite a bit in addition to the Urdu we learned before we were commissioned and I thought it just possible that they might have had some dealings with the Gurkhas at some time or other. It was a pretty remote chance but it seems to have come off. They're scared stiff of them—and scared stiff that we might be able to fight like Gurkhas.'

'We haven't done too badly,' Couldridge said. 'But I think it's time we cleared out now.' He gave some more rupees to the whores smiling hesitantly at them. 'Thank you ladies,' he said, 'you were a knock out.'

One of them said, 'Perhaps you would like . . .'

'No,' Couldridge said, 'we wouldn't. Thanks all the same.' He examined the knife wound in his arm. 'And now I think we'd better go and get patched up. I know of a very good doctor—

his name is Bose.' They walked out into a lane leading to the docks. 'Do you know,' he said, 'I feel much better now.'

'Do you? I wish I could say the same. My shin hurts like hell and my stomach aches.' But there was a glow of cameraderie and friendship fulfilled.

'What did you say to the Bengalis?' Couldridge asked.

'Among other things I called each of them a jhanta. It's a Gurkha insult which no Gurkha takes very seriously.'

'And what does it mean?'

'It means one pubic hair,' Spenser said.

6

MRS FULTON tried to persuade him to go on the Durbar. Over weak tea and desiccated cakes, beside morose potted palms in the lounge of the hotel, she said: 'Honestly, John, I implore you to go. You'll only jeopardise your career if you don't. And it's so silly to miss an opportunity like this out of piaue. Joanne meant well. And'—she added artfully—'I believe there's a conference in Delhi on the control of cholera.'

Couldridge knew she was right. But he had committed himself.

Spenser tried again to persuade him to go. As they sat on the hotel verandah, proudly feeling the throb of their wounds, joined in the special friendship of two men who have successfully done battle together, Spenser said: 'You're crazy. If you go you'll probably get promotion and before you know where you are you'll be in a position where you can officially carry out your research. And'—he added artfully—'we might even find a bar in Delhi . . .'

Couldridge knew he was right. He wondered vaguely if there was any escape clause in his commitment.

Fulton tried to persuade him to go. 'It could be a court-martial offence if you refuse,' he said as they strolled around the hotel garden and watched a lizard doing press-ups in the sun. 'I know because that's the sort of thing I have to deal with. As a senior officer and a friend I strongly advise you to go.'

Couldridge knew he was right. But how could he come to terms with his pride? Or vanity, perhaps.

Charlotte Spenser tried to persuade him to go. Shyly examining his meagre equipment in the laboratory after accepting his invitation to visit him, she said: 'I wish you would change your mind. I know it's none of my business but I thought you ought to know that Neville is really upset. It seems such a shame to part the two of you when you're such wonderful friends.'

Couldridge knew she was right. If perhaps he could discover that there was a passenger on the train suffering from an ailment which he thought required his special attention. . . .

Joanne Pinkerton did not try and persuade him to go. Which helped. And when he heard that she had told the Fultons that she now hoped that he wouldn't go he began to seek justification for boarding the train.

The justification was provided by Major Little in two ways. He implied one day that Couldridge had been chosen because someone with influence had exerted pressure on the Viceroy and that a certain subaltern called Spenser had been similarly selected.

Couldridge put it to her as she sat writing a letter in her room. 'My,' she said, 'the intrepid Dr Couldridge visiting a lady. Did you think I was suffering from the vapours?'

'Did you use your influence to get Neville Spenser chosen for the Durbar?'

She went on writing, a little more quickly than before.

'Did you?'

She put down the quill. 'I mentioned that he seemed to be a very competent officer, just I mentioned that you seemed to be a very good doctor. I thought it would be pleasant for you to go together. It's the last time I try and help anyone.'

He sat down on the side of the bed and laughed hugely and helplessly.

'What's so funny?' she said.

'Nothing yet. But Neville's face will be when I tell him.'

'Spiteful as well as arrogant,' she said. Her fists were clenched and she was breathing quickly. 'Now you've had your fun perhaps you'll leave me to get on with my letter.'

'Most certainly,' he said. 'Most certainly.'

But Spenser took the news stoically. 'I don't give a damn,' he said. 'I've been chosen and that's it as far as I'm concerned. I suppose there are often reasons that we don't know about for postings and promotions.'

'But why did she pick on us?'

'That's simple,' Spenser said. 'She wanted you along and thought that if I were going it would be an additional incentive because we're friends.'

'And you're still going even though you know that your services have been corruptly obtained?'

'Of course I'm going. I wouldn't miss this opportunity for all the tea in India. And in any case it's an order.'

Then Major Little provided the second justification. He said: 'Water. Purification. You'll be responsible for that I believe.'

'What's that, sir?'

'What's that?' Major Little said.

'What did you say, sir?'

'You'll be responsible for seeing that the water on the train is pure, I'm told.'

And in the hot little laboratory behind Dr Bose's surgery Surgeon Second Lieutenant Couldridge set about manufacturing Chlorogen from the prescription of Dr Nesfield.

7

THE special train steamed out of Calcutta on Christmas Eve
for the Great Durbar in Delhi to commemorate the Coronation
of Edward VII. It was to be the superlative flourish crowning
Lord Curzon's reign as Viceroy of India. An occasion of un-
paralleled splendour and dignity that would remind the Indian
people of the 'higher ideal' of the British Empire. It was also
Lord Curzon's act of thanksgiving to his American wife for the
love, happiness and wealth she had brought him. There was
to be a procession to the Great Mosque and a State ball in the
Dewan-i-Am, the public audience hall of the Great Mogul.

The train gathered speed through the rabble of suburbs. In
the carriages the diplomats, Army officers, civil servants and
their ladies noted that, outside, the Indians, occupied with taxes,
a plague of rats and an outbreak of cholera, paid little attention
to its passing. And some of the Viceroy's guests, sitting primly
in the tall carriages, felt a little annoyed that their dignified
progress was unobserved and unappreciated.

But as the suburbs thinned into villages, each as turbulent
beneath its deceptive torpor as India itself was within the Empire,
they began to relax. The men smoked with permission from the
ladies and the ladies cooled themselves with silk and bamboo
fans. And soon they began to talk among themselves; about
Lord Curzon, whose unbending stature of mind was attributed
to childhood experiences with a formidable governess, about
suggestions that Indians should be appointed to the legislative
councils (more pandering to trouble-makers), about last night's
rubber of bridge and the latest follies of their servants.

The Spensers, John Couldridge and Joanne Pinkerton had

a compartment to themselves so that Neville Spenser would have room to organise security in the event of danger and Couldridge would have room to organise first aid if he failed. Sepia photographs were screwed above the seats—Howrah Bridge, the Viceroy's summer residence at Simla, and Hindus bathing at Benares.

Outside the dusty countryside moved lazily past to the rhythm of the wheels on the track. Dry brown hills, occasional paddy fields watered by hidden irrigation, Indians in dhotis standing knee-high in mud-grey waters fishing with big sagging nets, an elephant stripping a sapling. Above small clouds grazed in blue pastures.

Joanne Pinkerton took off her straw bonnet, toyed with her hair and gazed down a village street where three Hindus were carrying a black-painted god with a blood-red tongue, tusks protruding from the mouth, a garland of skulls around its head. The train slowed down reverently.

Charlotte Spenser shivered and said: 'I'll never really get used to India as long as I live.' Her face was pale and her eyes were luminous and green in a shaft of dusty sunlight.

'Nonsense,' Neville Spenser said. His voice conferred an encouraging pat on the back.

'I think it's a wonderful place,' Joanne Pinkerton said.

Couldridge, who had determined to limit conversation with her, accepted the bait. 'Wonderful at Viceregal Lodge,' he said. 'And, I suppose, wonderful at Simla. Wonderful on this train with your tame doctor and your tame security officer.'

The sharp, pretty face beneath the sepia point of Simla was as serene as its alert features would ever allow it to be. 'Why don't you say what you mean? That I know nothing of the tragedy of India. Of the starving illiterate millions.'

'All right,' Couldridge said. 'You don't. Not that it matters. You've made your imprint—your footprint perhaps—in Indian history.' He lit his pipe and smiled into the blue smoke. 'Even a tragedy should have an element of comedy I suppose.'

Joanne Pinkerton said: 'You've still got a black eye from that brawl in Calcutta you were involved in. We never did hear too much about that little comedy.'

Spenser said: 'We were defending the honour of two ladies.'

'Coloured ladies,' Couldridge said. 'Or perhaps they're not regarded as ladies in Viceregal circles.'

'You really are an idiot,' Joanne Pinkerton said.

The train grunted up an incline and paused triumphantly at the top before accelerating down the other side. Below them they saw a sudden expanse of teak and sandalwood and a slow fat river. An hour later they stopped for lunch beside a wadi cemented with hard red mud and cossetted by bushes as round as cabbages.

Joanne Pinkerton opened one of the hampers. Cold turkey with chestnut stuffing, cold game pies and brandy butter.

Couldridge ate hungrily and savagely. Joanne Pinkerton, sitting on a small canvas chair, said: 'I know what you're thinking.'

'I feel guilty,' he said.

'So do I,' she said.

'About what?'

'The same thing as you. Us eating like this and the Indians in the villages we've come through existing on a handful of rice.'

Couldridge hurled a leg of turkey on to the hard mud. 'Then why the hell don't you do something about it? Either do something or go back to the United States of America where you belong. Stop patronising India with your fine aristocratic English friends. Stop gloating.'

He noticed a quiver of the lips and knew that for once he had struck home.

'I'm not gloating,' she said. She went on chewing at a slice of game pie but she didn't look as if she were tasting it.

They spent that night in tents put up beside the exhausted train by Indian servants brought from Calcutta. Luxurious tents complete with charcoal stoves, lamps, table, chairs and beds. Jackals barked and bats wheeled beneath the thick stars. The night air smelled of canvas, hot oil from the engine and wood-smoke. The charcoal glowed comfortably in the stoves by the flaps of the tents.

They ate in the Spensers' tent. Peppery kebab and fruit salad and coffee. Charlotte Spenser listened to the jackals and tried to follow the flight of the bats. Couldridge sensed her unhappiness reaching him across the glowing charcoal. Why the hell didn't Spenser put his arm round her? Or at least say something kind. But that wasn't part of his image. 'Don't worry,' Couldridge said. 'Bats don't get in your hair. It's an old wives' tale.'

She smiled, grateful for the kindness in his voice. 'I'm not worried about the bats. Not really. It's just the whole setting.' She spoke nervously as if expecting a reproof.

Spenser said: 'For heaven's sake there's nothing to worry about. There are sentries posted all around us.'

'I know,' she said. 'It's silly of me.'

The bats disappeared and the stars shone more brightly.

Joanne Pinkerton said: 'India doesn't seem very big tonight looking up at the stars.'

They knocked the dregs from their coffee cups; they yawned and stretched and said good-night.

'I'll see you to your tent,' Couldridge said to Joanne Pinkerton.

'You needn't bother.'

'It's the least I can do as you're responsible for me being here.'

Spenser said: 'I'd better have a look round. After all I'm supposed to be responsible for security.'

'Do you have to go?' Charlotte Spenser said.

'I won't be long,' he said. 'Don't worry.'

The scream came as Spenser undid the flap of the tent and let it fall back, closing her inside. A gurgling cry of fear and pain.

'What the hell was that?' Couldridge said.

'It was an Indian,' Spenser said. 'Come on—over in that direction.' He pointed to where the Indian bearers were camped about fifty yards from the main concourse.'

A sepoy, rifle at the ready, came running up. 'Sahib,' he said. 'Tiger. He's got one man pretty bad.'

Spenser spoke briskly, with new authority. 'Where is it now?'

The soldier said: 'I don't think it has gone very far. The men are very frightened.'

'Right,' Spenser said. 'I'll get over there.' He ducked back into his tent and fetched a pistol for Couldridge. Couldridge grabbed a first-aid box and ran to the man whimpering in the firelight. Spenser took six soldiers and moved cautiously into the darkness with them.

The wounded man was trying to cover the raking wound in his abdomen with his hands. One of the tiger's claws had caught the intestine and pulled out a grey tube of it. The blood pumped steadily on to the dust, black in the darting light.

Couldridge looked at the man hopelessly. Very gently he touched the glistening intestine and it slid back into the abdomen. The pulse of the escaping blood was growing weaker. Couldridge cut a piece of lint and lay it across the soldier's waist, trying to give him a little dignity in death.

Joanne Pinkerton said: 'Isn't there anything you can do?'

He turned on her. 'What the hell are you doing here?'

'I thought I might be able to help.'

'You shouldn't be looking at things like this.'

'If I were a nurse I would have to.' Her voice was almost apologetic.

He hesitated. 'All right. But there's nothing we can do.' He spoke softly so that the dying man could not hear.

Behind them the tall train rested in the occasional moonlight. To their right, in front of the train, men in unbuttoned jackets and open-neck shirts loaded guns, peered into the night and reassured the women that they were safe. To their left Spenser and his men explored the darkness with torches.

'You'd better get back to your tent,' Couldridge said.

'There's no point,' she said. 'I'll stay with you.'

The wounded soldier sighed, stopped breathing and departed to await rebirth into the world on his journey to ultimate salvation from the vale of tears.

Couldridge covered the body with a blanket. 'There's no point in us staying here,' he said.

'I've never seen a man die before,' she said. In the firelight he could see tears gathering at the corners of her eyes. She had, he thought, behaved very well. He put his hand over hers. She stared at him and two tears ran down her cheeks. 'I'm sorry,' she said.

'There's nothing to be sorry about.'

Out in the darkness Spenser shouted an order. Two shots cracked out; there was a snarl of pain and a shadow streaked for the line of tamarisk bushes directly in front of Couldridge and Joanne Pinkerton.

Spenser ran back. 'The bloody thing's more dangerous than ever now. We'll have to go into the bushes and finish it off.'

Couldridge said: 'Can't you leave it until dawn?'

Spenser shook his head. 'No. I don't know how badly it's wounded but it's certainly very angry. It could easily make a run for one of the tents as soon as we slacken off.'

'Even with guards?'

'Even if a guard got in a shot first the tiger could still reach him.'

Spenser sent in a line of soldiers as beaters. Behind them the half-dressed audience waited tensely in front of their luxury tents. Spenser stayed with the rest of the troops in between the camp and the bushes. The only sounds were the crackle of twigs and dry leaves behind the beaters' feet and the hoot of an unperturbed owl. It occurred to Couldridge that, since the soldiers had left that part of the camp, he and Joanne Pinkerton were exposed to an attack by the tiger. It occurred to him too late.

As a cloud crossed the moon the shadow came from the bushes fast and low, a ripple of darkness. The sepoys got in two shots, orange coughs in the night, and then stopped firing because the tiger was between them and the camp.

Then it was in the air, stripes black and grey in the phantom light, and Couldridge's pistol was in his hand and his finger was squeezing the trigger. But even as he aimed and squeezed he knew that, even if he shot it, the tiger would still reach the girl. As he aimed and fired he swung his left arm at her face, knocking her to the ground; but the movement dragged his shooting arm wide of its target and the bullet sped towards the stars.

The tiger landed beside Joanne Pinkerton and crouched in the firelight, classic and snarling and beautiful. Blood seeped from a wound in its side fusing the dark stripes.

Joanne Pinkerton lay in front of the tiger. One cuff from the tiger's steel claws and she could be dead. She lay still, mouth swollen from Couldridge's blow.

Couldridge spoke evenly, almost conversationally. 'Don't move a muscle,' he said. 'Not a muscle.'

Around him all movement was frozen. The owl called again and the tiger coughed, a bubbling sort of cough as if the bullet had perforated the lung.

Slowly, casually, Couldridge raised his pistol. The tiger watched him and Couldridge wondered if it realised that the gun was an instrument of execution. He knew he had to shoot before it tautened its muscles to spring again.

The bullet hit the tiger between the eyes. But there was no text-book hole neatly drilling a third eye. Just smashed bone and fur—and waste.

He knelt beside her and said: 'Are you all right?'

She nodded. 'I think so.'

'I'm sorry I had to hit you.'

'British to the end,' she said, and fainted in his arms.

Spenser ran over. And Charlotte and all the men with their guns from the main camp. Couldridge loosened the neck of her dress and bathed her forehead with cold water.

'Is she all right?' Charlotte said. She was trembling. Again Couldridge willed Spenser to put his arm around her, but the message didn't reach the soldier.

'She'll live,' Couldridge said.

Spenser said: 'I'm sorry.'

'Sorry about what? It wasn't your fault for God's sake.'

'I was supposed to be in charge of security.'

'You couldn't be expected to anticipate the intentions of an anti-British tiger.'

'They say it's a man-eater. It was getting old and found that human prey was easier to kill than animal. It must have been pretty hungry to attack a camp like this.'

'Or proud,' Couldridge said.

'How do you mean proud?'

'I prefer to think that it knew it would die. But it wanted to die fighting.'

'Pretty fanciful,' Spenser said.

Joanne Pinkerton said: 'It's a nice thought.'

Couldridge said: 'I always knew I'd end up treating you for the vapours.'

8

THEY ate Christmas lunch àt Dinapore where 140 years earlier 200 Englishmen had been massacred.

Blue jays perched on the telegraph wires watching them eat more turkey and mince pies washed down with white wine which no one had managed to keep cool. After they had drunk the wine they tried to sing carols but soon their voices faded in the thin sunshine, overawed by the incongruity of it all. Then they packed up their hampers and climbed back into the train remembering Christmases which they believed had always been white, questioning as they did at this time of the year their presence in this big brown alien land.

The train chugged along happily, making sleepy rhythms

with its wheels, blowing clouds and haloes of smoke into the tranquil sky. Couldridge, dreamy with turkey and wine and the rhythms of the wheels, gazed at a herd of buffalo moving along the skyline on their way to fresh pastures, at a scattering of crows in the sky, at a village dozing around a marble bull beneath a banyan tree, at a tree chattering with monkeys, at a boy sitting in front of a clump of bamboo fishing in still red water, at a procession moving with lethargic solemnity towards a temple. He gazed at the responsibilities of Britain, an amber lantern-slide projected beside him, and was moved with affection.

And he gazed upon the girl sitting opposite him, eyes closed, lips slightly parted, and thought about a girl he had always loved—a girl he had never met, never seen. A girl with long hair and a blue dress, as innocent as spring and as trusting as youth; a girl waiting for him in an orchard with blossom falling like snow. Sadly Couldridge said good-bye to the girl in the orchard and saw the pain in her eyes. When he awoke the train was braking and Joanne Pinkerton's smoke-grey eyes were searching his face.

'What were you dreaming about?' she said.

'About a girl in an orchard.'

'Was she pretty?'

'Very pretty,' he said.

Outside the tents were rising.

'Let's go for a walk,' she said. 'This is a darned unhealthy way of travelling.'

And so they came to the ruins of a town. Half a mile away from the train. A mossy, patient place that had died centuries before when its wells had run dry. Now its bastions, its towers, the tooth-stumps on its guard house and the tombs of princes were inhabited by hyenas and owls. By day its musky graces were shrivelled by the sun, by night it was theatrical in the moonlight. Its true time was dusk.

Joanne Pinkerton sat beside the stump of a pillar furred with dark moss. 'I guess it's going to be very difficult to talk,' she said. 'This place isn't meant for voices.'

'They made a mistake,' Couldridge said. 'They thought there wasn't water. But there was—look at the greenery.' He sat down beside her, suddenly aware that when the dusk thickened, when the fireflies were switched on, he would make love to her.

'What are you going to do?' she said. 'About the Army, and your research. You can't go on wasting your time.'

He put up a last puny resistance to the inevitable. 'Why should it concern you? This isn't your country. You can't possibly be interested in what I'm trying to do in the back streets of Calcutta. As far as you're concerned India is just a safari from New York. And your India is Viceregal Lodge.' But his antagonism had lost its bite.

'You know that's not true,' she said. He noted that the sprightly, assertive twang had left her voice. He remembered her lying beside the tiger, trusting him. As the girl in the orchard had trusted him.

'Why should you care about India?'

'Because you do.'

'But not before? You only care about suffering and muddle and hopelessness because I do?'

She shook her head. 'I felt it from the moment I arrived. But it wasn't a very fashionable topic of conversation. At least not in the officers' mess.'

He moved to the defence of the British. 'They're not all such fools, you know. They've done a lot for India.'

She leaned forward and kissed him, her lips dry and warm, and then retreated. 'The point is,' she said, as if the kiss had never taken place, 'did the Indians want anything done for them?'

'That's hardly the point. One of my patients might not want treatment. But it's my duty to cure him.' He was surprised to hear himself speaking for the defence: defending Colonel Hatherley, Buckingham, Little. He pointed in the direction of the train. 'The British have given them railways. Relieved famine. Cured sickness. Built schools.'

She smiled at him so that he felt clumsy with his words. 'I'm not arguing with you,' she said. 'But I want to know what you are going to do.'

'Go on heating test tubes,' he said. 'Cultivating microbes like pets. Hoping I'll stumble across something.' He stiffened his resistance. 'No, that all sounds defeatist. I don't quite know how I'll achieve it but I will find a way to get a proper lab. To search and experiment and perhaps contribute something towards medicine.'

'Towards medicine? Not towards helping humanity? You sound very clinical, Dr Couldridge.'

'Does it matter? If I contribute towards medicine then I contribute towards the betterment of Mankind.'

'It's just that your motive, your incentive, is kind of interesting. A clue to the man. And what field do you want to concentrate upon?'

'I don't,' he said. 'That's one of my crimes.'

The afternoon hastened away and they smelled the moisture on the moss, smoke from the fires beside the train. A star arrived and the crumbled past integrated around them: it was the time of the ruins.

He reached for her in the twilight and she came to him willingly. It seemed to him in the fanciful dusk as if it had been written thus when the tombs were still open, when the pillars supported roofs, when the princes played and water flowed in the wells.

'John,' she said.

'Yes?'

'It happened when we first met.'

'I know,' said John Couldridge who had been fighting it ever since.

He helped her to remove her clothes, laid his head upon her breasts and stroked the warm flatness below and then the oiled warmth beneath. Momentarily physiological awareness lingered—the maps and charts of the female body; then Dr

126

Couldridge retired in the dominant presence of John Could-ridge, lover.

'It's only you,' she said. 'It will never be anyone else.'

'Only you,' he said.

She cried out first in pain because he had been the first, and then in love because she was his and it was as she had always hoped it would be.

'Love,' she said. 'My love.'

The stars crowded above them and the past was quick in the dusk as together they arrived at the summit of love on the carpet of moss above the long dead princes.

A long time afterwards he said: 'That damn tiger. That's what did it.'

'What?' she said.

'This,' he said.

'Are you sorry?' she said.

'Will you marry me?' he said.

'Yes,' she said.

They lay quietly absorbing their decision. Peering ahead. Seeing their homes and their children; their love and their quarrels.

'I suppose you figured I was a pushover,' she said. 'Well, you were right. I'd never met anyone like you before. You were the first person I had met with any purpose. You were also more rude than anyone I had met before.'

'I haven't any more purpose than most people. It's just a different channel of purpose.'

'Let's say I hadn't met anyone quite as forceful in their purpose before. Or quite as conceited.'

'Is that conceit? Believing in what I'm trying to do?'

'Being so darned sure of your ability to achieve what you're trying to do—that's conceit.'

'You're wrong,' he said. 'I'm not sure of anything.'

She examined the thin knife-wound on his arm, not quite healed. 'I guess you were being pretty forceful that night.'

'I was drunk,' he said.

'Do you often get drunk?'

'Not often. That might even have been the last time. I think maybe I said goodbye to my wild youth that night.' He grinned at her. 'Or maybe I've just said goodbye to it.'

'I've said goodbye to mine. Why shouldn't you?'

'Has it been very wild?'

'Very,' she said. 'Can't you imagine the orgies at the Vice-regal Lodge? Nights of lechery after pig-sticking and polo. The men, you know, go pig-sticking to get rid of all their lusts. One of them told me one night.' She kissed him. 'I can tell you don't stick pigs.'

'I just shoot tigers,' he said. 'It's quite possible there's one here tonight. Come to think of it anything's possible. We should have gone back to the train hours ago.'

'Nothing will happen to us tonight,' she said. 'You see.'

'What are you doing in India?' he said. 'Living with society people whom you seem to despise.'

'I despised the people I knew in New York even more. Syco-phants trying to make the grade in my father's company through me. I used to get a proposal a week.'

'Of marriage?'

'Of marriage. Or anything else if they thought it would help. So finally I accepted an invitation from Mary Leiter—Lady Curzon to you—got myself engaged, met you and got myself unengaged as soon as I could. Then I made a fool of myself up in the hills, caught pneumonia and got well just in time to see you charging off to Calcutta to rid India of disease.'

'Why didn't you follow me?'

'Come on,' she said. 'A girl's got her pride. You showed no interest whatsoever. The nicest thing you ever said to me was that I was short-sighted. So I went back to New York instead and promised Mary that I'd come back in two years' time. I dropped off at Bombay, went to see the Fultons and found that they were coming to Calcutta. So here we are sitting among some ancient ruins somewhere in India engaged to be married.'

Couldridge felt vaguely irritated. 'So you wouldn't have come to Calcutta if it hadn't been for the Fultons.'

She finished buttoning her dress. 'Would you have cared if I hadn't come?'

'I wouldn't have cared then. I do now.' He stood up. 'Come on let's get back to the train. And mind the snakes.

She jumped into his arms. 'You don't think there are any, do you?'

'There's one called a krait. A little fellow. One nip from him in the ankle and you're dead in a minute.'

'I don't believe it,' she said.

'They'll be getting out search parties by now. Poor old Spenser will be going crazy. He's already let a tiger into the camp.'

Dusk thickened into night and the jagged walls, the stumps of pillars and the tombs, posed in the moonlight. Ahead the train waited for them like an illuminated seaside pier.

'You really like Neville, don't you?' she said.

'Don't you?'

'He's all right. I don't dislike him.'

'But you arranged for him to come on the train.'

'Only because I thought it would make your mind up for you. I knew you liked him very much. I couldn't really make out why.'

'Because he's vulnerable,' Couldridge said. He put his arm around her waist and steered her through the last suburb of ruins. 'We were in it from the beginning together. He can't deceive me at all. I feel like his mentor sometimes even though we're the same age. I hope he makes a success of it. But vulnerable people can do some pretty stupid things sometimes if they think they're showing weakness.'

'He doesn't seem vulnerable to me. He seems strong. And perhaps a little cruel.'

Couldridge shook his head. 'He's strong now but he wasn't once. And he's still vulnerable. I know and he knows I know.'

'John?'

'Yes?'

'You do love me?'

'I do.'

'Then will you do something for me?'

'Perhaps,' he said. 'I love you but I'm not besotted. What is it?'

'Will you swallow your vanity for once?'

'I might' he said. 'And I might not.'

'For me. Just this once.'

'Just tell me what it is,' he said. He sensed the disappointment; but he knew he was doing right; if you capitulated once you were beaten for ever.

'You know I'm rich.'

'That's why I want to marry you,' he said.

'I know that's not true. All of a sudden my money is an embarrassment.'

He took his arm away from her waist. 'What are you getting at?'

'You won't get mad?'

'I will if you don't spit it out.'

'I'd like to finance a laboratory for you in Calcutta.' She spoke rapidly. 'I know it's the sort of thing that makes you mad. But don't you see if I put the money into a lab we would both be helping to fight disease. In India, everywhere. We'd be doing it together like we should be doing everything together in marriage. Don't you see that if you turned the money down just because of your damned pride you'd be holding back progress, encouraging sickness?'

Couldridge saw the laboratory. The gleaming instruments, the test tubes and flasks and beakers, the cultures and serums and a new powerful microscope. He smelled chemical cleanliness, found the cure of tuberculosis at 4 a.m., heard the applause of his elders.

'What pride?' he said.

'You mean you'll accept the money?'

'I was only after your money anyway,' he said.

They met the search party setting out just as they reached the train.

9

Next day Couldridge happily told the colonel in charge that there was only enough fuel for the engine and not enough for boiling.

The colonel, a fair-minded fighting soldier who was bored with his present assignment, said: 'It was your job to make sure that there was enough fuel.'

Couldridge said: 'That wasn't how I interpreted my orders.'

The colonel stared gloomily at a woman throwing crumbs to a puzzled blue jay and said: 'What the devil are you talking about? Talk sense, man.'

'I presumed that my only duty was to ensure that the drinking water was free of infection.'

They were sitting in the colonel's carriage watching the night camp being dismantled. It was a grey, thoughtful morning.

The colonel said: 'And that means boiling it.'

'Not necessarily, sir.'

The colonel regarded him suspiciously. 'Please be good enough to tell me what the devil you are talking about in two crisp sentences.' He played with the points of his fierce moustache.

'I have brought with me a cylinder of chlorine which I made in Calcutta. A Dr Vincent Nesfield has discovered in London that chlorine effectively purifies water and is more practicable than boiling on a journey such as this.'

The colonel nodded understandingly. 'What you are trying to tell me is that you intend to use everyone under my care as guinea pigs for your experiments.'

Couldridge detected humour creasing a line from nose to

mouth on the colonel's face. 'Proven experiments, sir,' he said.

'Does this Dr Nesfield know that you are implementing his research?'

'No, sir. Surgeon Second Lieutenant Nesfield in fact. He's in the I.M.S. as well.'

The colonel lit a cigarette and inhaled deeply. 'What happens if we all catch cholera?'

Couldridge smiled warily. 'Then all of us will be beyond caring.'

'You are very reassuring, Lieutenant Couldridge. You must have a wonderful bedside manner.'

'Shall I go ahead, sir?'

'There's no alternative?'

'I'm afraid not, sir. There's no good burning wood in this area.'

'I don't believe you,' the colonel said. 'Permission granted.'

'Thank you, sir.'

'Before you go I should like a little medicine.'

'You're ill, sir?'

'A hangover,' said the colonel.

Couldridge went away and returned with a flask of whisky. 'A proven cure, sir,' he said.

'You'd better have a taste of your own medicine,' the colonel said. He poured an inch of whisky into two glasses and added water. 'To the successful completion of our duties as nurses and nannies,' he said. They drank. The colonel stared into the amber liquid and said: 'It tastes a trifle strange.'

'I'm afraid I didn't add quite enough sodium thiosulphate,' Couldridge said. 'You can still taste the chlorine.'

'Do you mean to say this water had been treated with chlorine.'

'Sir,' Couldridge said, 'I'm afraid you are not going to like this. In fact I've been treating the water with chlorine for two days.'

'Without permission?'

Couldridge swallowed the rest of his whisky. 'As I explained,

132

sir, I took it that my orders were to purify the water. Nothing else.'

'Then why the devil are you asking me for permission now?'

'Because I've discovered it works, sir.'

The line between mouth and nose wavered and finally broke into a crease of laughter. 'Surgeon Second Lieutenant Couldridge,' the colonel said, 'I shall follow your career with interest. One day you will either be knighted or court-martialled. We will drink to that—and that's an order.'

He poured two more shots of whisky.

Couldridge said: 'Water, sir?'

'No,' said the colonel, 'soda if you don't mind.'

10

LORD KITCHENER, soldier and celibate, did not look as if he were enjoying the ball. Nor—because he was not a man capable of disguising his feelings—did he look as if he were enjoying his conversation with Lord Curzon of Kedleston.

He was the son of Engish Protestant stock from County Kerry in Ireland, austere, brilliant and ruthless. Lord Curzon was an old Etonian, a former Tory M.P., a man who loved luxurious living and paperwork.

Lord Curzon was Viceroy. Lord Kitchener was C.-in-C. They had one quality in common—ambition.

The ball in the audience hall of the Great Mogul was the most lavish in the history of Imperial India. A galaxy of red, blue and green uniforms, tinkling medals, champagne corks popping like sporadic gunfire, satin and lace gowns swirling and curtseying—the Duchess of Portland wore diamonds in her skirt—crackling white shirt-fronts, a buffet of grouse and wildfowl bagged by the Viceroy's guests in one sunlit day of slaughter. Flirtations, quarrels, engagements, arguments about military strategy—all took place around the marble pillars inlaid with jade and cornelian.

Plague, poverty and starvation seemed a long way away. Even though they existed immediately outside the building.

Spenser said to his wife: 'Shall we dance?'

'If you like.' She had been drinking champagne to try and stop the nervous fluttering of her lips.

'You don't have to.'

'No, I'd like to.' She was very pale and her eyes were wide and lustrous with apprehension. Spenser looked at her and remembered their day of commitment in suburban London. Of promises and avowals of devotion and loyalty. Now he suspected that it had been a mistake, but he still hoped that their promises would endure.

They waltzed to the Blue Danube and above them the fans seemed to pick up the rhythm. They danced as they had learned together in a *salon* at Norbury under the flamboyant tuition of an Italian with pommaded hair and a pasta-plump wife.

'Do you remember?' he said.

'Of course,' she said. He sensed regret in her voice. He tried to suppress his irritation.

Couldridge and Joanne Pinkerton twirled by laughing at each other. She in a gown of green silk with jade at her neck and on her ears, her sharp pretty face softened by love.

Spenser watched them and wondered: Were we like that when we first met?

'They're very happy, Charlotte said. 'I'm happy for them.'

'I would never have believed that they would become engaged.'

'It was obvious from the moment they met.'

'Do you think she'll be good for him?'

'Yes,' she said. 'She'll be good for him.'

Spenser felt his wife waiting for him to say that she was good for him. Perversely the words would not come. Perhaps because he had never been a good liar.

Charlotte said: 'Look, John and Joanne are talking to Lord Kitchener and Lord Curzon.'

Spenser said: 'John will always be able to speak to people who matter now. He will almost be one of the family. Strange, isn't it, that Kitchener is one of the few men in the world I really admire, and there he is talking to Couldridge who couldn't give a damn about soldiering.'

'Maybe John will call us over,' Charlotte said.

Spenser, who knew that she was praying that he wouldn't, said: 'I shouldn't think so. It's hardly his place to call us over to the Viceroy's table.'

The musicians stopped the flow of the Blue Danube and the perspiring men escorted their partners off the floor. John Couldridge joined Spenser and Charlotte and said: 'Lord Curzon has invited you over to his table.'

Charlotte said: 'There, I told you so.' But her voice was frightened.

'I suppose Joanne arranged this,' Spenser said.

'I'm afraid so. She got me over there, too. But I shouldn't let that worry you. You've always wanted to meet Kitchener, haven't you?'

'Yes,' Spenser said, 'I have. Just as you would have liked to have met your Robert Koch.'

The two lords rose as Charlotte took her seat, Lord Curzon stiff and straight in the unseen steel corset that he always wore. Beside him sat his wife, Mary Leiter, the daughter of an American millionaire, who had warmed his cold nature. They talked about the sixty illustrious years of Queen Victoria's reign, of the partitioning of Bengal, of the powers of the military member of the Viceroy's Council, of the mounting insistence of many Indians that they should help fashion the future of their country. Joanne Pinkerton spoke a little, Spenser and Couldridge answered questions as briefly and non-committally as possible, Charlotte spoke once and used her fan to hide her nervousness.

135

Kitchener turned to Spenser and said: 'I suppose you've followed the Boer War?'

'Yes, sir.' He felt the man's strength, the singleness of purpose that was sometimes interpreted as brutality.

'Do you think the Boers got what they deserved?'

'Yes, sir. There was no other way as I see it.'

'I wonder,' said Kitchener, 'if you really mean that. Do you approve of burning farms and establishing prison camps?'

Spenser wondered if he would have replied honestly if he had not agreed with Kitchener's measures in South Africa. 'If the situation warrants it, sir.'

Kitchener nodded. 'I suppose I shall never really know what my young men think. If they disagree with me they daren't tell me. The only criticism I hear is from politicians who have never explored the Empire further south than Bournemouth or Torquay.' He stared at Spenser. 'But I think you're telling the truth.'

'Thank you, sir.'

Lord Curzon turned to Couldridge. 'I hear,' he said in his scholarly voice, 'that you've discovered a revolutionary method of purifying water.'

'Not me, sir,' Couldridge said. 'I'm merely implementing some research carried out by an I.M.S. doctor in London.'

'And that you implemented it on the journey from Calcutta to Delhi?'

'That's right, sir.'

Kitchener said: 'I presume you were carrying out orders.'

'Not exactly, sir.'

Lady Curzon said swiftly: 'I believe it was immensely successful.'

And Joanne Pinkerton said: 'There was only one case of cholera and that was on the first day before John—before Lieutenant Couldridge—started purifying the water with chlorine.'

Kitchener said: 'You seem to be very well informed, Miss Pinkerton.

Lady Curzon said: 'She should be—she's engaged to be married to Lieutenant Couldridge.'

Lord Curzon said: 'You didn't tell me, Mary. Is that so, Miss Pinkerton?'

'Not officially,' Joanne said. 'But we hope to make an announcement soon.'

'I hope,' said Kitchener, 'that when it comes to marriage that you are better at obeying orders than your fiancé appears to be.'

They all laughed uneasily.

Lord Curzon said: 'If this system of purifying water is so effective I wonder why it has not been introduced throughout India. Throughout the British Army. Throughout the world for that matter.'

Couldridge said: 'Perhaps because those who are in a position to put successful research to good use are jealous.'

'Or careful,' Lord Curzon said.

'I trust young man that you are not referring to the Army,' Kitchener said.

'No, sir. I was thinking of the medical councils that prevail in London, Berlin, Paris, New York.'

Charlotte spoke her only sentence. 'I think perhaps Lieutenant Couldridge is right,' she said. But her words were whisked away by the orchestra tackling The Lancers, and she retired once more behind her fan.

Kitchener turned the questioning to Spenser. 'What do you think, Lieutenant Spenser? Do you think your friend Lieutenant Couldridge was right in purifying the water in this way when the accepted Army method is boiling?'

Spenser was aware that he was on trial. And that Couldridge, who had always known his true character, was wondering whether loyalty to army or friend would prevail. 'I think he showed initiative, sir.'

There may have been a suggestion of a smile on the bleak face—Spenser wasn't sure. Kitchener said: 'A good answer, apart from the fact that it didn't answer my question. How-

137

ever there are times—even in the Army—when diplomacy is required.'

Lord Curzon started to speak, but applied himself instead to his champagne. Spenser suspected that he had been about to ask Kitchener when he had last bothered with diplomacy. But such remarks were not made in front of very junior officers. Spenser decided that it was time they left the table. He smiled at Joanne. 'Perhaps,' he said, 'I might have the pleasure of the next dance.'

'It would be a pleasure,' Joanne said.

They rose to dance and Couldridge completed the escape by asking Charlotte to dance.

Kitchener said: 'Lieutenant Spenser?'

'Sir?'

'I think you will make a very good soldier.'

'Thank you, sir.'

And as they took the floor Spenser felt an exultant surge of pleasure. The pleasure that a boy experiences when he meets a sporting hero who does not tarnish on close inspection.

Joanne said: 'I was very happy for you then, Neville. You were loyal to John and yet you still got your accolade.'

'Thank you,' he said. 'It's funny—he's quite a kind man, really.'

'I don't think the Boers would agree with you,' Joanne said.

'Perhaps you're right. But he did what he had to do.' He nodded in agreement with himself. 'Yes, he did what he had to.'

And together they danced the Military Two-step.

11

It was the day of the elephants. Dominant and deliberate, they seemed to be towing the procession. As if all the princes, the emirs, the maharajas, the guns and the horses with manicured hooves, were on one long float pulled and pushed and guided by them. Nothing diminished their dignity; not the paint on their trunks nor the silk skull caps nor the howdahs perched on their backs and the peacock personages inside them. The elephants, trunks swinging with pendulum movements, little eyes bright and wise, did more than physically dwarf the brown and white men around them: they dwarfed all human vanity.

There were five regiments of cavalry in the procession, police on horseback, Imperial cadets, heralds in gold silks, noblemen's sons on black chargers with leopard skins covering their flanks. Hindus and Moslems, tribesmen and princes, polo-playing playboys and Nationalist zealots, Old Etonians and graduates of the Mahabaleshwar Academy for Advanced Education. Lord and Lady Curzon rode in a howdah on an elephant sheathed in gold and silver majestically accepting on behalf of His Majesty King Edward VII the homage and hatred of the inhabitants of 1,800,000 square miles of Asia.

John Couldridge and the Spensers and Joanne Pinkerton watched from a platform near the Great Mosque. Couldridge was at first overawed with the splendour of the procession, hypnotised by sunlight splintering on diamonds, rubies and emeralds; the clatter of hooves; the metronome movements of ropes and pearls around brown satin throats. Then, quite un-solicited, a picture of a boy blinded by quackery inserted itself into his vision. And he thought how the fortune spent on the splendid arrogance strung out before him could have been spent on the provision of hospitals or schools or laboratories for medical research.

The contribution of the state of Rewah to the procession passed in front of them. Elephants with painted trunks pulling a coach—half railway carriage, half gypsy's caravan—with lace curtains at the windows. And boys self-consciously strutting beside it carrying lances.

'What are you thinking?' Joanne asked. She wore a straw bonnet trimmed with pink lace and twirled her parasol as she spoke.

'You know perfectly well,' he said.

Spenser said: 'It makes one very proud, doesn't it?'

Charlotte said nothing.

As the last elephant pushed the procession past them Couldridge said: 'I think I'm going for a walk.'

'Where?' Joanne said.

'Down the back streets somewhere. To see the other India.'

'I'll come with you,' she said.

Spenser said: 'You must be crazy. You'll get your throats cut.'

'Why should we?' Couldridge said. 'It's a proud day for Britain and all the Indians will be too busy salaaming to cut our throats.'

'Well for God's sake don't take Joanne with you.'

'I'm going,' Joanne said.

Couldridge shook his head. 'No, you're not. Nor is Charlotte. Neville is right—there might be trouble if they saw you dressed up like that. Particularly as there's a lot of bad feeling around today.'

'Then I'd better go with you,' Spenser said.

'Funny, isn't is?' Joanne said. 'The whole idea of the Durbar is to spread good will.'

Couldridge and Spenser struck off down a side street which might have been in Bombay or Calcutta. It wasn't crowded but Couldridge sensed the hostility from inside the leaning terraces of poverty. 'You needn't come, you know,' he said.

'You needed me that night in Calcutta,' Spenser said. 'I shouldn't be surprised if you don't need me again today.'

'I could have managed without you that night,' Couldridge said.

'And I would have come to your funeral.'

Couldridge smiled. 'That wasn't very gracious of me, was it. I couldn't have managed without you that night. But there won't be any trouble today.'

A small boy with a starved, swollen belly clawed at their

140

legs. Couldridge gave him the change from his pockets and the boy stared at the money, joy and disbelief jockeying with each other on his hollowed face.

They walked on. 'Now we'll have all the beggars after us,' Spenser said.

'I told you to go back if you wanted to.'

'I didn't say anything about going back. It's just that once you give money to one beggar then you get them all round you.'

'Do you call that boy a beggar?'

'That's what he was, wasn't he. Probably starved and sent out by his parents. He's lucky they didn't cut one of his limbs off at birth so that he could earn them even more money. You know some of these beggars are supposed to be as rich as the Maharajas?'

Couldridge said: 'I see you did your research pretty thoroughly in Streatham Library before coming out here.'

'It's a well-known fact,' Spenser said. The good humour had left his voice.

The rickshaw overtook them as they were about to turn down a dozing alley where brown limbs protruded from the shadows on to squares of sunlight spotted with betel-stained spittle.

Joanne Pinkerton climbed out, dismissed the rickshaw and said: 'I would have caught you up quicker except that I had trouble finding a rickshaw. They seem to have been cleared off the route of the procession like the beggars.'

Anger coarsened Couldridge's voice. 'I told you to stay behind. What the hell have you come down here for? This isn't Boston, you know. You might get your throat cut.' He spoke with exaggerated menace. 'Or something worse.'

'Gee,' she said. 'Something worse than having my throat cut. Whatever could that be?'

Spenser said: 'Where's Charlotte?'

'She's gone to have a lie-down.'

Couldridge said: 'Why couldn't you have a lie-down? We're

only having a stroll for God's sake. You're not achieving anything.'

'Just because I'm a woman I don't have to be left out of everything.'

Couldridge stabbed his finger at her. 'Just get this straight—if we're going to get married you've got to obey me. Love, honour and obey. Right?'

'Right,' she said. And added: 'When we're married. Now come on—I don't want to spoil your walk.'

'We're going back,' Couldridge said.

She appealed to Spenser. 'Can't you stop him bullying me?'

'You shouldn't have come,' Spenser said. 'You know you shouldn't. It was a stupid thing to do.'

'But it's something to write home about,' Couldridge said. 'Something to maintain the image. Bright tomboy all-American girl whose exploits are the main topic of conversation among stuffy old British Imperialists.'

'I couldn't have put it better,' she said. But the tilt of her head told him that she was angry.

'I should have thought you'd learned your lesson by now.'

She didn't reply.

He went on: 'Making an idiot of yourself up in the hills.'

Spenser said: 'I should leave her alone if I were you. We're almost back now.'

Joanne Pinkerton rounded on the two of them. 'You stay out of it,' she said to Spenser. And to Couldridge she said: 'And as for you—you're just a darned British stuffshirt. I don't know what I ever saw in you. Rude, arrogant and so stuffy that you should have been a taxidermist.' Her lips trembled but Couldridge wasn't sure whether it was suppressed laughter at her own humour or contained anger.

He said: 'If you feel like that then there's no sense in us getting married.'

'You're darned right there isn't.'

'Thank God we found out in time.' But the sudden desolate glimpse of life without her belied his words.

As they neared the spot where Couldridge had given the money to the starving boy an old Indian with a straggle of beard and an autumn-leaf face emerged from a doorway. He moved with a skewer movement because he had no legs. He salaamed grotesquely and asked for money.

'Come on,' Spenser said. 'Let's get out of this.'

'Haven't you got any money?' Joanne asked.

'I gave it to a hungry boy,' Couldridge said. 'But you've got money. You're very rich. Why don't you give him some?'

'I will,' she said.

'I shouldn't,' Spenser said. 'We were lucky once. We won't be so lucky again.'

But she was already picking around in her purse. She found a few coins and gave them to the grovelling trunk of humanity at her feet.

Couldridge thought again of the ball—the champagne and the game meat in aspic; and he thought of the procession minted with gold, silver and diamonds.

'There,' Joanne said, 'that's all I've got.'

'Quite a sacrifice,' Couldridge said. 'I hope you don't have to account to your father for it.'

'I wish I could have given him more.'

'He wouldn't have known what to do with it,' Spenser said.

'Streatham Library,' Couldridge said.

The sun shining from the narrow sky above found blue lights in the hair of the youth sidling up to them from the shadows. He moved the stump of his arm with eloquence.

'I told you what would happen,' Spenser said. 'Let's get out while we can.'

Couldridge looked at the arm which ended just above where the elbow should have been. 'How in God's name did that happen?' he asked.

'You've got to harden yourself to this sort of thing,' Spenser said. 'It's the only way. Otherwise you'll never survive India.' He glanced at Couldridge and allowed himself a twitch of a smile. 'And that's not Streatham Library. It's true. If you start thinking about all the suffering around you then you'll never survive. You can't cure it, no one can. All you can do is try and ignore it.'

Couldridge said: 'Even if you have it within your power to ease the suffering of one man?'

'A few rupees isn't going to do that,' Spenser said. 'For one day, two perhaps. You aren't solving anything.'

'Your trouble,' Couldridge said, 'is that you're too damn logical.' He was still looking at the young Hindu's arm. 'It looks as if it's been amputated surgically.'

Spenser shook his head. 'It was chopped off when he was a child. He's a professional beggar.'

'I know,' Couldridge said. 'And he's as rich as a maharajah.'

Joanne Pinkerton said: 'There are worse cases approaching.'

There was a boy with festering sores, a man with no nose, a shrivelled old woman limping with a stick, two boys leading their sightless masters, a leper and a lunatic and others.

'Come on,' Spenser said. 'Quickly.'

'Oh God,' Joanne said.

'Spenser's right,' Couldridge said. 'There's nothing we can do.'

But they were too late.

The beggars pleaded, cajoled, clutched, whimpered. And when there was no benificence began to growl.

'I warned you,' Spenser said.

Couldridge tried to speak to them with the few words of Hindi that he had learned. He showed his empty pockets and opened Joanne's empty purse. The lunatic began to scream hysterically.

Joanne said in a frightened voice: 'What are we going to do?'

'Just keep walking,' Couldridge said.

But the old woman grabbed at Joanne's rich silk skirts.

Couldridge said: 'At least it will teach you a lesson.' He tried to pull the old woman away but she clung on tenaciously. Other beggars gathered around them and began to shout.

They pushed on for a few yards with the woman still attached to Joanne's skirt. Then, with a snarl of gibberish, the lunatic threw himself at Couldridge's knees. The force of the tackle overbalanced Couldridge and he fell on to the betel-stained ground.

The rest of the beggars were crowding Joanne. She struck out with fear and fury with her parasol, but it was as effective as a sprig of blossom.

It was then that Spenser drew his pistol.

Couldridge managed to stand up and shouted at him. 'It's not necessary. Put the bloody thing away.'

'Do you want Joanne to be killed?'

'You don't have to shoot them.'

Joanne screamed as a sinewy arm clutched beneath her skirts. Spenser fired his pistol into the air. The explosion was as loud as a cannon shot in the narrow alley. It assaulted the ear-drums and froze all movement with shock. The beggars were momentarily statues.

'Get going,' Spenser said. Then he attacked the beggars with his swagger stick. One fell and he slashed him around the face and neck. The beggar whimpered, then screamed. The rest of the beggars stood uncertainly around and then dispersed.

Couldridge grabbed Spenser's shoulder. 'They've gone,' he said. 'They've all gone.'

But Spenser went on hitting the beggar. Couldridge pulled him round and bunched his fist. Spenser's face was glaring and sweat was running down his cheeks. Couldridge rammed him up across the wall. 'That's enough,' he said. 'No more. That's enough.' He kept his fist ready.

Spenser found a handkerchief and wiped the sweat from his face. 'It had to be done,' he said.

Joanne ran to Couldridge and he put one arm round her. 'John,' she said. 'I'm sorry.'

He tightened his grip on her. 'Never again?'

'Never again,' she said. 'My love—never again.'

'Love, honour and obey?'

'Love, honour and obey.'

'I love you,' he said.

145

Spenser put his pistol away. 'It had to be done,' he said.

'I know,' Couldridge said. 'You probably saved our lives. It had to be done.'

'I told you not to give the money to that boy.'

'I know,' Couldridge said. 'Everything you said has been right. If you hadn't fired your pistol and lammed into that beggar we would all probably be dead.'

'But you don't understand really, do you? I can feel that you don't understand. Even though we would all have been killed if I hadn't done what I did.'

'I understand,' Couldridge said.

'Then what's the matter? For God's sake, what's the matter?'

'The man you were hitting was blind,' Couldridge said.

They walked back to the site of the morning's Imperial glory in silence. It had been the day of the elephants. No one else's.

12

JOHN COULDRIDGE cared for his new laboratory more deeply than an artist or author cares for studio or study. And in it—like other crusading and inquisitive doctors all over the world—he experimented with vaccines. In the process he found another hero— Waldemar Haffkine who had undertaken research into plague, once known as the Black Death. But when fourteen people died from tetanus after he had vaccinated them against plague he had been suspended from his work. He claimed that his vaccine had been contaminated when it had been outside his care. He had been vindicated and reinstated as head of the Biological Laboratory, Calcutta.

To Couldridge the reinstatement of Haffkine was a victory of the pioneers over the reactionaries personified to him by Buckingham and Little. And it infused him with fresh lusts for work.

In the evenings he worked with Dr Bose, whom he now employed, and watched the two children that Joanne had borne him, playing with the ayah on the small patch of grass behind the laboratory. Sometimes he felt guilty that he was not spending enough time with Joanne, but she rarely complained: she had chosen a man with a purpose and she knew the price.

He worked with samples taken from patients—and from bodies—at the hospital. At first the officers in charge contented themselves with distant reproof, treating him like a youth whose whims had to be indulged. Couldridge knew that they suppressed their anger because Joanne was a friend of the Viceroy's wife. He accepted the shelter of her parasol but he didn't like it. Their only quarrels were about her friends in high places whom she had used to get him on the Durbar and the money with which she had bought him the laboratory. But in moments of introspective truth, as he peered at his smears and cultures, surveyed his retorts and tubes and cages of condemned rodents, he knew that he wronged her. Then, as the ayah gathered up his son, Neville, and his daughter, Mary Joanne, he hurried next door to the square house with the verandah—as regal as any building could be in the centre of Calcutta—took his wife in his arms and thanked her for what she had given him.

And when she looked at him and blinked mistily he said: 'I really must treat you for that astigmatism some day.'

'No,' she said, 'you just get on with your research. Whatever it is.'

But he couldn't tell her, not specifically. Because his mind and his notebooks were crammed with so many theories, so many possible contributions to the ultimate succour of Mankind.

One other aspect of discovery also worried him as he grew his cultures on potatoes and jellies in the city where the world's bacteria gathered from their eternal convention. He was worried about the value of any victory over a disease. If Man succeeded in defeating cholera or tuberculosis then other executioners would

147

take their place. If this were so then it meant that the work of Pasteur, Lister, Koch, merely prolonged life, prolonged the ultimate pain. Was there, he wondered, any point to this?

None of the worries, however, none of the disappointments, none of the patronising observations of his seniors, ever kept him from his laboratory and the company of Dr Bose.

The reproof of Little and, above him, Buckingham, hardened with the departure of Lord Curzon. Curzon quarrelled with Kitchener over the powers of the military member of the Viceroy's Council. Curzon offered his resignation which, to his mortification, was accepted. Because, although Kitchener was not a diplomat, he had friends in Whitehall.

Another Old Etonian, Lord Minto, became Viceroy of India. Eton, Trinity, Scots Guards. Whereas Lord Curzon had only suffered from a curvature of the spine Lord Minto had once broken his neck in a riding accident. He worked in uneasy alliance with the Secretary of State for India, Lord Morley, who was known as Honest John and pursued his passion for the truth to the extent of spelling god with a small 'g' because he was an atheist.

When Buckingham and Little and other members of the Indian Medical Service in Calcutta were satisfied that Lord Curzon no longer had any influence in the sub-continent they set about curbing the precocious activities of Surgeon Lieutenant Couldridge. Little changed and re-arranged his duties so that he was often so exhausted that he could hardly see through his microscope; he was constantly being upbraided for minor infringements of regulations; he was put in charge of casualty where he would not come into contact with any of the diseases that he was studying.

'Why don't you leave the I.M.S?' Joanne asked. We've got enough money.'

'You've got enough money, you mean.'

'All right,' she said. 'Then I've got enough money. I didn't think we were ever to argue about that.'

'All right,' Couldridge said. 'We won't argue about it. But

148

I'm not leaving the I.M.S. just because of people like Little and Buckingham. I've got to fight prejudice just as much as I've got to fight disease. These days I sometimes wonder which is the harder fight.'

So he continued to joust with authority at the hospital and fight bacteria with Bose in the laboratory. And one evening when he was very tired he sipped a glass of lime juice in the laboratory and told Bose about the doubts he sometimes had about the necessity for research and about his own motives.

Bose, his hair blue-black and his skin very dark against his white coat, looked surprised. 'I didn't know you ever had any doubts,' he said.

'Well I do,' Couldridge said. 'I sometimes think that it's just my vanity that keeps me going.'

'Perhaps it is,' Bose said. 'But it doesn't seem to me to matter. Many great scientists have been vain men.'

'So you think I'm conceited, do you Bose?'

Bose evaded the question. 'I think you are dedicated.'

'I'm sure of one bloody thing,' Couldridge said. 'I'll never let the Buckinghams and Littles of this world beat me.'

Bose grinned. 'I'm sure of that,' he said.

Bose nodded and, restraint released by fatigue, elaborated. 'I admire your spirit. You do not often see it in the Englishmen I meet. Perhaps because they cannot be bothered to talk to me. If you don't mind me saying it John'—he paused in case Couldridge was offended by the familiarity—'I think we are perhaps kindred spirits. Kindred rebels perhaps I should say.'

'I think perhaps we are.' Couldridge tinkled the ice in his lime juice. 'I think perhaps we've got to be if we're to succeed in what we're doing.' He surveyed the used test tubes, the un-stoppered flasks, a broken slide—the aftermath of the evening's work. 'Although I'm not sure what that is.' He threw some stained litmus paper into the bin. 'How old are you Bose?'

'Twenty-eight,' Bose said. 'Why?'

'You don't want to throw your youth away here. You're too good a doctor, too good a research man, to waste your time here.'

149

'You don't understand,' Bose said. 'You don't understand at all, John.' He pronounced the Christian name with pleasure. 'There is nowhere else I could work like this. There is no other white doctor who would be bothered to work with me.' He gathered confidence. 'You treat me almost as an equal.'

'Almost?'

'It is always almost. Even with you, John.'

'Piffle,' Couldridge said. 'Absolute piffle.'

Bose shook his head. 'No, John. Not piffle. You treat me better than any white man I have ever met. But I shall always be an almost-equal.'

'All right, then,' Couldridge said. 'I'll promote you above me. I always did think Bose was a damn silly name. It doesn't suit you. From now on you're Boss.'

'All right, sahib,' Bose said.

'Are you really serious about the way the other white doctors treat you? I hadn't noticed it particularly.'

'John, my equal, there are many things that you do not realise. Most of the time because you are too occupied with your cultures and your serum to see what is going on around you.'

'I think you've got a bit of a complex,' Couldridge said.

'We all have a complex,' Bose said. 'All Indians have a complex. We are born with it. The Brahmins have an inferiority complex about white people. We have an inferiority complex about Brahmins—and white people. Moslems have a complex about Hindus, Hindus have a complex about Moslems and Buddhists. Moslems, Hindus and Buddhists have a complex about white people. White people like to think we are simple: in fact we are the most complicated people in the world.'

Couldridge peered through the microscope. 'Boss,' he said, 'I didn't realise you felt as strongly as this. I just thought of you as a doctor.'

Bose poured himself more lime juice and held it to the light as if he had just titrated it. He said: 'Even now you are more concerned with your microbes.'

Couldridge pushed the microscope aside. 'I didn't realise you felt so strongly about the Europeans here.'

'Europeans? You mean whites.'

'All right,' Couldridge said. 'Whites then. Make it pigment rather than race if you insist. All this is a revelation to me. I didn't dream that you've felt this way all the time I've known you. How have you kept it all to yourself, Boss?'

Bose sat on a high stool beside the bench holding his glass tightly in one hand. His face was quick and eager; Couldridge didn't recall ever seeing him so alert, ever sensing such animalism.

Bose said: 'I have often felt like talking about it to you. I didn't know whether I should. I didn't know how you would react. I didn't want to disturb—if that's the right word—our relationship.'

'Boss,' Couldridge said, 'we've known each other a long, long time.

'I know, sahib,' Bose said.

'And you really couldn't talk about all this?'

Bose shrugged. 'What was the point? There is nothing you could do about it. There is nothing you can do to influence Mr Morley and your Government. Your work is medicine not politics.'

'And isn't yours?'

Bose swallowed the rest of his lime juice and thought for a moment. 'It is all very well for you to speak, John. Medicine is everything to you. You are an Englishman, a ruler, a sahib. Nothing else need matter to you. I am an Indian—other things must matter to me. I have to help my people attain equality.' He smiled. 'Or almost-equality if you like.'

Couldridge again surveyed the debris of an evening of abortive research. His eyes were sore and there was a tic in one of his eyelids. 'To hell with your politics and equality,' he said. 'What about helping to keep your people alive rather than equal? Do you know what the deaths from plague were in the last year?'

'I do not know the actual figures,' Bose said.

'I'll tell you,' Couldridge said. 'They were 940,821. Isn't it more important to find an answer to figures like that than to achieve equality for all Indians?'

Bose was silent.

'Well, isn't it?'

Bose's voice was quiet and strong. 'They are two entirely different arguments, John. Both are important. We must try and save lives, I agree. We must also try and preserve our dignity.'

Couldridge said: 'I believe that the battle against disease is more important.'

'Perhaps.' Bose was tentative. 'But from what you told me earlier, John, I am not so sure that you are wholly concerned with human suffering. You said, I believe, that your own vanity might enter into it.'

'And you said that didn't matter.' Couldridge realised that he was talking to Bose as an equal and that he had never done so before. 'In any case it's the end product that matters. By concentrating on research I am at least contributing towards alleviating human suffering. By playing with politics you are merely causing bloodshed. As a doctor you're supposed to be dedicated to stemming it.'

'I wish it were as simple as that, John,' Bose said.

'Isn't it?'

'Perhaps one day I should explain to you what I'm trying to say. Perhaps one day I should explain to you what it means to be an Indian.'

Couldridge took Bose's glass and refilled it with lime juice. 'There's no time like the present,' he said. He raised his glass. 'Here's to almost-equality.' He drank half a glass of lime juice. 'Now tell me all about it.'

'Now you have made me embarrassed.'

'Tell me.'

'There's nothing much to tell. I won't bore you with the details. I would like to tell you what it's all about. If, that is John, you won't be bored.'

'You've never been bored with all the dead-ends of my theories.'

'This isn't a dead-end, John.'

'I'm sorry.'

'It's just a feeling. Something in the bloodstream perhaps. But it's always there and there's nothing people like myself can do about it. We want equality and we want freedom to rule ourselves. Such things are as much our birthright as they are the birthright of the British. Why should we be patronised by white people? Why should we be servants? We have the Indian National Congress and that is a start. But that is not enough—our progress will be too slow. I want to see an independent India in my lifetime, so we must do more than just talk. Do you understand what I mean, John?'

But John Couldridge didn't reply. He was looking through the microscope again. 'Sorry, Boss,' he said. 'What did you say? I just had to have another look at those damned little cholera bugs of Koch's.'

By the time he looked up from the microscope the hurt and the anger had left Bose's face.

'It doesn't matter,' Bose said. 'It doesn't matter at all.'

13

GRADUALLY Couldridge found that he was specialising—despite his beliefs that a doctor could become expert in more than one field. All around him he saw glazed and cloudy eyes, pink eyes, dead eyes; and he remembered the whore who was going blind in Bombay, the boy blinded by a quack in the village in the Punjab. He read that 1.72 out of every 1,000 Indians were in fact blind: and shortly before his thirtieth birthday he determined to specialise in eye surgery.

He sent to England for a glossy coloured chart of the human eye which he pinned on the wall of the laboratory. It was beautifully drawn, a cross section, with black lashes, cornea, blue iris, colourless lens and glistening white optic nerve leading from the retina. In front of the eye stood a tiny ballet dancer; lines passing through the lens showed how her image was transmitted to the brain.

He bought books on ophthalmology and, with the help of Joanne, returned to his student days. He started at the beginning and, when the children were in bed, recited his homework to her. 'The eyeball is made up of three coats. The exterior sclerotic and cornea made of strong fibrous tissue. The middle muscular and pigmented layer forming the choroid and iris. The internal nervous and epithelial layer called the retina which contains the end of the optic nerve.'

'Very good,' said Joanne. She moved closer to him on the sofa of their tiger-skinned lounge and kissed him.

'It couldn't be more elementary,' he said. 'I feel a bit ridiculous. But if I'm really going to specialise then I've got to begin at the beginning.' He peered into her eyes. 'How's your myopia and astigmatism?'

'Doing nicely, thank you.'

'At least you haven't got any symptoms of strabismus.'

'What's that when it's at home?'

'A squint,' Couldridge said.

'Your eyes are quite hard,' she said. 'Hard and blue. They used to frighten me. Then you'd smile. And they would kind of smile as well.'

Couldridge lit his pipe. 'Impossible. An eye can't smile any more than this pipe can.'

'Yours do,' she said.

After he had relearned the physiology of the eye he progressed on to its diseases, its weaknesses and defects.

'Do you know the definition of a blind person?' he asked Joanne.

She shook her head.

'Someone who can't count his fingers at a distance of one metre.'

'I know one of the saddest things about blind people,' she said.

'What's that?'

'They say that people speak of them as if they were not present. As if they had been deprived of their hearing as well as their sight.'

'That's interesting,' Couldridge said. But his voice wasn't interested.

'Smile,' she said. And then: 'That's better—your eyes were hard again.'

He frowned. 'I'm a doctor. I can't afford to be a sentimentalist as well.'

'You've got to have feeling if you're going to be a successful doctor. And you have got feeling. I should know. But I sometimes think it gets left behind in the rush for learning.'

He bit hard on his pipe. 'Do you really think that?'

'I've noticed it lately. You still show feeling to me and the children. But I'm sometimes scared that the scientist is taking over from the doctor. Don't let him take over completely, John. Because then one day you might find that you haven't any feeling for me and the children and I couldn't bear that.'

He slid his arm round her waist, felt her warmth and smelled her hair. 'That will never happen,' he said. 'God, when I think how we fought when we first met. I nearly lost you through my stupidity.'

'I wonder what you would have done if that tiger hadn't happened along.'

'There would have been something else. A leopard or a rogue elephant.' He squeezed her and kissed her. 'Let's go up and have a look at the children.'

The children's eyelids were tightly gummed with sleep. But as they dreamed their eyes moved beneath their lids. Mary Joanne who was four, Neville who was five. The girl with her pretty pointed face, the boy with his Irish face and dark hair.

John Couldridge and his wife looked with awe and humility upon their healthy children with their healthy eyes flickering beneath their lids.

'Thank God,' she said.

He nodded. 'When you think of all the kids going blind out there.' He pointed into the night.

'You still have feeling,' she said.

'I still have feeling,' he said.

And after he had studied the sicknesses and anomalies of eyes he narrowed his learning to blindness in India. To the illnesses that could cause it—measles, meningitis, scarlet fever, smallpox; and the diseases of parents that could blind their children—leprosy, tuberculosis, scrofula, syphilis. Then on to the actual eye conditions—cataracts, glaucoma, trachoma, corneal ulcers, ophthalmia neonatorum, atrophy of the optic nerve; and quackery.

He lingered over trachoma because this was the most common curable cause of blindness in India. Curable if the inflammation and tiny eruptions beneath the eyelids were treated before there was any scarring or vascularisation of the cornea. He also lingered there because both the whore and the small boy had suffered from trachoma and he knew that he could have cured them.

He was also fascinated by glaucoma because again it was curable when diagnosed early enough; but he had not yet been presented with a case that was still in that early stage of hope. He read about the symptoms of acute suffering; pain in the mornings and evenings, nausea, vomiting, prostration, semi-dilated pupils, hazy cornea, photophobia. And all because of an obstruction to the drainage system of the eye that caused high fluid pressure. If they weren't treated in time, all children suffering from glaucoma became blind.

'And all because of blocked drains,' John Couldridge said.

'I beg your pardon?' his wife said.

'Blocked drains,' he said. 'That's what causes glaucoma. It's supposed to be the worst pain known to man.' He smiled at the tiger laughing at death on the floor. 'I once thought I had a case and it turned out to be a hangover. Did you know that glaucoma can be caused by emotion?'

'No,' she said, 'I didn't know that.'

Outside the monsoon rain sluiced against the windows and small scents of watered earth and ravaged blossoms wandered into the room. The watering of the cracked earth, its release and its sappy joy, engendered release and extravagant emotion in many humans; especially in those who sought an excuse. Women contemplating infidelity became unfaithful with the first fat blob of rain; men gambled their savings and lost, beat their wives, sacked the servants, got drunk, exulted, mourned.

White men, that is. Indians merely rejoiced that their gods had removed the umbrella from their country. They watched atrophied crops take on green flesh, they caressed the wet earth and prepared to plant more seeds and roots. The Moslems thanked Allah, the Parsees thanked the Prophet Zoroaster, the Hindus thanked Shiva and looked with gratitude upon cows, bulls, monkeys, tree squirrels and, in some parts, rats. Such was the frenzy of the rejoicing that Moslems and Hindus often killed each other when their celebrations impinged upon each other.

John Couldridge smelled the damp fertile scents and said to his wife: 'You are happy, aren't you, Joanne?'

'Of course,' she said. Her eyes, he thought, were the same colour as the smoke drifting from his pipe. 'It's just that I get worried about you sometimes. I guess it's silly. You find a man with a purpose in life and then you start getting scared that the purpose will take him away from you.'

'You're crazy.'

'Oh no I'm not. Women only have one real interest in life when they're young. The man they love. And their kids, of course. But men—men like you—always have two reasons for living. The woman they love and their purpose. I figure I know which is the stronger with you John Couldridge.'

'You,' he said scraping intently at the hot bowl of his pipe with an old scalpel.

She shook her head and walked across the room to the

window. The rain streamed across the panes so that it seemed as if they were in the cabin of a ship. 'You don't have to lie,' she said. 'I understand.'

'Because I have two reasons for living it doesn't mean to say that one is stronger than the other.'

'I don't mind you working late every night,' she said. 'I knew what I was taking on when I fell in love with you. But I get very scared. I'm such a little part of it all. Why, I reckon you confide in Bose more than you do me. None of it seemed to matter when you didn't really know where you were heading. But all of a sudden I've got a feeling that you do. You'll be a great eye surgeon, John.'

'If you're right you'll be a great eye surgeon's wife. If you're right....'

'That sounds kind of superfluous. Like a handmaiden or a pet dog.'

'Nonsense.' He laughed, and refilled his pipe; blue smoke the colour of her eyes drifted across the cabin in the rain. He told her about the delicate feats of surgery he hoped one day to carry out. The transplanting of healthy corneal tissue from the eyes of the dead to the eyes of those going blind. 'I shall take a sort of plug from the cornea of the dead man,' he said. 'And make a socket in the scarred cornea of the patient.' He smiled. 'How do you like this technical jargon?' She didn't reply and he went on: 'And then I shall suture the plug into the socket. And after a while the patient will have a healthy cornea once again. Or in other words he'll be able to see. I think we'll be able to prevent blindness caused by trachoma, dystrophy and ulcers that way.' He sucked enthusiastically at his pipe. 'It's an exciting prospect, isn't it? Except, of course, that I'm not the only surgeon working at it.' But still she didn't reply. He crossed the room and turned her round and saw that there were tears in her eyes. 'What's the matter?' she said. 'I don't ever remember you crying before?'

'No,' she said. 'It's the first time. At least it's the first time with you.'

158

'But why?'

'Because I'm scared,' she said.

He slipped his arm round her waist and together they stared out through their porthole in the monsoon.

14

THEY came for Bose one spring evening when all the honeyed scents of the dying day were suspended in the air waiting to be distilled into dew.

There were two white policemen in plain-clothes. Light grey suits and high white stiff collars exhausted by the day. Moustaches, ragged haircuts and speech like recitations.

'Surgeon Lieutenant Couldridge?'

'Yes,' Couldridge said. 'What can I do for you?'

He was conscious that behind him in the laboratory Bose, who had been testing a solution with litmus paper, was taking off his white coat.

'Do you have a Doctor Bose working for you?'

Bose said: 'They know perfectly well you have.' He hung up his white coat on a peg. 'Don't worry, John'—he was still self-conscious about the Christian name—'I expect they want a few words with me.'

The second policeman spoke. His manner of speaking was identical with that of his colleague. 'We want more than a few words with you, Dr Bose.'

His companion said: 'You seem as if you expected us, Dr Bose.'

'One always expects the police in India,' Bose said.

Couldridge said: 'What the hell are you talking about Boss? You've never expected them before.' He remembered the sudden vitality in Bose's face when they had been talking about Indian self-determination. 'Look, Boss,' he said. 'I don't know what all this is about but I would strongly advise you to say nothing at the moment.'

'Thank you, sahib,' Bose said. But there was no humour in his voice.

The first policeman spoke, anger strengthening his voice. 'I should be most grateful, Lieutenant Couldridge, if you would leave this to us. We merely want to ask Dr Bose to accompany us to police headquarters to answer a few questions and see if he can assist us in a certain matter.'

'Isn't he entitled to contact a solicitor?'

'He isn't being arrested,' the second policeman said. 'And in any case ...'

'And in any case what?'

'And in any case I'm only an Indian,' Bose said.

'You sound as if you're pretty touchy on the subject,' the first policeman said. 'Are you a member of any Nationalist organisations by any chance?'

Couldridge said: 'Take my advice and don't answer that.'

'What do you care?'

Couldridge looked at him in surprise. 'I care because you're my colleague and a good doctor. And because of lots of other reasons.'

'You're not interested in anything I care about. You don't understand and you don't want to. You are just protecting me as any white sahib thinks he should protect his Indian servants.'

Couldridge sat down on the tall stool beside the work bench and listened to Bose with astonishment. He pointed at the evidence of their work together; at their cultures, their text books, the glossy cross-section of the eye peering from the wall. 'What the hell are you talking about? Since when were you treated as a servant? And in any case I thought we were both interested in medicine.'

'We are,' Bose said. 'I tried to explain to you once but you didn't listen. I have another interest because I am an Indian.'

One of the policemen took out a notebook and began to write.

Couldridge said: 'Is that necessary?'

The other policeman said: 'I should be most grateful, doctor, if you would confine yourself to medicine. We are merely doing our jobs. We wouldn't presume to tell you how to cut out an appendix.'

'What is Dr Bose supposed to have done?'

One policeman stood with pencil poised while the other, who appeared to be his superior, picked up a flask containing hydro-chloric acid. 'Do you have any other acid in this laboratory, Lieutenant Couldridge?'

'I might have. Why?' Couldridge noted the hard face behind the luxuriant moustache, a face that was rarely creased by laughter. The moustache, black and curled, was a good disguise of character.

'Don't be so suspicious, doctor. A perfectly reasonable question. Perhaps Dr Bose knows why I am asking.'

Bose shrugged. 'I think Lieutenant Couldridge has given me good advice. I want to see a solicitor.'

'And so you shall. When we get to headquarters.' He returned to Couldridge. 'Have you, for instance, any picric acid here?'

Bose said: 'Don't you think *you* should have a solicitor, John? Or perhaps you think it is not necessary because you are British.'

'I don't know what the hell's come over you,' Couldridge said. 'Can anyone tell me what this is all about?'

'Can you tell me if you have any picric acid here?' said the policeman.

Couldridge shrugged. 'I might have. But I doubt it. I can't see that I would have much use for it.'

'You don't know what chemicals you have in the laboratory?'

'I know most of them. But Dr Bose here does the ordering. If there's something we need that I've forgotten he buys it.'

'Perhaps,' said the policeman from behind his disguise, 'we could see the invoice.'

'I don't see why not.' He turned to Bose. 'Go and get the file for them.'

'If you insist,' Bose said. His dark face was expressionless.

The policeman said: 'I shouldn't advise you to try and make a break for it. The building is surrounded.'

Couldridge thumped the bench with his fist. 'Look here,' he said, 'this is going too far ... inspector, sergeant, whatever your rank is.' He paused. 'Do you have any identification with you?'

The moustache twitched as if it had been waiting for the request. The policeman produced a card from a snakeskin wallet. His name was Robinson and he was an inspector.

Couldridge said: 'That still doesn't give you the power to surround my laboratory without a good reason.'

'We have a good reason,' Robinson said.

'Then perhaps you would be good enough to let me know what it is.'

The other policeman looked at Robinson expectantly. Robinson said: 'I should have thought you would have understood by now. One of the ingredients of the explosives which the anarchists are using is picric acid. They have to get their supplies from somewhere, just as they have to get their detonators and dry batteries. We have been checking every possible source. Your laboratory is an obvious possibility, especially as you have a very bright and potentially very dangerous Bengali working for you.'

Couldridge sat down on his stool. 'Very bright certainly. I don't regard him as dangerous in any way.'

The other policeman, who had hardly spoken since Robinson took charge, said: 'He's a real sneaky bastard, that one.'

Robinson stared at his subordinate thoughtfully, as if he were already phrasing a reprimand. The subordinate returned to his notebook. Robinson said: 'He's a very active member of one of the nationalist movements. We have a file on him but so far he has not committed any offence.' He fingered his disguise and added: 'So far.'

Bose came back with the file. Robinson thumbed through the invoices. 'On May the fifth,' he said, 'I see that you ordered some picric acid. That's two days ago. Where is it?'

The three men looked at Bose. 'I'll come down to police headquarters with you,' he said.

15

AFTER Bose had been sentenced to two years' jail Couldridge worked by himself in the laboratory. But he found that some of his zest had evaporated. His research into the diseases bred in Calcutta and disseminated throughout the world always lagged behind the work of other doctors. Because, he believed, his Army duties didn't allow him enough time for his own work.

He was also disconcerted by the absence of Bose. And sometimes when he was absorbed watching the wriggling commas and question-marks of disease in his microscope he would stretch out his hand and ask Bose to pass him an instrument.

When he wasn't working he sat on the verandah inside the cage of mosquito mesh smoking his pipe and wondering why it had never occurred to him that Bose had another life outside the laboratory. A life that, with its ambitions towards bloodshed, negated all their evenings of work together. And he brooded on the occupational blindness that prevented him from appreciating the feelings and crises of people around him; but he knew that the blindness would re-occur.

Then the Army decided to rearrange John Couldridge's life. He was summoned to the office of Colonel Buckingham, who had finally abandoned *all* interest in medicine and devoted himself to military bureaucracy. Everyone agreed that he excelled at it.

Buckingham told him that the I.M.S. was perturbed that he had given evidence for the defence of Bose, a convicted anti-Imperialist agent and a saboteur.

'Only character reference,' Couldridge said. 'I wish I could have done more for him.'

'Such as what?' The freckled fingers sought the swagger stick lying on his desk. 'You could hardly have done more. Except, perhaps, commit perjury.'

Couldridge didn't tell him that he had contemplated perjury; that he had been on the point of testifying that he had ordered the picric acid and used it. But Joanne had dissuaded him, and when he had tried to visit Bose in the cell after the conviction Bose had refused to see him.

'I could have done a lot more,' Couldridge said. 'If I had tried to understand him I might have been able to stop him.'

'You mean you knew about his activities?' Buckingham quivered with eagerness to snap up evidence against Couldridge.

'I didn't know about them. I should have guessed.' Couldridge remembered the vitality that had suddenly mobilised Bose's features when he talked about patriotism. 'It's strange, isn't it, that Bose regarded his actions as patriotic and we regard them as treacherous. Two sets of values for one set of emotions.'

Buckingham steam-rollered a dead fly with his stick. 'Just what are you getting at, Couldridge?' He flicked the small corpse off the stick. 'And would you be kind enough to call me sir. I seem to remember I had to draw your attention to this the first time we met.'

'I'm not getting at anything—sir. It just struck me as strange.'

An orderly came in with two mugs of treacly tea and Couldridge wondered if Buckingham was going to stir his with his swagger stick.

Buckingham said: 'An Inspector Robinson tells us that you seemed very sympathetic towards Bose when he came to take him to police headquarters.'

Couldridge grinned. 'So old moustachios is in on the act, is he?'

Buckingham sucked at his tea. 'This is no laughing matter, Couldridge. It could be very serious for you. Very serious indeed. There are one or two other matters as well. Frankly, Couldridge, we are all a little tired of your extra-curricular activities. It has

164

become quite clear that you are more interested in your private research than you are in your hospital duties. Although God knows why.' There was a blade of viciousness in his voice. 'Have you stumbled on any great discoveries lately?'

'Not great ones,' Couldridge said.

'Any at all?'

'Not really.'

Buckingham looked happier. 'All a bit of a waste of time, isn't it?'

'Perhaps. It's impossible to say. There has to be a long period of research before discovery.'

'I'm also told that you have been attempting to purify water at the hospital by the method introduced by this fellow Nesfield.'

Couldridge nodded. 'It works beautifully.'

'How interesting,' Buckingham said. 'How bloody interesting.' He leaned across the desk, gripping the stick at both ends. 'Now get this straight, Couldridge. Don't do it again. The method hasn't been approved. If you do then you will face strict disciplinary action. Possibly even a court martial.'

Couldridge said: 'What about the march from Lucknow to Delhi?'

'What march? What are you talking about?'

'I thought you would have known about it,' Couldridge said. 'Nesfield was given permission to use chlorogen on a march— I think it was the 1st Royal Dragoons—from Lucknow to Delhi and there wasn't a single death from any water-born disease. I understood a report had been sent to Simla.'

'I don't give a damn what report has been sent to Simla,' Buckingham said. 'You're not using chlorogen while you're in the Indian Medical Service.'

'But why not for God's sake?' Couldridge felt anger expanding inside him, but he knew that he must control it. 'It's been tested and proved. What's the matter with you people? Are you jealous? Don't you care about stopping the spread of disease?'

Buckingham's knuckles were white around the stick, the stringy muscles on his forearms taut. 'You seem to forget, Couldridge, that we're military doctors not Pasteurs or Listers.'

'Or perhaps doctors who know they can't make the grade anywhere else.'

Buckingham cracked the stick across the desk. 'Call me sir, Couldridge. Any more insubordination and I will take instant steps to see that you are severely disciplined.' He gnawed at a dry piece of skin on his bottom lip.

Couldridge felt the sweat of anger greasing his hands and running down his chest. 'I suppose you know I talked to Kitchener about Nesfield's method of water purification.' Despite his anger he felt ashamed of the small threat.

'Kitchener isn't a doctor.'

Couldridge almost said, 'And nor are you.' But he stopped himself.

Buckingham said: 'How long have you been in Calcutta now, Couldridge?'

'A few years. I don't know exactly how many.'

'You're about due for promotion, aren't you?'

'I don't know,' Couldridge said. 'To tell you the truth I don't really care.'

'You've only called me sir once since you came into this room.'

'I don't really care, sir.'

'Well, you're going to be promoted,' Buckingham said. He relaxed his grip on the stick and sat back to observe Couldridge's reactions.

'Why, for God's sake, if my work has been so unsatisfactory?' He tried to lean back so that the air from the fan would reach his sweating chest.

'I'll tell you,' Buckingham said. 'Because I want you out of Calcutta. You're a mischief-maker and a nuisance. And'—he paused to give more effect to the ultimate insult—'I'm not at all sure that you're such a good doctor.'

Couldridge frowned. 'You may be right,' he said. 'About not being a good doctor.'

'We're turning you over to a new field of operation. We're putting you in charge of the medical aspect of famine relief.

The rank for the job is captain and therefore you will have to be promoted. You will no longer be based here and you will be constantly travelling. The monsoon has failed again and things look pretty bad. You will have a busy time ahead of you, Couldridge. And I'm afraid it rather looks as if you will have to abandon your laboratory here.' There was a snigger of triumph in his voice.

Couldridge took out his pipe and began to fill it slowly. Inside him a great bubble of happiness was slowly inflating. The Calcutta experience was over; it had been necessary experience, part of his maturing process. He had come to the putrescent seat of disease and seen the enemy at work. Here bacteria were always the victors aided by ignorance, poverty and filth. Elsewhere in the world doctors were scoring victories over cholera and typhoid and plague. But in Calcutta he could not hope to compete with them.

'Well,' Buckingham said impatiently. 'What do you say?'

'What can I say? I have to obey orders.'

Now he would be able to wander the dry plains and bowls of India, its crests and canvasses, its creased white mountains where the valleys were filled with frozen echoes, its soupy rivers and whispering fields of young green rice. Luxuriously Couldridge allowed his mind to explore his territory and alight at the point to which it seemed that he had always been heading. It was a small neat laboratory beneath high arid skies. To this laboratory would come patients suffering from eye diseases from all the famine areas that he visited. They would not have to pay him: their fee would be their contribution to the progress of eye surgery—the most delicate, the most rewarding, the most beautiful of all surgical skills. It would, perhaps, be somewhere near Lahore; that sounded a good place for it to be.

'So you don't mind?' Buckingham said.

'Mind? I think it's absolutely wonderful news.'

'Oh.' The sandy face was petulant with disappointment. 'What will you do with your laboratory?'

'Burn it,' Couldridge said. 'Is that all—sir?'

Buckingham nodded, his negative face thwarted and sullen. 'That will be all.'

Couldridge walked joyously out of the administrative headquarters and sniffed the doubtful scents of Calcutta with pleasure. Captain John Couldridge, an officer with only two more years in the I.M.S. if he didn't want to sign on again, a man with a cause once more. It wasn't until he was almost home that he realised that he hadn't once considered what Joanne might think about his plans.

BOOK THREE

1

CORPORAL Albert Duckham from Camden Town, London, rarely talked without some reference to the sexual act. When he was pleased by something he said, 'Fucking good oh.' When he was displeased he said, 'Fuck off.' When he was arguing with a friend who had scored a point he said, 'And fuck you too, mate.' When he agreed with an observation he said, 'Too fucking true.' When he was astonished or deeply moved he said, 'Fuck me.' When he was mildly irritated or furiously angry he said, 'Fuck.' All officers were 'Fucking bastards' except one or two who were not bad 'Fuckers'. Occasionally Corporal Duckham who was a sapper serving with the Indian Army varied his conversation with references to defecation.

Now his limited vocabulary was directed at one Private Harold 'The Boot' Williams from Merthyr Tydfil in Wales, who was trying to kick one Private Ronald 'The Shin' Hutchinson from Burton-on-Trent until he either submitted through pain or gravity of injury or passed out. For this purpose he wore ordinary shoes because it had been found that the injuries sustained during shin-kicking contests were too severe if boots were worn.

As Corporal Duckham had put his money on Private Williams who was hopping around holding one bleeding shin he was moved to shout, 'Come on you fucking Welsh bastard. Pull your fucking finger out and get fucking kicking.'

Corporal Duckham was not alone in his emotional agony. About twenty N.C.O.s and privates from a nearby British Army unit were gathered around the combatants under a banyan tree near a marble statue of Nandi the Bull, as far away as possible from authority because the sport had been banned after two soldiers had suffered fractures of the tibia.

A few Indians watched with lethargic interest because they were too hungry to be interested in anything but food. The monkeys in the tree watched with chattering interest—as if they had placed bets—because it was the sort of thing they understood.

Private Williams finally stopped hopping and took a kick at Private Hutchinson. 'Take that you fucking bastard,' he said. Private Hutchinson grunted but stood firm—the idea was that you took your turn to receive and mete out punishment; no dodging was allowed.

Corporal Duckham said: 'Williams, you miserable fucker, you couldn't kick a dent in a fucking Christmas pudding.'

'The Shin' aimed a savage kick at 'The Boot', who collapsed squirming on the ground. Blood from his dented shin-bone stained the dust.

'Get up,' said Corporal Duckham. 'Get up you yellow pig.' Sometimes when he was really angry Corporal Duckham forgot to swear.

'Bugger that,' said 'The Boot'. 'I've had enough.'

The spectators who had backed 'The Shin' were moving forward to congratulate him. The monkeys in the tree, as thick aphides on a rose bush, applauded the victor.

Corporal Duckham bent down to 'The Boot' and spoke softly and venomously in his ear. 'Get up on your feet, Private Williams,' he said, 'or else you'll answer to me. I've got a week's fucking pay on you.'

'I can't,' said 'The Boot'. 'Honest I can't, Corp. He's got shins like fucking railway lines.'

'I thought you said that because you got bow legs from being down the mines you'd be able to take more punishment.'

'I always have,' said 'The Boot'. 'Until I met this bastard. I reckon he pickled his bleeding shins.'

'Shut your fucking noise,' said 'The Shin', who was looming

over him. 'Or I'll put one into your gut. If you've given up just give up and fucking shut your face.'

'I give up,' said 'The Boot'.

Corporal Duckham lifted one foot as if to implement 'The Shin's' threat. Then he stopped himself, swore once more, and walked morosely away in the direction of the hut from which, unobserved, Major Neville Spenser had been watching the contest.

Spenser had wandered away from the tented camp in the Punjab to think about his promotion, his reunion with Could-ridge and the disintegration of his marriage. And he had come upon the scene of brutality that a few years ago would have appalled him. Now he merely wondered whether to take disci-plinary action against the men. After a while he decided not to, because although shin-kicking was banned, the men had to have an outlet to their frustrations in a famine emergency station. But his decision worried him: he did not like failing to implement King's Regulations. He had intended to try and forget what he had seen, but now Corporal Duckham was walking straight towards the shadows at the side of the hut where he was standing. He moved into the sunlight. 'Good afternoon, corporal,' he said.

'Sah.' Corporal Duckham cracked his heels together and saluted.

'At ease, corporal. I've just been watching the contest. I gather that you lost your money.'

'Sah.' It was the only word Corporal Duckham ever used when addressing officers. He relied on intonation to get his meaning across.

Spenser considered his predicament. He knew that he should have Duckham up for disciplinary action in the morning. And the other spectators and participants. He wished he hadn't ling-ered in the shadows. And, to his annoyance, he found himself wondering what Couldridge would have done. Couldridge, still only a captain, but absolutely self-assured. A born leader—if he hadn't been a doctor. But was he a born leader? According to reports from Calcutta, Couldridge had been carpeted for insubordination. Insubordination was, Spenser thought, unforgiveable. And yet here he was, Major Spenser, wondering how an insubordinate captain in the I.M.S. would have dealt with one guilty, inarticulate corporal. A slap on the back, he imagined, a nod and a wink, a tacit understanding that no more would be heard about the incident. All done with a confident familiarity that in no way endangered the officer-N.C.O. relationship. All done with breeding.

'You know it's against orders, don't you?'

'Sah.'

'And you know I should have you up in front of me tomorrow.'

'Sah.'

There was a small silence to which even the monkeys contributed. By now Couldridge would have left the corporal; there would have been no embarrassment, no loss of face. Spenser said, 'All right, corporal'—and hoped that would be the end of it. He began to walk back to the tents and found to his annoyance that Corporal Duckham was walking stiffly beside him. He stopped again and said: 'That will be all, Corporal.'

'Sah?' The intonation said, 'What about tomorrow morning?'

'Forget it, corporal. But don't let it happen again.'

'Sah.'

Spenser turned and walked towards the district officer's bungalow, angry with himself for doing what Couldridge would have done instead of what he knew he should have done.

He walked on through the town of Baipur, starving in the afternoon sunshine. The monsoons had failed—the devil had kept his umbrella up—and then the famine relief grain was a week overdue. As in the case of the Orissa Famine of 1866 the onset had been swift and complete. One day there had been 'no cause for alarm': next day people had been starving. According to the district officer there had been just enough grain to keep the people alive until the relief supplies arrived; but the moneylenders and merchants had bought up the meagre reserves.

Spenser had sent patrols into the town with orders to break into the homes of known crooks. But they had found no grain, just the silver bangles and ivory heirlooms that peasants had been forced to surrender to buy back the sustenance they had sold for a few annas.

In distant fields there had still been a little grain. But the bullocks were too weak to fetch it and Spenser's troops had become farm labourers. What little grain they had harvested had now been distributed. But only today a subaltern had told Spenser that he found a peasant with an emaciated face and fleshless hands selling his cupful of grain to a merchant with painted fingernails.

There were rumours in the town on the edge of the Thar Desert, just outside the shade of the Aravalli Hills, that the ship bringing the relief grain had foundered off the coast of Goa. Whatever the cause of the delay the Indians blamed the British with the same easy conscience that they accepted the schools, health services and railways.

Outside the brown and yellow houses children sat against the walls, bellies distended so that the navels looked like brown nuts, bush-baby eyes staring from skeletal faces. A gentle wind loaded with sand and hot dust singed the trees, and the leaves rustled plaintively. The railhead was deserted, its single track reaching away into the distance as if it were divining for water.

Neville Spenser walked on towards the district officer's bungalow, angry at the plight of the people, angry at himself for reprieving Corporal Duckham. The town was predominantly Moslem but near the bungalow there was a Hindu temple in which they worshipped rats. In the middle of the temple stood a stone rat, as big as an elephant, covered with gold leaf. Spenser peered into the warm dusk of the temple and saw the phantom shapes of worshippers gathered around their rodent god. When the grain came, Spenser thought, they would thank the rat for delivering them from the famine caused by the British.

He arrived at the bungalow and sat down with Couldridge and the district officer, Clifford Chambers. Chambers was a good and dreamy bachelor who loved India and its people and his job which he did well when there was no big crisis. With small

174

crises he was very adept—he settled complicated land tenures in which maps of fields were drawn in ink on grimy cloth, he adjusted the books of thieving village accountants, he organised the shooting of tigers and the arraignment of murderers.

'Can I get you a drink?' he said.

'Please,' Spenser said. 'A whisky and soda if you have one.'

Chambers poured the drink and stared for a moment down an avenue of withered poinsettia. All over the town he had planted lanes and avenues of trees and bushes and from the peaks of the distant hills Baipur looked like a cartwheel with green spokes. He loved his garden and, because the soil was fertile despite its proximity to the desert, it prospered. Its ramparts were embroidered with sweet peas, its grounds were spired with lupins and starred with dahlias. Now it was brown and dead. He turned his kind and decent face away from it and handed Spenser his drink.

'Aren't you drinking?' Spenser said.

'No, I feel guilty even drinking gin or whisky. You see they've got nothing out there. Absolutely nothing. And they think it's my fault.'

'I shouldn't worry about that,' Spenser said. 'We all know it isn't your fault. You can't be held responsible for the hoarding of grain, for the weakness of the bullocks and for a storm which seems to have grounded the supply ship. Nor can you be responsible for the failure of the monsoon.'

'I should have realised what was happening,' Chambers said. 'I should have warned Calcutta earlier.' He picked up the pair of secateurs with which he nipped off dead blossoms in the evenings—the time when he made his decisions for the following day, the time when, as night crept over the hills and the scents of his flowers crowded around him, he reavowed his love for the beautiful muddled land in which he had chosen to live.

Couldridge, who was slumped in a wheezing wicker chair, his legs resting on the balustrade of the verandah, said: 'It's not your fault. It probably isn't anyone's fault. It's India, that's all.'

'They always trusted me,' Chambers said.

'For heaven's sake,' said Spenser who was still brooding over

Corporal Duckham. 'Any minute now you'll be saying they're just like children.'

Couldridge said: 'Aren't they?'

'If you have the outlook of a schoolmaster—yes. I don't—I'm a soldier. Nor do you. They're all just patients to you. Or'—the thrust of perspicacity was sudden and malicious—'subjects for research.'

Couldridge was too tired to argue. He struck a match on his shoe, lit his pipe and retired behind a grey curtain of smoke.

The thirsty day died and the distant hills crouched like a sleeping lion. But there was no dew, the hot dryness merely cooled.

Chambers stared down the single track of railroad searching the twilight for the furnace of an engine. 'When?' he said. 'For God's sake when?'

'Soon,' Spenser said. 'It must come soon. A day or so perhaps.'

'But how many dead will there be by then?' Chambers turned to Couldridge. 'How many dead are there now?'

'About fifty,' Couldridge said. 'Mostly old people and children. There's not a lot I can do. But I can try and inoculate them against cholera because when the monsoon comes that will be the next killer.'

Spenser said: 'The next killer will be rebellion.'

'Well I can't inoculate them against that,' Couldridge said.

Chambers sank back in his chair, tragic with the prospects of new crises for which he had never been briefed.

Spenser sniffed the evening air. 'I can smell burning flesh,' he said. 'Funny. They surely don't practise suttee at a time like this.'

Couldridge said: 'Are you sure it's not my pipe?'

'It's not your pipe. Put it out anyway.'

Couldridge knocked out his pipe and Spenser knew that they were both thinking the same thing.

'What is it?' Chambers said. 'What's the matter?'

Spenser said: '*Do* they practise suttee around here?'

'It has been known. But not for a long time. I managed to

stop a lot of their more barbaric practices. You see they respect me. Or at least they used to.'

'Then they're practising something worse,' Spenser said.

They left the rambling bungalow and ran down the deserted main street seeking the source of the smoke scented by roasting flesh. As he ran, unbuttoning the holster of his pistol, Spenser, who knew that he had identified the smell correctly, thought that it didn't smell too badly; just the smell of roasting pork.

They stopped outside the entrance to a courtyard opposite the temple of rats. In the temple the light from burning candles flickered over the gold teeth of the big rodent and its eyes seemed to glow with pink albino depths.

'In here,' Spenser said. He took out his pistol and gestured into the mouth of the courtyard. The smell was strong now, mixed with autumn bonfire scents.

As they moved down the alley leading to the courtyard sinewy arms grabbed them. Spenser clubbed to his right and felt the butt of the pistol smash a mouthful of teeth. The arms relaxed their hold. Spenser followed the other two, who had reached the courtyard. Ahead of him he saw flames spurting in an open fire. Couldridge had an Indian pinned to the wall by the neck; he pulled the man forward and cracked his head against the wall; the man slumped to the ground.

Chambers was lying on the ground with a dark body crouched over him. Spenser brought the butt of his pistol down on to the back of the man's skull.

It was a child's body that they were roasting on the pyre of blazing wood. It was trussed and the head had been removed. Now the smell of burning flesh made Spenser want to vomit.

There were no cannibalistic rites. Just a group of silent, slavering men the other side of the fire. One of them leaned forward to prod the small body. Spenser raised his pistol and took aim.

'No.' Chamber came charging at him from behind. The Indians looked up at the sound of his voice and stood still for a moment as if they were being photographed. Only the flames moved, their light finding the hollows in the ravenous faces. Then they ran.

177

Spenser pulled the trigger and the Indian who had been prodding the body pitched forward into the fire. The flames ran along his white cotton clothes like orange liquid.

Couldridge pulled the body from the fire but he was dead.

'Oh God,' said Chambers. 'What have I done?'

Spenser's fingers were clutched tightly around the butt of his pistol. His teeth were clenched; the horror and exaltation seething inside him were inseparable.

Couldridge destroyed the fire with a pole and pulled the small skewered corpse into the shadows. 'It wasn't necessary to shoot,' he said.

Spenser put his pistol back into its holster. His voice was dry and hoarse. 'Wasn't necessary? They were going to eat that child. Is everything permissible to you?'

'You could have stopped them without shooting. They hadn't murdered that child—it had died of starvation. There was hardly a scrap of flesh on it.'

'Christ,' said Spenser. He leaned against the wall wiping the sweat from his forehead. 'Now you're condoning cannibalism.'

'I'm not condoning it. These people were starving. They had lost their reason. If someone has died there is a certain logic to using the body to save the lives of others. It's not the first time after all—it happened in Orissa.'

'This was a child.'

'It makes no difference.'

Spenser tried to control his shivering limbs. 'You're a funny kind of doctor.' He turned to Chambers and said: 'What do you think? Should I have appealed to their better natures?'

'I don't know,' Chambers said. 'I don't know.' The tears were trickling slowly and steadily down his cheeks.

'Christ,' said Spenser.

'You're very tough,' Couldridge said.

'What are you going to do about it? About the shooting.'

'Don't worry. Just another famine fatality—if Chambers agrees, and I imagine he will.'

Spenser and Couldridge stared at each other across the spars

of smouldering wood, across the corpse of the Indian, in a courtyard beneath milky stars in a starving town called Baipur, in the
primitive heart of the country they both served. And they both
knew that the friendship born of immaturity and green cameraderie was over. Each had grown up in his different way.

'What about the Indians who were there?' Spenser said. 'You
don't think they'll miss an opportunity to say a British officer shot
one of them, do you?'

Couldridge shook his head slowly as if it were weighted with
fatigue. 'Don't worry,' he said. 'They won't say anything. They
won't admit that they've become cannibals. Come on, let's get
back to the bungalow. I want a bath.'

Chambers wiped the tears from his face. 'You can't,' he said.
'There's no water.'

As they walked back past the entrance to the temple the eyes
of the giant rat seemed to glow with deep furtive knowledge.

2

CAPTAIN John Couldridge and Corporal Albert Duckham found
to their mutual surprise that they made a good working partnership. Couldridge sensed sound obdurate qualities behind the
monosyllabic exterior, the sort of stony qualities on which the
British Army was founded. If ever the Army fought to the last
man, Couldridge thought, then Corporal Duckham would be
that man; cursing, whimpering, self-pitying, he would be there
snarling obscenity into the breach of his rifle and clubbing as
many skulls as he could after his ammunition had run out.

Now, as he swabbed brown arms ready for Couldridge's needle,
his boxer's face was frowning with concentration.

'Not the sort of work you expected when you signed up,' Couldridge said.

'Sah.' Corporal Duckham shook his head to give added emphasis to his reply.

'How do you like this sort of work?'

'Sah?' Couldridge watched Corporal Duckham's features contort as he tried to avoid answering with more than one word.

'I said how do you like this sort of work?'

Corporal Duckham shrugged and frowned. Finally he said: 'It's all right, sah.' He frowned again, irritated that he had been tricked into an extravagance of words.

'Where are you from, corporal?'

Again the trick. 'Sah?'

'I said where are you from? You're not deaf, are you, Corporal Duckham?'

'Sah.' He shook his head.

'Then where do you come from?'

'Camden Town, sah.'

'There are a lot of Irish there, aren't there?'

'Sah.' Affirmatively.

'I thought so.' Couldridge plunged a needle into shrinking brown flesh and Corporal Duckham slapped a dressing over the puncture. 'I'm half Irish.'

Corporal Duckham thought fiercely for a few moments. Then he said: 'Some Pads are all right.'

Couldridge accepted the compliment gracefully. By the time they had finished inoculating the Indians who had trusted themselves to the needle, Corporal Duckham had become expansive. Some Pads were all right, so were a few Scouses. Taffys were a shower of bastards.

About fifty Indians had reported for inoculation. A tired, shambling queue of suspicion. Pot-bellied children, men with ribs sharp beneath their skin, no women. Couldridge doubted whether any of them understood what he was doing: they probably imagined they were receiving some form of nutrition.

That morning Chambers had received word that a train carrying supplies of grain was coming. But no time of arrival had been given. And they all knew that it might have been attacked by bands of starving Indians on the way. So they waited helplessly in the hot mocking sunshine.

Five more Indians died that morning. Other corpses lay in dark rooms, mouths and eyes swarming with flies. Moslem-Hindu enmities were temporarily forgotten. Prayers were offered to Allah, and the big gold rat.

Spenser, who had been seconded from the North West Frontier area and put in charge of famine relief in Baipur, strolled up as Couldridge was plunging the needle into the last thin arm. Corporal Duckham retired into monosyllabic reticence.

'All right, corporal,' Couldridge said. 'You can hop it now and play cards with some of the other Pads.'

'Sah,' said Corporal Duckham.

When he had gone Spenser said: 'That's hardly the way to talk to an N.C.O., is it?'

'Why not? We got on rather well together. My orderly has gone sick and Duckham did the job competently, I thought.'

'I don't doubt it,' Spenser said. 'But you can't afford to be over-familiar.'

'You mean you can't.'

'I am the commanding officer.'

'I know. I keep forgetting.'

They walked down a street lined with Chambers' dying poinsettias. Hostile eyes gazed at them from the hutch-like shops of the bazaar. The barber's chair at the side of the road was empty, the moneylender had stopped counting money, the medicine man lay asleep among his bones and snake-skins. The bazaar was still.

'How's the new laboratory?' Spenser said.

'It's fine,' Couldridge said. 'Just fine.'

'You won't have much time for your research doing this job.'

'I know. But sometimes I feel that this is the sort of work that I should be doing.'

But he was far from sure. The desire to return to his new surgery on the outskirts of Lahore was strong inside him. So was the fear that, when he returned, he would sacrifice all humanitarian instincts to research.

'There doesn't seem much future for you then in the research field.'

Couldridge sensed his satisfaction. 'I don't know about that. I've only got another two years in the I.M.S.'

'Won't you sign on again?'

'I doubt it. Before I got this job I was thinking about trying to get out.'

'I forgot that you had a wealthy wife.'

'What the hell is that supposed to mean?'

'The only way you could stay in India before was to be in the Army. Now everything is very easy for you.' He paused on the steps of Chambers' verandah. 'But then I suppose it always has been. You're a very lucky man, John.'

On the verandah Chambers' cook had laid out two plates of pistachio nuts and candied sugar. It was lunch. They also drank whisky and soda because there was no beer and hardly any water.

Chambers had recovered his equanimity and something of his idealism. He sipped his warm whisky and recalled some of his shrewder moves during his administration. 'We had a little political trouble here recently,' he said. 'Some of the important chaps in the town decided to organise a procession seeking more powers in local government. There might have been trouble. But they had named the day and I knew that they could not lose face by postponing it. So I summoned them here for a little pow-wow in the morning and gave them tea laced with laxative. They tried to lead the procession but after a few steps they had to leave hurriedly. Their followers were so put out by their rapid exit that the procession was as quiet as a funeral.' He laughed with gentle delight.

Spenser, shorts and jacket crisply pressed despite the heat, said: 'You shouldn't have much trouble now. They're getting all they want, aren't they, under Morley and Minto? Indians in the legislative councils. Elections. Indians on the Secretary of State's Council and the Executive Councils of the Viceroy himself. What more do they want?'

'Rather more than that, I'm afraid,' Chambers said. With his celibacy, his occasional touches of schoolboy wit, his intuitive leadership of his charges, his idealism and his lonely torments, he reminded Couldridge of a type of Irish priest.

'What more do they want?' Spenser said.

'Food,' Couldridge said.

Spenser ignored him. 'We've given them enough concessions for God's sake. And they're nowhere near ready for self-government. Another hundred years, I should think. Or more.'

'I agree we've given them a lot,' Chambers said. 'Railroads, hospitals, education. But is there any reason why they should be content with that? Human aspirations are part of evolution—you can't halt them.'

A young man in a soiled dhoti walked past the end of the garden, thin and bowed. The words of a London surgeon's son who had once come to India to help with famine relief came back to Couldridge. Describing a starving Indian, Herman Kisch had written that you could 'readily conceive a skeleton walking.' That, Couldridge remembered sadly, had been written in 1874. Nothing had changed: the wounds of India defied suturing.

He stared across the brown vistas of Chambers' endeavours, along the dry vein of the railroad. He sucked at his cold pipe and thought about his wife and children, now in America staying with relatives of Lord Curzon's wife, Mary, who had died leaving behind an inconsolable father and widower. He lit a match and let it burn out without applying it to his pipe. The dry breeze stirred his long hair and the chequered sunshine piercing the bamboo ceiling of the verandah found a few strands of silver.

A few hundred yards away he saw a group of exhausted Parsees taking a body to a small tower of silence just outside the perimeter of Chambers' scorched avenues of vegetation. They wore dark brown turbans and sacred shirts. He remembered the day many years ago when Surgeon Second-Lieutenant John Couldridge had witnessed a parsee funeral with Second-Lieutenant Neville Spenser.

Spenser said: 'I know what you're thinking.'

'Just remembering,' Couldridge said.

'You've changed.'

'We've both changed.'

The mourners disappeared and the vultures flapped lazily down from their observation posts. There was a lot of meat these days but it was poor quality.

Couldridge said: 'You realise we're going to meet a lot now that I'm doing this job.'

'Our destiny perhaps.'

'I don't know about that. But don't worry—I'll probably leave the Service in a couple of years' time.'

'What will you do then?'

'Carry on my work at the surgery. You don't have to tell me again—I'm lucky to have a wealthy wife. I know it—I am.'

Chambers said: 'As soon as the grain has arrived and the men are strong enough I'm going to get them working on irrigation canals.'

Spenser said: 'It's a bit late, isn't it?'

Chambers nodded. 'No one ever thought it would be necessary just here. The short rains have failed before but there's always been enough water in the wells to get to the crops by watercart. But I was always frightened that this might happen one day. I tried to warn people but no one seemed to care.'

Spenser said: 'Perhaps you didn't warn the right people.'

'No,' Chambers said. 'You can't get me on that one. I warned everyone. Even the Army—although it wasn't their business.'

Couldridge crossed his legs on the balustrade and returned to his contemplation of the leonine hills and the railroad. He wondered how many more inhabitants of Baipur had died since the last count, how many more had died in the surrounding villages. He was appalled at the inability of medical science, of British bureaucracy, of civilisation, to halt the death toll.

From somewhere in the town they heard the chant of prayers. Couldridge looked at his watch. It was just after noon. So it

184

would be the Moslems praying towards Mecca, Allah, King Rat, Jehovah, Buddha. Did the name really matter? Couldridge, who had been without proper food for several days, felt lethargic. 'They were, after all, praying to one deity with different names. "Whatever God a man worships, it is I who answer the prayer".'

Couldridge stared deeply and lazily into the landscape rippling with heat. And vaguely became aware of a wisp of smoke like a single grey curl on a sun-burned pate. After a few moments he became aware that the curl had an orange root. A spark, a flame, a furnace.

He leaped to his feet and shouted. 'The train's coming. We're saved.'

Chambers picked up his topee. 'Thank God,' he said. 'Thank God.' But he didn't specify which one.

3

THE grain was in sacks, each tightly stitched at the top. Despite the stitching some of it had escaped to wander around the floors of the freight trucks. Children burst through the ranks of British soldiers and sepoys and leaped into the trucks stuffing the grains into their mouths. Queues patrolled by troops stretched along the parched avenues of Chambers' garden city.

Spenser stood in anxious command at the railhead—a wooden waiting room for passengers and a new goods shed ringed with dead bushes.

'If there's trouble,' he said to Chambers, 'I'll have to shoot.'

'Shoot? What in God's name for? There won't be any trouble. If any of them become troublesome just leave it to me.'

Spenser gazed down the lines of Indians, each carrying a bowl. 'You can't give them laxatives this time, Mr Chambers.'

'There won't be any trouble. They're too hungry.'

'That's just why there might be trouble. And another thing—how do we know whether they'll come round again for another helping?'

'We don't know,' Chambers said. He smiled down upon his people from the platform outside the freight shed.

'I'm not having any of that. We've got to get a lot of grain to the outlying districts.'

'Don't worry, Major Spenser,' Chambers said. 'It will all be taken care of.'

'And the water. We've got to keep at least one wagon of water away from them.'

'Don't worry, Major Spenser.'

'Well,' Spenser said, 'I've warned them. They know what to expect if they get out of hand.'

But, apart from the children, none of the Indians showed any sign of getting out of hand. They were listless, docile, famished. They moved on spindle-legs and supported themselves with sticks.

The soldiers stood at ease, rifles held ready. The driver and fireman of the engine rubbed their brown faces black with greasy clothes and polished the brasswork of their engine which hissed as if it were about to subside on the track. Its name was 'Lord Curzon'.

Couldridge, who had been tending an old man too near death to be saved by a bowl of grain, joined Chambers and Spenser on the platform. 'We'll have to be very careful,' he said. 'Too much to eat could kill some of them.'

'Don't worry,' Spenser said. 'There won't be too much. We're keeping eight wagon-loads here. The rest is going on to other centres. We're also keeping two tankers of water.'

As he spoke a dozen monkeys leaped from a banyan tree on to the roofs of the wagons.

Chambers grabbed Spenser's arm. 'Watch out—they'll steal enough to feed twenty people.'

Spenser grabbed a rifle from a sepoy. The sepoy remained statuesque, arms still outstretched holding an invisible weapon.

Spenser fired the rifle into the air. The monkeys returned to the trees as if they were attached to elastic.

The puff of blue smoke lingered in the air. The queue of starving Indians gazed at the British officer without interest.

'Well done,' Couldridge said.

'Are you being sarcastic?'

Couldridge looked surprised. 'No,' he said. 'I wasn't.'

'All right then. Let's get this stuff unloaded so that the train can get along.'

The troops dragged the sacks off the trucks and stacked them in the shed. Once there was a disturbance in one of the queues. Spenser's hand went to his pistol. 'What happened?' he said.

'A man died,' Chambers said.

'I can't get it done any quicker,' Spenser said.

'I know,' Chambers said. 'No one said you could.'

Couldridge came back from the corpse. 'He died from a heart attack,' he said. 'Perhaps he was too excited at the prospect of food.'

The sky faded and the hills darkened to mauve, then, as the sun escaped, to black. A few pink tendrils of cloud remained in the sky festooning the first star.

The troops lit flares and started doling out the grain into the bowls. The engine coughed loudly, emitted three puffs of white-beard smoke and moved ponderously away. For a few moments the evening air was streaked with flying smuts and sparks. Then the train was away taking nourishment elsewhere, a glowing cheroot in the eternal distance of India.

At the head of one of the queues Corporal Duckham rationed out the grain, sibilantly informing himself what he thought of the task. Beside him stood Couldridge.

'Greedy lot of fuckers?' Corporal Duckham said.

'What's that?' Couldridge said.

'Nothing, sah.' And then because of his special relationship with Couldridge he added: 'Joking, sah. You can't help feeling sorry for them.'

'You're a humane man, corporal.'

187

'Thank you, sah.'

The soldiers lit more kerosene torches which oiled the night air with their fumes. For two hours they fed the grain to the Indians, but the queues seemed as long as ever.

'Captain Couldridge, sah.'

'Yes, corporal?'

Corporal Duckham pointed at a tall, gaunt Indian in clean white cotton standing at the head of the queue. 'He's jumped the queue, sah.'

Couldridge pointed towards the end of the queue and spoke to the Indian in bad Hindi. The Indian shook his head and thrust forward his wooden bowl.

Couldridge spoke again in Hindi and the Indian answered in the brand of English spoken by many Indians—as if they had been taught by Welshmen. But the lilt, which so often sounded servile, remained as arrogant as the man's manner. 'I am wanting to receive my grain now,' he said.

'You'll just have to take your turn like everyone else,' Couldridge said.

The Indian shook his head. 'It is impossible. I am a Brahmin, you understand. I cannot join a queue with these people. Many of them are menials.'

Couldridge said: 'Then it's very simple—you won't get any grain. Now get back to the end of the queue if you want to be fed.'

'You do not understand.'

'I understand all right.'

'These people understand.' He gestured towards the queue. 'They know that I cannot take part in any endeavour with them. It is part of our way of life, captain. If they don't mind why should you?'

Couldridge said: 'If you come from such priestly stock then why can't you wait until these people have been served?'

Corporal Duckham said: 'Because he's a greedy bastard.'

The Brahmin said: 'Because my children are dying from hunger.'

Couldridge clenched his fists. 'So are these people's children dying from hunger.'

The Brahmin took a step forward. 'Serve me, please.'

Couldridge hit the bowl with the side of his fist. It flew through the flaring light like a discus and fell into deep dust. The landlords, the farmers, the leatherworkers and the untouchables gazed with embarrassed interest at the Brahmin. 'Then my children will die,' he said. He walked, thin and erect, across the perimeter of the kerosene light into the darkness.

'Serve him fucking right,' Corporal Duckham said. But his voice wasn't sure.

Couldridge felt his anger fade. 'I don't know,' he said. 'I don't know.' He pictured the Brahmin's children waiting for him to return with food—eyes large, stomachs inflated, bones showing white beneath their skin. 'It's not their fault,' he said.

'Who's fault, sah?'

'His children.'

'No, sah.'

'How much grain left in that sack, corporal?'

'Not much, sah. Enough for three or four.'

'Open another sack and give that one to me. Can you cope here for a while?'

'Sah.'

'I'll be back in twenty minutes.'

Couldridge took the sack that was almost empty and walked past the unquestioning queue into the dark town looking for the street where the Brahmin lived.

Much later he returned to Chambers' bungalow and poured himself a whisky and soda which he drank while undressing. On the chest of drawers painted with tacky varnish he found a week-old newspaper. On the second page was an account of a shoot in which the Viceroy and some of his friends had participated near Srinagar. On the first day one guest had bagged 152 ducks; the Viceroy had come second with 121. The next day the total bag had been 913 of which a Maharajah had shot 172 and H.E. 138. The article also gave statistics for the previous year.

189

The Viceroy and his guests had claimed 3,888 sandgrouse, 2,790 wildfowl, 43 bears, 17 pigs, three tigers, two panthers and one hyena.

Couldridge slept with the paper still in his hand.

4

NEXT day a small grey cloud appeared in the noon sky. It came from nowhere; not from the desert, not from the hills. It was created as the first molecule of life was created. It loitered for a while savouring its importance and the attention it attracted. Then more procreation took place and more clouds, darker and heavier, materialised. They drifted together, then fused, then grew as if summoning every tendril of mist suspended over ocean and continent. Within half an hour Baipur was shadowed by grey, convoluted pastures and there was no blue to be seen.

Beneath the cloud they prayed to their respective gods. The clouds darkened and a cold breeze that, to the thirsty and the fanciful, smelled of water found its way over the hills and nosed around the town. Dried leaves and pods whispered, dogs patrolled restlessly. The belly of the clouds sagged closer to the ground and its grey muscles moved. On the outskirts of the town an elephant that had been stripping bark from a tree as dry as a telegraph pole trumpeted.

Far away, somewhere over the hills, the townspeople noticed a belch of light. And a few seconds later heard a grumble of thunder. They prayed louder and beat the dust with their hands, the dogs howled with fear at the noise of the thunder—and the praying. The elephant trumpeted once more.

The first blob of rain fell beside a dog patiently dying under a banyan tree. He sniffed at the smell of wet dust and then closed his eyes to continue dying.

Lightning and thunder synchronised overhead. The lightning forked a dead tree near the rogue elephant. The cannon-crack silenced the prayers and the wail of the dogs. Then the rain fell, as strong and as heavy as a wave.

The townspeople thanked their deities who were possibly one and the same god. And beneath the banyan tree the dog who had smelled the first drop of rain died without realising it.

5

IN the bungalow which she hated Charlotte Spenser prepared for the return of her husband from Baipur without enthusiasm. The preparations did not take long because the servants did most of the work. The Spensers employed a sweeper, a bearer, a cook, a dishwasher, a gardener and a watchman. Charlotte had once tried to dispense with all but two of them; but Spenser had become angry because, he said, a major should have at least five servants. Charlotte failed to understand the prestige involved because even a subaltern could afford to pay five servants little more than £1 a month.

As the servants went about their tasks with lethargic inefficiency Charlotte arranged a bunch of zinnias and cosmos in a vase, drank from a tall frosted glass filled with lime-juice laced with gin and gazed across the verandah at the remote white battlements of the mountains. She had never reached them because women were forbidden to cross the intervening hills. They weren't always visible, and sometimes in the mornings when their crumpled peaks surfaced above the cloud they seemed to be floating. Then the cloud dispersed and the mountains were once again aloof and invulnerable. Sometimes the sight of the mountains brought tears to Charlotte's eyes.

She poured herself another gin and lime-juice and sat on the sofa lined with chintz sent from a store in Streatham. Soon she would have to prepare herself for her husband who always wanted to make love to her immediately on his return after a long absence. The prospect disgusted her: she had been alone for three months and her body had healed from his attentions. Not, she supposed, that he performed the act—that was how she always thought of it—more brutally than any other man. Except, perhaps, when he returned from the hills after shooting and killing; then his movements were more frantic and more painful to her, and as he reached his completion he whispered strange words in her ear. Charlotte Spenser had always presumed that the real purpose of the act, the unpleasant adjunct of marriage, was the conception of children; so far there had been no children. She sometimes wondered whose fault it was; but when she tried to discuss it with him he became angrier than he had ever been before.

Because of the imminence of the act Charlotte decided to strengthen her drink with more gin. In this way she could simulate pleasure—and that always pleased him. Once when she had drunk too much gin she had found herself imagining that it was John Couldridge performing the act and had experienced a sudden spasm of pleasure. Afterwards she had been disgusted with herself and had consigned the memory to the dark recesses of her mind where it could not be examined; but the memory occasionally escaped in sleep.

Neville was bringing Couldridge with him to their bungalow at Jinjabad because tomorrow Joanne was arriving from New York. The knowledge that Couldridge was coming helped to lift her depression a little.

Across the hills the mountains shed the last lingering strata of cloud and assumed their majesty. Beneath the verandah the gardener hosed the couch grass—so different from the honey-sweet blades of the English meadows—and the arc of water shed rainbow drops in the late-morning sunlight. Faintly she heard the staccato voice of a havildar drilling his men.

She tinkled the ice in her glass and wondered when she had stopped loving her husband; wondered if she had ever loved him. Perhaps she had once in the hansom-cab days of their courtship. Before the consummation, before the terrible conversations in the bungalow about discipline and killing. Before she had learned how he had summarily executed two Pathans on the orders of Colonel Hatherley as a reprisal for atrocities committed on captured Gurkhas. She did not presume to pronounce on military justice but his self-justification that night sickened her.

She went into the bedroom, taking her gin and lime-juice with her, and began to take off her clothes to prepare herself for her husband. She looked shyly at her body in the long speckled mirror on the wall. At the small firm breasts with the schoolgirl nipples that had never burgeoned with motherhood, at the flat belly and sharp hips. And, because she had drunk sufficient gin, she looked upon the downy hair of her pubes with interest and wondered why men regarded this secret little triangle, so innocent and inconsequential, with such passion.

Then she washed herself. Powdered herself with talcum and watered herself with her most powerful aphrodisiac—lavender water. Then she dressed and went to the kitchen to see what progress the cook was making with lunch.

But while Charlotte had been bathing and dressing the cook had admitted a girlfriend to the kitchen. He must have presumed that Charlotte had left the bungalow because he was copulating with enthusiasm on the kitchen table.

Charlotte departed unseen, poured herself another drink and retired to the verandah to gaze upon her mountains. After a while she began to cry.

6

COULDRIDGE said: 'Do you think we'll get there in time for lunch?' The formality of the question occurred to him and he laughed. But conversation between Spenser and himself had been like that since they left Baipur.

He felt gay and vaporous as if he had just emerged from a fever. In fact the fever was exhaustion. For three weeks after the arrival of the rain he had worked sixteen hours a day, sometimes more, trying to help the people of Baipur and the surrounding towns and villages.

He had helped supervise the distribution of the rest of the grain that had arrived soon after the first delivery. He had curbed outbreaks of cholera and typhoid, he had helped Chambers to chart irrigation canals, he had delivered several babies.

When he and Spenser and the troops left the town it was covered with green moss that was hourly maturing into stalks and leaves and food.

Spenser said: 'I think we'll just make it.'

They were riding from the railhead at the base of the hills to Jinjabad just as they had once ridden together on the blameless days of early friendship.

Conversation dribbled away again and Couldridge thought about his wife and children whom he would see next day. He was happy with the thought of their family togetherness, happy with the thought of her healthy love. He saw her lying beside him, face a little swollen with passion, eyes and lips slightly apart; he felt her breasts nuzzling his chest and smelled her hair, her warm scents. And because he was a doctor and received many confidences he knew they were very lucky that it was so.

He squeezed the flanks of his horse with his strong thighs and tried to channel his thoughts in other directions. To the new clinic and surgery on the outskirts of Lahore and the beautiful diagram of the human eye on the wall.

Now, he thought, he was ready to perform some of the more simple ophthalmic operations. And soon he would be able to join the ranks of the surgeons still experimenting with theories of corneal transplants started by de Quengsy in 1789. It was incredible, he thought, that progress had been so slow: that since those first conceptions of eye grafting, involving fragments of glass, Lister's theories of antiseptic surgery had been accepted and yet keratoplasty was still in its infancy. John Couldridge wished that he had been a little older so that he could have accumulated the knowledge that had enabled Edward Zrim in 1905 to cure blindness with a graft from the cornea of a boy whose eye had had to be removed to the eye of a man blinded by lime.

But the principal problem, Couldridge realised, was the supply of donor tissue. If blindness was to be cured on a large scale by the transplanting of healthy tissue then the only possible source of supply was from the recently dead. And he knew that it would be a long time before the moral issues were accepted either by the medical establishment or by the layman. He also knew that many other surgeons in the world were experimenting with grafts taken from the eyes of cadavers.

But John Couldridge's enthusiasms were not confined to ophthalmology. They brimmed over to embrace diseases of the ear, nose and throat and the endemic diseases of India. Even though he knew that doctors were not supposed to specialise in more than one subject.

Spenser spurred his horse to a canter and Couldridge followed. Gradually as they climbed the countryside assumed a patina of green, the air cooled and sweetened and in the distance they saw the white mountains. As they approached Jinjabad Couldridge urged his horse into a gallop. Along a stream of steel-blue water, hooves splashing wings of spray, up a hillside balding on its

195

rocky scalp.

Then in front of them was Jinjabad. They galloped the rest of the way to the bungalow. But when they arrived Charlotte Spenser was drunk.

Couldridge didn't realise what was the matter with her at first. She was more talkative than he had remembered her being, and some of the words she used were incongruous. It was 'stupendous' to see him and she hoped that the journey had not been too 'sapping'.

Spenser was polite, as if he were talking to an old friend recovering from a nervous breakdown. He kissed her on the cheek and said: 'How have you been, Charlotte?'

'I've been fine, Neville,' she said. 'There's been so much to do directing my servants and sitting on the verandah looking at the mountains. It's all been ... delicious.' She smiled crookedly. 'And how have you been, Neville? Has there been any fighting? I know you won't have been very happy if there hasn't been any lovely fighting.'

Spenser said: 'I was in charge of famine relief. I was supposed to be saving people not killing them.'

Charlotte giggled. 'Did you like that, Neville?'

He nodded. 'It was all right.'

Charlotte picked up her tall frosted glass and drank from it. It was then that Couldridge realised that she was drunk. He should have realised before but it was so unlikely. He tried to divert the conversation and said: 'When do you think Joanne and the children will be here?'

'Tomorrow,' she said. 'Sometime tomorrow. Would you like a drink? Neville usually likes a drink before he tells me all about the fighting.'

'No thanks,' Couldridge said. 'Not just now.'

'I'm sorry I'm a little indisposed.'

'Perhaps you should lie down.'

Spenser said: 'Yes, Charlotte, why don't you do that?'

'I think I'll have just one more glass of lime-juice,' she said. 'It's so delightful.'

196

'Delicious,' Spenser said.

'Tell me about the trip,' she said. 'You've been away three months. You must have got a lot to tell Charlotte about.' She turned to Couldridge. 'You tell me, John. You'll tell me about different sorts of things.' She frowned and put her glass to her lips, clicking it against her teeth. 'Nice kind things.'

Couldridge wondered when she had started drinking. There had been no signs of it in Calcutta. Perhaps it had been the loneliness while Spenser had been away. Although, if that were so, it was hardly likely that she would drink herself stupid on the day of his return. He supposed it was something to do with their marital relationship. He felt sorry for her, but he had an aversion to women who drank. Too much liquor coarsened men and women—but it showed more with women. The opening of the pores, the blurring of the features. In India women drank more than they did in Britain. But the thought of Charlotte Spenser, so shy and nervous, drinking too much was more incongruous than anything else. Should he, as a doctor, speak to her? The idea was as bizarre as her drinking.

Spenser said: 'Perhaps John's right. Perhaps you should have a lie down.'

'No,' she said, 'it's early days yet.' She peered closely at her thin gold wrist-watch. 'It's only three o'clock.' She giggled again. 'Whatever happened to lunch?'

Couldridge said: 'I think perhaps I'll have a wander round and come back later. Although the old place won't seem the same without Colonel Hatherley.'

'Poor Colonel Hatherley,' Charlotte said. 'Poor, poor Colonel Hatherley. He drank, you know.'

Spenser eagerly pursued the topic of Colonel Hatherley. 'It was more than drink,' he said. 'He was a little mad. When he left here he couldn't speak at all.'

Couldridge remembered the first time he had prescribed drugs for Colonel Hatherley. 'He's not alone. There have been several cases of men serving for long periods in the hills being deprived of their speech.'

Charlotte smiled conspiratorially into her drink. 'But not Neville,' she said. 'He hasn't been deprived of his speech.'

Spenser said: 'I wish you would take John's advice and have a lie down.'

'I think I'll be off,' Couldridge said, almost breezily.

Charlotte said: 'Not yet. You don't have to go yet,' There was a touch of desperation in her careful speech.

'John wants to have a look around his old haunts,' Spenser said.

'You want him to go,' she said.

'Don't be stupid.'

Couldridge said: 'I really must go.'

Charlotte gulped the rest of her drink. 'You'll be round to lunch tonight?'

'You mean dinner?'

'Yes, dinner. But you'll be round?'

Couldridge saw the plea in her face and said: 'Of course I will.'

He smiled at her, clumped Spenser on the back without enthusiasm and escaped into the mellow afternoon.

Little had changed. The mess still seemed to be suspended in time, brown and comfortable and lost; the same tiger's head snarling with impotent fury, *The Times*, the trophies. It was a tired and gentle place, this haunt of fighters.

Outside his former quarters he found an old man sitting on the doorstep staring across India. He was sure it was Bhawansing Rai. He spoke to him but there was no recognition on the obdurate face.

He looked closer and saw that the old eyes were afflicted with presbyopia and were unable to focus. He sat down on the doorstep and counted the man's fingers: there were nine: undoubtedly it was Bhawansing Rai.

Couldridge tried again in his immature Ghurkali. 'Do you remember me? Second Lieutenant Couldridge? You were my first batman.'

But Bhawansing Rai had been the first batman of many a

198

subaltern. He stared ahead of him without answering, five fingers interlocked with four.

Couldridge said: 'They still talk about the fight when you lost that finger in the mess.' He decided to exaggerate a little. 'They even talk about it in Calcutta. How you bit it off and brought it back to be sewn on again.'

An event then occurred that seemed to Couldridge more miraculous than anything that modern surgery could achieve: Bhawansing Rai smiled. His wrinkles extended into creases; his mandarin moustache twitched. The process looked painful; but nevertheless it was a smile—the first that Couldridge had ever seen on the walnut features.

Bhawansing Rai said: 'They talk of it in Calcutta?'

'Yes,' Couldridge said. 'And Delhi and Bombay.'

The smile lingered. 'I remember you,' he said. 'Second Lieutenant Couldridge. I liked you. I was unhappy when you left.'

It was the longest statement Bhawansing Rai had ever made to Couldridge. Couldridge stood up and said: 'I'll see you again before I leave.'

'They really talk about that fight?'

'I wouldn't lie to you, Bhawansing Rai.'

A trace of the smile still adhered to the corners of Bhawansing Rai's eyes as Couldridge walked away. Couldridge was astonished at the pleasure that the old man's smile had engendered: it was as strong almost as the emotion he experienced when he saved a man's life. Because he had made one recalcitrant ancient happy. John Couldridge frowned because sentimentality was not an emotion to be encouraged by an ambitious surgeon and hastened his footsteps.

That night at dinner he asked Spenser if Bhawansing Rai had ever been known to smile.

'Good God no,' Spenser said.

And both Charlotte and Neville Spenser looked puzzled as a content and stupid smile settled on Couldridge's face and lodged there in between courses.

7

CHARLOTTE dressed by herself in the bedroom while her husband drank a whisky and soda in the lounge. Her hands and her lips trembled slightly at the prospect of the social evening ahead at Colonel Willoughby's house. To subdue the fluttering nerves she drank from a glass concealed behind their wedding photograph; after each drink she popped a peppermint into her mouth to disguise the perfume of the gin.

She brushed her long pale hair, pinned it up and looked at her white face in the mirror. It had been a pretty, passable face in her teens, now it was ordinary and resigned and the skin around the eyes and mouth was creased with tiny lines of worry. She had another drink and felt courage burn in her stomach.

Spenser knocked and came in without waiting for her to answer. He looked very handsome in his green uniform—in a crisp and military way.

He walked across the room and stood behind her. 'You seem to be very fond of peppermints these days,' he said.

She fastened a necklace of smooth amber beads around her white neck. 'Yes,' she said. 'I like them.'

He glanced around the dressing table but not behind the wedding photograph. 'I hope you'll be pleasant to everyone tonight.'

'Aren't I always?'

'And don't drink too much.'

'I never do.'

'You were drunk when I arrived with Couldridge the other day. It was disgusting.' He put his hands on her shoulders and she shivered. 'Why were you drunk, Charlotte?'

She fingered the smooth warm beads. 'It was a mistake. I had been so lonely. And you know how it is with me sometimes—the pains in my back.'

'Did you really have pains that day?'

'You know I did. I said I did. That's why we couldn't . . .'

He nodded impatiently. 'I know about that. Let's not discuss it. I'm merely asking you to stop drinking so much. You know how they gossip here.' His thumbs massaged the muscles at the nape of her neck.

'You don't have to tell me about the gossip, Neville. I've been here alone for three months. I know all about the gossip. That's all they do. And play bridge, of course.'

'You could play bridge.'

'You know I hate it. You know I always make a fool of myself. Especially when you get angry. You're getting angry now.'

His lips beneath his moustache were thin and pale. 'I am not getting angry. But it seems to me that you've never tried to get on with these people. You were determined to dislike them from the moment you arrived. You've never made any attempt to settle down in India.'

'I've been a good wife to you,' she said. Her lips were beginning to flutter again and she wanted another drink from the glass behind the photograph. It was ironic, she thought, that it should be lurking behind a picture of them looking so self-consciously happy.

'A wife? I don't know that you've ever been a wife.'

'What do you mean by that, Neville?' She frowned because she thought she had been a good wife to him.

'You know what I mean.'

'I've always tried to be nice to your friends. I've done my best with the servants if they do sneer at me behind my back.'

'I didn't mean that,' Spenser said.

'You mean . . .' She found difficulty in finding words to describe the act of love.

'You know damn well what I mean. You make me out to be some sort of maniac. I'm just a man with ordinary healthy appetites, a man who's been away from his wife for three months.'

The tears gathered in the corners of her eyes. 'I'm sorry, Neville. I suppose I'm just inadequate. I don't know—I can't help it. I'm just not made that way. Perhaps you should have married someone else.'

'Perhaps I should.' He sat down on the edge of the bed. 'But it's too late now. And if you can't be a proper wife to me perhaps at least you can try and be pleasant to my fellow officers and their wives.'

The two tears accelerated down her cheeks. 'I do my best, Neville.'

'By walking around stinking of gin?'

'I don't walk around "stinking" of gin. I drank too much the day you arrived back, that's all.'

'That surprised me,' he said. 'I didn't think you would make a fool of yourself in front of your precious John Couldridge.'

She put her hand to her throat. 'My precious John Couldridge? He's your friend, Neville. What on earth do you mean?'

'I know that you admire him because he's everything I'm not.'

She took a lace handkerchief from her sleeve and dabbed at her eyes. 'I don't know what you're talking about. You're more successful than he is. You're a major and he's still a captain.'

He went into the lounge and returned with another whisky and soda. 'Sometimes it feels like a conspiracy,' he said.

Suddenly she felt very sorry for him, for both of them. 'Conspiracy? Don't be so silly, Neville. What on earth could we be conspiring about?'

His military back was bowed. 'I don't know. Somehow he seems to do everything right. I don't mean by the book, not by King's Regulations or anything like that. But I know he represents everything you admire.' He drank half the whisky. 'And I represent everything you abhor. You might not believe this but Couldridge is responsible for a lot of my actions. I

202

suppose it's because we started together. Somehow I always seem to be trying to impress him.'

She went and sat beside him, feeling affectionate—almost maternal—for the first time for years. 'I wish you had talked to me like this before, Neville.'

'I don't like talking like this. It's not very masculine.'

'You should talk like it more. Then perhaps we'd be closer. I want to be a good wife to you, Neville. If you had been more understanding perhaps I could have learned to put up with this place and these people.'

'There's nothing wrong with them.'

'There is, Neville. They've created a false existence for themselves—with false values. They can't enjoy themselves anymore. Servants, bridge, duck-shooting.' She paused. 'If only someone would go for a walk. An ordinary walk in the hills. Just as we used to go for walks on the common.'

'Perhaps John Couldridge will go for a walk with you. You could stop and pick flowers.'

She stroked his hair. 'Don't be silly,' she said. 'Why should I want to go for a walk with John?'

'I can think of a lot of reasons,' he said. 'You may not know it but you talk in your sleep.'

The buried secret stirred. 'What do I say?'

'Nothing very much. Nothing that makes much sense. But you sometimes mention his name.'

'Because he's one of the few people I like out here. He's a good man, Neville. You mustn't make him your enemy. He's a doctor and you're a soldier. You're both very good at your jobs but you're completely different.'

'He patronises me. That time in Delhi with the beggars. It had to be done. We would have been mobbed if I hadn't struck out. But he made me more vicious than I need have been. He was right, you see—I shouldn't have hit the blind man. I sometimes wonder about this violence in me. . . .'

'You wouldn't be a very good soldier if you didn't have some violence in you.'

203

'I don't even know if it's genuine. Perhaps I've made myself this way.' He finished the whisky. 'God knows why I'm talking like this.

'I'm glad you are.'

'I'm sorry about the way it's worked out, Charlotte. You weren't cut out to be a soldier's wife.'

She smiled and the little lines of worry wavered. 'I can try.'

He looked at his wrist-watch. 'What time have we got to be at Colonel Willoughby's?'

'Seven-thirty, I think.'

'We've got an hour, then.'

She nodded. 'About an hour.'

He went to kiss her on the lips but she turned her head away instinctively. 'What's the matter, don't you like being kissed by me?'

'Of course I do,' she said. 'But I've just been getting myself ready for the party.'

'We've got an hour.'

She shrank away from him. 'No, not now. It's not that I don't want to. It's just that it doesn't seem right at this time of the day. And just when I've got myself ready.'

'Nonsense,' he said. 'There's plenty of time. We are husband and wife.'

'No,' she said. 'Please.'

'Have you still got the pains in your back?'

'A little.'

'You told me this afternoon that they'd gone. They seem to be lasting a long time.' He put his arm around her and she felt its tallon strength.

'Please, Neville.'

'Show me that you love me.'

She made a last small resistance. 'Show me that you love me by being patient.'

'I'll show that I love you by not being patient,' he said. There was a growl in his voice. 'That's all I ever have been—patient. Am I so repulsive to you? What do you think I should do,

Charlotte—go out and find myself a whore?'

She shook her head.

'Take your dress off then.'

Still she shook her head.

'Then, by God, I'll take it off for you.'

She fought him briefly. But he tore the dress off, and her bodice and the rest of her clothes. She lay back on the bed, red weals showing on her schoolgirl breasts, waiting for the final assault, her thighs open baring her shy sex. Then he entered her and she heard him grunting, his breath coming faster. God, she thought, dear God, is this truly love? Then in one grotesque spasm it was over and he was rolling away from her.

'There,' he said. 'Did you like that, my precious lady? Or was I too rough for you?'

She could see that shame was replacing desire. 'You were rough,' she said. She felt the weals on her breasts.

'Did I do that?'

'No one else,' she said.

'I didn't mean to hurt you.'

'It doesn't matter. As you said—I am your wife.'

'You should have let me make love to you. I didn't want to hurt you.'

She covered her body with the counterpane. 'It doesn't matter. Now perhaps you would go in the other room while I get ready to be nice to your friends.'

He was buttoning himself up, smoothing his hair. 'It should never have happened like that. We are man and wife.'

'Don't worry,' she said. 'Please don't worry, Neville.'

'I've said I'm sorry.'

'I know you have. I accept it.'

He walked back into the lounge. And Charlotte took the glass from behind the wedding photograph.

8

JOHN COULDRIDGE said to his wife who was glossy with being loved: 'Charlotte isn't looking very well. I wonder what's the matter?'

'If it wasn't Charlotte I would have said she had been drinking.'

'You may be right.'

The new commanding officer, Colonel Willoughby, introduced himself and his wife. He was young to be a colonel. Very ambitious and very handsome. His hair was black and curly and his teeth white and sharp. He was reputed to be an unorthodox tactician and Couldridge wondered how the older officers to whom orthodoxy was inviolate would react to him. One defeat in the field and they would be at him—behind his back. His wife was tall and dark and capable, a woman who revelled in her husband's ambition.

Colonel Willoughby showed his sharp white teeth to Joanne and said: 'I believe that you two met in this house.'

Couldridge nodded. 'For better or for worse.'

Colonel Willoughby delivered one of his boyish smiles to Joanne. 'For the better—without a shadow of doubt.'

'You're very kind,' Joanne said. Couldridge hoped that only he could detect the sarcasm.

Colonel Willoughby turned to Couldridge and the boyish smile faded a bit. 'They still tell a few stories about your service here.'

'Really?' Couldridge said. 'I'm flattered.'

Mrs Willoughby said: 'Apparently you mistook a hangover for some obscure eye complaint.' She favoured Couldridge with the same sort of smile that her husband bestowed on Joanne.

'Quite true, I'm afraid. I thought it was glaucoma.'

'I hear that you're chucking the I.M.S. in soon,' Colonel Willoughby said.

'Really,' Couldridge said. 'Who told you that?'

'One of our chaps was holed up in hospital in Calcutta with cholera. A Major Little told him. I gather you did some pretty unorthodox work over there.'

Couldridge tried to assess Willoughby. Unorthodox people did not necessarily condone unorthodoxy in others. 'I tried to prove that there were easier ways of sterilising water than boiling it. Especially on a long march. It wasn't my own idea—it was the brain-child of another doctor in the I.M.S. And it works.'

'But they wouldn't have it?'

'No,' Couldridge said. 'They wouldn't have it.'

Colonel Willoughby nodded thoughtfully. 'I know just what you mean. I've had similar experiences. But you have to use diplomacy as well as initiative, Captain Couldridge.' He put on his smile for Joanne. 'I fear that you have a very impetuous husband, Mrs Couldridge. Perhaps impetuosity is not always a desirable quality in medicine.'

Joanne said: 'From what I've seen enthusiasm and dedication aren't rated too highly either.'

Colonel Willoughby turned to Couldridge and narrowed the smile by a couple of teeth. 'And you, Captain Couldridge, have a very loyal wife.' The smile expanded again. 'And a very pretty one.'

Couldridge looked at his wife and agreed with the colonel. She was mature now and the sharp points had been smoothed from her face. Her smoke-grey eyes were content and there was a creamy look of fulfilment about her. He thought about their reunion after her return from New York and momentarily closed his eyes with pleasure. He was very grateful to the tiger who had interrupted their lives on the way to Delhi. He smiled at her. 'I agree with you, sir. Although I don't think I was quite so impressed when we first met in this room.'

207

'You were a boor,' Joanne said. 'All you could do was tell me that I was short-sighted.'

'Well you are,' Couldridge said. He said to Willoughby: 'You have doubtless heard about my wife's exploits in this part of the world before we were married.'

'Who hasn't? She has become part of the lore of the land. These days you have to see the Taj Mahal by moonlight and Miss Joanne Pinkerton's footprint in cement.'

Most people were on to their second drink. Conversation had accelerated and the misdemeanours of the servants, the Morley-Minto reforms, Asquith's refusal to make Kitchener Viceroy and Lord Kensington's triumph in the Kadir Cup, fused into a droning babble.

Willoughby said: 'I believe you're very friendly with Major Spenser.'

'We were great friends,' Couldridge said. 'We arrived here together.'

'*Were* great friends?'

'We don't see so much of each other these days.'

'Ah.' His face was shrewd. 'Major Spenser talks a lot about you.'

'Does he?' There didn't seem to be anything else to say.

Willoughby drew Couldridge away from the two wives. 'I get the impression that he may be a little jealous of you.'

'Jealous? That's ridiculous. I'm a doctor and he's a soldier. In any case he's done better than me—he's a major.'

Willoughby nodded. 'And a very good one. But even if you're a professional soldier promotion isn't everything. I think perhaps he is a little aware of his background.'

'Then it's even more ridiculous,' Couldridge said. 'My mother was an Irish barmaid and my father was a missionary. Hardly aristocracy. In any case, sir, if you don't mind me asking— I don't quite see where all this is leading.'

'I'm talking to you as a doctor and therefore in confidence. You know this man better than anyone. It is my duty to know my officers. Especially one as senior as Major Spenser. I have noticed lately that he has been a little preoccupied. You know, Captain Couldridge, how this part of the world can affect men. You know what I think his trouble is?'

Couldridge shook his head.

'I think it's very simple. He believes that he should never have been a soldier—despite the fact that he's a very good one.'

'And why should that make him jealous of me, for God's sake?'

'Because you were born to be a doctor.'

'You're not blaming me for Major Spenser's preoccupation, I trust.'

'Not really,' Colonel Willoughby said. 'But I think you play a symbolic role.' He gave his man-to-man smile. 'There is one thing I would like you to do as a doctor and a friend of the Spenser family.'

'What's that, sir?'

Willoughby looked around him. 'Perhaps you would have a word with his wife. The gossips are starting, Captain Couldridge. You know what it's like in these parts. They can finish a man. My motives for seeking your help are purely selfish—I don't want to lose a good officer.'

'What is the gossip, sir?'

'They say she's hitting the bottle.'

'Perhaps it's because she doesn't like bridge, duck-shooting or watching polo, and they can't think what else she can be doing.'

'Perhaps it is,' Willoughby said. 'But I'd be grateful if you would see if there's any truth in it.'

'Very well,' Couldridge said. They returned to the two wives.

'I hope you've settled that amicably,' Mrs Willoughby said.

'Settled what, my dear?' Willoughby said.

'Whatever it was,' she said.

'We must move on and mingle,' Willoughby said. 'Here come your friends the Spensers.'

Charlotte Spenser looked sober enough, Couldridge thought. Except, perhaps, that her powder had been carelessly applied and she was smiling too much.

Charlotte said: 'Joanne, you're looking wonderful.'

It was not the sort of thing Charlotte said, Couldridge thought.

'Thank you,' Joanne said. 'It's being back again, I guess. Back with the father of my children.'

Charlotte smiled knowingly. 'You're a very lucky girl.'

Spenser said: 'Can I refill your glasses for you?'

Charlotte said: 'Yes please, dear. I'll have a little gin and some lime-juice if you can find any.'

'You haven't finished that one,' he said.

'We'll soon see to that,' she said. She drank it in three swallows and a little of the drink trickled down her chin. 'I'm enjoying myself,' she said. 'Are you enjoying yourselves?'

'It's like old times,' Couldridge said.

'Not quite,' Charlotte said. She frowned. 'No, it's not quite like old times.'

Spenser said: 'I think perhaps we'd better be getting back. I'm not feeling myself today. A touch of fever I think.'

'All right, dear,' Charlotte said. 'You go back home. I'll stay on for a while. I'm having such a wonderful time. And you did ask me to be pleasant to everyone.'

The remark hung for a moment before them. Then Couldridge suggested that he should examine Spenser to find out the cause of the fever. 'Do you suffer from malaria at all?'

Spenser shook his head. 'I've been lucky. I think it's just a touch of flu.'

The Fultons joined them. He was still unpromoted, still adjutant, still apparently happy. She was still the perfect soldier's wife. 'How are you both?' she said.

'We're fine,' Couldridge said. 'How is Mrs King?'

'Divorced,' Mrs Fulton said. 'She started to take her clothes off in front of another young subaltern. Unfortunately this one wasn't even a doctor and her husband caught her.'

'Who's Mrs King?' Joanne asked.

'You mean to say your husband hasn't told you about her?' Mrs Fulton said.

Joanne turned to Couldridge. 'Tell me,' she said. And he told her.

'My,' she said. 'You're not quite the open book I thought you were.'

'I sometimes suspect,' Couldridge said, 'that you haven't told me everything about those young men in your father's office.'

'I wish there was more to tell,' she said.

Fulton came over to Couldridge and spoke softly. 'I don't think Charlotte is too well,' he said. 'Perhaps you can do something. Without drawing too much attention to it, that is.'

Couldridge looked at Charlotte. Her face was pale and there was sweat on her forehead. He went to her side and she swayed and leaned against him. 'Are you feeling all right?' he asked.

'You know I'm not,' she said. 'I feel terrible, John.'

'Then don't you think you should leave now and have a rest?'

She nodded. 'I think so.'

Couldridge looked round. Spenser, who did not look as if he had a fever, was talking to Colonel Willoughby. Joanne was chatting to the Fultons. 'Come on,' he said. 'I'll see you back to your quarters. If we slip away now no one will notice.'

Her body was heavy against him and he thought she was going to faint. 'I feel so terrible,' she said. Her voice was plaintive and fragile.

'Don't worry,' he said. 'You'll be all right. Just keep close to me.' He eased himself through the chattering groups taking Charlotte with him. Then they were out in the warm night air. 'Where are your quarters from here? I forget.'

'Not far,' she said. 'Just across there.'

He hoped she wouldn't be sick. 'Can you make it all right do you think?'

'I can make it with you, John.' She clutched his arm. 'I wish we were walking across the common together. Ten years ago.'

'What common?'

'The common at home. Where Neville and I used to go courting.'

Fireflies danced in the scented darkness and a shooting star sped on its melting trail towards the dark mountains. A couple of Gurkhas passed by on their way to find the women and the rum and gambling tables of Jinjabad. Their eyes and their teeth glistened but their faces were barely discernible.

Couldridge said: 'How do you feel?'

'A bit better in the fresh air. I think the heat of the room was affecting me.' Her hand was tight around his arm. Once or twice she staggered on the rough grass.

Couldridge said: 'When did it begin, Charlotte?'

'When did what begin?'

'You know what I mean. Don't forget I'm a doctor. When did the drinking begin?'

'Oh' she said. 'Is it so obvious?'

'To me it is. But then I've known you a long time. And it's out of character. Is there anything I can do?'

'No,' she said. 'There's nothing you can do. It's my fault. I'm inadequate, I suppose.'

'You're nothing of the sort. You're a beautiful and sensitive girl. Much more sensitive than any of these other wives up here. It's they who are at fault, not you.'

They went into the bungalow, waking the dozing watchman as they entered. Charlotte lit a lamp and sat in a big leather easychair that sighed as she moved. Moths fluttered at the window and a mosquito hovered briefly around them before alighting on the ceiling.

'Do you really mean that?' Charlotte asked.

'That you're more sensitive than the other wives?'

'No.' Some of the colour had returned to her face but her head was nodding slightly. 'Did you mean that you thought I was beautiful?'

'Of course I did.' Couldridge searched his pockets for his pipe. The defensive mechanism that he had developed when treating women patients began to work. But surely not with

Charlotte—it was too ridiculous.

'Shall I tell you something?'

He gave the reassuring smile that he employed when telling hypochondriacs that they weren't going to die. 'It depends what it is.'

'Neville has never once told me that he thought I was beautiful.'

'Then I must treat him for myopia.'

'What's that—myopia.' She was speaking very carefully and too loudly.

'Short-sightedness.'

'But you think I'm beautiful?'

'I want to see if I can help you, Charlotte. Only very unhappy people drink too much. Why are you unhappy?'

'Don't you know?' She took a handkerchief from her handbag and dabbed at the sweat on her forehead.

'I know you don't like India. But lots of women don't like the place where their husbands have to work. They just have to put up with it because they love them. And I'm sure you have a lot of affection for Neville.'

She giggled. 'Then it's you who suffer from this myropia.'

'Myopia.'

'Then it's you who suffer from this myopia. It's you who are short-sighted, John. Can you love someone who hurts you?'

'Many women do.' He applied a match to his pipe and sucked the frail flame into the bowl. Blue smoke rose disturbing the mosquito on the ceiling. 'In fact it's been my experience that the more a husband hurts his wife the more she loves him.'

'When he really hurts her?'

'Do you mean physically?'

'Yes, John. Physically.'

'I'm sure Neville hasn't been hurting you physically.'

'He's been hurting me for a long time.'

'Physically?'

'No. It's only been physically recently.' She had difficulty pronouncing physically.

'I'm afraid I find that hard to believe.'

'You think I'm drunk, don't you?'

'I think you've had a little too much to drink. I think you need a good night's sleep. Then perhaps we'll have a talk.'

'You don't believe me?'

'I said I found it a little hard to believe that Neville had been ill-treating you.'

'Then look at this.'

Before he could stop her Charlotte Spenser had jumped to her feet and ripped at the neck of her grey silk dress.

'For God's sake,' Couldridge said.

'So you don't think he's ill-treated me...' She was muttering to herself as her hands tore down to her waist. Then she ripped at her bodice. For a moment the strong material resisted; then it split down the middle and her small white breasts with the little nipples were exposed. Around the nipples were red weals and bruises turning blue. 'Look at that Dr Couldridge,' she said. 'Just look at that. What's your diagnosis?'

'Did Neville do that?'

'I would hardly do it to myself.'

He took a step forward and examined the small wounds around the puckered nipples. Such small, vulnerable breasts. He experienced a pulse of sorrow and compassion. 'I'm sorry' he said.

Then she was in his arms and he was soothing her with his hands, feeling the sharp shoulder-blades and knuckles of her spine. She tried to speak again but the words were overcome by her sobs.

'There,' he said. 'There. Don't cry.' It was, he thought, like soothing a heart-broken schoolgirl.

But her sobbing was uncontrollable. And as he stroked her bare back and murmured into her hair he failed to hear the door open behind him.

Spenser spoke first. 'Good evening, Dr Couldridge,' he said. 'I am very grateful to you for attending to my wife. I presume

214

it's in a professional capacity.'

Joanne, who was behind him, said: 'I thought for a moment that it must have been Mrs King.'

And because there was no humour in her voice Couldridge searched her face for it. But there was none there either.

9

Two years later John Couldridge left the Indian Medical Service. There was no display of grief among his superiors and he received a polite but brief note from Buckingham who was now well-placed in the hierarchy of the I.M.S.

In his surgery at Lahore not far from the Shalamar Gardens, Couldridge worked hard at his ophthalmic studies. There was plenty of material for him to work on: conjunctiva as glistening red as the meat on butchers' slabs, corneas hazed by glaucoma, cloudy cataracts, caruncles, columba, presbyopia, eyes butchered by quacks. Often he managed to cure: often he was unable to help: sometimes—or so he believed—he blinded patients who might have continued to see if they hadn't consulted him.

Despite his failures his surgery became famous in the Punjab. Noblemen journeyed to him to have their eyesight improved or returned; and he journeyed to cities and villages to treat the poor. But when he tried to sleep, after excessive work, he was still troubled by his motives. He could not treat everyone who came to him for help; and as he lay beside Joanne awaiting sleep he accused himself of accepting only those with the most interesting conditions. And he wondered, as he had often wondered before, whether it was the quest for achievement rather than the easing of suffering that absorbed him. Often he worked until two or three in the morning observed by the section of the blue eye on the wall. When he went to bed Joanne slept on undisturbed: when he awoke she was busying herself about the house tending to the children.

To help him with his work Couldridge employed a young Sikh doctor who claimed to be descended from Ranjit Singh. He was proud and studious and fond of explaining the equipment of his belief—the comb, the steel bracelet, the sword, the long hair and the short drawers. But his pride was too strong for his duties: instead of an orthoptist he wanted to be a surgeon. Also he had profound contempt for many of the patients.

Couldridge longed for the sullen efficiency of Bose. Especially now that he understood the smouldering fires of nationalist discontent—and Bose's predeliction for picric acid. One day, after the Sikh had lectured him about British perfidy in taking the Koh-i-Nor diamond for Queen Victoria, after he had wrongly diagnosed a simple case of atrophy of the eye due to lack of nourishment, after he had explained at length his connections with Ranjit Singh who was immortalised by a tomb in the Shalamar Gardens, after he had informed a Hindu patient that his eye condition was caused by congenital syphilis which it wasn't, Couldridge decided to write to Bose in Calcutta.

A month later he received a reply. Bose said he would come to Lahore provided that his conviction was not held against him and provided that their relationship continued as it had been before his arrest. There was no suggestion of an apology. It was as if Bose sensed Couldridge's predicament; as if he were making the terms. Bose also suggested that Couldridge should pay his fare across India. Couldridge agreed and told the Sikh that he thought his talents were too promising for him to be a subordinate any longer. The flesh and blood of Ranjit Singh agreed immediately and departed.

When he was not completely absorbed with his work, Couldridge found time to be worried about his marriage. Not too worried because he believed that no two people were so completely suited to each other as Joanne and himself. But he knew that his work was isolating him from his family; he was also aware that their relationship had been subtly different since the incident with Charlotte Spenser.

'You're not still thinking about that, are you?' he had asked one night when he sensed that she was shrinking from him in their big bed beneath the mosquito net.

'It's difficult to forget the scene when you find the wife of your husband's best friend bare-busted in his arms.'

'I am a doctor. It wasn't the first naked bosom I've seen.'

'That's quite irrelevant.' She shrank a little more. 'And it wasn't exactly a doctor-patient relationship, was it?'

'I've explained to you what happened. And it was two years ago or more, for God's sake.'

'I know. I also know it's stupid of me. But it's difficult not to react when you see a half-naked woman in the arms of your husband.'

'She was a poor creature.' Couldridge slipped his arm round his wife's waist. 'So is Neville in a way.'

'I know.' She didn't move away from his arm. 'I wonder what they're doing now.'

'I expect they've settled down a bit now. They've had their leave. Charlotte's got her baby.'

'That's another thing,' Joanne said. 'The baby—it was born exactly nine months after that awful scene.'

'You can't blame me for that.'

'No, but it's strange. Horrible really. It's not nice to think of a baby being born as the result of rape.'

'You don't know,' Couldridge said. 'You can't possibly know. All we saw were the marks on her breasts. She never really explained.'

'I think she was crazy to stay with him.'

'She married him. For better or for worse.'

Joanne allowed him to move closer to her. 'To hell with that,' she said. 'Not if your husband is a rapist.'

'You just don't know. And don't say a woman can always tell or anything predictable like that.' He watched a mosquito

217

lancing away at the white gauze above them. 'But what does it matter? Charlotte wanted a baby. It will make all the difference to their marriage.'

'It depends.'

'Depends on what?'

'It depends on how they regard the child. She will never forget how it was conceived. He will never forget her half-naked in your arms. The arms of the man he's envied since you first met.'

'How do you know he envied me?'

She turned and smiled at him in the vague light. 'A woman can always tell.' She paused. 'And so would you have been able to tell if you hadn't always been so immersed in your work.'

'Do I shut myself away too much?'

'Your children are growing up and you don't even notice it.' She turned to him in the big, hard-mattressed bed. 'How old are your children, John?'

He thought for a moment. 'Neville's eight and Mary Joanne's seven.'

She shook her head, a blur in the darkness. 'Nine and eight. They're growing up, John, without you even seeing it.'

He stroked her thick soft hair. 'I'm sorry,' he said.

'You're a clever, sensitive man,' she said. 'And yet you didn't notice that Neville was growing to hate you, that Charlotte was falling for you, that Bose was plotting to blow up the Viceroy and—dammit all—using your chemicals to do it.'

His hand moved from her hair to her shoulder. 'I'll try and pay more attention to the children.' And from her shoulder to her breast.

'And pay more attention to me?' He fondled her breasts, already awakening to his touch.

'Yes,' he said.

'Those damned doctor's hands of yours,' she said, and pressed her body close against him.

For two or three weeks Couldridge made an effort to pay more attention to the wife and family whom he loved. He showed them the attractions of Lahore—the Fort and Mosque of Wazir Khan, the tomb of Emperor Jahangir across the Ravi River and the Shalamar Gardens with their terraces and fountains. As in other Indian cities he was struck by the contrast between the European and the Indian quarters—the leisurely bungalows with their tranquillising fans and watered gardens beside hot, tottering slums. The European quarter seemed to have been laid out by the colonial architects as an invitation to a rampaging mob to unleash its fury—bare feet swathing through blossom, the tinkling of glass, the cries of frightened children.

Soon the quests and lusts, the small victories and defeats, in his surgery began once more to draw his attention from the family whom he loved. And when Bose arrived one summer afternoon, sullen and exuding unrepentence, it seemed to Couldridge that their partnership was once again converging upon achievement.

He took Bose into the room behind the gleaming surgery where he kept his rats and rabbits. 'Soon,' he said, 'I shall be ready to put some of my ideas into operation.'

Bose looked at the twitching faces of the animals in the cages. 'I thought you British loved animals,' he said.

'So we do. But we get our priorities in the right order. Don't tell me you're an anti-vivisectionist, Bose. Not you of all people.'

'No,' Bose said. 'But the hypocrisy of the British has always puzzled me.'

'Surely it would be more puzzling if I refused to make my contribution towards helping humanity because I objected to experimenting on a few animals.'

'Perhaps,' Bose said. And added: 'If that is indeed the purpose of your work.'

'What do you mean by thát?'

'If your only concern is helping humanity.'

Irritation mounted to anger. 'Does it matter a damn about my motives? The fact remains that the work I'm doing may help to ease suffering irrespective of whether I want a knight-hood.'

'You're right, of course,' Bose said. But his accusation lingered between them.

But it wasn't only Bose who accused Couldridge in his new surroundings. Other doctors practising in the area showed their hostility and made it clear that his principal crime was un-orthodoxy. They might have been prepared to forgive him if he had been an abortionist or a drug-peddlar. But a non-conformist—never. Stories reached them from Delhi and Cal-cutta about his work with Nesfield's Chlorogen and his disagree-ments with Buckingham and Little. There were rumours of unorthodox practices and vivisection at his surgery.

His second crime was the breadth of his interests. If a doctor chose to specialise in eye surgery then he should not stray into other fields. And there were stories that in one village he had performed two operations in one morning—one on an eye, the other on an ear. Unforgiveably, both had been successful.

His third crime embraced the other two. He would not have been able to afford either of them if he hadn't found himself a rich American wife. More simply he was a kept man.

Couldridge was at first hurt by the animosity. But when he had assessed the calibre of his critics the hurt was replaced by contempt.

He and Joanne were invited to another doctor's home only once. Their host was a small, dry man whose linen suits were always freshly pressed. All his patients were Europeans and he was a great advocate of 'sweating out' a fever. If 'sweating out' failed he called in a specialist. He made a point of never telling a patient what he was suffering from—a necessary pre-caution because there were many times when he had no idea himself. If a patient tentatively suggested that perhaps he was suffering from a touch of malaria Dr Benjamin Emmerson looked up from the prescription he was writing with a conspira-torial smile which the patient interpreted as confirmation. Dr

Emmerson's five Indian servants went elsewhere for medical treatment.

He gave Couldridge and Joanne gin and lemon squash jostling with ice on his verandah, crossed his legs clad in linen that still seemed to be steaming from the iron and said with banter and accusation in his voice: 'I hear you're carrying out a few experiments in that wonderful new surgery of yours.'

Couldridge said: 'I'm trying out a few ideas on ophthalmic surgery. Nothing very revolutionary. Surgeons with far more experience than me are pursuing similar ideas all over the world.'

Dr Emmerson tinkled the ice in his drink. 'Must be very interesting work,' he said.

'It is,' Couldridge said.

Mrs Emmerson said: 'My husband doesn't find time for experiments. He's much too busy looking after his patients.' She was a plump, squashy woman whose flesh looked as if it would dent if you poked your finger into it.

'I do have my hands full,' Dr Emmerson said. 'I'm surprised you find time for experiments, with all those patients of yours.'

Joanne said: 'John sometimes works till two and three in the morning.'

Dr Emmerson said quickly: 'Does that leave him in a fit state to look after his patients next morning? There's nothing like a good night's sleep you know. Much better than any drugs we doctors can prescribe.'

'I find I can cope,' Couldridge said.

Mrs Emmerson said: 'I suppose it's different with Indian patients.' The dimple at her elbow closed like a little pink mouth as she flexed her arm.

Couldridge laughed with his mouth full of gin and lemon-squash and nearly choked. 'What on earth do you mean, Mrs Emmerson? What difference can there possibly be?'

'Well, I should think it's much easier to diagnose their complaints, isn't it? You know—cholera, typhoid and some of those more unpleasant diseases.'

Couldridge said: 'Do you mean venereal disease, Mrs Emmerson?'

She examined a small hand with rings embedded deep in the fingers. 'That sort of thing,' she said.

Couldridge said: 'In fact venereal disease is much trickier to treat than cirrhosis of the liver. And that, I imagine, is one of the principal complaints of your husband's patients.'

Emmerson ran one finger down the sharp crease in his trousers. 'Come now, Couldridge,' he said. 'That's no way to talk. I asked you and your wife over for a friendly chat. A bit of advice, in fact. After all I am the older and more experienced practitioner.'

'I'm sorry,' Couldridge said.

In the garden an Indian was hosing a bed of roses. In the kitchen they could hear an Indian washing up the luncheon dishes. In the nursery an Indian nurse cooed over the Emmersons' fleshy baby.

'We must all stick together,' Emmerson said. 'I know that you're a bit of a rebel, Couldridge. But I don't think India is the place for a rebel doctor—there's enough rebellion in the place already.'

'But am I a rebel? Just because I seek advancement? Do you want medicine to stop still? For God's sake, Emmerson, you're the sort of person who derided Simpson when he introduced chloroform, the sort of person who opposed Lister. If doctors like you had your way we'd still be pouring boiling oil over the raw stumps of limbs to cauterise them.'

Emmerson held up his neat hand. 'Please,' he said. 'Mrs Emmerson may be the wife of a doctor but she can't stand gruesome talk like that.' He leaned over and patted the yielding flesh of his wife's arm. 'Are you all right, Mollie dear?'

Mollie Emmerson indicated that she would survive.

Joanne said: 'Can I get you another gin and lemon squash, Mrs Emmerson?'

Dr Emmerson frowned, shook his head and rang a handbell. An Indian shuffled on to the verandah, head bowed in perpetual servility.

They all had more gin and lemon-squash and played a little music with the ice. Then Emmerson tried again. 'I really think, old man,' he said, 'that you should try and conform a little more. For your own good, you understand. Word gets around, you know. You're still a young man and you don't want to endanger a promising career by being obstinate, do you?'

'I'm thirty-six,' Couldridge said. 'And if I'm a young man why do you call me old man?'

Emmerson tried to laugh but his voice cracked like a school-boy's. 'Wasn't there some trouble in Calcutta?' he said. 'Using chlorine or something to purify water instead of boiling it?'

'There was a difference of opinion about its value.'

Emmerson nodded. 'Nothing wrong with boiling water,' you know. It's always worked in the past. Why bring in new methods if the old ones work perfectly well?'

'Because it's more practicable. Because on battlefields water could be purified in a matter of minutes. Because it could save thousands of lives. Are those sufficient reasons, Dr Emmerson?'

'Certainly—if you can prove them.'

'Nesfield proved them years ago in London. And they're still not in general use in the Army.'

Emmerson said: 'This eye surgery that we keep hearing about. What exactly are you trying to do, Couldridge?'

'I'm trying to help people who are going blind to keep their sight.'

The gardener with the hose moved behind a bush so that, with his body hidden, it looked as if he were urinating over the rose-bed.

Mrs Emmerson said: 'Don't you have to pass special exams to practice eye surgery, Dr Couldridge?'

Couldridge smiled at her over the top of his glass. 'I am a qualified surgeon, Mrs Emmerson.'

Joanne said: 'John's patients trust him.' Mrs. Emmerson began to speak and Joanne said quickly: 'I know they're only Indians.'

Emmerson said: 'I didn't want to bring this word into the conversation, Couldridge, but you've forced my hand. Isn't your behaviour a little... unethical?'

'That's almost defamatory,' Couldridge said.

Mrs Emmerson patted her husband's knee in return for the pat on her arm. 'Don't say anything that could in the least bit be misconstrued, Benjie. I suspect that Dr Couldridge is something of a lawyer as well as a doctor. Perhaps a better lawyer than a doctor....'

Couldridge said: 'If that isn't defamatory I don't know what is. But don't worry, Mrs Emmerson, I abhor litigation.'

Emmerson made one last effort. 'Perhaps the word unethical was a little strong. There's nothing personal in this, Couldridge. I'm not speaking for myself at all. A few of us got together and decided that for your own good...'

'You mean you ganged up on me?'

'Nothing of the sort. We decided that we doctors should stick together.'

'You mean we white doctors?'

'Interpret it how you wish.' Dr Emmerson gave the sad smile with which he confirmed patients' fears that they were suffering from an incurable disease. 'These are my last words on the subject. We think that for your own good you should stop these experiments, stop trying to specialise in more than one field, and conform a little. I know you don't like the word but there's nothing wrong with conformity in our profession.'

Couldridge stood up. 'Well, thanks for the warning anyway. But I shall go on experimenting. If I didn't, if Nesfield didn't, if Koch hadn't, if Lister hadn't...'

'You are comparing yourself with Lister?'

'No, Dr Emmerson, I'm not. My words were badly chosen. But at least I am a doctor and not a male home nurse.'

Emmerson stood up. 'Very well,' he said, 'at least we know how we stand. These things have a way of reaching influential quarters in London, you know. We have tried to help you...' He pinched at the creases in his trousers where they had been blunted by sitting down.

'You mean they might just happen to hear about unethical practices in a letter signed "a friend"?'

'I didn't say that.'

Couldridge advanced upon Emmerson, looked down upon him and said: 'Don't try and threaten me, Emmerson.'

Mrs Emmerson said: 'Oh dear, oh dear.' She dabbed at her face with lavender water and looked as if she were about to faint, but no one took any notice.

Emmerson said: 'Keep your hands off me, Couldridge, or you will find yourself in court.'

Joanne said: 'He hasn't got his hands on you, Dr Emmerson.' She took her husband's arm. 'Come on,' she said. 'There's no point in this any more. It's becoming a trifle unseemly.'

Couldridge allowed his muscles to relax. 'You're right,' he said. 'I mustn't lose my temper. I might get apoplexy and I'm not on Dr Emmerson's list of patients—thank God.'

As they left the bungalow the gardener waved his jet of water as if he were saluting.

But Couldridge didn't pursue any more unorthodox practices that year and Emmerson didn't carry out his threats because two months after the conversation on the verandah Britain and Germany went to war.

10

SURGEON Captain John Couldridge was posted to France with the Indian reinforcements and at Marseilles met for the first and only time his hero, Vincent Nesfield. Nesfield—handsome, intense and moustached—had found that the water piped to the Army camp from the French port was polluted. As embarking troops were also taking this water with them to Gallipoli they were transporting two powerful allies to the Turks— typhoid and dysentry. Nesfield persuaded the French to add sodium hypochlorite to the reservoirs and the bacilli vanished.

Then Nesfield sailed for Basra and Couldridge went to Northern France where the Army had finally been persuaded to chlorinate its water. But they didn't bother to dechlorinate it and the water had a strong green taste about it. It was immediately damned in the eyes of the British soldiers because it flavoured their tea—a worse hazard than dysentry, cholera or typhoid.

Couldridge was at first infected with deep melancholia at the grey muddy suffering around him. At the relentless carnage dogmatically arranged by tacticians in London, Paris and Berlin. He was numbed by the haemorrhage of manhood around him; numbed by evidence of humanity's inhuman capabilities. The scale of it seemed to utterly negate the small alleviations of suffering that he and all the doctors of the world managed to achieve.

He saw lines of men advancing through dawn mist towards inevitable death; he saw the death snarls on their faces and fancied that in those frozen expressions he saw relief. And he thought of the generals who must have known that the German machine-guns were waiting to chop them down. In his melancholy he equated the generals with the elders of medicine who were more concerned with ethics and dogma than the wounds of Mankind.

In field hospitals behind the ravaged lines he removed shell splinters and bullets, sutured, incised, amputated. And he found a certain satisfaction in his aseptic record. Like Nesfield he used Listerian techniques, painting his hands with iodine, cleaning the wounds with percholide of mercury and using carbolic and Lysol to protect his instruments and clothes. And he never had a single case of sepsis.

Gradually the old dormant enthusiasms began to fight back against the melancholia. They drew his attention to the bravery and chivalry in the blood-stained mud; they reminded him of the succour he brought to the few; they suggested that the work of the doctors in France might lead to fresh discoveries in medicine. Gratefully he accepted the suggestions and closed his mind to their fallibilities. He became so familiar with the remorseless suffering that he accepted it as a casualty officer accepts his daily allocation of bloodshed. And pride at his small surgical victories overcame his horror of the systematic slaughter around him.

One day during a pause in mending bodies, he sat outside a dug-out trying to infect a young doctor in the Royal Army Medical Corps—it served the British Army in the same way that the I.M.S. served the Indian Army—with his new enthussiasms. Spring sunshine was drying the mud and the air smelled of rivers and paint. Ahead of them tiny lemon leaves uncurled furtively in decimated tree-trunks. In a farmyard soldiers with superficial wounds which they hoped were tickets to Blighty hunted rats with a stolen air-rifle.

'It's overwhelming,' the young doctor kept saying. 'Just overwhelming.' He had been qualified for six months, a conscript for three. The hair on his pink cheeks was still downy and while he spoke he cleaned his fingernails with a file from a leather manicure case.

'You'll learn to accept it,' Couldridge said. 'You'll learn to take pride in what you achieve rather than mourning what's going on around you.'

'It makes it all so pointless,' the young doctor said, pushing back the quick from his forefinger. 'I mean what's the point of saving one man's life while thousands are dying over there.' He pointed towards the barbed wire, the drying mud and the tree-stumps.

'You could put up the same argument during a plague.'

'But this isn't a plague. This is men killing each other and not even knowing why.'

'Maybe it is a plague of sorts. A sort of mass madness.'

The young doctor snipped a minute particle of skin from

beside his thumbnail. 'I don't know,' he said. 'You may be right. It's all so overwhelming.'

But the generals were bored with the sunlit oasis in the fighting. Somewhere a thrush had the temerity to begin singing. Somewhere a big gun opened up: Couldridge never knew whether that first detonation was German or British. One thing was certain—the Germans had brought up guns with a longer range. A shell exploded fifty yards in front of the dug-out and a chunk of metal with rifling on its shining surface opened up most of the young doctor's abdominal cavity killing him almost immediately. A smaller piece dug itself into Couldridge's thigh fracturing his femur.

A tourniquet was applied and before he lost consciousness Couldridge gave instructions about the antiseptic precautions to be taken before any field surgery was performed. He was then put on a hospital train to the coast and ferried to England. The bone was set again in London and, after convalescing in a nursing home overlooking the harbour at Torquay—where he read about Kitchener's death by drowning off the Orkneys— he was put on a ship bound for India.

There, as he hobbled around with a stick, nursed by Joanne and regarded with pride and curiosity by his two children because it was not everyone whose father had been shot in France, he followed the course of the war-to-end-wars and the career of Vincent Nesfield.

In Mesopotamia Nesfield managed to persuade the general officer commanding the expedition that chlorination of the drinking water would stamp out cholera, typhoid and dysentry. The enlightened general empowered Nesfield to manufacture his own chlorogen; this he did on board a captured Turkish steamer. When he ran short of containers he paid the Arabs to collect bottles which he filled with chlorogen.

Then Nesfield himself fell sick with typhoid. He, too, was brought back to India and put in charge of the mounted field ambulance service at Peshawar. There he composed a paper for the *Indian Medical Gazette* about the delays in implementing his discovery of chlorogen that had caused so many deaths.

He was transferred to another hospital at Indore. There he was told that he was under arrest under the Defence of the Realm Act for publishing unauthorised information about the conduct of the war. He was told that if he didn't retract what he had written he would be court-martialled.

While he was under open arrest Nesfield lived in a riverside tent because he was not allowed to use his mess or club. He took with him a dog, a horse and a servant and stayed there for six months.

Then an inquiry was ordered. Senior officers were sacked and Nesfield was released and promoted to major.

In Lahore and Bombay where he treated the returning wounded, Couldridge followed the story of injustice and vindication with anger and pleasure. It would, he knew, be the pattern of his life, injustice followed by success. In his beautiful aseptic surgery in Lahore he raised a glass of purified water and toasted the cross-section of the big blue eye on the wall.

BOOK FOUR

1

THE girl was about fifteen. Her hair was black and polished and pigtailed. Her skin was brown and pliant, her teeth white and even. Her eyes were dull and cloudy.

'What do you think, Bose?' Couldridge asked.

Bose looked into the brown iris and the pupil. 'It is for you to say,' he said. 'But it is obviously scarring from trachoma.'

'You know what I mean, Bose. Should I operate?'

'It is not for me to say.'

Up in the banyan tree the monkeys sensed conflict and hushed their noise. The afternoon sunlight filtered through banyan and acacia throwing a moving mosaic of shadow and light on the baked mud of the village's only street. The air smelled of onions flowering in dust patches; of honey and dates and butter from dark shops. Down the street a youth rode perilously on the village's first bicycle: it was the only movement outside Couldridge's mobile surgery.

The surgery consisted of two tables set up beneath a tent made of mosquito netting, and the big black boxes containing his lotions, ointments, liniments and pills. If there was nothing wrong with a patient he dispensed lots of white pills—usually ascorbic acid. European hypochrondriacs favoured coloured potions: Indians preferred white pills. His instruments, boiled and sterile, lay in carbolic.

Twice a month Couldridge harnessed three horses—one for himself, one for Bose and one for the pack—and set out from his surgery in Lahore on his rounds of the villages. He told himself and Bose that he was fulfilling his obligations as a physician. But neither believed that this was the complete truth: during every tour a handful of patients were persuaded to attend the surgery in Lahore—and nearly all of them suffered from eye defects.

Once Bose pointed this out and Couldridge lost his temper. 'You make me sound like a Glasgow body-snatcher,' he said.

Bose, who nowadays confided nothing, said: 'I am merely pointing out that although we come across tuberculosis and tumours and weak hearts it is nearly always those with troubles of the eyes who come back to your surgery.'

Couldridge said: 'Are you suggesting that the rest of the work I do in the villages is worthless? The fractures I reset, the dysentery and the cholera and the typhoid I treat, the hernias I operate on, the overdue babies I produce?'

'I am not suggesting it's worthless,' Bose said. 'I am merely questioning the real reason for these journeys. But I agree that it does not matter because you do good work whatever the motive.'

'Bose,' Couldridge said, 'I think you're just trying to rile me.'

'Just seeking the truth,' Bose said. 'But it does not matter.'

This morning, watched by the monkeys and the parrots and all the population except the very young, the very old and the youth on the bicycle, Couldridge had performed one operation on a woman suffering from acute appendicitis, snipped out a pair of infected tonsils, done his best with a case of cholera, and disinfected the local well, removed several warts and re-set a fractured tibia that had been set with cow dung.

The girl had not really been a patient at all. She had come in with a boy of twelve who had a greenstick fracture of the radius and Couldridge had noticed her hesitancy of movement and the cloudy tissue in her eyes. She had sat on a chair, shy and frightened, while he examined her eyes.

He looked up at Bose and said: 'She'll be blind soon'

Bose nodded, hand straying to the patch of white on his

hair and patting it. The rest of his hair was still as blue-black as it had been when he was a young man. His brooding face had aged only slightly with a single line stretching from his nose to the corner of his mouth. But there were no webs of laughter at the corners of his eyes.

Couldridge said: 'Don't you care?'

Bose said: 'There are a million such cases in India. And in any case...'

'And in any case she's a girl? Is that what you were going to say?'

Bose shrugged. 'Perhaps. It does not matter. What do you want to know?' He hadn't called Couldridge by his Christian name since his arrest and trial.

'You know what I want to know. Do you think I am ready to perform the sort of operation I've been preparing for? This girl will go blind anyway.'

'You must do what you think right,' Bose said.

'But do you think I can do it?'

The girl looked at them with frightened, half-seeing eyes.

'The question,' Bose said, 'is not whether you are capable of carrying out such an operation. It is whether you think you should carry it out.'

'You sound like Dr Emmerson. For God's sake, Bose, what's happened to you? What's happened to that spirit of adventure you once had in Calcutta?'

'That was a long time ago. I have had good reason to distrust the spirit of adventure as you call it.'

'But not in medicine. I'm trying to cure people, Bose, not blow them up.'

'As I say,' Bose said, 'you must do what you think right. It doesn't seem to me that you have bothered with my opinions in the past. Why should you now?'

'Because I need advice.'

Down the street the youth fell off his bicycle and cursed modern invention.

Bose said: 'This sort of operation is not fully accepted. You may find a lot of opposition. You will also have to persuade the girl's parents that the operation is necessary. That will be difficult.'

'I would be prepared to pay them,' Couldridge said.

Bose shrugged non-committally.

'But you still don't think I should go ahead with the operation?'

'If you do I am hoping for your sake that you are successful. If you fail your profession will turn on you.'

'Tell the girl that I may be able to make her see again and see what she says. Is she the last patient?'

Bose nodded. Couldridge left his gauze surgery and lit his pipe. The village, one of the few where Moslem and Hindu lived together amicably, awaited his next move. Couldridge emitted small puffs of smoke from the side of his mouth and limped along the main and only street. He was over forty and still there had been no achievement. Plenty of progress but no achievement. He believed that he was now ready to attempt a corneal graft using donor material from a dead body. He was aware that he was not alone in his ambitions. Before the war Magitot had demonstrated that a clear graft could be made from donor material stored for eight days; in Russia and at the Elschnig School in Prague surgeons were making great progess in keratoplasty. But still the successes were being recorded with grafts from the eyes of living people: the next breakthrough had to be the use of tissue taken from the dead to help the living. The obstacles, Couldridge knew, were not only surgical: he and the other pioneers would have to contend with a great outburst of anger over the moral and ethical issues involved. The dead should not be disturbed. Were the donors, in fact, dead before the 'butchers' got to work on them?

Couldridge believed that most medical authorities now accepted the reality of corneal grafts from cadavers. But they were waiting for action from one or two intrepid surgeons: if the surgeons were successful there would be guarded and qualified praise: if they failed they would be damned for their impetuosity. Happily for medicine there had always been the few eager for recognition; Couldridge was one of them and he saw no shame in his eagerness. He was also aware that pioneering surgery and irresponsible surgery were separated by barriers as thin as skin: one false cut from a scalpel and they were indistinguishable.

Having considered the devious paths of advancement Couldridge stopped and considered a scene that had not been affected by progress since the invention of the wheel. A sacred cow chewing the cud outside a hut that had no sanitation, no comfort and little substance. In it lived three members of the population of a country containing a sixth of the world's population. If statistics were to be believed all three of them stood a good chance of being dead before they were thirty-five. Plans for the development of surgical techniques were, Couldridge thought, somewhat incongruous in these surroundings. The cow went on chewing and regarded Couldridge with minimal interest.

Couldridge returned to the gauze tent and said: 'Well?'

Bose said: 'She is very frightened. I have tried to explain to her that she has nothing to lose. That she will go blind in any case.'

'I hope you put it to her in a more comforting way than that.'

'I told her the truth. I am a doctor not a missionary.'

Couldridge knocked out his pipe on his boot. 'I sometimes wonder, Bose,' he said, 'why we put up with each other.'

'Because we suit each other's purpose.'

'It wasn't always like that.'

'No,' Bose said. 'It wasn't always like that.'

Couldridge looked hopelessly at him for a moment. Then he said: 'Well, what is the verdict of the girl?'

'She says it is up to you. But first you will have to get the permission of her parents. She doesn't think there will be any trouble there if you are prepared to pay. But she doesn't think you should have to pay. She says she should be paying you money to cure her.'

'She has a point,' Couldridge said. He stuffed more tobacco into his pipe. 'Why does she leave the decision to me?' He looked into the hazed, trusting eyes of the girl.

'She has confidence in you. She says that you have a kind voice and clever hands. I think she has a feeling for you.'

'Feeling for me? Are you crazy, Bose? I'm forty-six, going grey and developing a gut.'

Bose permitted himself one of his rare smile. 'You forget,' he said, 'that she can hardly see.'

Couldridge said: 'The fact that she transfers the decision to me makes it more difficult.'

'Perhaps you should go and see her parents now.'

'What's the point if they can be bought as easily as that?' He paused. 'Tell her that the operation might not be successful.'

'I've already told her that.'

'Then tell her again.'

Bose spoke rapidly and irritably to the girl. She listened carefully, head bowed, afternoon sunlight shining in her polished hair. Around the flimsy tent the villagers waited expectantly. A monkey dropped from the banyan tree and vanished behind the yellow and brown cottages. Down the street the youth fell off the bicycle again.

Bose said: 'She repeats that it is up to you. But she wishes to say that if it will make you happier then she agrees to the operation.'

'She means if it will ease my conscience.'

'She would not understand that.'

'But you and I do, Bose.'

'Perhaps.'

Couldridge put his hand on the girl's shoulder and she looked up at him, trying to focus her eyes on his face. 'We must go and see your parents,' he said in his dreadful Hindi.

She nodded.

Her parents lived a few hundred yards away near the sacred cow which was still masticating thoughtfully. Her father was

237

the village money-lender. He was fragile, bow-legged, ingratiating and wealthy.

Through Bose he told Couldridge that under no circumstances would he permit his daughter to be operated upon. It was, he said, against his beliefs and his religion: he didn't elaborate. He waited expectantly and Couldridge presumed that one of the listening villagers had told him that he was willing to pay money for the privilege of trying to restore the girl's eyesight. It was incomprehensible to the old man that anyone should want to restore his daughter's eyesight; but if they did and were willing to pay money for the privilege then who was he to protest?

Bose mentioned cash and the money-lender looked shocked as if it were a commodity in which he didn't trade. Bose shook his head at Couldridge and they started to walk out of the old man's quarters at the top of a flight of bending wooden stairs. He was drinking coffee and in one corner of the room, which smelled of pepper, stood a lacquer spinning wheel.

The old man spoke quickly to Bose.

Couldridge said: 'What did he say?'

'He said that if he is contributing to science then he is willing to consider an offer of money. Or words to that effect.'

'Canny old devil, isn't he?'

'He's a money-lender,' Bose said.

Thirty minutes later a price had been agreed.

Bose said: 'I hope you are satisfied.'

'You make it sound as if I've committed a crime.'

As they rode back to Lahore Bose said: 'One problem remains. Where are you going to get a section of a healthy cornea from?'

'I shall have to wait until I can find someone fatalistic enough to accept that they are going to die and sensible enough to realise that it doesn't matter what happens to their bodies after death.'

'You may have to wait a long time,' Bose said. He rode well, body upright, thighs gripping, hands loose on the reins. But whereas some riders seemed to merge with the horse until together they became one sinewy movement Bose remained independent of the horse. Withdrawn, strong—like his character.

'Why for God's sake? Don't be such a bloody pessimist, Bose.'

'You may think that it does not matter what happens to your body after death. I'm telling you that there are a lot of people who would disagree with you. And there are a lot of people who are going to say that it is not right to transplant tissue from a dead man to a live one.'

'There will always be people who try and stop progress,' Couldridge said.

They rode on through the brown countryside, their horses' hooves making dry noises in the dust. Couldridge glanced at the dark, self-contained man beside him and remembered the days when he had called him Boss. If he had listened to what Bose had to say in those early adventurous days what would their relationship have been like now? Too late now to wonder. He said: 'One of these days, Bose, doctors are going to transplant many organs from one body to another. Kidneys, livers, perhaps even hearts. One day they might even find a way of joining two alien optic nerves and transplanting a complete eye.'

'These are not the sort of things that doctors were intended to do.'

'Why not, for God's sake? It's healing, isn't it? Stopping suffering, prolonging life.'

'I think,' Bose said, 'that doctors can help nature and allow nature to help them. If you take the organs from one man and give them to another then you are interfering with nature.'

They trotted into the suburbs of Lahore, along a wide baked road crowded with Sikhs.

Couldridge said: 'Any revolutionary idea is rejected at first because it shocks. But humans soon absorb the shock.'

'I have said what I think,' Bose said.

'You will change your mind when the operation succeeds. When the girl's sight returns to one eye. Are you going to assist me in the operation?'

'Of course,' Bose said. 'I work for you.'

'Don't overdo the enthusiasm,' Couldridge said.

But in Joanne he found the encouragement he sought. 'I can't say how ready you are to perform such an operation,' she said. 'Only you know that. But if you think you are ready then you must go ahead. I guess there will be a lot of criticism, a lot of condemnation. But there always is for the one with the courage to take the initiative.' She smiled at him knowingly. 'In any case you aren't really seeking advice. You just want confirmation of what you're going to do anyway. I know you, John. Nothing on God's earth would stop you from carrying out this operation.'

He grinned affectionately at his wife, mother of his three children. She was still beautiful, he thought: the outlines of her sharp prettiness slightly padded now, the waist thickening after the birth of their third child. He went and sat beside her on the settee, held her hand and reflected on her loyalty that had triumphantly survived the discovery of a half-naked woman in his arms and the long parting of the war.

'Who would have guessed it?' he said.

'Guessed what?'

'At Colonel Hatherley's that evening.' He gestured around the room and pointed to the nursery where the ayah was singing to the baby. 'Who would ever have guessed that all this would happen?'

Joanne touched his cheek. 'A year ago I wouldn't have guessed that would happen.' She pointed towards the nursery.

'Colonel Willoughby told you I was an impetuous man.'

'Then kindly curb your impetuosity in future. The way we work it we'll always have an infant crawling around our feet.'

'Don't you like it that way?'

'Sure I like it. But you don't know what it's like having them.'

'I more than most men know what it's like for a woman to have a baby.'

'You less than most men,' she said.

'What do you mean by that?'

'I mean that you're an explorer not a doctor. A scientist not a family physician.'

He leaned back, hands behind his neck, pipe smoke eddying around him, long legs crossed. 'I know,' he said. 'It used to worry me. Now I've accepted it. But just the same I'll go on dispensing quinine, castor oil and aspirins around the villages. Does it worry you—what I am?'

'It only worries me when you forget your family. I sometimes wonder if you even realise that your other two children are at school in England.'

'I wonder how they are,' he said. 'We'll give them a term each and see how they like it. If they tell us they hate it when they come back on vacation then we'll let them stay here.'

'But you said Neville must have a proper education.'

'Then we will have to go and live in England.'

'And leave the surgery? Leave all your work? The doctors around here are unpleasant enough. I dread to think how they'd react to you in England.'

'You make it sound very complicated.'

'I figure that the elements of a happy marriage and good parenthood *are* complicated. You can't just make vague utterances and then disappear into your surgery.'

'I know,' he said. 'I'll try a bit harder in future.'

'Like hell you will,' she said. She kissed him and rubbed her cheek hard against his.

He gazed comfortably around the lounge which might have been transported in its entirety from Calcutta—the tiger-skins, the rich fading furniture, the water colours of the Ganges. He envisaged it in a museum in a hundred years' time. The home of John Couldridge, surgeon, pioneer....

'What are you thinking, John?'

He was ashamed of himself. 'Nothing much,' he said. 'Nothing at all, really.'

'You're lying, John Couldridge.'

'All right then—I was thinking that perhaps we should have

an early night.'

She sighed happily. 'As I said—the way we work it we'll always have an infant crawling about our feet. But hell, who cares?'

2

FOR three weeks Couldridge searched for a suitable donor. He found several but they all refused—or their next-of-kin refused. Convincing them of the inevitability of death without emphasising its immediacy was the most difficult task: he was there to cure them not to anticipate their demise. Even the Hindus who professed indifference to mortal life objected to his presumption. There were angry scenes, tearful scenes, threatening scenes.

Soon the European doctors heard about his quest. They held a meeting at Dr Emmerson's house and Couldridge was summoned to attend. He ignored the summons. He later received a letter signed by Emmerson on behalf of them all deploring his intentions. Couldridge didn't reply. He suspected that they were delaying taking any action until the result of the operation was known.

One day when he was relaxing with Joanne after an abortive day's search he picked up a copy of *The Lancet* and read a paper by Nesfield about a surgical cure for deafness. A few days later he received a letter from a friend in London telling him that Nesfield had been asked to resign from the Bethnal Green hospital where he was ophthalmic surgeon because, according to Couldridge's friend, the medical committee had decided that an eye surgeon had no right to pronounce upon surgery of the ears. But subsequently he had been vindicated.

Couldridge folded up the letter and said: 'I still find it difficult to believe that doctors can be so petty. When you're young you never suspect it. You know pettiness exists among writers, poets, lawyers, civil servants. But not somehow among doctors. You don't actually sit down and think, "Doctors are above this sort of thing". The possibility is too remote for that. You think of them like priests, like parents.'

Joanne said: 'I shouldn't have thought you found it difficult any more. Not after Buckingham, Little and Emmerson.'

Couldridge stared into the dry garden where the nurse sat beside their son who was incredulously discovering and examining his hands. Bolting roses and tired delphiniums waited for the rain.

'I know I shouldn't find it difficult,' he said. 'But I still do. And I wonder at the motives of such men.'

'Try jealousy,' Joanne said. She was settled comfortably in an easy chair embroidering a tablecloth—she the girl who had once blackened her face and ridden through Pathan territory.

'Perhaps. But at this moment Emmerson is probably accusing me of ambition. Perhaps ambition is just as bad as jealousy in medicine.' He looked hopefully at Joanne.

'Perhaps,' she said.

'You weren't supposed to say that.'

'I know I wasn't.' She finished sewing a yellow silk petal on a daisy. 'And you shouldn't fish for compliments.'

'But do you think I'm ambitious?'

'Sure you're ambitious. But you're giving the word an unpleasant meaning. There's nothing wrong with ambition: without it there wouldn't be any achievement.' She looked at him fondly. 'In any case whether or not I say you're ambitious it won't make the slightest bit of difference to what you do.'

Next day Couldridge found his donor. She was a youngish woman—a Sikh who had once been a schoolteacher and was dying from a heart condition. A pious woman who had been an invalid for ten years. Couldridge examined her eyes and found that the tissue was in perfect condition. He wondered how to make his request with its morbid implications. He first

243

approached her husband, a small sad man whom a turban did not suit.

The husband said: 'If my wife can help to give sight to others then you have my permission. But first you must ask her. I cannot allow anything to be done to her body if she has not given permission before death.' He sat cross-legged on a mattress in a corner of their hot, clean home; subdued and fatalistic.

'How can I ask her? I cannot anticipate her death. I am supposed to be here to help her to live.'

'You must be brave,' said the little Sikh, like a doctor talking to a patient.

But his wife said: 'The doctor need not be brave. I agree to his request.'

Couldridge turned to the woman in the doorway. 'You shouldn't have come in here,' he said. 'You should be lying down.'

'Does it matter, doctor?'

'Of course it matters.'

She smiled and shook her head. 'I do not think so. I have not much longer to live. I do not think that a day or two matters when there is no longer any hope left.'

'There is always hope,' Couldridge said. 'There is hope until the moment of death. Now please lie down again on your bed.'

From the bed she said: 'I feel sorry for you, doctor.'

'Why?' he said. He was ashamed of himself and his motives and he was glad Bose was not present.

'Because you have a conflict inside you. One part of you wants to keep me alive, the other wants me dead.'

'You mustn't say that.'

'But it's true, isn't it? If I live then you will not be able to operate on this poor girl's eyes.' She waved aside his protests. 'Do not deny it—I heard what you were saying to my husband.'

'It is only true that I want to help this girl if ... when you die. But I would rather that you lived.' This, he thought, was true; his voice gained strength. 'You will probably live for a long while yet.'

She shook her head. 'I do not think so. I have been an invalid too long. I am tired of this life.'

'You shouldn't say that.'

'Why not, doctor? It is true. For a long time now I have been lying here occasionally walking from one room to another. Now I find that I have a use—if not in life then in death.'

Coulridge wiped the sweat from his face. He was not too much a man of science to believe that factors other than physical deterioration could hasten death. If this woman willed herself to die because of what he had told her then he was responsible for her death.

'You mustn't talk like that,' he said weakly.

'I am sorry. I see that I grieve you. Do not be afraid, doctor. I know that you are trying to do what is right. Perhaps one day the world will be grateful to you. And perhaps they will even remember the person who helped you.'

Couldridge held her hand and squeezed it. 'You're not going to die,' he said.

'I am,' she said. 'But perhaps that girl will be able to see again.'

Couldridge's next action appalled him. Despite his remorse and compassion for the woman he asked the husband if he would sign a statement confirming that he and his wife had agreed that an operation could be performed on her eyes after her death. The husband agreed but Couldridge thought he detected cynicism in his voice.

Couldridge said: 'Let's hope that she will not die.'

The husband said: 'Do you hope that, Dr Couldridge?'

'Of course I do,' Couldridge said.

And he hastened from the house bewildered by his conflicting emotions, frightened by the cold, sharp determination that was never deviated. A black shark-fin knifing through the seas of compassion.

3

COULDRIDGE worked with speed and precision immediately he heard that the woman had died. He removed the donor material within two hours of her death and stored it in liquid paraffin at a temperature of two degrees centigrade. Then he collected the girl from the village and brought her back to the clinic where she stayed the night. He decided to operate next morning because, even though Magitot and others had proved that the donor eye could be preserved for eight days, he believed that the graft stood more chance if the corneal tissue were used as soon as possible.

That night he sat in his consulting room and re-read his books about the progress of keratoplasty from the time of de Quengsy in the 18th century. The progress, he thought, had been very slow when you considered that as long ago as 1879 Wolfe had carried out the first corneal graft in Scotland. And as far back as 1841 Marcus had stated the conditions necessary for a successful transplant—exact correspondence in the shape of the graft, rapid transference with quick fixation, and precautions to ensure that there was no loss of the internal structures of the eyeball. The advice had not changed radically. The introductions of general anaesthetics and the isolation of cocaine had aided the ophthalmologists; they now used trephines and corneal splints and grafts from humans rather than animals. But surgeons must have been aware of the possibilities of grafting tissue from the dead for decades. Had they really been too scared of public reaction to implement their knowledge? In particular the British seemed to have been over-cautious: in between 1872, when Henry Power from Barts published his last work, until 1922, when Tudor Thomas expressed his views, there had not been a single article in the literature of of British ophthalmology on corneal grafts.

Now, after the long maturing process, the time had come to confound prejudice. In a way Couldridge envied the Russians who were making rapid advancements in the practice of grafting eye tissue from the dead because they wouldn't meet opposition: in a way he didn't because he relished the challenge from the moralists. At 11 p.m. he put away his books because he wanted to be rested for the operation.

Early next morning he visited the girl and administered eserine drops to contract the pupil of the eye. He had decided to give the girl a general anaesthetic and in his tortuous Hindi he tried to explain to her that she would lose consciousness and that when she awoke the operation would be over. He warned her about the danger of touching the eye afterwards; later he prepared an injection to make sure that on her return to consciousness there would be no spasm of the eyelids.

At 8 a.m. Bose and a middle-aged sister from the hospital—the only member of its staff who would acknowledge Couldridge as a surgeon—arrived at the clinic. They scrubbed up at a sink in the theatre and painted their hands with iodine. Then the sister, who according to Joanne admired Couldridge in more than a professional sense, laid out the sterilised instruments. Cataract knives, scalpels, scissors, trephine, probes and forceps. Above the fierce lights and fan scythed away at the heavy air.

Couldridge saw Bose looking at the liquid paraffin and said: 'I suppose you think this is a bit ghoulish.'

'Not particularly,' Bose said. 'Just a little unorthodox.'

'Chloroform was unorthodox when Simpson first introduced it.'

'I don't think the comparison is quite valid.'

Couldridge turned to the sister, a sturdy, greying-haired woman whom everyone described as sensible—a description which she hated. 'What do you think, Miss Benson?'

She looked at him with unconcealed admiration and affection. 'I can't see anything ghoulish in it,' she said. 'Not if we're going to help this poor girl to see properly again.'

'There you are,' Couldridge said to Bose.

Bose shrugged. 'Shouldn't we start as soon as possible—while the woman's tissue is still alive? If it's alive now, that is.'

'It should be. It stays alive for eight days or more.'

'If you say so. If you believe that tissue is really alive after the heart has stopped beating.'

'There's no reason why it shouldn't be.'

'Then how do you know the exact moment when such tissue dies?'

'Frankly I don't,' Couldridge said. 'But I'm surprised you haven't asked the other question.'

'What other question?' Bose looked surprised that there was something that he had forgotten to ask.

'I'm surprised you haven't asked how I knew at what precise moment the woman was dead. In other words is it possible that I could have removed the eye while she was still alive?'

'I presume you knew she was dead because her heart had stopped beating.'

'Yes,' Couldridge said. 'I presumed she was dead. But do any of us really know that a human being is dead because the heart has stopped beating? Is the mind necessarily dead? Is the soul dead? What about her soul, Bose?'

Bose's expression was momentarily uneasy. 'I don't know about her soul,' he said. 'I'm a doctor, not a man of religion.'

'So am I,' Couldridge said. 'So am I.' Sweat was already beading his forehead. He turned to Miss Benson. 'You'll have to keep mopping me,' he said. 'We don't want sweat dropping in the girl's eye.'

'Of course, Dr Couldridge.' She looked pleased at the prospect.

He went into his consulting room where the girl was sitting quietly on the edge of his leather couch. She was trembling with fear. 'We're ready now,' he said. She looked at him uncomprehendingly with her brown scarred eyes.

Bose joined them and translated.

Couldridge said: 'Just make sure that she hasn't eaten any-thing. I know we told her not to but you can't be too sure. We want as little disturbance as possible if this graft is to take.'

Bose spoke to her again and she shook her head. He said: 'She says she hasn't eaten since this time yesterday.'

'Has she brought the affidavit signed by her parents authoris-ing me to carry out this operation?'

'She says she has.'

'Then we'd better start. Tell her not to worry. She will feel nothing. When she wakes up her eyes will be covered. Tell her not to touch them or rub them. I've already told her but I'm not sure whether she understood. And tell her that, when I finally take the dressings off in about a fortnight, we hope that she will be able to see through one eye.'

'Only hope?'

'Only hope. That's all it ever is, Bose. You know that.'

Bose spoke to the girl again. She nodded and smiled hesi-tantly in Couldridge's direction.

Couldridge said: 'Are her parents here?'

'They certainly are,' Bose said. 'They're waiting in the house with Joanne.

'Like vultures?'

'Like parents,' Bose said.

After Miss Benson had dressed her in a gown the girl lay down on the operating table and Couldridge made his last examination of the eye. The pupil was contracted and he had already verified that the conjunctival sac was free of pathogenic organisms.

Bose administered the anaesthetic.

When the girl was fully anaesthetised Couldridge asked Miss Benson for the first instrument—a pair of scissors with which to cut the eyelashes. 'This is it, Bose,' he said. 'Wish me luck.'

'I wish the girl luck,' Bose said.

'You haven't previously shown much interest in the girl.'

He asked Miss Benson for a suturing needle and sutured the eyelids so that the eye was bared. Then he put sutures under the four recti muscles to control the eye, and marked the cornea with a Graefe knife at the point where the graft was to be inserted.

He worked with complete absorption, occasionally calling for instruments and asking Miss Benson to swab the sweat from his forehead.

After marking the cornea he loosely inserted two silk mattress sutures in the cornea which were subsequently to hold the graft in place. Then he turned his attention to the donor eye.

'Everything all right?' Bose said.

'So far,' Couldridge said. He paused and looked at his two assistants, their eyes watchful above their masks. Miss Benson nodded reassuringly. The only sounds were the swishing of the fan and the regular breathing of the girl.

Couldridge removed the cornea from the donor eye, washed it in saline solution and placed it on a bed of paraffin wax already moulded to the curve of the cornea. Then he punched out the graft.

He said to Bose: 'I had thought of performing a lamellar graft instead of a penetrating because of the girl's age.'

Bose's eyes looked up from above the mask. 'Then why didn't you?'

Couldridge shrugged. 'They've never really been considered practicable since Von Hippel. And you know I always like to conform...' He was, he knew, delaying the final irrevocable incision on the girl's eye.

He looked down at the brown sutured eye. One eye, one girl. Seven years ago it had been estimated that there were 2,390,000 blind people in India. For a moment Couldridge imagined that he could see trust in the scarred eye with the pinpoint pupil. But that was succumbing to sentiment—the only quality that all blind people detested. That and being discussed as if they weren't present—as if they were also deaf.

He took a 5 m.m. trephine. Sweat was again running down his forehead. 'Bose,' he said, 'see if you can speed up that bloody fan.' The fan rotated quicker and Miss Benson pressed a piece of lint against his forehead. Now there could be no more delays.

He applied the trephine, remembering that only his sensitivity of touch would determine when he reached Descemet's membrane. The eye no longer seemed to be part of the girl: it was impersonal—a tough ball of muscle, fibrous tissue, liquid and nerve cells. And he was mending it. He forgot the girl, forgot that he was trying to restore eyesight: he was merely repairing the most beautiful organ of the body.

When the bed for the graft with its shelving margins was ready he removed the sutures from under the recti muscles.

'Nearly done,' he said. No one answered.

He placed the plug from the donor cornea into the bed in the girl's eye and tied the cobweb sutures over it. 'Finished,' he said. His eyes stung and he could taste blood where he had bitten the inside of his mouth.

He released the eyelids and closed the eye. He placed tulle gras dressings and eye-pads over both eyes. Then he went into the consulting room and lay on the couch. The nervous tension faded and exhaustion settled throughout his body; he closed his eyes. It would be a long time before they knew whether the operation had been successful.

Bose said: 'She's beginning to come round. She will be sick, I expect.'

Couldridge didn't open his eyes. 'Be very gentle. Try and stop her from vomiting because the movement might shift the graft.'

A wave of sleep passed over him; he jerked and was awake again. 'When she's ready we'll put her on a stretcher and take her into the house—Joanne has made up a bed for her there.'

The second wave of sleep drowned him. Vaguely he heard Bose's voice and the girl moaning. He held a scalpel in his hand and he was slashing away at brown reproachful eyes

251

lying on slabs. Two strokes to each so that they fell into four quarters. The scalpel became a sword and he was jousting with Emmerson. Emmerson's face dissolved into the brown dangerous features of Bose. Couldridge knew that he was fighting for his life. Bose had him against the wall, scalpel at his throat. Couldridge jerked again and awoke to find Bose bending over him. Bose said: 'The girl is conscious now.'

She lay on the operating table without moving. A small frown on her smooth brown forehead. Couldridge held her hand. 'How does she feel?' he said.

'She is all right. Just as one would expect a girl to be coming out of general anaesthetic.'

'Is she in any pain?'

'She says not. But she is very frightened.'

'Tell her not to worry. We will look after her.'

'She thinks she may lose her eye.'

'Her eyesight in that eye can be no worse than it was before. She was practically blind.'

Couldridge gently touched the dressings. 'We'll leave them like that for forty-eight hours,' he said. 'Let's pray that she doesn't develop a cough.' He turned to Miss Benson. 'Thank you,' he said. 'You were wonderful. I hope it won't affect your position at the hospital.'

'I don't care if it does,' she said. 'Being here today has been the most wonderful experience of my whole career.'

He said to Bose: 'Let's put her on a stretcher then and confront her parents.'

Her father was sitting in the lounge with Joanne.

Couldridge said: 'Where's the mother?'

Joanne said: 'She was dispatched home. Apparently she shouldn't have been here anyway. It wasn't her place. How is the girl?'

'She's all right. We shan't know the result of the operation for a long time yet.'

They lifted the girl on to a bed in a spare room. A fan moved gently and the breeze ruffled yellow curtains printed with blue flowers.

Couldridge pointed at the curtains and said: 'Perhaps she will be able to see those soon.'

Joanne nodded. 'I'm sure she will. But I think her father is a bit upset about something.'

Couldridge looked at the frail avaricious Indian with the bandy legs and said to Bose: 'Ask him what he wants.'

The father talked excitedly mixing servility with histrionic grief and bursts of anger. He appeared to be incoherent until his preamble reached its point—money. Then his voice became sharp and incisive.

Bose said: 'He wants more money.'

'What the hell for?'

'He says he didn't realise his daughter was going to kept away from him like this. He says his wife is sick and he has no one to look after his house. He wants money to recompense him for his loss.'

'Tell him to go and ...' He stopped himself because Joanne was there. 'Tell him he's had all the money he's going to get. We shan't keep the girl here for very long. Then he can have her back. She could hardly see before so he can't claim that he's suffered any loss there.'

'It's not as easy as that,' Bose said.

'What the hell do you mean?'

'He is very cunning. He knows that there was something very unusual about this operation. I think that he has been finding out what other white men think about the use of tissue from a dead woman.'

'You mean he's trying to blackmail me?'

'I think it is something like that,' Bose said.

'Just how does he think he can blackmail me?'

Bose's face was impassive. 'I think he would spread rumours that you had taken the girl and operated on her without his permission.'

'But I have a signed affidavit from him.'

'I know.' Bose's hand strayed to the patch of white hair. But think what damage he could do. First the rumours that would have to be investigated. Perhaps even by the police. They would vindicate you, it is true. But only up to a point because then the information would be made public that you had paid for the girl—almost as if she were a guinea pig—because he made a duplicate of the receipt.'

Couldridge smashed his fist down on the table. 'Paid for her, for Christ's sake? I'm curing her of blindness, am I not?'

'I think you will agree that it is unusual for a doctor to pay a patient.'

Couldridge kicked a chair. 'Are you with me or against me, Bose?'

'I am neither. You must know that by now. Once I was with you. Once we were together. Now I do my job and you pay me. It is as simple as that.'

'It shouldn't be as simple as that.'

'You have only yourself to blame. You are blind to everything except your work. A form of selfishness, perhaps?'

The girl's father launched another speech on to the hallowed subject of money.

Bose said: 'He is beginning to get more threatening.'

Couldridge said: 'If I give him more money then it will be more evidence against me.'

'There will be no evidence that you have given *more* money. But it will keep him quiet while the girl recovers.'

Joanne came in from the spare room. 'What's going on? Chairs being kicked, voices raised in anger. I thought the patient was supposed to convalesce in peace and quiet?'

Couldridge said: 'I'm being blackmailed.' He sat down on the couch and stuck out his long legs.

'I thought you might be,' she said. 'What is he threatening to do?'

Couldridge told her.

'Does he want much?'

'I don't know. The whole thing disgusts me. I'm giving his daughter a chance of recovering her sight and all he can think

254

about is depositing a few more rupees in the bloody bank.'

'If it's only a few then I think we should pay him.' She turned to Bose. 'Does he want much?'

'Not much,' Bose said. 'It is a question of principle with him. He is a money-lender after all. He has suddenly realised that there is a way open to him of making more money. He would consider it dishonourable if he did not take advantage of this opening.'

'And I shall feel dishonourable if I don't give him a kick up the arse in a minute.'

'Why Dr Couldridge,' Joanne said. 'What a delightful bedside manner you have.' She laughed; then Couldridge laughed. Bose and the money-lender waited. 'Here,' Joanne said, 'I'll settle this question of honour.' She picked up her handbag and gave the father some money. He counted it, smiled and departed without speaking again to his daughter.

'Did you give him much?' Couldridge asked.

'Never you mind.'

They went into the other room to see how the girl was. But she was asleep with a pattern of liquid sunshine, filtered through leaves outside the window, playing on her face.

4

SEVERAL people in and around Lahore waited impatiently to hear the outcome of the operation.

While he paced the house and garden Couldridge considered the many complications that could follow the transplant. Of these the greatest threat was vasularisation. And the most unfortunate was a cataract caused by damage to the lens during the operation. In addition to the complications from known causes there were the grafts that clouded for no apparent reason: in these cases the only possible treatment was another graft—and Couldridge knew that this was out of the question.

Forty-eight hours after the operation he dressed the sutured eye. The graft was clear beneath the spider-legs of the mattress stitches, but Couldridge knew that it was far too early to ascertain whether the operation had been successful. Before applying the dressing he cleared the mucus from the cornea and took cultures from the conjunctival sac.

Among the others waiting anxiously for the verdict on the graft were Emmerson and the other doctors. Each tried to convince the other that he hoped for success because he was dedicated to healing; but each talked more about irresponsibility than surgical progress.

Emmerson betrayed his true feelings more transparently than the others. And when he was alone with his wife he didn't bother to maintain the hypocrisy. 'They won't like it in London,' he said. 'Mark my words.'

His wife sat in front of the dressing table applying rouge to her plump cheeks. 'I don't know why you let him get away with it. Most unethical I should say. And the way he talked to you that day at our house. No respect at all.'

Emmerson tied his bow tie with neat movements. 'It will only become unethical if the operation fails. He is after all trying to cure the girl.'

'So he says.' She clipped a gold bracelet around her fat wrist with difficulty. 'I think he's just using that girl as a guinea pig.' She paused, momentarily hushed by the astuteness of her next thought. 'Just because she's a poor Indian girl.'

'Come now Mollie,' Emmerson said, well pleased with his wife's observation. 'I don't think we can hold that against him.'

'He's not like you and I,' his wife said. 'He was born out here remember. That's the way he would think about an Indian.'

'If the operation is a failure then we'll all have to get together and get in touch with the authorities in London. It's our duty.'

'I should do it anyway,' his wife said. 'It's no more than he

256

deserves—living off that Yankee wife of his. I think it's disgraceful. You would think he had more pride. I hope that the operation is a failure. Not that I wish the girl any harm. But any other guinea pigs he tries to get his hands on should be safeguarded.'

Emmerson completed his bow and regarded its neatness with pride. He slipped on a white dinner jacket as creaseless as when it had first been made. 'I rather think I agree with you,' he said. 'But don't repeat that in company. However, you're quite right—the public has a right to be protected from doctors like him. And he can't say that I didn't try to warn him. Anyway I think this conversation is pretty academic because I can't see that there's much hope of the operation succeeding. Transplanting tissue from a dead eye. What next I wonder? I shouldn't be surprised if he doesn't imagine that one day surgeons will be trying to transplant human hearts.' He tucked a silk handkerchief into his breast pocket. 'The fellow's a butcher and a crank, not a doctor.'

'I hear that he paid the girl's father money to allow him to perform the operation.'

'I heard that too—but we can't prove it.'

'I hear that there may be some sort of document in existence that proves he paid money. His Yankee wife's money, of course.'

'Is there?' said Emmerson hopefully. 'I hadn't heard that.'

At dinner that night he passed on the information to two other doctors and their wives. Over port, while their wives chattered in the lounge, the doctors discussed the ramifications of Couldridge's initiative. And with solemnity and frank hypocrisy each expressed the hope that the operation would succeed.

The girl's father also waited impatiently for the verdict. If his daughter's eyesight was not restored then there would be fresh material for blackmail: if the eyesight was restored then he would have to find fresh ways of extracting money from Couldridge. 'When?' he kept asking Couldridge through Bose. 'When will I know whether my little girl will be able to see again?'

257

'Tell him soon enough,' Couldridge said. 'Tell him anything but keep him quiet.'

In the house he snapped at Joanne and grumbled at his son crawling around the floor. Joanne didn't seem to mind. 'It will be all right,' she said. 'I know it will.'

'You have more trust in me than I have.'

'You're a fine surgeon,' she said. 'In any case other corneal grafts have worked. Why shouldn't yours?'

'The percentage of successes is still low,' he said. 'Even when surgeons aren't using tissue from the dead.'

The person involved who seemed to worry the least was the patient. A new serenity had dawned on her. She smiled at Couldridge when he went to her bedside and invited him to sit down. Suddenly she was important and she acted like a pregnant woman who is loved.

Every day he dressed the sutured eye. But he never asked the girl how much she could see or if she could see at all. For one thing, he feared the answer; for another, she would not have been able to discern much in the glare of the lamp. The graft still looked clear and healthy but that didn't prove that it had taken.

On the fourteenth day he removed the sutures under local anaesthetic. He knew then that the graft had taken: there remained the final test—her eyesight.

The sun was burning away the morning mists as he took her into the consulting room. 'The time has come,' he said to Bose and Joanne. He felt more like a conjuror than a surgeon.

He took her into the surgery and made her sit on the couch. 'Now,' he said to Bose. Very gently Bose removed the eye-pad from the grafted eye.

'Tell her to open her eye,' Couldridge said. He noticed that her knuckles were clenched tight and sweat was beading her forehead. There was no movement from her eye.

'Open your eye,' he said in his slow Hindi.

Her lips trembled. Then the eyelid raised and he gazed into the deep brown iris and the pupil already contracting from the new light. He held up a yellow rose in front of her. 'Ask her what colour this is.'

The girl spoke. Couldridge said: 'What did she say?'

'She said it was yellow.'

Couldridge said: 'Ask her what it is.'

'She says it's a rose.'

Couldridge walked ten paces away. 'Can she see it now?'

Bose said: 'She says she can see it. She says it's a yellow rose and it's beautiful.'

Couldridge nodded and because the tears were starting in his own eyes he walked into the operating theatre. Joanne joined him. 'She said it was a very beautiful yellow rose,' Couldridge said.

'It is,' she said.

5

DURING the next six months John Couldridge discovered that the medical authorities of London, New York, Paris, Berlin were not particularly interested in the success of his operation.

He submitted papers to several medical journals; each was rejected. One editor pointed out that many other surgeons were pursuing similar lines of research and it would not be in the best interests of the development of surgical techniques to publicise one isolated operation—but perhaps he would like to contribute to a general assessment of corneal surgery in the future. Another, with judicious observance of the laws of libel, suggested obliquely that Couldridge may have acted irresponsibly in performing such an operation without consulting other ophthalmic authorities. Another returned the manuscript with a printed rejection slip. No one commented on the success of the operation.

Couldridge admitted to himself at this stage that he craved recognition. The fact that he had restored a girl's sight and had probably contributed to the progress of medicine was not enough. The knowledge saddened him but at the same time dispelled much of his worry about his motives. After all pioneering instincts and a desire for recognition were not incompatible. Couldridge was not aware that he was also in danger of adopting the guise of a martyr.

As the manuscripts returned he reminded Joanne that the elders of medicine had always belittled the achievements of crusading doctors. Robert Koch had been reprimanded instead of being praised because he hadn't published his findings through the proper channels—and had even injected himself with tuberculosis vaccine to prove his theories.

Joanne said: 'You can hardly operate on your own eye.'

The local doctors were non-committal. The success of the operation had disrupted their plans to disgrace Couldridge and sharpened their spite. So they continued to ostracise him and wait for him to make a mistake. He made one within the year. He wrongly diagnosed an illness; but they could do nothing about it because a diagnostic mistake was not necessarily irresponsible and was certainly not a breach of ethics. The patient was Couldridge's elder son.

The boy and his sister arrived in Lahore for the summer holiday when Couldridge was at the height of his martyrdom and searching for another patient willing to undergo a corneal transplant, and another donor. He greeted his children with love and pleasure and entertained them for two or three days. But gradually he retired into his surgery for longer and longer periods.

One evening Joanne came to the consulting room when he was composing a letter to 'The Lancet'.

Joanne said: 'John, could you come and have a look at Neville. He's got stomach pains and a touch of diarrhoea.'

Couldridge looked up from his desk and said: 'All right, I'll come over in a minute.'

A small frown creased Joanne's forehead. 'Can't you come now? It's time he was asleep.'

'All right. I'll be over in a minute. I told him not to eat that mango.' He put down his pen. 'If I successfully pull off one more corneal transplant I don't see how they can ignore me any longer.'

'No,' she said. 'I don't see how they can.' She stood looking at him, the crease still on her forehead.

'I found another girl today with scarring and vascularisation of the cornea.'

'I sometimes wish,' Joanne said, 'that the operation had been a failure.'

'What the hell do you mean?'

She turned to the door. 'I didn't really mean that. I'm glad that poor girl can see.'

'I should bloody well hope so. What's come over you, Joanne?'

'I don't know,' she said. 'But whatever it is you would never be able to diagnose it.' She closed the door.

Couldridge stared after her for a few moments, then picked up his pen and started writing again. It was fifteen minutes before he remembered his son.

Neville was tall and very thin. But, like his father, he had a broad bone structure which would be clothed with sufficient muscle and flesh when he was older. He was fourteen and was trying to summon the courage to tell his father that he hated England and the school where he was boarded. Now his forehead was moist and his hands were clasped across his thin abdomen. At his boarding school they had taught him not to complain about pain.

'How bad is it?' Couldridge asked.

'Not too bad.' Neville smiled at his father from his bed.

Couldridge took his temperature. 'Just below normal,' he said. 'Nothing to worry about there.' He took the boy's pulse and felt his abdomen. 'Have you been sick?'

'No. In any case I didn't want to disturb you. It was mother who decided to fetch you. It's nothing really—that wretched

261

mango that you advised me not to eat, I expect. It *was* a bit rotten.'

Couldridge nodded. 'Nothing from the other end?'

'From the other end?'

'You haven't had any diarrhoea?'

Neville said in an embarrassed voice: 'Nothing to speak of.'

'I'll mix you up some medicine. You'll be as right as rain tomorrow.'

Later on the verandah Couldridge said: 'If I can persuade the parents of that girl to permit the operation then I must find another donor immediately.'

Joanne said: 'How's Neville?'

'He's all right. Gyppy tummy. We've all had it from time to time—especially when we're fresh out from England.'

'He seems very restless. He keeps saying he isn't in pain but I'm sure he is. His hands keep straying down to his stomach.'

'Has he drunk the medicine I gave him?'

'Yes, but I think he brought it up again.'

'Don't worry,' Couldridge said.

But next day the boy was worse and Couldridge asked Bose to examine him.

Afterwards Bose said: 'You must know what's the matter with him.'

'I thought it was mild dysentery yesterday,' Couldridge said.

'I may be wrong,' Bose said. 'And after all you're the expert. But I think your son is suffering from cholera.'

'Oh God,' Couldridge said.

'Didn't you see the stools?'

Couldridge shook his head. 'He said there was nothing to speak of.'

'He meant that it was almost clear fluid. But he was too embarrassed to elaborate.'

'My own son too embarrassed?'

'Yes,' Bose said, 'your own son.'

'Oh God,' Couldridge said again.

He went back into the bedroom and saw with sudden clarity

all the early symptoms of the disease that he had studied for so long. 'How do you feel?' he said.

'Not too good.' The boy's skin was cold and clammy—there was no mistake. 'And I feel so terribly thirsty. And I get these awful pains every time I go to the lavatory.'

Couldridge said: 'Don't worry. You'll be all right soon. A few pills and medicine will put you on your feet again.'

Outside the room Bose said: 'We'd better get him into hospital.'

'And have him treated by the likes of Emmerson? No bloody fear.'

'I really think you should get him to hospital,' Bose said.

'And you can mind your own business,' Couldridge said.

Bose's features tightened. 'I was only giving you good medical advice.'

'I'm sorry,' Couldridge said. 'You're right of course. But I'm not having him treated by those doctors in town. Especially when they realise he's my son.'

Bose said: 'I do not think they would be quite as heartless as that.'

'Maybe not. But I'm not risking it.'

Joanne came into the lounge and said: 'Well, how's the patient?'

Couldridge stared out into the garden. 'I made a wrong diagnosis,' he said.

'What's wrong with him?' Fear sharpened her voice.

'We think he may have a cholera. But it's not as bad as it sounds. We've caught it early.'

She ran to the bedroom and they heard her talking to the boy. When she came out she said: 'You told me it was a stomach upset.'

'I know,' he said. 'I made a mistake.'

'Made a mistake? With your own son? You could hardly be bothered to look at him.'

'That's not true,' he said.

'Oh yes it is. You were much too occupied with your damned

263

letter to "The Lancet". Much too occupied with yourself to give a damn about your son.'

'Don't talk like that,' he said. 'I was wrong. I admit it. But he's not going to die.'

The tears slid down her cheeks. She tried to speak again but the words were drowned and she went on to the verandah.

Couldridge said to Bose: 'What do you think the chances are?'

'He's a strong healthy boy,' Bose said. 'But you should know more about the chances of survival with cholera than me.'

'I'm too involved,' Couldridge said.

They fixed up the summerhouse as a sickroom and scrubbed it with disinfectant. They administered hypertonic saline and oral permanganate and waited while the boy's body mustered all its resistance to fight the crescent-shaped bacilli which Couldridge had once nourished on beef broth and blood serum jelly.

But Neville visibly weakened as the fluid poured out of him and his body began to dehydrate. And it always seemed that more fluid was escaping than the volume of saline they were able to introduce into his system. His thirst was terrible, his pulse was weak and his eyes were sunken. But, as Couldridge knew, one of the worst aspects of the disease was the cold clinical awareness of the patient to his plight: there was no escape in fevered dreams: just detached observation of physical deterioration.

Occasionally Neville talked about his school. Couldridge imagined its bleak disciplines so alien to a boy nurtured among the warm muddles of India and promised his son that he need not return. One night when the air outside was alive with glow-worms and the stars were soft and bright Couldridge sensed that his son had conquered the first stage of the disease. His forehead was warmer, his pulse was stronger. Joanne joined Couldridge at the bedside and he told her to wait on the verandah. Then Bose came to the bedside and Couldridge joined Joanne. But their love for each other which should have blended with their love for their son and strengthened their courage had faded since

Neville's illness. Couldridge tried to take her hand but she moved it. 'He'll be all right,' he said.

'I've been praying,' she said. 'Just now in the bedroom. Do you think God gets tired of people who only pray when they're in trouble?'

'I don't know,' he said.

'I would,' she said. In the bedroom behind them their daughter walked around restlessly, infected with adult fear.

'I should have made a more thorough examination,' Couldridge said. 'But an earlier diagnosis wouldn't have made much difference. I've done my best for him.'

'I should hope you have,' Joanne said. 'He is your son.'

'Don't punish me,' he said. 'There isn't any point.'

'Have you prayed?'

'I'm not a religious man.'

'Don't you think it's still worth a try?—even if you don't believe.'

'I've never prayed,' he said. 'I'm a doctor.'

'What has that got to do with it?' she said. 'I think you should pray. Millions of people believe that their prayers are answered. Yours might be even if you don't believe.'

'All right,' he said, 'I'll pray.' He went into their bedroom, knelt beside the bed and prayed to God to whom he had not spoken since he was a child. To God, to Allah, to Krishna. 'Whatever God a man worships, it is I who answer the prayer.'

He returned to the verandah and said: 'I prayed.'

'So did I,' she said. 'While you were in the bedroom.'

'He will be all right,' Couldridge said. But he knew that there was still doubt. 'It's difficult,' he said, 'for a doctor to accept that God is really the healer.'

'Does it matter?' she said. 'All that matters is that our son gets well again.'

They saw the door of the summerhouse open. Bose came striding across the lawn and, as he climbed the wooden steps to the verandah, they searched his dark face for his verdict. But his features told them nothing—they never did.

265

Couldridge said: 'Well?'

'He's in the reaction stage,' Bose said. 'He has a slight temperature. His pulse has recovered and his bile has reappeared.'

'Thank God,' Couldridge said.

Joanne said: 'What does it mean?'

'It means that he's over the worst. The reaction stage is still serious. There are certain complications which can occur. And even when he's over this stage he mustn't sit up too quickly because there is a danger of cardiac failure. But Bose and I can handle all that. He's going to be all right.'

'Thank God,' Joanne said. She paused. 'And I mean just that.' Then she went into the house to tell their daughter that her brother was going to be all right.

6

FOR several months John Couldridge abandoned his search for eye donors. He left the surgery to Bose, he enjoyed the companionship of his children, and he waited for his wife to forgive him. But the gentleness and passion seemed to have left their marriage. They made love quickly and fiercely, but there was no burgeoning of feeling, no entwined aftermath: they made love because they were married. She never mentioned his mistake over their son's illness, but the reproach was always there. To John Couldridge, physician, it seemed as if she were experiencing a premature menopause: to John Couldridge husband and lover it seemed as if their long courtship was finally, unbelievably, over.

Sometimes as he went on his rounds or went riding with his son in the dusty countryside or wandered around the scented garden in the evening, he wondered who had saved his son.

Because if it was God then there seemed little point in any research. He knew all the arguments against such thinking— that as a pioneering surgeon he was acting for God, that without the drugs discovered by his predecessors his son would surely have died. But the sudden suspicion of divine guidance removed his incentive. If he hadn't prayed that evening would his son still be alive?

Some of Couldridge's worry was diverted to the civil problems of India. Little of the great new freedom which Indians had expected as a reward for fighting for Britain in the Great War had materialised and Mahatma Gandhi's civil disobedience campaign had started. There were mass strikes, boycotts of British goods, riots and assassination attempts. And there was Government retaliation: in less than one year 103 people were killed, 420 injured and 60,000 imprisoned. And one of the Congress leaders, V. J. Patel, said that all hope of reconciling India with the British Empire had gone.

On one occasion Couldridge was called out to give medical help at a village where there had been a riot. It had started as a demonstration in front of the sub-district officer's bungalow. The officer had been unimpressed by the demands of the demonstrators and had continued with his fork lunch of fried fish, curried fowl, roast kid, and mango-fool which he had been giving for a handful of guests.

The Indians shouted and threw stones. The officer telephoned for troops encamped ten miles away and told one of his servants to serve brandy to anyone hardened enough to drink it in the heat of the day. The guests, two of them women, took their lead from the officer and chatted intently about the Kadir Cup, and about the bow-legged little trouble-maker Gandhi. Married at twelve, they said, pushed off a train at Pietermaritzburg by a guard; pity he hadn't fallen under the wheels, they said, and laughed anxiously. One American guest recalled that Gandhi had learned civil disobedience from the American hermit philosopher Henry Thoreau.

Outside the crowd paused and debated what to do as seconds

of mango fool were served. They were mostly Moslems, but a minority of Hindus committed to the non-violent policy of Satyagraha lurked at the back. The Moslems favoured razing the bungalow and butchering the occupants. The Hindus objected to violence but suggested that the courthouse to which the officer drove in his buggy once a week to dispense injustice should be burned down. Disagreement intensified engendering its own violence and saving the lives of the officer and his guests.

While Hindu and Moslem fought each other in the town the officer who was famed for his sartorial elegance and his dislike of Indians strolled through his garden to see if his four horses were safe. They were, but he found three of his servants hiding in the stables and chased them out. By this time two Indians were dead and half a dozen were injured and the troops were on the outskirts of the town.

The Muslims cried, 'Allah Ho Aklar' and the Hindus cried 'Har har Mahadio' and the troops charged. After the charge there were a dozen dead and about thirty wounded.

The sub-district officer informed his guests that there had been a small classic riot and he would have to leave them for a while. The Indians dispersed and set about trying to burn down each other's homes; by the end of the day there were 20 dead and 50 wounded. By then it was time for dinner in the sub-district officer's home and he apologised to his guests for the poor fare because his servants had not returned to prepare it.

Couldridge helped an Army doctor to treat the wounded. Skulls cracked by sticks and rifle butts, broken limbs, gaping flesh wounds caused by crude lead bullets that had spread on impact. He worked until he was exhausted; and yet for the first time since his son's illness he felt happy. The troops retired, the flames of the fires died, the sub-district officer made out a brief report and Couldridge departed reluctantly for Lahore.

He rode through the night against the advice of security officers and felt some of his confidence return as the night air flowed past his face like liquid. Once, just before dusk finally thickened into night, he saw a fire burning, heard the cries of a woman and smelled burning flesh. He slowed his horse because he knew that on the fire a Hindu widow was allowing herself to be burned to death. But the smell of roasting was strong and he knew that if he intervened the woman would suffer greater agonies before she finally died of shock and third degree burns.

He urged his horse on and considered the savagery, the muddle, the ignorance and the arrogance, of India; and the devotion that it perversely instilled into Europeans such as himself. An exhilaration concocted of the racing night, the straining sinews of his horses and the thud of the hoof-beats overcame him. He charged a village sleeping beneath the stars, galloped on through a wadi and only stopped when he realised that his horse needed a rest. As he stroked the horse's streaming flanks he decided that he would start looking for another eye donor. He rode on more slowly and fed and watered his horse in Lahore as the stars were retiring and the sky was turning green on the horizon.

Joanne was in bed. She turned to him, warm and incoherent, and allowed herself to be kissed. Then turned away and slept again. For the first time in his life John Couldridge thought, 'To hell with her'. Anyone could have made a wrong diagnosis and their son *had* lived. He smiled to himself and conceded that God might have aided and abetted in the boy's recovery.

He made himself some coffee and waited for the servants to materialise. He noticed an envelope on the table and opened it. It was from Charlotte Spenser and it confirmed his resolve to attempt another corneal transplant. To hell with Emmerson and his cronies. To hell with jealousy and medical protocol. To hell with everything except the sharp clean knife of surgical progress.

John Couldridge was cured.

7

JOANNE sliced the crown off her tiny egg and read the letter from Charlotte Spenser with care and interest. When she was half-way through she turned the eggshell upside down, smashed it with her spoon and said to her husband: 'I think poor old Charlotte has gone out of her cotton-picking mind.'

Couldridge said: 'I don't see why you should think that. Just because she has found someone who seems to have some faith in my ability as a surgeon.'

'Not just because of that,' Joanne said. She urged their two elder children to eat up their eggs. 'All this theosophy business. It's just plain crazy.'

'Theosophy started in the States,' Couldridge said.

'And why is she writing to you after all that awful affair? She should have more pride. She knows I can't stand her because of it. Perhaps she's on the booze again.'

Couldridge said: 'Do you have to?' He pointed at the children.

'Well, honestly,' Joanne said. 'You must admit it was a bit thick.'

'She wasn't well,' Couldridge said. 'You know she wasn't well.'

'And she's not much better now by the sound of it.'

The servant removed the eggs and Joanne buttered thick slices of grainy bread and regretted expressing her opinions of Charlotte. Just as she regretted—but could not melt—the frigidity of feeling towards her husband.

She knew she was being unfair. She knew that the wrong diagnosis of their son's illness was a mistake that any doctor could have made. But the sudden hatred that night of his consuming ambition—which she had previously condoned—had remained. It was as if it had been petrified in her soul by the grief and fear during the days of her son's illness. She had always maintained that there was nothing wrong with such ambition because it was the spearhead of achievement, but now it antagonised her. It was, she knew, unreasonable and it pained her because she had always revelled in the familiarity of their relationship, in the friendship, and in the physical love which they never tried to confuse with the spiritual: the act was gratification shared by two people who were attracted to each other—no more. There were many other aspects of love, and these they also possessed. But they had always agreed about the practical aspects of the procreative act. Now, because of that one mistake concerning their son, their love-making was intense and ugly. A sneeze of the loins. And with the disappearance of sexual understanding all other understanding had vanished too. It was, she knew, her fault; but there was nothing she could do about it. Except wait for an act, a gesture, a consideration, that would dispel the hostility.

She remembered the moment she had found Charlotte Spenser in her husband's arms, small bruised breasts pressed against his chest. It had been more farcical than anything else, except that Charlotte was a figure of tragedy.

She said: 'I'm sorry about Charlotte—I didn't really mean it.'

Their son said: 'Are you talking about Major Spenser's wife?'

Couldridge said: 'Go into the garden and play with your sister.'

Neville said: 'I don't want to play with her. For heaven's sake, father, we're not five-year-olds.'

'I'm sorry,' Couldridge said.

Neville said: 'It's a bit much hearing mother talking about Mrs Spenser like that when you named me after her husband.'

But Neville and his sister left the table and Joanne considered her feelings towards Charlotte. Like her feelings towards her husband they were unjustified but inescapable. You could not find a bare-breasted woman in your husband's arms—even if he were a doctor—without reacting. Joanne wondered if perhaps the freezing of her feeling towards her husband had begun that day. She picked up the letter again.

Since the birth of her child, nursed by at least three servants, Charlotte had become a disciple of Madame Helene Blavatsky, the Russian who had founded the Theosophical Society in New York in 1875. The Society, purported to create 'universal brotherhood of men' and to develop 'divine powers latent in men'. In India where the belief both drew on the spiritual aims of Buddhism and received messages from mahatmas from the past, Charlotte had followed the teaching of the sub-continent's apostle of theosophy, Annie Besant. The movement was regarded by the British rulers as a puzzlement and an irritation.

Charlotte wrote: 'My dearest John and Joanne ...'

Even the greeting, Joanne thought, was presumptuous in view of their last meeting. But Charlotte seemed completely unaffected by the scene in which she had exhibited evidence of apparent rape.

The letter continued: 'As you know I have given birth to a son since I last saw you. He is a lovely little boy and looks just like Neville although Neville will not admit it. . . .'

Joanne said: 'Ugh.'

Couldridge said: 'I beg your pardon.'

'Nothing,' Joanne said. 'Just ugh.'

'It seems years since we last saw you and it must surely be time that we all got together again. Neville says that perhaps you do not want to see us again after what happened last time. But I know that this is nonsense. It was all just a dreadful misunderstanding. I am sorry if you were offended by anything that happened that day. But I have since come to realise how unimportant such superficial behaviour is. I enclose some literature which I hope the both of you, Joanne in particular, will read. It will show you just what nonsense our outward behaviour to each other is. It is the powers latent within us that we must explore and develop. . . .'

'Oh hell,' Joanne said.

'What's wrong?'

'This stuff about theosophy.'

'Ah yes,' Couldridge said.

'Didn't you read it?'

'I'm afraid I skipped a lot of it,' Couldridge said.

'No wonder you don't think she's out of her mind.'

'Read on. There's a lot of sense later.'

The letter went on: 'I have heard a lot about John's success with eye operations. I have a proposition to put to him which I think will interest him. There is a man in Peshawar whose son is suffering from an affliction of the eyes. From what I can gather it is similar to the complaint which the girl you cured was suffering from. The boy's father is very rich and very important. I have told him that I know you, and that you may be willing to perform an operation on his son's eyes. I have not been so presumptuous as to *promise* him that you will examine the boy. But I have given him hope. He is a very wonderful and influential man and his son is a fine little boy. Do you think, John, that you could come up here and examine the boy without obligation? Then perhaps you could tell the father one way or the other whether there is any hope. I know that I have no call on you, John, but I do assure you that this is a deserving case. Perhaps in any case you would let bygones be bygones and come up here to see us once more.'

Joanne looked up from the letter. 'You're not going, are you?'

'I might.'

'Then you're crazy as well. Neville hates you for what happened—and for what you are. He probably always has although you've been too obsessed with your work to realise it. Charlotte is clearly crazy. And you don't have to go all the way to Jinjabad to find someone whose eyes you can operate on. It's getting the donor that's the trouble, isn't it?'

Couldridge lit his pipe and said: 'Read on.'

Joanne picked up the notepaper embossed with a military crest. Charlotte's backward-sloping handwriting went on: 'I realise that one of your troubles must be finding someone from whom you can make the transplant—you see I have been keeping myself up to date with the details of your work.'

Joanne said: 'I can't for the life of me think how she's been keeping herself up to date seeing as no one has published any details about the operation.'

Couldridge sucked on his pipe and stared out of the window. 'Well they haven't, have they?'

'I wrote a letter to a magazine,' Couldridge said.

'Ah yes,' she said. 'I remember.' She paused remembering the letter he had been writing the evening their son was taken ill.

'Read on,' he said.

The letter continued: 'As I say the man whose son is going blind is very rich and powerful in Jinjabad. He has a servant whose wife is dying. We think he will be prepared to help. If you think you can come please let me know as soon as possible so that I may reassure the father. I know that you may both feel embarrassed at the thought of seeing us again after what happened last time. Please believe me all that is in the past. Neville says he has forgiven you, although, of course, there was nothing to forgive. We have our beautiful child, Neville is hoping to be promoted soon and, of course, I am wrapped up with my work for the Theosophical Society. So please say you will come.'

Joanne thoughtfully poured herself another cup of tea. 'I suppose this means we're going?'

'I don't see why not. The children will love it up there. It seems a pity to deprive them of a chance to ride and hunt in the hills.'

'Don't be dishonest,' she said. She stared at him and tried to see the forceful and eager young man she had married. And she realised that he had not changed much. Was it she who had changed? Or was it perhaps that while he hadn't changed she had matured? Or was it merely a lingering trauma that would in time cure itself.

'I'm not being dishonest,' he said. 'I want to go to examine this child's eyes. I'm not disguising the fact. But it would still be good for the children.'

274

'And you want me to come too?'

He looked at her through the tobacco smoke. 'Once upon a time you would have come with me to a leper colony.'

'Once upon a time you would have taken me to places just to be with me. You only want to go to Jinjabad because of your work.' She stood up knocking over her tea-cup. 'Your damned, damned work.'

'You knew what I was when you married me.'

'I must have been crazy.'

'Or in love? You weren't crazy in those ruins near the railway, were you?'

She stood by the window staring out at the garden where the children sat in long canvas chairs bought from a retiring cruise ship. She felt the moss of the ruins and remembered how she had been surprised at the hardness of his muscles. She had not expected such strength because his surgeon's hands were so clean and well-manicured. She felt again the first thrust of love, painful and wonderful, and she remembered how happy she had been that there had been no one else. She felt the sting of tears in her eyes. 'No,' she said, 'I wasn't crazy.'

'What are we to do about ourselves, then?'

'Stay married. Wait. Perhaps it will return.' She turned to him. 'Do you still love me?'

'You know I do. I always have and I always will.'

She nodded. 'It's my fault. I know it. But what can I do about it?'

'You can come with me up to the hills. Because, Joanne, I think you still do love me.'

The tears overflowed. 'I'm sorry,' she said.

'Don't be. It was my fault.'

'It was a mistake any doctor could have made.'

'Not with their own son,' he said.

She opened the window and the dry scents of straw and dust flowed into the room. 'I'll come with you,' she said.

He came over and put his arm round her waist. 'It will be all right,' he said.

She moved away from him. 'I'll come with you,' she said, 'and we'll wait.'

He took away his arm. 'Very well. We'll wait.'

But it was a long time before they went to the hills together because once again famine came to the land as suddenly and as devastatingly as a plague of locusts. And once again Couldridge was called in to help.

When he arrived in Baipur, where he had once helped to distribute grain, Colonel Neville Spenser was waiting for him.

8

THEY sat in Spenser's tent sipping whisky and water and searching for conversation.

Spenser said: 'It's worse this time. We think there may be serious rioting.'

'Why?' Couldridge said.

'The agitation here has always been bad. Now they've got a good excuse to cause real trouble. They're blaming the British for deliberately holding up deliveries of grain.'

'And are they?'

'That's a bloody stupid thing to say.'

'I suppose it is. I think we've got to face the fact that we're going to find it difficult working together. Especially as I am now a civilian.'

'You were never a soldier.' Spenser sipped his whisky and tried to dispel the image of his wife in Couldridge's arms. But the image stayed and he thought: You shit. You bloody shit.

'You're probably right. The wonder of it is that we got on so well together when we first met.'

'Did we? I can't remember.' But he could—the tall, handsome young man with the easy ways and the breeding, and the natural authority which he had never possessed.

'We seemed to.'

'Perhaps. It doesn't matter any more. What we're concerned with now is stopping these people from rioting.'

'I thought I was concerned with giving them medical treatment for starvation.'

'And treating them for their wounds.'

'You seem very certain that there's going to be bloodshed.'

Spenser nodded. 'It looks pretty much like it. I'm doing my best to stamp it out before it gets out of hand. But there have been some nasty incidents.'

Couldridge said: 'I don't see how they can get too nasty if they're starving.'

'I don't think they are,' Spenser said. 'Not in this town anyway. There was plenty of grain only a few days ago. But it vanished overnight. I think it's been hidden somewhere. Those who are young and strong enough to start a riot are being fed while the rest of them are being allowed to starve. So they think they'll win all round. The old and the useless will fall sick and die and give the young the justification for causing trouble which will be strong enough to participate in. More whisky?'

Couldridge held out his glass. 'What are you doing about it?'

'That's rather my business, isn't it.' Spenser tugged at his greying moustache. He noticed that one of his legs was jogging up and down. He stopped it and hoped that Couldridge hadn't noticed. In the centre of the town they would be tying the three Indians to the posts now. Couldridge, he knew, would object to the punishment but he would be powerless to intervene. The knowledge gave Spenser pleasure. Although the punishment itself did not; it was just something that had to be done; an example that had to be made if bloodshed was to be averted.

'I suppose it is,' Couldridge said. 'But I'll know sooner or later, won't I?'

Spenser glanced at his watch. Outside the heat rose from the

baked ground in wavering fumes. 'You'd better come with me,'
he said. 'Sergeant?'

'Sah?'

Sergeant Albert Duckham materialised at the entrance to the
tent.

'I'm going to the centre of town. Make the necessary arrangements. Tell the men to load their rifles.'

'Sah.'

Couldridge said: 'Hallo, Duckham. Remember me?'

'Sah,' Duckham said affirmatively.

'For heaven's sake you can forget all that now. I'm a civilian.'

Duckham's waxed moustache twitched. 'Sah.'

Spenser said: 'That will be all, sergeant.'

Duckham saluted briskly, turned, cracked one heel against
the other and vanished.

'Cheerio, Duckham,' Couldridge said.

'I wish you wouldn't,' Spenser said. 'It doesn't help discipline.'

Couldridge grinned at him. 'It doesn't harm it,' he said. 'Now
tell me what this is all about. Why all the secrecy?'

'There isn't any secrecy. It's just that a woman was assaulted
this morning.'

'An Indian woman?'

Spenser looked at Couldridge with surprise. 'No, a European
woman. A British woman called Mrs Montgomery, in fact. The
wife of the chap in charge of the railway here. She was walking
down one of the side streets in the late afternoon on her way
to collect a pair of shoes when three Indians tried to rape her.'

'Good God,' Couldridge said. 'Do you want me to have a look
at her?'

'No, she's all right now. My doctor looked after her. He wasn't
so busy then. It was only yesterday that we decided to call in
another civilian doctor to help.'

'Was there any medical evidence of rape?'

'I said they tried to rape her, I didn't say they succeeded.'

'Then how do you know they even tried?'

Spenser stood up and buckled on his belt. 'Does it matter, for

God's sake? She's a respectable woman and she says they tried to rape her. Isn't that enough?'

Couldridge said: 'It isn't and you know it isn't.'

'To hell with your high and mighty attitudes. I've got to maintain law and order. The only way to do it is to set an example. You know as well as I do that there's been a lot of trouble in the Punjab and there's going to be more. If we don't act firmly there'll be bloodshed. There might even be another rebellion on the scale of the Mutiny. What do you expect me to do? Make it seem as if a white woman was making false accusations?' His hand strayed to the pistol at his hip; he unbuttoned the holster, then rebuttoned it.

Couldridge said: 'Is Chambers still district officer?'

'Yes, but he's completely ineffectual in a crisis like this.'

'Chambers is a good man. One of the best types of British civil servants. The Indians respect him.'

'Do you call this respecting him?' Spenser gestured vaguely out of the entrance of the flat towards the parched town. 'Rioting, attacking European women?'

'I thought only one had been attacked.'

'One then.' Spenser remembered the last time the three of them had been together in Baipur; the smell of roasting flesh, the small body on the spit, the shot and the body pitching into the embers. 'In any case it's out of Chambers' hands. Martial law has been declared.'

'What does Chambers think about it?' Couldridge was filling his pipe with slow irritating movements.

'If you must know he thinks there should be more proof.'

'More proof before what?'

'Before what you're about to see.'

'For God's sake spit it out,' Couldridge said. 'Let's forget that we were ever friends. We're on opposite sides of the fence now. It would be a bloody farce if we pretended otherwise. I'm sorry about what happened with your wife. But I've said that before. Now we're just doctor and soldier. But as I'm here at the request of the Army—even if you didn't know it was me who was coming

—then we'd better co-operate.'

'I'm having them flogged in public,' Spenser said. He waited tensely for Couldridge's reaction and found to his annoyance that he was waiting guiltily.

'Christ,' Couldridge said. 'Having who flogged?'

'Three Indians.'

'The ones who raped—sorry tried to rape—this woman?'

'We believe they were concerned in the attack.'

'But you don't know.'

'They can't account for their movements at the time of the attack.' He paused. 'In any case proof of their guilt is immaterial. They are known trouble-makers and they cannot account for their movements. Yesterday afternoon a British woman was attacked. Whether or not these are the actual culprits doesn't matter. An example has to be made.'

'And if I try to stop it?'

'Then you will be arrested. As I say we are under martial law. A state of emergency if you like. And I am in command. Now you'd better come with me. The Army doctor is occupied elsewhere and these men will need medical attention from a civilian doctor after their punishment.' He emphasised the word civilian.

The whipping posts had been erected in the centre of the bazaar. There were six of them—two for each flogging. Each Indian was tied between the two thick posts like a letter X. Their backs were bared and their white cotton clothes hung from their waists. Their chests and backs looked muscular and thin. The monkeys had gathered overhead in the branches of the banyan and acacia trees and the leaves hung limply in the heat. Around the square formed by the small dark shops stood sepoys, rifles at the ready. A group of Europeans, including two women, stood at one side of the square.

'Well?' Spenser said.

'It makes me feel sick,' Couldridge said.

'It made the woman feel sick when they tried to rape her.'

'Why? Because they didn't succeed?'

'A singularly tasteless remark,' Spenser said.

280

'I agree,' Couldridge said. 'But these are singularly tasteless proceedings.'

'You don't have to watch. Just be in attendance if they need medical treatment.'

'Is it necessary to have those women watching?'

'It's up to them. They seem to want to stay. I expect they were friends of the victim.'

'It's more like watching an execution than a flogging. Catching the heads under the guillotine. Take my advice, Neville and drop the whole bloody thing. It will only bring you trouble. Don't forget that Chambers was present at that last incident.'

'Are you referring to the time when I stopped cannibalism?'

Couldridge nodded. 'The time when you shot an Indian in the back.'

Spenser said: 'That sounds suspiciously like blackmail to me. I won't be blackmailed, Couldridge.' He looked at the glistening backs of the Indians and prepared to give the order. Colonel Hatherley would have had no compunction. He tried to visualise the three crucified men attacking the woman; but the image would not clarify. What had she said? 'They ran their hands over my body and made obscene suggestions.' Hardly attempted rape. 'One of them put his hand up my dress and I could see that he was in a state of excitement.' Then she had run into a garden where a white woman and her husband were drinking coffee under a coloured umbrella. The only witnesses—and they had not even seen the incident. But the woman wasn't the type to lie; she came from the London suburbs—like himself—and had married a paunchy, outspoken Scotsman dedicated to whisky and railways. But Spenser knew that frustrated women could behave in a peculiar fashion. The picture of Charlotte in Couldridge's arms replaced the hazy image of the woman being attacked. He called out to Sergeant Duckham.

Couldridge said: 'I wasn't trying to blackmail you. I was trying to advise you.'

In the dark shops all was quiet. The crowd was growing, filling the lanes and alleys of the bazaar. The sky was dark blue and hot. Only the ring of sepoys separated the Europeans and those about to be whipped from the crowd.

On one side of the square there was a disturbance as Chambers pushed his way through the throng of bodies, ducked between two sepoys and strode across the hard ground.

Chambers' kindly face was working with anxiety. He said to Spenser: 'Isn't there any way this can be stopped? I know these men—I don't think they would do the things she said they did.'

Spenser said: 'It's too late now. I can't back down now. It would be regarded as a sign of weakness.'

Couldridge said: 'That's hardly the point. You needn't have done it in the first place.'

Spenser blinked the sweat from his eyes. 'Don't you tell me what I should have done. I'm a soldier and you're a doctor. This had to be done. In any case it's irrelevant now. I've got to go through with it.'

Couldridge said: 'Then for Christ sake get on with it—those poor bastards will pass out from heat exhaustion before they've been punished.'

Chambers said: 'Don't be too hard on them. There is a famine on.'

Spenser said. 'You know as well as I do that the famine in this town is faked.'

'I know that a lot of grain has been hoarded,' Chambers said. 'Are you against this flogging?'

'I don't like it.'

'But are you against it?'

Chambers looked helplessly at Couldridge.

Couldridge said: 'Well, tell him.'

'It has to be done, I suppose,' Chambers said. 'If it isn't there will be bloodshed. We must make an example. But I don't like it, Couldridge. Believe me, I don't like it.'

Couldridge said: 'For Jesus Christ sake, Spenser, get on with it.'

Spenser turned to Sergeant Duckham. 'Sergeant.'

'Sah?'

'Six strokes each. And be quick about it, man.'

'Sah.' Hesitantly.

'Yes, sergeant?'

'I'd rather not,' Duckham said.

Spenser swore softly. 'Why not, sergeant?'

'Sah—it's not the sort of job I like. Not in front of the men, sah.'

'You know the penalty for disobeying an order?'

'Sah.'

'Then get on with it, man. And make sure you use that cane properly. I shall know from the weals.'

Couldridge said: 'You sound as if you've been to a public school.'

Spenser said: 'You know damn well that I haven't.' If he had he might have known better how to handle the situation. To hell with it, he thought. 'All right, sergeant, administer the punishment. And be quick about it.'

They walked across the square, in front of the silent crowd, in front of the awed monkeys under the hot sky.

When they reached the three men Duckham said to himself softly: 'I don't fucking like it.'

Spenser said: 'What was that, sergeant?'

Couldridge said: 'Don't worry, Duckham. It's not your fault. There's nothing you can do about it.'

Spenser heard Duckham speak once more. 'Poor fuckers,' he said. Then the cane struck the first prisoner's back with a fleshy, cutting noise. Spenser said: 'Don't try and be lenient, sergeant.'

'Don't spare the rod,' Couldridge said. Duckham finished whipping one Indian and moved on to the next. 'Isn't this a bit melodramatic?' Couldridge said. 'After all you're only giving them six of the best. Was it really necessary to have them tied up in public like this?'

'There had to be an example,' Spenser said. The cane cut into the back of the second Indian, a thin red line of blood. Spenser looked at the two white women in the square; they were staring intently at the Indian who was being flogged. One of them appeared to be smiling to herself, the tip of her tongue, as small

283

as a kitten's, playing along her lips.

The first two Indians were released by sepoys and taken to one of the shops. They showed no emotion, no sign that they were enduring pain. The third whimpered as the cane cut into his flesh; he was younger than the other two, about seventeen or eighteen, and his face was bewildered.

Duckham stopped after three lashes.

Spenser said: 'Why have you stopped, sergeant?'

'I think he's had enough, sah?'

'It's up to me to decide when he's had enough, sergeant. Proceed with the punishment.'

'Sah?'

'Yes, sergeant?'

Duckham stared at the cane in his hand. The quiet and the heat fused into a single force. Duckham spoke very quickly making a sentence into a word. 'I don't think he's the sort to attack women, sah.'

'Proceed with the punishment, sergeant.'

Duckham looked at Couldridge.

Couldridge said: 'Better do as he says. Three strokes one way or the other won't make much difference. You're just making it worse for him at the moment.'

Spenser said: 'You know what will happen if you disobey an order, sergeant.'

Duckham nodded. The next three strokes were very quick. The boy began to cry. The sepoys released him and he stumbled towards the shop helped by half a dozen young Hindus.

Spenser looked around the square measuring the reaction. The crowds stared back. It seemed to Spenser that he had asserted the authority that was needed. Without bloodshed, at the cost of eighteen strokes of the cane. The wounds would heal within a week and many British schoolboys had endured worse.

He went over to the shop, which smelled of curry and ginger, with Couldridge and Chambers. He wanted to speak to the men who had been whipped, but he was not sure what he wanted to say. He wanted to warn them, he wanted to placate them, he wanted to assuage a vague feeling of guilt that lingered although he knew he had done right.

Couldridge opened a military first-aid kit and approached the first Indian who had been whipped to bathe the wounds. The Indian turned and spat in his face. Couldridge used the white lint to wipe the spittle from his face.

Spenser said: 'Do you see what I mean?'

'No,' Couldridge said. 'I don't. What are you talking about?'

'You see the sort of people we're dealing with.'

'If I had just been flogged for something I hadn't done I'd enjoy a good spit.'

Chambers said: 'I'm afraid there will be a lot of trouble now. You've insulted and humiliated these men. They will become martyrs. And you didn't even allow them a trial.' The kindliness on his face had been replaced by worry.

'This is martial law,' Spenser said. 'And if there is more trouble then I shall have it put down even if really brutal measures are necessary. If we don't stamp out trouble now then we'll have another full-scale rebellion on our hands.'

Couldridge said: 'If *you* carry on like this then we most certainly will have another rebellion on our hands.'

Spenser said: 'I don't think it is very seemly to argue in front of these men.'

Outside the crowd began to disperse. The troops stood by, their rifles hot and greasy in their hands. Spenser experienced a small stirring of pride and pleasure. They walked across the square to the gathering of Europeans.

Chambers said to the two women: 'You needn't have come, you know. It must have been very upsetting for you.'

Cruelty still lingered on the face of the one who had been smiling. 'We thought it was our duty,' she said. She had a small, greedy face and there was a beading of sweat above her upper lip. 'We're really here representing poor Mrs Montgomery.'

Spenser said: 'It was a very decent gesture on your part.' But he wasn't so sure that it was.

The woman said: 'It was horrible to watch.' The tip of her tongue flickered across her upper lip. 'But they deserved what they got. In fact I think you were very lenient—and fair—to them Colonel Spenser.'

Spenser accepted the compliment without enthusiasm. 'It had to be done,' he said.

'I like a man who stands up for his principles,' she said.

'Thank you ma'am,' Spenser said.

'You made a hit there,' Couldridge said as the women walked away.

Spenser shrugged uneasily. 'They came because of Mrs Montgomery,' he said without conviction.

'They came because they knew they'd enjoy it,' Couldridge said. 'And they did. Now she wants to go to bed with someone. Preferably you.'

'You're very crude,' Spenser said. And once again he saw Charlotte's naked breasts pressed against Couldridge. The hatred spurted. 'But of course it's that crudeness that has always enabled you to have such success with women.'

'It's what enabled me to get you that Indian girl in Bombay that time,' Couldridge said loudly enough for Chambers to hear him. 'Do the young blades under your command still sleep with Indian girls?'

Spenser snapped an order at Sergeant Duckham. The hatred had never been so strong before. He wished he had disciplinary powers over Couldridge.

Chambers said: 'Let's go back to my place for a drink. I think you've won this round but you certainly haven't won the battle.'

9

It was true, Couldridge thought, that despite the famine most of the younger men in the town seemed to be fairly robust.

The troops found one cache of grain hidden in a school storeroom. There was a skirmish and one Indian was shot dead. At dusk crowds began to gather again and Spenser imposed a curfew. But still the relief train with the grain didn't come. Then they heard that the railroad had been sabotaged forty miles away.

'Why for heaven's sake?' Chambers said.

'God knows,' Couldridge said. He sipped at his whisky on the verandah and looked at Chambers. A good servant of the Government and of India who had been able to cope with the complications of previous famines because he expected petty cunning and hoarding: but now there were darker and deeper undertones. He was the type of officer, Couldridge thought, who regarded his charges as unruly children—but never delinquents. Now for the first time since his arrival in India twenty years earlier he was probably longing for England; for the tranquility of villages at dusk with the mist deep on the meadows. It was a pity that he didn't have a wife in whom to confide his fears.

Chambers said: 'But why should it be sabotaged?'

Spenser said: 'The Indians say we did it.'

'Why on earth should we do it? It doesn't make sense.'

'We didn't do it. But they're saying we're deliberately withholding the grain to keep them weak so that they can't cause trouble.'

'But we'd hardly blow up the railway line.'

'The people here don't know the line was blown. All they know is that the grain hasn't arrived. And all they hear is the story the trouble-makers are putting out that we're deliberately holding it back.'

Chambers shook his head sadly and lit a cigarette. A bat wheeled and dived so fast that it seemed to be chasing itself. 'It was never like this before,' he said.

Couldridge gazed out towards the crouching shapes of the hills. 'I'm afraid it was,' he said. 'This is India. It always will be so.'

'It wasn't like that here,' Chambers said.

'You didn't notice it.' Immediately he regretted his brusqueness. 'But I suppose it's a tribute to you that real trouble has never broken out here before.'

'I tried to guide them rather than rule them. Was that so wrong?'

Spenser gestured around him. 'You must judge for yourself.'

Couldridge knocked out his pipe with deliberation. 'It remains to be seen how effective your ideas are,' he said to Spenser.

'They're not doing too badly at the moment.'

'But for how long?'

'It won't take the troops long to repair the railway. They're taking up the track from behind and putting it where the explosive went off.'

'And what happens when they blow up the next stretch?'

'We've got troops out on patrol to stop them.'

Chambers said: 'I think there might be trouble tonight.'

Couldridge said: 'You'd better get your car out of the way then. It's the sort of target they'd love to have a go at.'

The car, Couldridge thought, was the only sign of progress in Baipur. Apart from that everything was as it had been for a hundred years and more—disease, religious feuding, dreaming dogs, the Temple of the Golden rat, the distant mountains, drought, malnutrition, beggars, the pot-bellies of the children,

288

the arrogant Brahmins, the dusty torpor, matchbox shops imprisoning eternal dusk, the monkeys in the spectator branches of acacia and banyan, the rogue elephant and the annual man-eating tiger, vultures and crows, the eternal drone of prayers, smells of curry and pepper and brilliantine, paper kites in the hot sky, servility and hostility and occasional unshakeable loyalty. The only interloper was the big open Rolls-Royce that Chambers had bought instead of a wife and a house in Frinton.

And it looked incongruous waiting outside the shambling bungalow. It was built to wait for a King or a prime minister or a munitions-maker. In London or New York, Paris or Berlin. Instead of that it had been bought with savings and a small inheritance by District Officer Clifford Chambers and shipped to a small town in India of which few people in London or New York, Paris or Berlin had ever heard. But if the car didn't have the dignity of a drive, gravelled and watered, and a garage and prestigious passengers and a chauffeur as smart as a Prussian officer, it did have love. Before he pruned the roses and supervised the watering of the lawn—in the pre-drought days—and perhaps planted a few more trees in his avenues, Chambers dusted and polished and caressed his Rolls. He attended to it before breakfast, lunch and dinner; if he could not sleep he gazed upon it from his bedroom window. Occasionally he drove it.

From the verandah they could see its black, square-nosed shape beyond the garden fence. Light from the bungalow glowed on its big lamps. Chambers looked towards it and shifted in his seat as if he wanted to give it a pat. He said: 'Don't worry about the car. They won't damage that—they know how fond I am of it.'

Couldridge said: 'I wouldn't be too sure. A mob doesn't take much account of sentiment.'

Chambers sipped confidently at his whisky and soda. 'We'll see,' he said.

Spenser said: 'You both seem very sure that there's going to be trouble. I've got men posted all over the town. They've got orders to shoot any Indians who don't answer them when challenged after curfew.'

'That should help,' Couldridge said.

The rifle shot came from the direction of the bazaar. It was followed by a scream. Then silence. Spenser said: 'I'm going back to my headquarters.'

Fists hammered on the door and a servant opened it to let in a British corporal. 'Sir,' he said, 'Captain Julian says to tell you that it looks as if there's going to be trouble in the bazaar.'

'All right, corporal. What's happening there?'

'I don't know, sir. Nothing that anyone can actually describe, sir. Just a lot of movement. Shadows and things, sir. We don't yet know what that shot was.'

As Spenser left the bungalow to cross the road to his headquarters set up in a merchant's house they heard shouting. Then a volley of shots.

'This is it,' Chambers said. The lines of worry had set overnight on his face.

Chambers said: 'I'm going up to the bazaar. Are you coming?'

Couldridge hesitated. 'If there's going to be trouble I should be at the hospital.'

'You can take a look and then go back to the hospital if it's bad.'

'I mightn't be able to get back in time.'

'You would,' Chambers said, 'in the Rolls.'

'You're not taking that surely.'

'I think it will have a calming effect.'

'You're crazy,' Couldridge said.

Chambers shook his head with benign obstinacy. 'It will impress them no end,' he said. 'It represents dignity and all that British rule has stood for. It will do more good than a hundred troops.'

Couldridge shrugged. 'I still think you're crazy. But if you're determined to take it then I'll come with you.'

The engine started immediately and, despite its muted throb, Couldridge could feel the power. They backed out, turned outside the Army HQ, and headed towards the bazaar as if they were on their way to a wedding—or a funeral.

10

THE agitation in the bazaar started with anti-British intent. But soon its purpose became muddled and Hindu and Moslem began once more to settle scores they had been trying to settle for centuries.

Troops fired at shadows and occasionally drew blood from them. Occasionally they fired at each other by mistake and drew blood. Police with old muskets fired at anyone.

The fire started on the borders of the canton of thatched sheds where Hindus spun silk for Moslem weavers when a bullet hit an oil lamp. The first shed flared up and was destroyed as quickly almost as burning magnesium. The hungry flames leaped from shed to shed and drought-dry wood and bamboo burned joyously. Looters ran among the flames, moths of fire flickering in their cotton clothes. On the edge of the blaze troops and police waited uncertainly, firing spasmodically into the flames.

Spenser acted as swiftly and as efficiently as the confusion allowed. He had planned to prevent attacks on British property: now he was dealing with domestic bloodshed. And trying to stop the flames engulfing the whole town. He consulted the police and the fire chiefs. They pointed out that the blazing suburb was joined to the rest of the town by a single street of wood and mud huts. They could isolate the fire by blowing up the street.

When he arrived with two of his officers, three N.C.O.s and a score of sepoys, the flames were moving towards the street with

crackling deliberation. Spenser ordered the N.C.O.s to get everyone out of the houses.

One of the officers said: 'Surely they're out by now, sir.'

Spenser said tersely: 'You're in India not Knightsbridge, lieutenant.'

As the troops moved from hut to hut the rats from the silk-
spinners' quarter decided on mass evacuation. They came down
the street in a grey verminous tide, eyes beady bright in the
light of the flames. Some of them were burning as they ran
in the direction of the Temple of the Golden Rat.

The soldiers carried and coaxed old women and children
away from their homes. The old women screamed and clawed
and shuddered.

Behind the rats, in front of the flames, came a Hindu. He
was screaming and waving his hands with futile butterfly movements.

Sergeant Duckham who was supervising the laying of the
explosives said: 'What the fuck's the matter with that fucker?'

The man dropped to his knees, praying to the stars and the
plumes of sparks drifting dreamily overhead. As he fell forward
on the baked ground they saw that he had been speared from
behind with a spindle. He was dead when they reached him.

The flames explored the perimeter of the canton, found the
entrance to the street and began to advance on the rest of the
town.

Spenser crossed the road to a hut where Duckham was crouched
in the flickering light. 'How long, sergeant?'

'Five minutes, sah.'

'If you take five minutes the whole town will be destroyed.'

'Four minutes, sah.'

'Three,' Spenser said.

'Sah.' But Spenser couldn't tell whether it was affirmative, negative or interrogative.

On either side of the road stood the town's two fire engines.
The hoses had been uncurled and the firemen were directing
the nozzles in the general direction of the flames. But because

of the drought there wasn't any water.

Chambers arrived in his Rolls and parked it between the two huts on either side of the road where the explosives were being laid. The flames reflected on the gleaming black bodywork looked like a coal fire in a grate.

Chambers said: 'It looks pretty hopeless, doesn't it?' He looked unhappily at the flakes of grey ash settling on the car's leather upholstery.

'We're going to blow up the road so that the flames will have nothing to bite on. It might work provided the wind co-operates with us.'

'The Moslems and Hindus are fighting back in the main part of the town,' Chambers said. 'I'm afraid the Hindus will be wiped out.'

'Whoever gets wiped out we'll still be blamed for the fire,' Spenser said. He grabbed Duckham's arm. 'How's it going, Sergeant?'

'Two minutes, sah.'

'Make it one.'

'Sah.'

The flames leaped from hut to hut. The moneylender's premises disappeared in a snuff and crackle of orange hunger; a murky pharmacy specialising in cures for waning virility exploded in a bluish cough of light that discharged tablets like buckshot; a barber's, a bookshop and a letter-writer's office vanished with the first lick of the flames. The fire was now prancing half way down the street that linked the blazing suburb to the town like a string linking a balloon to its owner. It was about a hundred yards from Duckham and his men.

Spenser said to Chambers: 'You'd better get your car out of here. There's no point in getting it blown up.'

'Is there nothing I can do?'

'Nothing. This is a soldier's job.'

'I suppose so.' Chambers climbed into the Rolls and turned in the narrow street as the last of the evacuated families, a woman and three children, came running past. He stopped, opened the doors and called out to them. They looked at the big black car mirroring the flames; the woman put her hand to her face, whimpered and ran on shouting to the children to hurry. Chambers shut the doors. The big dignified car moved slowly and incongruously down the street.

Duckham presented himself to Spenser and said: 'You'd better move now.'

'Is the explosive ready?'

'Just about. But you'd better get the rest of the lads well out of the way.' There was authority in his voice and he seemed to have forgotten that he was addressing an officer.

'What are you going to do, sergeant?'

'I'll stay on in case the bloody fuses go out.'

'I'd better stay as well,' Spenser said.

'I shouldn't if I was you,' Duckham said. 'It's going to be a fucking great bang.'

Spenser looked at him angrily. 'I still think I'll stay, sergeant.'

'Suit yourself,' Duckham said. 'Just as long as you get the other poor bastards out of it.' He pointed at the other officers, N.C.O.s and sepoys.

'Look here sergeant,' Spenser said. But Duckham had dodged across the street to the hut where a corporal was setting the fuse.

The flames were about fifty yards away. Embers and ash danced in the air like fireflies and the voice of the fire had become stronger and throatier, a roar of destructive greed.

Spenser shouted across the road. 'Everyone away now before it's too late.'

Officers and soldiers looked questioningly at Spenser. 'Right,' he said. 'At the double.' They sprinted 200 yards into the darkness outside the glare of the fire. Spenser spotted a brick building, a Baptist missionary chapel, and shouted to them to get behind it. Then he ran back towards Duckham. As he got closer he saw Duckham's silhouette running towards him. The flames were a few yards from the huts with the explosives in them.

There were two explosions, sharp and painful and brutal.

294

Debris scattered high into the starlit night and the ground shuddered. Wood and stones showered down around Spenser. Ahead of him he saw Duckham fall. He continued running towards him.

There was a gap about thirty yards wide in the road. The flames reached one side of it and stopped uncertainly. But, Spenser thought as he ran, it only needed a few wind-blown sparks to cross the gap and ignite the rest of the street. As he ran the wind turned and began to blow the embers back into the flames. And he knew that they had won.

He knelt beside Duckham and tried to cradle his head. But there was no hope: a jagged chunk of cement—probably the only cement in the whole street—had cracked open the back of his skull. 'We did it, sergeant,' he said. But he didn't know if Duckham could hear him. 'Sergeant.'

'Sah?' His eyes opened wearily.

'You did it sergeant. You stopped the flames.'

'Sah.' Neither interrogative nor affirmative nor negative. And never again.

11

COULDRIDGE jumped out of the Rolls near the hospital when he first saw the flames in the distance. Moslems and Hindus were fighting in the streets around the hospital and troops were firing haphazardly at the skirmishing shapes.

He flung himself to the ground as a bullet ricocheted and sang around the street like an angry bee. In the shadows beside him two Indians fought with desperate intensity. He heard bone thudding against bone, heard a knife puncture flesh, heard a sigh and a bubbling cough and knew that the knife had penetrated a lung. Again he heard the knife strike home and guessed that it had been aimed at the heart. He sprang to his feet and, keeping low, ran towards the grappling shapes. He wished he had a pistol with him. One shadow reared up and vanished. The other lay in the black shadow of his blood; he was dead.

Couldridge ran on towards the hospital. Once he stopped to look at a body lying in the road. It was the body of an old woman who had been shot in the back. The old score, Couldridge thought, must have been very old. Or perhaps she had been killed by a stray bullet.

Once he saw a Sikh running from a house. His turban had been pulled from his head and his long hair was pinned in a bun on top of his head. The kirpan in his hand was dripping with blood.

Couldridge arrived at the hospital as the first casualty was being brought in. A young Hindu with his arm almost severed by a cut from a-knife. He was followed by an older man trying to plug a bullet hole in his abdomen with his fingers; he collapsed as he reached the stone-floored entrance hall. Most of the casualties were Hindus, but there were a few Moslems.

The young Army doctor whom Couldridge was helping was nervous at first. But the nervousness was soon dispelled by the sweating intensity of the work. Although he had been in the North West frontier he was still appalled by the pointless violence and suffering of India.

They worked beside each other in the casualty department. The town's only European doctor worked in a kitchen which they had drenched with disinfectant and converted into a surgery. But because he was drunk they only allowed him to treat minor wounds: he couldn't manage stitching but he did some bandaging, although most of the bandages slipped off soon afterwards. Three Indian doctors worked in the other wards. Couldridge feared the two Moslem doctors would only treat their own kind leaving the bulk of the work to the remaining Hindu; he was happy to find that he had misjudged them.

Despite their labours the waiting room and corridors were soon filled with casualties.

'What are we going to do for God's sake?' said the Army doctor whose name was Ellis.

There's nothing more we can do,' Couldridge said. He plucked a .303 bullet from a bicep, swabbed the wound with antiseptic and tied a field-dressing around it.

'They're dying out there before we can get to them.' He brushed the soft brown hair from his forehead with an agitated movement.

'If you'd been in France in the war you would have got used to this sort of thing.'

'I was too young,' Lieutenant Ellis said.

Couldridge glanced at him. 'Of course you were. Far too young.' He smiled because of the lieutenant's youth and because he was trying so hard. 'I'm sorry.'

Ellis stood away from the operating table for a moment while an orderly cut away a Hindu's blood-stained dhoti. 'Is that where you got your limp?'

Couldridge nodded. 'A shell splinter. It fractured the femur.'

'Someone told me that you have your own clinic now and that you're experimenting in eye surgery.'

'Who told you that? It hasn't exactly been over-publicised.'

'A patient of mine.' Ellis looked embarrassed as if he shouldn't be disclosing a patient's name. 'It was Major Spenser's wife, actually.'

'Charlotte? How is she?'

'She's all right,' Ellis said guardedly. He returned to the operating table and said: 'Christ, look at this.'

Couldridge glanced over his shoulder. The Indian had been castrated. 'Just try and stop the haemorrhage. There's nothing much more you can do.'

Ellis applied himself to the wound. 'How can men behave like this?'

Couldridge felt very cynical and middle-aged. 'I suppose someone took the opportunity to exact revenge. I expect he had been sleeping with someone else's wife. He certainly won't do it any more.'

'You're just being deliberately callous.'

'What else can I be? I don't know the answer to your question.'

Ellis sighed, stepped back and called an orderly.

'What's the matter?' Couldridge said.

'I'm operating on a corpse.'

Their gowns were stained bright red and their feet slipped on the blood on the floor. Overhead the fans lazily sliced through the soupy air. There were now ten bodies in the morgue.

Couldridge said: 'We'll have the first burn cases any minute now. There's going to be a hell of a lot of them. We'll just have to cover the burns with lint soaked in saline, give morphine to the third degree cases and hope the bloody Army turns up with relief medical supplies within the next twenty-four hours.'

The first burn case was not too bad. His hair had gone, and his eyebrows; but the burns to his face were superficial.

Couldridge said: 'He'll live. Don't waste any morphine on him.'

The Indian writhed and clawed at them imploring them to take away the pain.

Ellis said: 'Can't we do anything?'

'Just lint and saline. There's worse to come. We'd better get a couple of soldiers to wait outside in case any of them decide that they're not receiving proper treatment.'

'You sound very cold-blooded about it.'

'Just practical,' Couldridge said.

'Doesn't all this make you wonder about your work on eye surgery? It must make it seem a bit futile.'

'It makes me wonder,' Couldridge said. He told an orderly to cut the hair away from a head wound. 'You know what's going to happen next, don't you? We're going to run out of water.'

A few flies had found their way into the theatre of the old hospital painted in bureaucratic brown. They circled the bright lights before settling on the viscous blood on the floor. In the corridors and wards the flies crawled greedily over the open wounds. Cockroaches peered from the cracks in the walls that had been put up seventy-five years ago. No one could recall the hospital being decorated or renovated since then.

The skin of the next burn victim was blistered and patched with charred clothing stuck to his chest and belly. 'Poor bastard,' Couldridge said. 'There's not much we can do for him. But he'll live—provided he survives the shock. He looks strong enough. As if he's had access to the hoarded grain.'

'Do you believe that?'

'I think so. I don't agree with a lot Major Spenser says and does. But I'm afraid he's right on this one.'

'I gathered that you didn't always see eye to eye.'

'Who told you that—Charlotte?'

'I shouldn't have said it.' Ellis looked with despair at the third-degree charring of an old woman's chest and arms. 'What can I do here?'

Couldridge looked at the old woman. 'Nothing,' he said. 'Speak kindly to her.'

'She's dying,' Ellis said.

Couldridge turned and looked at the lined and frightened old face. She didn't speak as life departed from her.

Couldridge said: 'What did Charlotte say?'

'You know I can't tell you.'

'Did she say anything about an incident a few years back at Jinjabad?'

'Nothing specific. As a matter of fact she just said that you and her husband were totally different. She seems to be a great admirer of you, though. Although I don't think she's always quite herself ...'

'Really? Do you mean this theosophy caper?'

'You know about it, then.'

'She wrote to us about it.'

'It's a bit sad really. She believes she receives messages from the past—mahatmas and what have you. She believes that the society will eventually achieve a brotherhood of men throughout the world.'

'She should be here right now,' Couldridge said. The man on the table had a compressed fracture of the skull on which they

299

would have to operate later. He told the orderlies to take him to a ward on a stretcher.

Ellis said: 'She believes that she has been chosen to achieve this brotherhood in India.'

'Poor Charlotte,' Couldridge said.

They went on talking as they sutured and incised, injected and amputated. Life regained hope or died at their fingertips. They worked with brutal efficiency, and to Couldridge it seemed that they were more like butchers operating on live meat than surgeons. His eyes stung and his iodine-stained fingers ached. He looked at his wrist-watch: it was 1 a.m. Outside the sounds of violence had faded.

He went over to the sink and rinsed his face. 'What's the score?' he said.

'I don't know.' The soft hair was matted now. 'About a hundred wounded I think. Probably about thirty dead.'

'Many more to come?'

'A few. Not many.'

At 1.30 the other European doctor came in. His face was sticky and pale and his breath smelled of whisky. He was about fifty-five years old—emaciated from a diet of liquor and occasional food. 'Does anyone have a drink on them by any chance?' he said. He smiled feebly. 'For medicinal purposes only of course.'

Couldridge shook his head. 'Sorry.'

The doctor abandoned pretence. 'I've got to have a drink. I can't go on without one.'

Couldridge said: 'I'm sorry. I'd give you a drink if I had one.'

The doctor's face slipped into slyness. 'Sometimes when I forget my flask I make myself up a little something?'

Ellis said: 'What, for God's sake?'

'You might not like the idea being so young and conscientious.'

'What do you want?' Couldridge said. 'Drugs?'

'No, not drugs. I make myself up a little drink with some surgical spirit and one or two other things. A little juice sometimes and some sugar perhaps.'

Ellis said: 'Clear out of here.'

'You don't understand,' the doctor said. His mouth hung open in his parchment face. 'You're too inexperienced to understand. Dr Couldridge here understands, don't you doctor?' He looked at Couldridge hopefully, hopelessly.

'What's he mean?' Ellis said.

'He means he's a sick man. He means he's an alcoholic. He means he's got to have his medicine like any other sick man.'

Ellis said: 'But not surgical spirit—it will kill him.'

The European doctor nodded. 'I think we all know that.'

'Can't we get him some whisky or some other drink?'

Couldridge said: 'If he's been prescribing this stuff for himself all this time I don't think one more lot will make much difference.' He pointed at a bottle on the shelf. 'Help yourself, doctor. Don't mix it too strong. We need you.'

The doctor poured some into a beaker with shaking hands and took it away to the secret clinical bar where he mixed his drinks.

Couldridge said: 'Don't look so shocked. It's not uncommon out here. A lot of Europeans accept failure very easily. They can always blame India and the Indians you see.'

'But surgical spirit ...'

'How long have you been in the Army?'

'Three years.'

'Then you've got a lot to learn. I've treated soldiers who've drunk a mixture of metal polish, meths and lemon squash before now. Some add a little boot black for colouring.' Couldridge applied himself to treating the badly burned arm of a fiercely-bearded young Sikh; blisters were ballooning either side of his kara bracelet.

By 4 a.m. they had done their best with all the badly-wounded. Medical supplies were almost exhausted and there was hardly any water left. Outside the theatre it looked like a scene from the Crimean War. Bloody and bandaged they lay sprawled in the corridors, moaning, laughing in delirium, praying, dying. In the wards they lay on the beds, beside the beds, under the beds. The hospital smelled of ether and carbolic and burned flesh.

Couldridge looked at the wounded and wondered if they would be there if a white woman hadn't alleged that three Indians had tried to rape her. Ironically it now depended on her husband, the railway superintendent, to get many of them to Lahore for medical treatment; and to get medical supplies from Lahore to Baipur. If neither happened then within a few days he and Ellis would be fighting gangrene. Couldridge remembered the smell of gangrenous limbs from the war. He took off his gown, as stiff as cardboard with dried blood, and scrubbed his hands.

'Come on,' he said. 'We haven't got far to go—we might as well walk.'

On the far side of the town they could still see a faint glow from the gutted hovels. Troops patrolled the silent streets and a scimitar moon shone in the sky. The crowded stars seemed more remote than usual. The air smelled of charred wood.

Outside Chambers' bungalow they saw a black silhouette, humped and twisted like the outline of some stricken prehistoric animal. It was Chambers' Rolls-Royce, bent and buckled and wrecked. Couldridge's foot struck a hard object which went clattering along the ground: it was a headlamp.

Chambers was leaning against the wreckage smoking a cigarette.

'What happened?' Couldridge said.

'They blew it up,' Chambers said. 'The bastards blew it up.' He stamped on his cigarette and went inside the bungalow.

12

NEXT morning the Indians accused the British of almost everything that had occurred. The drought because they had failed to stock water, the famine because they had deliberately held back the grain, the fire because they had started it as a punitive measure, the riots because the British always tried to divide and rule. They also delivered a protest to Chambers about the flogging of the three Indians. Chambers tore it up.

The Moslem leaders retired to their meeting places to consider the next move. The town idled in the sun. A few more died from hunger, a few more died from their wounds. At 8 a.m. a train pulled out from the station. Its two carriages were filled with the Indians Couldridge hoped might be healed in Lahore; he didn't send any with third degree burns, or internal haemorrhages, because he knew they would die anyway.

The burning and the bloodshed had created a new sullen tension. Patrolling sepoys jerked their rifles in the direction of any movement; even the sleepy dogs hauled themselves into their masters' homes—and found to their pleasure that the old people and the children left behind were too weak to kick them out again.

Couldridge pushed aside the flap of Spenser's tent. Spenser was shaving in a metal mirror, lathering his face with an old badger-hair brush. He looked healthy and pleased with himself. He was almost polite to Couldridge.

Couldridge said: 'You look surprisingly happy. I shouldn't have thought there was much to be happy about.'

Spenser cut a swathe through the soap on his cheek. 'I don't know,' he said. 'We averted a catastrophe last night. The fighting has stopped.'

'In case you don't know,' Couldridge said, 'they are already seeking compensation for the blowing-up of their homes.'

'Ungrateful bloody lot.' Spenser applied his razor to the stubble at the extremes of his neat greying moustache. 'But I expected no more.'

'You don't like Indians much, do you Spenser?'

'Do I have any reason to?'

'Perhaps not. But you must be a bit of a masochist to stay here if you don't.'

'You like them all of course.'

'Yes,' Couldridge said, 'I do. And I like India. And the good we're doing despite ...'

'Despite what, John?'

Couldridge had been going to say, 'Despite people like you.' Instead he said: 'It doesn't matter. But I'm sure the good we're doing far exceeds the bad. The railways, the schools, the irrigation. And there is gratitude if you look for it and forget what the fanatics are saying.'

Spenser massaged the remains of the shaving soap into his jowels, then washed and dried his face. 'Are you sure you don't like Indians because they're suitable guinea pigs for your experiments?'

Couldridge contained his temper and occupied himself lighting his pipe. Finally he said: 'You know you're in for big trouble today, I suppose.'

'I shall control it. If they're stupid enough to start any sort of protest they know exactly what they can expect. I've posted notices all over the town forbidding gatherings of any sort. If anyone flouts this order then my troops have orders to open fire.'

'What exactly is a gathering?'

'I've stipulated more than five people.'

Couldridge gazed at the sun climbing to its zenith of heat. Even the sun seemed ominous today. The heat, the absence of dogs, the silence. But there were still the few oases of comedy that always flourished in the deserts of Indian tragedy. Down the road a shaggy-haired barber had planted his chair and his huge scissors and his jars of pink and green brilliantine outside the tented Army camp. He had, Couldridge presumed, heard of the reputation of Army barbers. Encouraged by the barber's intrepid spirit, a medicine man was squatting nearby surrounded by bones, a couple of skulls and a dried bat or two.

Couldridge said: 'I hear Duckham died very bravely.'

Spenser buckled on his belt, combed his hair and looked ready for anything. 'He did. I shall see that he receives a posthumous decoration.'

'He was the best type of soldier.'

304

'He was a good soldier.'

'The best. He was the sort of man the Indians respected.'

'Meaning I'm not?'

Couldridge looked at him with surprise. 'I didn't say that.'

'You meant it,' Spenser said. 'You've been saying it ever since we met. God knows how long ago that was. I suppose you think I've mishandled this situation.'

'You shouldn't have had those men flogged. If you hadn't done that we might not have had last night's rioting. But you handled the fire bloody well.'

'You think Duckham was responsible for saving the town.'

Couldridge stood up. 'For Christ sake,' he said. 'You were the officer in charge. Why the hell should I think Duckham was responsible? He was a good, brave soldier carrying out orders, that's all.'

'You think I should have stayed with him.'

'I don't think anything of the kind. Dammit you took the rest of your men to safety and then returned. It wasn't your fault that Duckham got hit on the head with a stray piece of concrete.'

'I know what you think,' Spenser said. He dusted a photograph of Charlotte on the table beside his camp-bed and looked at Couldridge with renewed hatred. 'I've always known what you think. But I'm a bloody sight better soldier than you are a doctor. You'll see—today I'll bring this town to heel the military way.'

A lieutenant materialised at the opening of the tent and saluted. Spenser said: 'Yes, lieutenant, what is it?'

'Signs of trouble in the bazaar area, sir. About two dozen people gathered there.'

'Then disperse them. Fire over their heads if necessary. If that doesn't do the trick fire into them.'

'Yes, sir.'

'Anything more, lieutenant?'

'Just a feeling, sir. I think we're going to have trouble on our hands. If we shoot them out of hand then the trouble will be really bad.'

305

'Lieutenant.'

'Sir?'

'Where did you do your training as a cadet?'

'Sandhurst, sir.'

'And didn't they teach you to obey orders there?'

'Yes, sir. I was just expressing an opinion.'

'Keep it for your letters home, lieutenant.'

'Yes, sir.' He saluted and walked briskly away across the baked mud, past the barber and the medicine man moving his bones around like chessmen.

Spenser said: 'They're breeding a different kind of officer these days.'

'He was right though,' Couldridge said. 'Believe you me I wouldn't continue this conversation if I didn't think I might be able to say something that might save this long-suffering bakehouse of a town from further suffering. You don't want a massacre on your hands, do you?'

'I don't want a massacre,' Spenser said. He sat down on the camp bed. 'But I don't propose to bow and scrape to a rabble of trouble-makers intent on starting a rebellion. You mustn't show weakness—that's the way to a massacre in the end. A massacre of defenceless British civilians as soon as we're gone. No, we must show strength and determination. That's why I've given the salaaming order.'

'What salaaming order?'

'I've given orders that all Indians must today salaam all Europeans.'

Couldridge bit hard on his pipe. 'You must be joking.'

'Joking? Why should I be? I've got to assert our authority again.'

'You've got to stop it before it's too late.'

Spenser's leg was bobbing up and down on the ball of his foot. 'I must ask you to mind your own business,' he said. 'If you try to interfere in any way then I shall have you placed under arrest. We are under martial law, remember.'

'You're crazy,' Couldridge said. He gazed into Spenser's taut face, at the slight twitch in one eyelid, at the teeth biting away at the military moustache, and realised with a shock that he was.

13

THE crowd was growing rapidly in the square where the three Indians had been caned. So quick was its growth that the military had no time to contain it. People multiplied as swiftly as moths gathering around a lamp that has just been lit. No one seemed to have been summoned: they just arrived drawn by a magnet compounded of grief, hatred and a sense of injustice.

The square was a gentle place cushioned with musty shops and lazy alleys. Along one side stood a high yellow wall on which copies of Spenser's order prohibiting gatherings had been stuck. They were now being torn down by youths.

Troops stood uneasily at the entrances to the square and waited for reinforcements. Occasionally they fired shots into the sky; but no one took any notice.

Near the wall a slightly-built Moslem with an excited face and nervous eyes was standing on a box talking energetically to a group of Indians. And still the crowd grew; there was no stampede of bare feet along the alleys; they slipped and sidled in until the whole square was filled.

The Indian on the box was becoming drunk with his own words. He told the crowd that their fathers and brothers and sons had fought for Britain in the Great War. What had they received as a reward? A few paltry concessions. Was that why Indians had spilled their blood? Just for a few patronising gestures from the Imperialists? It was no good arguing and negotiating any more. Britain had to be taught a lesson. She had to be shown that the era of the Sahib was over. That Indians were the equals of their European colonisers.

Some of the younger Indians shouted agreement, fists clenched and held high, sweat running in their wild eyes. The older and the wiser urged restraint. But the speaker, encouraged by the throaty approval of his audience, had no time for the wisdom of the old and the timid.

The monkeys sensing danger fled from the banyan and acacia trees; the dogs stayed in their homes and buried their noses beneath their paws. Outside the improvised HQ Spenser mustered a hundred troops and began to march on the square.

Forty-eight hours earlier, said the orator, the British had cruelly humiliated three men by having them publicly flogged for a crime they hadn't committed. A crime that had probably never happened.

'I say,' said the lieutenant who had reported the situation to Spenser, 'that's a bit thick.'

'What are we going to do, sir?' said a havildar with a greased and pointed moustache.

'We'll just have to wait for reinforcements. There's no good shooting into this lot—they'd murder us.' A flicker of satisfaction crossed his worried face. 'We'll just have to see what Major Spenser recommends. He had all the answers.' He brooded again. 'But that was a bit thick from that slimy little bastard suggesting that Mrs Montgomery made the whole thing up.'

The orator who never commanded the attention of the pupils at the school where he taught flung wide his arms again with newly-found eloquence. What did the British do after the flogging? He pointed towards the devastated suburb. Why, set fire to the homes and workplaces of hundreds more innocents. Then, when the fire seemed to be getting out of hand, they blew up a few more houses for good measure.

The murmur of the crowd thickened to a growl. Anyone dissenting was punched and elbowed, and trampled upon when he fell.

'Better do something quick, sir,' the sergeant said. He sharpened the points of his moustache with his fingers. 'It's going to get nasty in a minute.'

The lieutenant who had been ordered into the Army by his father and had spent all his service wishing he could have become a veterinary surgeon said: 'I suppose you're right—we'd better do something.'

The orator passionately recalled the latest humiliations and injustices. The order to salaam, the order not to gather in public places. There were now about five hundred Indians gathered immediately around him. They roared their approval.

The troops fired into the air and a few leaves from the trees floated to the ground. The shouting was switched off. Indian soldiers gazed grimly at Indian civilians as the gunshots around the edge of the square merged into a hedge of bluish smoke. The shots tried to echo but the noise was lost in the dark shops and the alleys. The sun settled itself directly above the square; somewhere a dog raised its mongrel head and barked with fear.

'What now?' the lieutenant said. He had green eyes and a squarish, friendly face.

'Pray to Allah,' said the havildar.

A few hundred yards away Spenser ordered his hundred men to proceed at the double.

The orator looked momentarily apprehensive, his newly-found eloquence shot to stammers by the crack of the rifles. Then he began to speak again and his voice regained its power, his hands their flamboyance.

That, he said, was the sort of reward Indians received for helping the British fight the Germans. They met to discuss their grievances and what happened? The British fired on them.

'We shot over their bloody heads,' said the lieutenant.

There were some five thousand Indians in the square now, a thousand of them gathered around the orator. Elsewhere in the sunshine other speakers tried to match the first orator; but their calls for action and their lectures on the infamy of the British were so devious and tortuous that few listened to them.

The smell of pomade and sweat and, very faintly, mimosa from Chambers' avenues, mingled with the cordite fumes of

309

the gunfire. The square was daubed in white and brown; glistening oil paints on a dusty canvas. But there was still a little room left to move around the edge.

Spenser sent a subaltern to tell all officers, N.C.O.s and sepoys to make their way to the side of the square on which he stood with his reinforcements.

Spenser then addressed the crowd in English through a loudspeaker. But the first orator, having gained confidence from his earlier victory over the gunfire, managed to shout louder. And his supporters shouted encouragement.

Chambers said to Couldridge: 'This is it. This is the end of everything I've worked for.'

'I hope you're wrong,' Couldridge said.

'Do you? I don't care. Not any more.'

Spenser tried Urdu. But the shouting increased. He handed the loudspeaker to a captain who was a linguist. 'Tell them I mean business,' he said. 'Tell them that if they don't disperse I'll be forced to shoot. I don't want to but I cannot allow this demonstration to continue.

The troops were lined up behind him three deep. The front line knelt, rifle butts pressed into their shoulders.

The linguist said: 'Shall I tell them something that might pacify them a bit, sir? Perhaps if we dropped that salaaming order ...'

'Tell them what I told you to tell them, captain. Can't anyone here understand a simple order?'

'Yes, sir,' said the captain.

But the crowd showed no signs of dispersing. The first orator had produced a grubby scroll of paper and was waving it in the air.

Couldridge said: 'I think it's some sort of representation they want to make to you.'

'I don't give a damn what it is,' Spenser said. 'I've given them an order. If they don't obey it then I shall fire at them.' His voice was loud and his hand was on his holster. 'Unless you want a rebellion on the scale of another Indian Mutiny.'

310

Couldridge looked at Spenser and remembered Colonel Hatherley. Hatherley and Spenser were, he realised, two classic cases of paranoia. With Spenser his diagnosis was too late.

The orator and about fifty of his admirers were pushing their way through the crowd.

Spenser said to the linguist captain: 'Tell them once more. Just once more. If they continue to defy me after that then I will give the order to shoot.'

Couldridge turned to Chambers. 'Can't you do anything? After all, they're your people. You say they respect you.'

Chambers shook his head. 'They don't any more. It's got beyond that. It's up to Spenser not me. It's a military matter. Purely a military matter.' His kindly face was hopeless.

The captain spoke into the loudspeaker but he might have been chatting across a garden fence. The words fused with the growl of the crowd and were lost.

Brown faces, white cotton clothes dusted with scarlet sandalwood powder, arms waving, mouths chanting. Yet not really threatening, Couldridge thought. Harmless units welded into a mob. But the word had the connotation of menace. Mob rule. That's what it was to Spenser: a mass threat to peace, to the Raj, to his own authority. And yet these people could be controlled. One man could do it. Step out in front of them, raise his arms, quell the clamour with commonsense and promises to consider their complaints. It wouldn't be difficult because many of their complaints were justified. He gazed into the eager, frantic faces and knew that this was not the time for a military solution.

The phalanx around the first orator pressed towards the troops on the high ground in front of a row of shops. A white, green and red Nationalist flag broke above them.

Spenser said: 'I warned them.' He spoke softly so that only Couldridge standing beside him heard the words.

'You mustn't shoot,' Couldridge said. Spenser took his pistol from his holster. Couldridge shook his head. 'No,' he said. 'No.'

He leaped in front of the officers and stood in front of the

311

crowd with his arms raised. Spenser snapped an order and two British soldiers grabbed Couldridge's arms and dragged him backwards. The voice of the crowd was momentarily stilled and Couldridge's voice sounded sharp in the hot motionless air. 'You're mad,' he said. 'You're bloody mad.'

The orator began to shout again and moved towards the troops. He stopped as a bullet from the first volley of shots hit him in the mouth. He stood for a moment frowning as if words should still be coming from the gaping lipless pink hole in his face; then the blood poured out and his body slumped; but the crowd was so thick around him that at first he did not fall and his blood stained their white dhotis.

The bullets from the first volley killed five and wounded half a dozen. So thick was the crowd that the bullets couldn't miss. The dead and wounded stayed suspended by the living. The growl of complaint was stilled. There was quiet, absolute quiet, for a fraction of a second. Then a great whimper of fear. They turned, or tried to turn, to fight, push and burrow their way to the mouths of the narrow alleys to the left and right. Slowly the dead sank to the ground to be pulped by bare frantic feet.

Couldridge experienced first revulsion, then a pity and compassion for humanity that he had never experienced as a doctor. He stood passively between the two soldiers and waited for the shooting to stop so that he could succour the men being shot down in front of him. But the shooting didn't stop.

The lieutenant who had wanted to be a vet grabbed Spenser's arm and said: 'That's enough. Surely, sir, that's enough.'

Spenser said: 'Take your hands off me, lieutenant, or I shall see to it that you face a court martial.' His voice was flat and unemotional and mad. He raised his pistol and pointed it at the lieutenant's chest. 'Did you hear me, lieutenant?'

'But you've got to stop the shooting, sir. It's a massacre.'

'For the last time, lieutenant.' Spenser cocked the pistol. The lieutenant let go of his arm.

Another volley of bullets ploughed into the panic of brown bodies in front of them. They screamed, writhed, prayed, they

312

tried to crawl and claw their way to the escape hatches, but the alleys were very narrow and only a few managed to get away. Some sank to their hands and knees and stayed there with heads bobbing like terrified insects: some stood imploring the military to stop shooting and fell as the bullets tore into their bodies.

'For Christ's sake.' Couldridge tore himself loose from the two soldiers and hurled himself at Spenser. 'For Christ's sake stop it.' Spenser held him off with one arm and cracked his temple with the butt of his pistol. Couldridge slid to the ground, hands ruffling Spenser's uniform as he fell.

And still the shooting went on. The sepoys' faces sweating, disciplined, hardly questioning. The ground was covered now with the dead, the dying and the wounded. A child came running from the bodies straight at the hot guns jerking in the soldiers' hands. They fired over her head and she ran on so that she was standing among the officers' legs. Couldridge saw her as consciousness began to return—a weeping, bewildered face with a fat-knuckled hand at the mouth. 'Hallo,' he said, and lost consciousness again.

Blue smoke hung over the square and the air smelled acrid. Vultures wheeled high in the sky, dropping lower as the bloodshed continued. One settled on the yellow wall overlooking the carnage, moving excitedly from one claw to another. Spenser raised his pistol, took careful aim and blew its head off.

The little girl moved nearer to Couldridge. He opened his eyes again and smiled at her between the officers' legs. He put his hand to his head and felt the lump growing on his temple. The firing continued and he remembered. He tried to jump to his feet but his head was weighted; the pain felt as if a scalpel was probing his brain. How long had the massacre been going on? He lifted a heavy hand but the face of his wrist-watch had been smashed. The girl stopped crying and stared at him from between two plump-carved legs. He smiled at her again and began the laborious business of trying to stand up.

The lieutenant who had wanted to become a vet suddenly

broke away from the rest of the officers and ran in front of the guns. The sepoys tried to avoid hitting him but one bullet struck him in the chest and killed him. It was the only British casualty.

Couldridge stood up, swayed and caught hold of Chambers' shoulder. Chambers, who had been vomiting, was trembling uncontrollably.

Couldridge said: 'How long?' Pains lanced his brain and he felt unconsciousness calling him.

Chambers said: 'Five minutes. God knows.' He turned away and vomited again.

Many waited now to be killed. Standing, sitting, on their hands and knees. The will of God, the will of Allah. The bodies on the ground twitched and the vultures sank lower in the afternoon sky.

Spenser shouted an order and the guns stopped. The Indians still fought to escape into the bazaar, trampling, crushing, suffocating. Those who had accepted death and found themselves still alive stared perplexedly at the smoking barrels of the rifles. The vultures glided down to perch on the wall overlooking the feast.

Spenser stood still, pistol in his hand, gazing at his achievement. There was no emotion on his face; he looked detached, almost content. The Indians looked back at him with horror and disbelief. No one moved except the wounded and the flies.

Spenser turned to Couldridge and said: 'I don't think there will be any more trouble now.'

Couldridge looked at Spenser's face and knew that there was no point in replying.

Spenser said: 'There will be no rebellion now.'

The Indians were taking away the wounded. Couldridge looked at the dead and the wounded and experienced an overwhelming sense of futility. He walked over to the nearest casualty; but it was almost a corpse with the last weak pulses of blood flowing from the femoral artery. He approached a youth clutching a shattered humerus. He tried to splint it, but it was so fragmented that he knew that the arm would have to be amputated. He stood up and bowed his head and considered the possibility that in ten minutes' shooting Spenser had probably terminated more lives than he had saved since he started practising medicine.

He thought about the hospital overflowing with wounded and burned. He looked at the whimpering bleeding multitude. The hopelessness of it made him want to weep.

He heard Spenser say to Chambers: 'It had to be done. You realise that, don't you? It had to be done.' Couldridge didn't hear Chambers' reply. He moved on to the next casualty.

On top of the yellow wall the vultures shifted their claws and opened their wings restlessly.

BOOK FIVE

1

THE inquiry into the Massacre of Baipur lasted twenty days. It became inevitable after intense Indian agitation and a speech by Gandhi demanding that the officer who had given the order for the 'mass execution' be court-martialled. An Opposition Member of Parliament picked up a report of Gandhi's speech from *The Times* and put down a question in the House of Commons. In Britain the possibility that a British officer could be capable of issuing such an order caused initial concern; but it *was* India, and the victims had been natives ... concern soon faded. In clubs and private hotels in St James's, Cheltenham, Bombay and Calcutta the massacre continued to dominate conversation. It was generally agreed that Spenser must have had private knowledge of impending trouble and that he might well have averted a large-scale insurrection; although some considered that he had gone too far whatever the strength of his information; a few who had known him said that there had always been something not quite right about him; one or two said he was a murderer and a disgrace to the uniform he wore, but few heeded them. The majority agreed that an inquiry would be a good idea and that Spenser would be vindicated. But none of them anticipated the calibre of Spenser's evidence: none of them realised—despite the fact that they had defended him—that Spenser really believed that what he had done had been right.

The inquiry was held in committee room of a civil administration building in Calcutta. The chairman was a High Court judge. On either side of him at a long mahogany table sat a General, an M.P. who had not spoken in the House of Commons since his maiden speech a decade before, a peer who had made his money out of biscuits, and an eminent historian making a study of the Indian Mutiny. There were no Indians at the table because it had never occurred to the conveners that there should be. The Indian Nationalists asserted that the inquiry was rigged and that Spenser, whose promotion had come through on the day of the shooting, would be found innocent. They, too, reckoned without Spenser's own evidence.

Fans moved lazily in the long brown room with its oil-paintings of noble and contented rulers of India and the M.P. had to be jogged awake several times during the proceedings. About fifty members of the public sat on upright wooden chairs. But even gunfire, bloodshed and suffering could beckon sleep, the public discovered, when it was repeated hour after hour. On the straw-coloured grass of the park outside young men and boys played cricket. And instead of concentrating on the testimony of tragedy many Englishmen found their thoughts transported to village greens and thatched pubs where the cool beer tasted of nuts.

At first there were some twenty journalists taking notes. But the evidence lost its impact after the first half dozen Indian witnesses had given their versions of the massacre and the numbers dwindled. Although all the Indian journalists stayed, receiving each new accusation of British brutality with noisy shock.

The casualty figures made the biggest impact because they had never been released officially. Dead—149; injured—386. In the public seats the Englishmen returned from their villages and their pubs and exclaimed softly; the Indians were unable to contain their outrage. The journalists talked loudly and excitedly and rushed from the committee room under the gaze of their oil-painted overlords. One Indian with a thin, wild face in the public seats stood up knocking over his chair and shouted:

'Shame on the British.'

The judge, a slight, very white man wearing rimless spectacles who looked suddenly fallible without his wig and the pomp of the High Court, said: 'If I have any further interruption from you, sir, I shall have you removed from the court. From the inquiry rather.'

The Indian ignored him—a rare experience for Judge Perryman. Palpably he longed for the funereal authority of his ushers, for the support of the tipstaff. He said: 'I have warned you once, sir. I shall not do so again.' He beckoned the paunchy police officer standing near the doors.

The Indian marched around the chairs, stood in front of the mahogany table and continued shouting. 'The British have blood on their hands.' A few droplets of spittle fell on the deep-shining wood. Judge Perryman saw more than forty years of precise and dignified law culminating in humiliation in this parched and alien land of muddle and madness. 'Officer, take this man away.' The Indian spat and the spittle skated across the table-top stopping in front of the biscuit peer who stared at it with embarrassment. The Indian was pulled kicking and screaming from the room and a young and dapper clerk mopped up the spittle with his handkerchief.

The incident briefly resuscitated the inquiry in the British Press. In the Indian papers the headlines were about the arrest of the man who had spat; and there were suggestions that he was being ill-treated in the police station.

In the long warm room the recitations and accusations continued. In elaborate English the interpreters described the shooting and the slaying and some witnesses still wore bandages and slings; one removed an eye-patch to prove that he had lost an eye. Some said they feigned death because they thought the troops would butcher the wounded. Such a suggestion, said the M.P., was scandalous. The judge whispered in his ear and he did not speak again throughout the inquiry.

The historian made exhaustive notes in skeletal writing. The biscuit peer sweated copiously, swatted invisible mosquitoes and

320

during the breaks for cold drinks retired to the lavatory to drink from his hip-flask of whisky. The general glared menacingly at the Indian reporters seated in front of him.

The inquiry aroused interest in Britain again when evidence about the whipping and the salaaming order was given. And there was much indignation about the alleged attempted rape of Mrs Montgomery; in some quarters it surpassed the emotions engendered by the massacre.

Then interest faded again. Until Spenser gave evidence. Then no newspaper could ignore the story because Spenser spoke in headlines.

It had been emphasised that the inquiry was not a trial; that, although the interrogator was a King's Counsel, he was merely seeking the truth, not cross-examining. And the K.C., tall and bony and deadly, did his best to oblige. But Spenser declined to be helped; and his own lawyer sat with hand histrionically clapped to his forehead at a desk in front of the public seats throughout most of his client's evidence.

The K.C. said: 'Please tell us, Colonel Spenser, in your own words, just why you gave the order to shoot. Take your time and do your best to be fair to yourself because it is your career at stake.'

'I do not need time. I shot them because they defied me.'

The journalists' shorthand flowed and they rushed for the telephone. In London sub-editors arrived at their offices and sharpened their pencils without knowing that in Calcutta the principal witness at the Baipur Massacre inquiry had composed their headlines for them.

The judge took off his rimless spectacles, pressed the ridge of his nose with two fingers, and reflected that it was the first time in nearly thirty years as a judge that he had heard such plain and brutal honesty. Throughout his career he had dealt with the various forms of dishonesty—evasiveness, hypocrisy, absolute lying and the wearisome embroidery of the truth by the self-righteous and the vindictive. Sometimes he had been powerless to prevent the triumph of dishonesty: now he was

321

hearing a witness destroy himself through honesty. The injustice of it perturbed the judge because it questioned the whole criteria of his life. 'Surely Colonel Spenser,' he said, 'you can be more explicit than that. I must remind you that you are not here in the role of martyr.'

The journalists flipped over the pages of their notebooks, and paused expectantly. The General stared at Spenser, considered having him cashiered and then decided to promote him to full colonel. The biscuit peer caught a non-existent mosquito on his neck a stinging slap, the historian filled his fountain pen from a small bottle of ink and the M.P. tried to keep his head above a tepid wave of sleep.

Spenser said: 'There is no need to elaborate, sir. That is the exact truth. I did have certain fears about the future but at the time I ordered the troops to fire because the crowd defied me.'

The barrister and the judge looked at each other. 'Tell us about those fears,' the barrister said.

'I don't consider they appertain to the incident.'

'Please,' said the barrister, 'answer my questions. You are doing yourself a lot of harm by not elaborating.'

'I knew that if the Indians were allowed to defy us there might be another rebellion on the same scale as 1857.'

'I see. Can you tell us why you thought that?'

'There was open defiance all over the Punjab. If the Indians in Baipur had been allowed to stay in the bazaar square despite my order then there would have been a complete break-down of law and order throughout the Punjab. Probably throughout India.'

The judge said: 'You are saying that by taking 149 lives you saved the lives of thousands more?'

'Yes, sir.' Spenser stood very straight, his back arched, his jaw thrust out. There was no emotion in his face or in his voice; no awareness that he was arraigned on an indictment of atrocity.

The judge led him gently in the direction of honest mitigation. 'And you suffered as you saw your guns shoot down these people in the square?'

Spenser answered crisply and immediately. 'Not really, sir.'

The pencils of the reporters raced across the pages of their notebooks. The room was silent except for the swish of the fans. Judge and counsel stared helplessly at Spenser. Spenser stared at a portrait of Lord Curzon in oils. The M.P. who had surfaced briefly from his torpor looked incredulously at him: for ten years he had kept a job without speaking, now he was witnessing a man throwing away a career with a few words.

The barrister spoke slowly and fatalistically. 'Why did you not suffer, Colonel Spenser?'

'Because I knew that what I was doing was right. It would have been pointless to suffer.'

The General spoke in his beautiful military voice. Authoritative, deep, refined. The voice of breeding. Spenser turned his head for the first time in the direction of a questioner. The general said: 'As I see it, Colonel Spenser, you did your duty as a soldier.'

'Yes, sir.'

'You knew it was your duty and there was no escape.'

'That is so, sir.'

'You acted as you would have done in battle?'

'I don't quite understand, sir.'

Irritation rasped the deep precise voice. 'You were protecting something. In this case the future of the Punjab, possibly the future of India. To do this you had to kill just as you would have done in battle?'

'That is so, sir.'

'The price was small compared with the price that might have been paid in human life if you had permitted this disobedience to continue?'

The judge said gently: 'I don't think we can permit the witness to be led in this manner.'

The General regarded the civilian judge beside him with disdain. 'I thought we were trying to arrive at the truth. This man is not on trial, is he?'

The judge said: 'Please accept my authority in this matter,

323

General Bishop.'

'I feel that we should give this officer every opportunity to present his side of the case. It seems to me that he acted with considerable presence of mind. The casualties were unfortunate but inevitable. It is my opinion that Colonel Spenser in all probability prevented a conflagration in which hundreds of thousands might have died.' He glanced at his companions. 'What do you think, gentlemen?'

The M.P. jerked upright and gazed inquiringly at the fan above him. The biscuit peer drummed his plump fingers on his hip-flask and said: 'I really think opinions are a little premature.' The historian said: 'In my opinion Colonel Spenser may well *be* responsible for a conflagration in which millions will die.'

The judge said to the barrister: 'Please continue with the questioning, Mr Baverstock.'

The barrister turned despairingly to Spenser. 'Why did you continue to shoot into the crowd for fifteen minutes?' It was a question he would have liked to avoid asking; but it really didn't matter any longer what he asked.

'Because the lesson had to be complete.'

'I don't follow you, Colonel Spenser.'

'A few shots killing a few people would have been interpreted as weakness.'

'Why, Colonel Spenser?'

'It would have appeared that we were just shooting to protect ourselves. That we were scared of them. In my opinion the situation merited more than defensive measures.'

The historian blotted a page and said in a gentle voice as incisive as a sergeant-major's bellow: 'Did you enjoy killing them, Colonel?'

Spenser's lawyer leapt to his feet but the judge anticipated him. 'Objection sustained,' he said.

The judge looked inquiringly at the K.C. 'Any more questions, Mr Baverstock?'

The barrister shook his head unhappily. 'None, sir.'

'Then I think we will have a short adjournment.'

The biscuit peer disappeared, and reappeared five minutes later looking happier, his pink face pinker. The other participants stood on the black and white marble squares of the hallway smoking. Fingers of dusty sunlight quivered on the squares. Outside the big studded doors beggars gathered to await the departure of the sahibs who always threw them coins when they were together: it was only when a sahib was alone that he ignored their pleas.

Spenser's lawyer, a toothy, pessimistic man, told Spenser that he should prepare himself to face a court martial.

Spenser appeared vaguely surprised. 'Why?' he said.

'Because you have just damned yourself in there.'

'I did what I thought was right. I told them so.'

'Are you that foolish, Colonel Spenser? Can't you see the headlines? *"Spenser: I didn't suffer as Indians died."* Why didn't you try and save yourself in there?'

'I spoke the truth. That's all there is to it.'

'Your remarks will go down in the history books as a catechism of British brutality.'

Spenser shrugged. 'I may go down in the records as the man who saved India from another mutiny.'

'In my opinion,' his lawyer said, 'you will go down in history as the man who made Indian independence or partition inevitable. The Nationalists have never had such a feast of propaganda.'

Spenser walked across the big chess-board of the floor and gazed through the shutters into the street where the beggars waited on withered limbs and truncated bodies. 'Independence? You're crazy. Look out there. Are they ready for it?'

'Not now. Not for another decade perhaps. But your case will never be forgotten and one day many people will say that independence dated from today.'

'The General was on my side.'

'He had to be. He was the only soldier there apart from yourself. He was defending his way of life as well as your actions.

But believe me you wouldn't stand a chance if he were presiding at a court martial.' His eyes flickered in his intelligent, rodent face. 'Now there's only one thing for it.'

'What's that?'

'We'll have to make a lot of your mental state at the time of the shooting. The strain of prolonged service in the hills, the famine, the fire.'

'Make out I'm crazy, you mean?'

'Nothing of the sort,' said the lawyer. 'Just emotionally upset at the time.' His quick face worked enthusiastically. 'In fact we might be able to turn sympathy your way. Recall what you did for the Indians during the fire and all that. Emphasise their ingratitude. Then weigh in with some good medical evidence about your condition.'

'Medical evidence? What medical evidence.'

The lawyer smiled proudly. 'I've discovered that you've got one or two good friends. One in particular. He's come all the way from Bombay to give evidence on your behalf.'

'John Couldridge?'

The lawyer nodded happily.

For the first time since the inquiry started the face of Colonel Neville Spenser showed emotion. His eyelid twitched and the skin on his forehead tautened. 'I am your client, right?'

'Of course.'

'And so you do what I instruct you, right?'

'Of course.' The happiness was fading from the sharp face.

'Then I instruct you not to produce Dr Couldridge as a witness. If you do then I shall publicly dismiss you.'

The lawyer backed away from Spenser. 'You are crazy,' he said.

'That', Spenser said, 'is what Dr Couldridge would have testified.' He strode across the black and white squares with the lawyer almost running beside him. 'And what's more,' he said, 'he would have enjoyed it.'

They left the stale-mate on the chess-board and went back to the committee room.

2

THE hotel, Charlotte Spenser thought, hadn't changed. It was like a dusty set from a play with a never-ending run. The garden with its painted hibiscus and sprinkler set in perpetual motion; the two beggars outside; the marble-floored reception and the white-jacketed waiters with the blue sashes across their chests and the potted palms standing beside the doors to the garden. Their room was the same one they had occupied years before and she suspected there would be curried chicken with chapattis and popadoms for lunch.

She left Pandit Chet Ram and his son in the lounge and went upstairs. Then she went to her room and sat on the bed remembering an evening years earlier when she had been lying beneath the mosquito net hating India and waiting for her husband to go out drinking with Couldridge. She should have returned then to her London suburb, to the kites and the carriages and the square substantial houses; but girls of her class didn't leave their husbands.

Now it no longer mattered. She had her child and she had her new beliefs. And since the scene with Couldridge, since the beginning of her pregnancy, her husband had not wanted her. This pleased her, although she had trained herself not to show her repugnance. Now he was in trouble and she was not bothered. Her new beliefs had taught her the unimportance of phenomena such as worldly disgrace. She was sorry about the suffering that Neville had caused; but again bodily misery played little part in the ultimate patterns of existence. Everyone had divine power latent in them: it was up to her to follow the example of Annie Besant in India and Helen Blavatsky in America and make people aware of these powers. Charlotte looked back with incredulity to the days before she had joined the Theosophical Society when she drank to escape the brutality of life—the days when her mind had not been receptive to such messages as the one she had received from a mahatma telling her to help Pandit Chet Ram, one of the brightest of the Nationalist leaders in the Punjab.

Then Pandit Chet Ram had told her at a dinner given by a senior civil servant for a Tory M.P., that his son was going blind and there was nothing the doctors could do. Progressive scarring of the cornea, or something like that. But the day before the dinner she had heard an Army medical officer talking about John Couldridge and some eye surgery he had been carrying out. The coincidence splintered in her mind into a bright star of realisation: this was the way in which the mahatma expected her to go to the assistance of the Nationalist leader. 'I believe I can help you,' she said.

Pandit Chet Ram looked surprised. 'In what way, Mrs Spenser?' He was a delicate-looking man with deep-set eyes and elaborate good manners that only emphasised the intensity of his hatred of the British.

'I think I know of a doctor who can help your son.'

'An Indian doctor?'

'No,' said Charlotte, 'a British doctor.'

Suspicion settled on the delicate features beneath the fragile forehead. 'What is the doctor's motive, Mrs Spenser, in wishing to help the son of an agitator?'

Charlotte smiled at his naïvety. 'There is no motive. There cannot be one. Dr Couldridge doesn't even know about your son.'

'Then what is *your* motive, Mrs Spenser?'

'It is my duty.' She didn't complicate his suspicion by telling him about the message she had received.

'You will forgive my cynicism, Mrs Spenser, but your concern for the son of a man hated by the British is a little hard to understand.' He ate his fruit-salad with quick, bird-like movements.

Charlotte ate more slowly and thoughtfully. It was, she thought, a little difficult to explain. 'You will just have to believe that I have only your son's interests at heart.' She sipped her coffee and realised vaguely that the Tory M.P. was on his feet talking about the sympathy of His Majesty's Government for the aspirations of Indian Nationalism.

Pandit Chet Ram sipped quickly at his coffee. 'It is more than sympathy that we need,' he said.

'What do you really want?' she asked. And was amazed at the incisiveness of her question.

Pandit Chet Ram said: 'Do you really care, Mrs Spenser?'

'Yes,' she said, 'I do.' And suddenly she found she did. Because the fragile little Indian pecking at his coffee had ideals, dreams of equality and independence. Whereas every instinct of her husband was repressive.

'You must not presume,' he said, 'that people like myself do not appreciate what the British have done for us. The railways, the schools, the hospitals. We are very appreciative. Very appreciative indeed.' Hatred sharpened his mannered speech. 'But we are not slaves, Mrs Spenser. We need actions and promises to sustain our pride—not His Imperial Majesty's sympathy. Nor do we consider ourselves to be objects of ridicule. We are, after all, only what the British have made us. In short, Mrs Spenser, we are neither slaves nor clowns—we are human beings.'

'I understand that,' Charlotte said. She always had, she thought.

'Do you, Mrs Spenser? I wonder. Or are you merely indulging His Majesty's sympathy?'

'It is not His Majesty's sympathy. It is mine. I can offer little else.'

He took a last sip of his coffee. 'We fought for the British in the war, Mrs Spenser. Thousands of us died to help protect you from the Hun or the Boche as you called the Germans. We didn't have to. It didn't matter to us who won the war. But we did expect recognition of our loyalty. There has not been much recognition, Mrs Spenser. A few concessions here and there. But

329

none of them will make any difference to the ordinary man. We have become a dominion. The Government of India Act is to come into force in 1937. We have negotiated with a few enlightened men such as the Earl of Willingdon. A great man the Earl of Willingdon.' He drained his coffee and smiled. 'Also a very strong man. As Viceroy he has always refused to discuss civil disobedience with law-breakers such as myself.'

Charlotte smiled vaguely because she couldn't distinguish his sincerity from his irony.

'Because of him a lot of people think that the subversive movement will die out. We shall see.' He paused. 'Do you know, Mrs Spenser, the single honour that was bestowed upon us at the end of the Great War?'

Charlotte shook her head helplessly.

'It was made possible for us to be awarded the King's Commission. We were overwhelmed with gratitude, Mrs Spenser.'

Charlotte glanced at her husband who was spooning into a jar of Stilton. She looked at the guests at the head table and saw mouths instead of faces: two dozen mouths feeding, pouting, pursing, talking.

Pandit Chet Ram looked too. With distaste and contempt. 'I had another son,' he said. 'But he was killed in 1918—the year the boy who is going blind was born.'

'I'm sorry,' Charlotte said.

'Do I embarrass you, Mrs Spenser?'

She stared into her empty coffee cup. 'I am not a very good conversationalist, I'm afraid.'

He was suddenly contrite. 'I am sorry, Mrs Spenser. I am afraid I am a little bitter. The fact of the matter is that he wasn't killed by the Germans, he was killed by the British. Two drunken British soldiers set on him in Peshawar when he was on leave. His skull was fractured and he died a few hours afterwards in hospital. The incident was witnessed but the two soldiers were never brought to trial. A question of identification, I believe.'

'I'm sorry,' she said again. She sank her fingernails into the palms of her hands because of her inadequacy.

He drummed his fingers on the table. His nails, she noticed, were daintily manicured, very pink against the brown of his skin.

Again she felt the prompting. 'Let me write to Dr Couldridge,' she said. 'At least let him see your son's eyes. He can give an opinion. I can write to him tonight, if you like.'

'What would your husband have to say about all this, Mrs Spenser?' He looked very knowing in his birdy way.

'He needn't know,' she said. 'It really isn't any of his business.'

'And this Dr Couldridge of yours. What makes you so sure that he would be willing to treat my son?'

'Because I know Dr Couldridge,' she said.

He put his manicured fingers to his forehead and looked at her shrewdly, almost coyly. 'You know him very well, Mrs Spenser?'

Her cheeks flushed as they had so often done when she had been a schoolgirl. 'He is just a friend of the family.'

'Ah.' He nodded without belief. 'And is he very British in his thinking, this Dr Couldridge of yours?'

'He's very humane in his thinking. He is a very good doctor.'

The mouths at the important table were being tended now after the eating and talking. Wetted with tongues and dried primly with the corners of serviettes. The dinner was almost over.

Pandit Chet Ram said: 'I suppose it would not do any harm.'

Charlotte said: 'You say he is going blind anyway.' She paused, frightened at the brutality of the statement.

'That is so.'

'Then it certainly cannot do any harm.'

'I agree.' They walked together towards the hallway. 'But I must warn you, Mrs Spenser, that any connivance—if that is the word—between you and me may get you into trouble. Even now the British are considering bringing a prosecution against me for inciting revolution. It is their phrase for awakening patriotism. And you, after all, are the wife of an Army officer.'

331

His concern for her welfare restored her confidence. 'Don't worry,' she said. 'It will be between the two of us. I shall write to Dr Couldridge tonight.'

But the famine came. And the massacre. Her husband was summoned to Calcutta for the inquiry. And when she heard that Couldridge would be giving evidence she caught the train to Calcutta ostensibly to be with her husband. Pandit Chet Ram and his son followed.

In the bedroom overlooking the perpetual sprinklers she dealt with some Theosophical Society correspondence and waited for Couldridge. In this same hotel she had once looked at him shyly and hoped that his friendship with her husband would continue because he was the only person with whom she had felt at ease in India.

She thought fleetingly of the episode in Jinjabad. But it no longer embarrassed her. She had been a different woman then. She watched the gardener, wearing khaki trousers severed at the knee to convert them into shorts, edging a rosebed with dazed concentration. She felt a great compassion for the gardener and all the bewildered people for whom Pandit Chet Ram and his like were fighting. She wanted to make her small contribution to the solution of India's torment—and thus a contribution to the 'universal brotherhood of men'. She smiled at the shabby figure of the gardener blurred by a veil of spray from the sprinkler; but her compassion didn't reach him and he went on slicing phlegmatically at the turf.

She pressed the bell for room service, waited ten minutes, ordered afternoon tea and considered the plight of her husband. It affected her less, she found, than the future of the boy losing his sight in a room down the corridor.

She added milk and sugar to her tea and bit into a desiccated cucumber sandwich. The taste of cucumber resurrected memories of Streatham. Of courtship. Of a handsome young man, not too sure of himself, who should have worked in a bank snapping elastic bands around white five-pound notes and leaving sharp on time to meet her on the common to discuss the mortgage and the three unborn children they planned to produce. The feeling was as short and sharp as the snap of the elastic. Her husband was a mass murderer.

She heard a knock on the door and became aware again of the room and the smell of scented wood and the thick-china cup of tea growing cold. She stood up, opened the door and said to John Couldridge: 'Why, hallo John, it's been a long time.'

3

JOHN COULDRIDGE looked warily at Charlotte sitting opposite him in the lounge. But there was no trace of embarrassment in her manner. The worry had left her face and her thin features were softer and more rounded. He made a business of lighting his pipe because he was a little embarrassed. A blue-sashed waiter brought them drinks and placed them on the table beside the potted palm.

Finally he said: 'How's it going with Neville?'

'Not very well. He's busy condemning himself.'

Couldridge drew at his pipe and tried to readjust himself to her new personality. 'It must be very worrying for you.'

'Not really. He believes what he did was right so he must take the consequences.' She sipped her lemon squash tinkling the ice against the glass. Then she smiled and said: 'It's nicer without gin in it.'

'You never looked entirely happy drinking gin.'

'I was completely unhappy,' she said. 'When I look back it seems as if it was someone else.'

'You should have some more children,' Couldridge said. 'They do you good.'

'No, never.' Her voice was hard and abrupt.

'It was just a thought.'

'I'm sorry. I didn't mean to snap. It's just that I'm too old now to have more children.'

Couldridge remembered the weals on her body and guessed at the truth. 'Is Neville very distressed?'

'Not really. He just sees himself as the man who saved India from destruction. I think he's reconciled to the fact that the inquiry is going to find against him. But he doesn't care. He's become a martyr.'

'He's in a very delicate mental condition,' Couldridge said. 'I can never forgive him for what he did but I could have given medical evidence that might have saved him from complete disgrace.'

Charlotte said: 'Poor Neville. He should never have been a soldier. And I didn't help him. He should have had someone like Joanne.'

'Yes,' Couldridge said, 'I suppose he should have done.'

'You needn't agree quite so readily.'

He smiled. 'I'm sorry. I didn't mean to. Neville should have appreciated you more. His trouble was that the standards of behaviour he set for himself were all the wrong ones.'

'I know,' she said. 'A bank clerk trying to be a soldier.'

'Some of the best soldiers in the war were bank clerks,' Couldridge said. He thought about the curt note from Spenser saying that he had decided not to call any medical evidence. 'I suppose the trouble was that we were never really close. It was just that we started together. We were almost friends then. That night when I got drunk and ended up in a brawl.' He smiled reminiscently. 'I enjoyed myself that night. So did he. It was afterwards that it all went wrong.' He applied a match to his pipe. 'Did he ever tell you about our first visit to Baipur?'

'He talked about it quite a lot. But nothing in particular. Why, what happened?'

Couldridge smelled again roasting human flesh and saw the body topple into the smouldering ash. 'It doesn't matter. Just

334

something that happened between us. It was the end of our friendship.

'Neville never really knew whether to admire you or hate you.' She paused. 'You know in a way you were responsible for what happened.'

'What on earth are you talking about?'

'He used to brood about you. I could sense it although he would never admit it. I know the word he would have used if he had discussed his feelings about you. He would have said that you had breeding. Poor Neville—he knew that he didn't.'

'You can hardly blame me for his break-down.'

'I'm not saying it was your fault. But you represented all that he knew he wasn't. And instead of directing his hatred at the Army, or at himself, he directed it at you.' She drained her squash. 'And at me sometimes—but for other reasons.'

Couldridge ordered more iced squash from the waiter. A breeze smelling of rain breathed through the window, a lizard chased a cockroach across the marble floor, stopping when he realised that he had been enticed indoors; he paused, throat pulsing, then dashed for the door in a darting run. Couldridge said: 'I think you exaggerate.'

She shook her new placid face. 'I had a lot of time to study Neville. We had nothing to talk about really so we could just sit studying each other.' She picked up the new glass already beaded with moisture. 'In a way we knew each other better than couples who get on well. I knew all about his ambitions and his desperate need to be accepted in the mess. I knew how hurt he could be at an imagined slight. Or if anyone was given an assignment that he thought he should have had. He would even get upset when the other officers talked about the schools they had been to because he imagined they were getting at him.'

'It's very sad,' Couldridge said.

'It *was* very sad because he was a far better officer than most of them. At least the Army recognised it by promoting him.'

'I didn't mean that,' Couldridge said. 'I meant it is very sad because if you were able to sense so much that upset him then

335

you should have been able to help him.'

'I know. It was sad in the early days. But he wouldn't talk to me, you see. He thought that the male had to be aggressive and proud. If I tried to ask him about the things that upset him he snapped at me. He couldn't admit to a single weakness. At first I wanted to help him. And of course I wanted help, too. I hated it here—the country and the way of life. With a little bit of understanding I could have put up with it and even been happy. But my unhappiness merely irritated him. Then I got frightened of him and, I suppose, hated him.' She looked suddenly embarrassed. 'I'm sorry, I didn't realise how I was carrying on. You wouldn't understand, you see, because you've got Joanne.'

'I understand,' he said.

'Is Neville very ill?'

'He's not himself. He hasn't been for a long time. I didn't fully realise how bad it was until just before the massacre. There are a lot of things I haven't realised.'

She nodded. 'You've always been pretty absorbed in your work.'

'Yes,' he said. 'I know.'

'You know, of course, that Neville doesn't want you to give evidence on his behalf?'

'He sent me a note. It's a pity—I could have helped him.'

'He thinks you would have testified that he was mad.'

'Not mad exactly. But certainly not fully in control of himself at the time of the shooting. He was in an acute state of paranoia. Mental derangement if you like—sometimes marked by delusions of grandeur.'

'I guessed he wouldn't want you to help him. That would have been the ultimate humiliation.'

'You're very philosophical about it all,' Couldridge said.

'I've changed a lot, John. Since the baby, since I joined the Theosophical movement. Nothing bothers me very much any more. Do you know I even went to a Dussenhra ceremony the other month with Neville? There were headless chickens running about. And they had to cut off a goat's head with one stroke. If they succeeded it meant it was going to be a good year. Can you imagine me going to a thing like that a few years ago? I didn't like it, but it didn't bother me. It's wonderful to have this new acceptance.'

'Doesn't it worry you that Neville will probably be disgraced? After all you knew he was a soldier when you married him. Brutality is part of a soldier's life. You can't blame him too much.'

'I didn't know I had married a murderer,' she said. She glanced at her watch and stood up. 'And now shall we go and see the boy?'

'Yes,' he said. 'Very well.' As they walked down the corridor he said: 'Tell me, Charlotte, why have you gone to such lengths to help me with my surgery?'

She smiled at him placidly. 'A lot of reasons. I loved you once, you know. You must know—after that incident. I also admired you. The love may have gone but the admiration hasn't. Also this boy needs your help.'

'You know his father has a pretty bad record?'

'I know. But that wouldn't stop you wanting to heal his son, would it?'

'No,' Couldridge said. 'It wouldn't.'

The boy, who was about sixteen, was sitting on the edge of the bed waiting for them. He was very handsome with long glossy hair and an arrogant expression mollified by premature creases at the corners of his eyes. The boy's father greeted them and said: 'There's the patient, doctor. Would you like to examine him?'

Couldridge opened the blinds and sat the boy in front of the window. He took his ophthalmoscope from its case; but already he could see the clouding of the cornea in both eyes. 'I'll have to carry out a more thorough examination somewhere else,' he said.

Pandit Chet Ram said: 'We are in your hands.' His voice contained no humility: his elaborate courtesy conveyed scorn, his fragility was parchment screening virility.

Couldridge said to the boy: 'Have you ever suffered from pink-eye?'

The boy was contemptuous. 'We do not have such complaints in our family. Pink-eye, as you call it, is associated with dirt.'

Couldridge said: 'Do you want to be cured of your blindness?'

'I am not blind.'

'If you are not treated you soon will be.'

'Of course I want to be cured. The question seems a little unnecessary.'

'If you want to be cured just answer my questions politely.' Couldridge glanced at Pandit Chet Ram and glimpsed ancient resentments and hostility. He said to him: 'Please tell your son to behave himself if he wants me to help him.'

The father hesitated. Then said: 'Please be polite to Dr Couldridge, my son. He is only trying to help you.'

The boy said: 'No other white doctor could cure me. Why should this one be any better? Why do we not go to one of our own kind? If, that is, we are equal as you say we are?'

His father spoke and his tongue was a flame immediately extinguished. 'Be quiet, my son. Do as you are told.' To Couldridge he said: 'Please do what you can for him, doctor.'

Couldridge gazed into the cornea, into the brown strands of the iris and the contracting pupil. The clouding was milky, almost opaque. The boy, he knew, would soon be totally blind.

Charlotte said: 'Do you think you can help, John?'

'Perhaps,' Couldridge said. He turned to the father. 'Your son has never suffered from any form of inflammation of the eye?'

'Not as far as I know. You do not seem very sure about his condition, doctor.'

'I shall have to examine him more thoroughly. If I decide that I can operate then you will have to bring him to my clinic at Lahore. I believe Mrs Spenser has explained to you what is involved.'

'She has put me in the picture completely, doctor. I have told her that we will put ourselves in your hands. You see, doctor,

338

some of us ordinary Indians trust the British even if you prefer to deal with the princes.'

Couldridge said: 'I am aware of what the Hindu leaders think of the India Act. I do not want to discuss politics with you. Just your son's health.' Couldridge hoped he had stemmed the usual flow of adjectives describing all British policies—futile, unacceptable, outrageous, perfidious. Currently the 'perfidy' was the India Act which had granted autonomy to the eleven provinces of British India but at the same time given disproportionate representation to the princes in the Upper House and the Federal Assembly.

Pandit Chet Ram's fragile face creased into reluctant submission. 'Please forgive me, doctor. I realise of course that you are not interested in politics. I can never forget them. They are as essential to me as food and drink. Currently I am very concerned with the British attempt to strengthen autocracy against the threat of democracy.'

Couldridge said: 'I should be grateful if you would leave the room.'

The smile froze and the exaggerated servility evaporated for a moment. 'Please continue with your examination, doctor. I shall not interrupt you again.'

Couldridge peered into the milky brown eyes. The cloudiness, he decided, had none of the characteristics of scarring from trachoma. He stood up and looked speculatively at the boy's father. 'You won't like the next question,' he said.

The ingratiating smile had returned and he held his hands in a prayer-like position. 'Really, doctor? I am pretty thick-skinned.' He implied that a lifetime of serfdom to British Imperialism was the cause.

Charlotte said: 'Would you like me to leave the room?'

Couldridge shook his head. 'No. The old Charlotte would have had to leave. But of course the old Charlotte wouldn't have been here in the first place.'

The boy sat with his hands clenching his thighs, arrogance tempered by the lost air of those who are blind or nearly blind.

339

Couldridge put his hand on the boy's shoulder, but the boy made a shivering movement of impatience.

Couldridge said: 'I think perhaps the three of us should go back to Mrs Spenser's room. You'—he pointed at the boy—'stay here.' His voice softened. 'And don't worry—I think I shall be able to help you.'

'I wasn't worrying,' the boy said.

Pandit Chet Ram said: 'I do not think I should go to Mrs Spenser's room. I am after all ...'

'You are after all an Indian,' Couldridge said. 'All right, if that's the way you want it let's go downstairs to the lounge. I'm certainly not pandering to your persecution complex.'

'You are a very outspoken man of medicine,' the boy's father said.

'I have to be,' Couldridge said. In the lounge beside the potted palm he said: 'I have warned that you will not like this question. I am only asking because I must correctly diagnose what is wrong with your son's eyesight if I am to help him see properly again. For his sake I would ask you not to become too upset.' He paused. 'I wouldn't normally make such a business of it but you are an exceptionally sensitive man.'

Pandit Chet Ram prayed again. 'Please do not concern yourself so much with my sensibilities, Dr Couldridge. What is it you have to ask me?'

'Have you ever suffered from venereal disease?'

Again the smile paused and again Couldridge glimpsed the hatred contained inside the delicate cranium.

Charlotte said: 'Dr Couldridge has to know. You must not feel insulted.'

'Of course I am not feeling insulted. It was merely a surprise. It is, I believe, a complaint to which the British soldier is particularly prone.'

'All soldiers,' Couldridge said. The waiter sighed beside them. Couldridge said: 'Would you care for a drink?'

'I do not drink, Dr Couldridge. I do not drink and I do not indulge in practices that would expose me to the risk of catching venereal disease. The answer to your question is, No.'

Couldridge dismissed the waiter and said: 'You must be perfectly honest with me for the sake of your son's sight.'

'I am not accustomed to lying, Dr Couldridge.'

'I'm sorry,' Couldridge said. 'But I had to make sure to eliminate the causes of your son's loss of vision. I thought at first that it was the aftermath of trachoma—there's so much of it in India. But the texture of the cloudiness of the cornea isn't right. There's no question of cataracts so I had to discover if it could be a condition of hereditary veneral disease.'

'Then what is it?' Charlotte asked.

'I can't be certain. There is another condition in which the eye becomes cloudy. It's called glaucoma. It's caused by fluid pressure inside the eye—obstruction of the natural drainage system. Often it's hereditary. But I don't think your boy is suffering from that. In fact I'm sure he isn't because he would have been in agony. The worst pain known to man, they say.'

The father nodded and waited with elaborate patience.

Charlotte said again: 'Then what is it?'

'I said I can't be certain. But I think he's suffering from a condition called dystrophy.'

Pandit Chet Ram said: 'And what is the cause of that, doctor?'

'I don't know,' Couldridge said.

'Ah.'

'What's more no one knows the cause. It's a progressive clouding of the cornea and it causes blindness.'

'Can you cure it, doctor?'

Couldridge stared across the marble floor into the hot afternoon screened by the feathers of date palms. The lizard had replenished its courage and was staring around the corner of the door. He didn't know if dystrophy could be cured by a homograft. And he knew that only one failure was required to stir the punitive spirit of the medical profession. On the other hand he didn't really think that the boy was suffering from dystrophy: he still suspected that he was suffering from interstitial keratitis which was a form of hereditary syphilis. Could he cure it? 'I

341

don't know,' he said.

'Then it would be foolish to try, would it not, doctor?'

Couldridge felt in his pockets for his pipe and his pouch. 'If I don't operate your son will go completely blind. If I operate now and the operation is a success then he will be able to see through one eye at least. After that we may attempt a similar operation on the other eye. But I must tell you that there is a strong element of risk. In fact if my treatment of my first patient had not been successful I know that many members of my profession would have leaped at the opportunity to damn me. On the other hand if I don't operate your son will lose his sight because my critical colleagues have not yet discovered any other cure for his condition.' He lit his pipe and blew out a jet of grey smoke that settled into strata between them. 'The decision is yours.'

Pandit Chet Ram gazed at him warily, suspecting an Imperialist trick. Finally he said: 'What do you think are the chances of success, doctor?'

'I cannot say. I believe that your son's condition *is* curable. I see no reason why his cornea should not react to a graft in the same way as a cornea scarred by trachoma or even injury.'

Pandit Chet Ram examined his little pink fingernails. Then he turned to Charlotte, 'What do you think, Mrs Spenser? Let the decision be yours.'

Couldridge knew then that he would perform the operation. Charlotte said: 'If he were my son I would authorise Dr Couldridge to go ahead.'

'Then it shall be done.' He parted his hands from supplication. 'He is my only son, Dr Couldridge. The future I am working for is his. I want him to be able to see it.'

Couldridge ignored a future governed only by politics. 'You understand the nature of the operation?'

'Mrs Spenser has been good enough to explain it to me. I understand that you need a donor.'

Couldridge said: 'I understand that you have one.'

'The person I had in mind died.' The incurable hostility spurted again. 'You were away at the massacre.'

'I went to Baipur to help treat the victims of the famine.'

'You must forgive me.' He smiled and Couldridge noticed that his teeth were very yellow. 'It is difficult to forget a lot of things that have happened.' He aimed his hatred at Charlotte. 'It is difficult to forget that your husband is the one who is accused of the massacre.'

Charlotte's tranquillity was unaffected. She said with the sweetness of an old lady knitting: 'He is not accused of anything. They are merely holding an inquiry.'

'Ah.'

Couldridge said impatiently: 'The sooner the operation is performed the better. If there is no possibility of a donor then the whole conversation has been abortive. I can find other people who are willing to have the operation to cure their blindness.'

Pandit Chet Ram said: 'I think I may have someone who will be able to help.'

The impatience rasped into anger. 'It's hardly a question of helping. We need someone who has accepted the fact that they are going to die shortly. Someone who is prepared to allow their body to be operated upon after death. Someone whose relatives are prepared to allow that to happen. There are not many such people. Now, do you know of anyone?'

'There is such a person. Although he doesn't know that he is dying.'

'Who is he and what's he dying from?'

'He also is a boy of about sixteen. He is dying from a brain tumour, I believe. His parents have agreed to allow one of his eyes to be operated upon after death. They raise no objection because they, too, want to help my son continue the fight for freedom when I in my turn die.' He paused. 'They are also in my employ.'

'How soon will he die?'

'Very soon. A matter of weeks.'

'I must see him and examine his eyes.'

'That will be quite in order,' Pandit Chet Ram said.

'Very well,' Couldridge said. 'Subject to a few provisos I am

343

willing to carry out the graft on your son.'

'Thank you, doctor,' Pandit Chet Ram said. 'You are very kind.' But there was no gratitude in his thin voice.

4

NEVILLE SPENSER, in fawn suit and military tie, walked purposefully through the babbling streets of Calcutta. Into areas he had never seen before, into areas where sahibs without escort were not expected. Thumb-sucking children, flies crawling on the sores on their faces, watched him from doorways; peddlars, vendors, knife-sharpeners, water-carriers, charcoal-burners, thieves and assassins observed him with curiosity which had no time in which to harden into hostility. A few beggars hobbled and heaved their way past him on their way to broader thoroughfares where white men with coins in their pockets sauntered from hotels and banks —a few lay down to die and be collected. The roofs crowded out the sky, smells of sewers and spices fused with heat rising from the concrete mud into a lazy entity—the sweat of the city. Spenser ignored it all because he was oblivious to it all. He walked swiftly and incisively and everyone except the dying moved out of his way because of his air of purpose. He reached the Hooghly river and leant against the iron railings watching the rusty cargo ships and the swinging cranes loading and unloading coal, wood, grain and railway track. The smell of paint and coal and smoke and hot funnels reached him, and faintly the saline draughts from the sea. The smell of the sea awakened sleeping thoughts from youth, aspirations that had swelled into ambition and lost their fine green bloom. The smell of the sea disturbed him. He shivered despite the heat.

A cargo ship eased its way out of a dock and stopped in front

344

of him, propellers churning yellow water. Bound for England no doubt. Gravesend, Tilbury. An evening beside the Thames when he had listened to a military band in scarlet and white with the setting sun imprisoned in a thousand gold buttons and told his parents that he wanted to be a soldier. And they had laughed so hugely that the scarlet and gold fancy in his mind had gained substance. To be different; to escape from shops and counters and grills and foggy coughing in the morning; bugles called and the Empire beckoned. To be brave and true and honest and to hear the medals jostling on your chest; to fight for the Queen and keep the natives at bay. To be an officer and a gentleman and finally a general.

Neville Spenser watched the rusty bows splitting the smooth water, knifing their way to England. He heard again the bugles, and the impassioned fury of the sergeant major's voice on the parade ground. He smelled polish being burned on black boots, the cordite reek of a rifle recently fired. 'What is the weight of a pull-through? Half a pound? It's the piece on the end, you stupid bastard.' The Sandhurst lectures and the instilled, indisputable knowledge that all Britain's enemies got what they deserved. The commission and the admiration—although the admiration was sometimes muted when you returned as an officer and gentleman to Streatham. India, putting down rebéllion, punishing the natives when they deserved it. Brutality, perhaps, when judged from afar; but really nothing more than the harsh justice the country deserved. Promotion despite the sneers in the mess, a victory over breeding. Captain, major, lieutenant-colonel. Famine, fighting, disciplining, massacre. Brown bodies and white cotton in the sunlit square with the vultures applauding. The Punjab, India, aflame if he didn't open fire. Keep on shooting. Bodies falling and guns repeating. Couldridge sneering, all of them sneering, patronising. Whimpering, crying, falling. No mutiny, his duty, a hero, mentioned in history books if not in dispatches. Promotion—full colonel, general.

The cargo ship hooted and slid from sight through the grey waters which reflected none of the blue lustre of the sky. Spenser

345

turned and walked proudly back through the streets. He smiled as he remembered the futility of Couldridge struggling in the square at Baipur. A lifetime of endeavour and application had triumphed over assumed superiority.

The Indians in the streets—arguing, gesticulating, resting, dying—stared with renewed curiosity at the Englishman marching past them as if he were on the parade ground. Pride pulsed inside him and he blinked his eyes because they stung. He smiled again as he thought of all the friends and relatives who had tried to dissuade him from becoming a soldier—and how he had confounded them. He slapped his thigh with an invisible swagger stick.

An Indian without a nose whimpered for money. Spenser marched past unnoticing and, arms rigid and swinging with thumbs to the fore, swerved sharply into a main street. Past a line of taxis manned by Sikhs, past a straw-coloured park alive with cricketers, past shops filled with imitation jade and Kashmir woodwork, past a bank, colonial and solid among the seething poverty, and so to the hotel.

General Bishop was waiting for him in the foyer. 'Spenser,' he said. 'A word in your ear, perhaps.'

'Sir?' Spenser's rigid body arched backwards.

'Relax man. Perhaps we could go up to your room. A glass of whisky up there perhaps.'

'Of course, sir.'

Charlotte was in the room. She greeted General Bishop placidly and left the room. They went on to the verandah and Spenser poured them whisky and soda. 'A very great honour, sir,' he said. 'You must be glad it's all over.'

The general nodded and gazed across the garden where the immovable gardener was edging the lawn. 'Quite,' he said. He seemed to have difficulty in finding words.

'I think it went quite satisfactorily, sir.'

General Bishop drank eagerly and thoughtfully. 'You know I shouldn't really be here.'

'I suppose it is a little unusual in the circumstances, sir.'

346

'I thought I'd come and give you a little advice.'

Spenser smiled. 'Let me replenish your glass, sir.'

The soda fizzed in the inch-deep measure of Scotch. The perfume of the roses in the garden reached the verandah, the evening began to settle.

The general said: 'You know, of course, that the findings of the inquiry are inevitable. It's just a question of what we can do.'

'What we can do, sir?'

'Yes, man, what we can do.'

'I'm afraid I don't quite understand.'

'The inquiry will inevitably find against you. I did what I could for you. But India is no longer a soldier's world. It's been taken over by the politicians. By the bloody do-gooders.' He finished his whisky and stared regretfully into the empty glass. 'I don't say that I completely agree with your actions. Why did you have to go on shooting, man? One volley would have been enough. A dozen dead, perhaps. We could have covered that up. You might have become a hero instead ...'

'Can I get you another whisky, sir?'

'No, dammit. Doesn't any of this mean anything to you, Spenser?'

'Oh yes, sir. It is after all my career.'

'The thing is we must try and find a way to avoid a court martial. The Army's suffered enough already.'

'A court martial, sir?'

'Yes, man, a court martial. Are you deaf?'

'No, sir.' He gazed at a silver biplane pottering through the fading sky.

'Are you listening to me, Spenser?'

Spenser didn't answer. A sound of bugles and a smell of cordite.

The general exclaimed in exasperation, stood up and left the room.

The biplane disappeared over the top of the telegraph pole palm trees. The sky darkened and the first star appeared.

347

5

In the consulting room beside the surgery in his clinic John Couldridge wrote out the case history of Pandit Chet Ram's son in a sprinting scrawl. He was almost sure that the boy was suffering from interstitial keratitis even though the father had denied suffering from venereal disease. Certainly it wasn't glaucoma or scarring caused by trachoma or congenital cataracts.

Couldridge was aware that some of his colleagues would be waiting even more tensely for the verdict on the operation than they had on the previous occasion. If the graft from the dead boy failed to take then he would be accused of irresponsibility: if it took then he might achieve recognition alongside Elschnig and Filatov. As far as Couldridge was concerned the final confirmation of the perversity of his profession had been their treatment of Nesfield. It had been some fifteen years before his theories on purifying water had been implemented. Now he had been struck off the register over some triviality involving the publication in a newspaper of details of a drug containing placenta. The offence, in the eyes of the disciplinary committee of the General Medical Council, had been more important than his discovery of chlorogen, his work on glaucoma, cataracts of the eye and deafness. But of course versatility—however successful—was further evidence of irresponsibility.

Couldridge picked up the latest literature on keratoplasty. In 1923 Elschnig had reported only nine clear grafts from 92 operations; in 1930 he had reported 34 out of 174. But it was the accompanying statistic that interested Couldridge. Seventeen out of twenty-six grafts carried out in cases of interstitial keratitis had been successful. Very encouraging. And in Russia Vladimir

Filatov was doubtless treating interstitial keratitis with grafts from cadavers.

Couldridge walked to the window and gazed into the garden where their youngest child was pestering the patient ayah. A wind stirred the parchment leaves of a banana tree announcing rain. The atmosphere made him restless.

He went back to his books. Albert von Graefe on iridectomy as a treatment for glaucoma, and linear extraction of the lens for cataract. Sellenbeck's attempts at grafting in 1872 with a special trephine and the first corneal splint. Bigger's early grafts with rabbits, pigs, and a blind pet gazelle. Reisinger, Thomé, Konigsfer, Kissam, Henry Powers, Zirm. And now Elschnig, Filatov and Tudor Thomas. Couldridge thumbed through a general textbook on ophthalamology illustrated with Hogarthian relish. Photophonia, presbyopia, ptosis, visual acuity, vitreous body, zonule. He closed the book and gazed at the cross-section of the eye on the surgery wall—feathered eyelashes, blue iris, the image of the ballet dancer reaching the optic nerve upside down. Even if his operation failed he knew that one day grafts from dead bodies would be accepted. It was like some sexual practices, he thought—at first they shocked, but after usage the shock was superseded by acceptance.

He closed the book, went out of the house and climbed into his new Morris Oxford.

Joanne opened the window. 'Where are you going?' she said.

'To see a patient.' Which was true up to a point.

'You didn't tell me you were going out.'

'I didn't know until just now.' Which was true up to a point.

'Will you be long?'

'A couple of hours.'

'You're being very mysterious.'

He waved and was off. He drove slowly through the city crowds, then accelerated when he reached the suburbs and the countryside waiting for the rain. He could smell the rain before it came. A fresh, exciting smell. The restlessness increased. He drove faster and wondered if Joanne would ever love him again.

He rammed his foot down on the accelerator but the car wouldn't go any quicker.

When he reached the village he drove straight to the home of the money-lender. 'How is your daughter?' he said.

The money-lender who was used to visits from the strange British doctor and suspected that he wanted to borrow money said: 'She is seeing very well. Can I help you perhaps with a loan? Small or large I do not mind and I do not desire collateral.' He was proud of the word and repeated it.

'I'd like to see your daughter.'

'You saw her last week. She has not changed. She still sees through the eye that you so kindly mended.'

'I'd still like to see her. Just to make sure that everything's all right.'

The moneylender who was by now convinced that the solicitude for his daughter was an elaborate subterfuge beckoned Couldridge closer. 'There is no disgrace in borrowing a few hundred rupees,' he said. 'No disgrace at all.'

Couldridge smiled for the first time that afternoon. 'Bring me the girl. I just want to have a look at her eye.'

The girl looked at him shyly. He looked into her eye, looked with tenderness and pride at its beautiful transparency. 'Perhaps one day,' he said, 'we will cure the other eye.'

He led her to the door and gestured around the village. At the dark green umbrella of the banyan, the fluttering lace of an acacia, a garden Catherine-wheeled with daisies and cosmos. 'You see them all?'

She nodded. 'I see them.'

'Good.' Pleasure and confidence elbowed aside the doubt. 'I'm glad I was able to help. Soon perhaps you will be married?'

'I believe it is so,' she said.

'Someone you like?'

'I do not know,' she said. 'I have not seen him.'

He sighed; such problems were beyond his scope. 'I hope you like him,' he said. He turned to leave.

The money-lender said: 'Sahib, are you quite sure that there is nothing you want?'

'I have all I want,' Couldridge said. He patted the girl's sleek head, climbed back into the Morris Oxford and drove back to his clinic as the first rain exploded on the windscreen and danced on the bonnet.

When he arrived home Pandit Chet Ram, Bose and Joanne were sitting in the lounge reading the local newspaper.

For the first time he noticed signs of ageing on Bose's strong face—a line from nose to mouth, a slight thickening of flesh under the chin, two small creases between the eyes. But his face was still virile, still self-possessed and secret. The self-possession only relaxed when he spoke to Pandit Chet Ram and adulation briefly lit his face.

Pandit Chet Ram said: 'I am afraid your friend has been found guilty. My sympathies to you because he was your friend.' The emotion most obviously lacking in his voice was sympathy.

'You mean Neville Spenser?'

Joanne said: 'They seem to have turned the inquiry into a court martial. He's been completely damned in the findings. The local paper's full of it and so I guess are the British papers because there are extracts from leaders in *The Times* and the *Daily Telegraph*.'

Couldridge read the headline. 'British Officer Blamed for Massacre'. No one, he thought, could argue with that. The only point at issue had been Spenser's motives. He read the front-page synopsis of the report. Only one paragraph dealt with mitigation —Spenser's belief that the savagery of his punishment had prevented a rebellion. The indictment of Spenser was as savage in its way as his own idea of a deterrent. An indictment, Couldridge decided, composed as a political appeasement to extremist Indian opinion. The report also deplored the lesser insults to human dignity—the whipping, the salaaming order. These seemed to condemn Spenser as much as the shooting. After reading the report only the most reactionary of colonialists sipping whisky and soda in Poona or St James's would have been able to condone the action. Only Couldridge knew that the massacre had been carried out by a sick man whom he had been unable to help. 'Poor bastard,' he said.

Pandit Chet Ram put his hands in their praying position. 'And all those who died at Baipur. Were they not poor bastards too, Dr Couldridge?'

'Yes,' Couldridge said. 'They were poor bastards, too.'

Bose's hand strayed to his tough white patch of hair. 'You will find,' he said, 'that Dr Couldridge is a very honest man. He always tells the truth even when it means that those close to him suffer.'

Pandit Chet Ram gazed fondly at Bose, one of the younger men upon whom the emergence and independence of India rested. 'You speak with some bitterness, Dr Bose. Do you refer perhaps to your trial all those years ago?'

'I was thinking of that. Dr Couldridge told the truth. I cannot condemn him for that. As a result I was thrown into a British jail for two years.'

Couldridge said: 'I'm surprised you weren't hurled, Bose.'

Joanne intervened with drinks. Pandit Chet Ram and Bose drank lemon squash, Couldridge sipped a whisky. But the two Indians couldn't let politics and their sense of injustice rest.

Pandit Chet Ram said to Bose: 'You must not be bitter about your sacrifice. We want no martyrs in our cause. I have been put—not thrown—in a British jail twice. Once in 1921 just before Gandhi was given authority to lead our movement. Once in 1930 when his civil disobedience campaign began.' The fanaticism was replaced briefly by ordinary pride. 'That year I took part in the march to Dandi when Gandhi made salt from sea water to break the Government's monopoly on salt. After that we had strikes and boycotts and demonstrations. I saw the police club hundreds of non-violent demonstrators with their steel-tipped lathis. The British imprisoned 60,000. I was one of those 60,000. Even now I believe that the British are contemplating imprisoning me once again. But I am not bitter about it. It will merely be another small segment in the attainment of our birthright and the furtherance of the aims of the Congress Party.'

'Not a small segment,' Bose said. His dark face glowed with admiration. 'But you are right—I must not be bitter.'

Joanne said: 'I think you're both crazy. Good grief, the Government of India Act will be passed. You're getting your own Government. What more do you want?'

Pandit Chet Ram took tiny sips from his glass of squash. 'I'm afraid you don't understand, Mrs Couldridge. The Government of India Act is going to be merely another Imperialist trick. It will give nearly as much power to the princes' states as it does to the rest of India. Divide and rule, I believe the system is called. There are, I believe, some 80,000,000 people in the princes' states whereas there are 270,000,000 in the rest of India. I think you will agree, Mrs Couldridge, that such a system is hardly fair.'

'So you're plotting further anarchy?'

Couldridge said: 'I suggest we drop the subject. It's all hopeless. Even the Moslems attack the Act because they reckon it's a plot between the British and the Princes to appoint a preponderance of Hindus to the Government and thus suppress Islam.'

Bose said: 'You used not to have time to discuss such matters.'

'We were both doctors,' Couldridge said. He smiled across the coffee table at his wife, remembering the time when Bose and he had been young doctors and she had loved him with passion. She was still beautiful, he thought—the sharp face softened with age, the body thickened with children, but the radiance still there, and the laughter lurking in the tiny line at the side of her mouth; and the passion still there awaiting release once more.

Pandit Chet Ram finished his squash and licked his lips. 'The trouble with Gandhi,' he said, 'is that his policy of non-violence is not a strong enough weapon.'

Couldridge poured himself another whisky and lit his pipe. 'That sounds a pretty treasonable statement.'

Pandit Chet Ram said: 'Only treasonable if you are British. Patriotic if you are Indian.' He leaned forward. 'Tell me, Dr Couldridge, how can mere civil disobedience have any effect against such men as your friend Colonel Spenser who are prepared to perpetrate mass murder to maintain British supremacy?'

353

Couldridge sucked comfortably at his pipe. 'Come off it,' he said. 'Spenser, the poor bastard, has been indicted by his own people. My guess is that he will be forcibly retired from the Army. And to someone like Spencer that is the same as a death sentence.'

Bose said: 'He should be court-martialled.'

Couldridge said: 'You want your pound of flesh, don't you Bose.'

Bose shrugged. 'I want justice. I received the British conception of justice. Why shouldn't he?'

'You were as guilty as hell,' Couldridge said. 'And you know it.'

'So is Colonel Spenser.'

'There can be no worse punishment for him than to be forcibly retired.'

Pandit Chet Ram stood up, neat and obsequious and contemptuous. 'I am sorry, Dr Couldridge, to have bored you with our problems. You are quite right, of course—our struggle has no place in a doctor's house. I shall bring my son to you tomorrow and he can rest here until the circumstances are right for the operation.' He extended his small thin hand to Couldridge. 'Come, Dr Bose, accompany me back to my hotel where we can plot fresh anarchy.' He smiled without humour.

When they had gone Joanne said: 'You're crazy if you go through with this.'

Couldridge listened to the rain peppering the dry leaves in the garden. There might be snakes out there now, a Russel viper perhaps, or a krait. Now that the rain had come he would have to get some serum from the hospital. 'I'd be just as crazy if I didn't,' he said.

'Supposing the operation goes wrong?'

'It might well go wrong. But if I don't go through with it now word will go round that I refused to operate because he was an Indian Nationalist. Or some sort of distortion like that. You can't win in India—you know that.'

She came and sat beside him on the old sofa that had accompanied them around India. 'If the operation fails you will be in real trouble. You know that but you're just obstinate.'

354

'Once upon a time you would have wanted me to operate.'

'I only ever wanted you to do what I thought was right. I don't think you should operate on this boy. The whole medical profession is against you and if anything goes wrong they'll finish you. Don't have any doubts about that—they're more vicious than any financiers or lawyers or actors. But they hide their jealousy and their pettiness behind the nobility of their trade. A lot of bunkum if you ask me. And I reckon they're worse than the cheats and liars in other professions because they're hypocrites as well.' Her cheeks were flushed and her knuckles clenched. 'But one of these days they'll have to climb down off their perches. One of these days people will realise that they're just the same as everyone else. Just as fallible, just as scheming.' She paused for breath and he gazed down upon her, loving her. 'One of these days doctors may even be forced to tell patients what's wrong with them—when they know, that is.'

Couldridge put his arm around her. 'Did you embrace me in that tirade?'

She moved closer to him. 'No, not you. You're a good doctor. But I'm frightened for you. I've got a feeling about this operation. Just as I had a feeling when I met you that I'd marry you.'

'That's a lie,' he said.

'No, it's not. I always knew I'd marry you from the moment we started arguing at Colonel Hatherley's party.'

'You didn't let me into the secret.'

'A girl doesn't tell a man that she's going to marry him. It just might scare him off.'

'It wouldn't have scared me off.'

'You're kidding. I never knew a man so oblivious of my charms.' She twirled the smooth gold wedding ring on her finger. 'Who did you say the donor was for the grafting?'

'A boy of about sixteen. He's about to die from a tumour of the brain.' He felt her muscles stiffen. 'I know it all sounds inhuman. But there's nothing we can do to save tne boy. Other doctors agree about that.'

'Is he a suitable case? I mean if he's got a tumour ...'

'As far as I can see there's nothing wrong with the cornea. I examined it when I pretended I was examining him for his headaches a few weeks ago.' Couldridge felt vaguely ashamed of himself. 'I know it sounds a bit gruesome.'

She shook her head. 'I don't think it's gruesome. I don't see any reason why the organs of the dead should not be used to help the living. But somehow this all seems wrong.' She paused. 'Do the other doctors in Lahore know what you're doing?—the ones who said there was no hope for the donor.'

Couldridge said: 'No, they don't. Well, not as far as I know.'

'Then the whole affair is a secret.' She put her hand to his chin and turned his face so that he was looking straight at her. 'Don't you think you should let it be known what you're doing?'

'If I did they might try and stop it.'

She stroked his cheek and his jaw with cool fingers. 'You know better than that. That's the last thing they'd do. They want to see you make a hash of the whole damned thing.' She ran a finger along his lips. 'I don't want to see that happen.'

'I don't like to think that you're right,' he said. 'The medical profession has to be cautious. Their caution is the public's only safeguard.'

'Nuts,' said Joanne. 'You don't really believe that. If you can't see the jealousy and pettiness then you're in need of ophthalmic surgery yourself. Do you really think the motives of people like Buckingham and Little are as honourable as all that? They're just mediocrities who are as angry as hell that someone they know is contributing towards progress.'

'Perhaps you're right,' he said. 'I only know that I must go ahead with the operation. If it fails then nothing is lost because the boy will soon be blind anyway. If I succeed then at least one boy will have his sight restored and the ultimate acceptance of grafting and transplants will be that much nearer.'

She moved nearer and kissed him gently on the lips affectionately, a token of experience shared, a seal of trust. 'All right,' she said. 'You must do what you think is right.'

He kissed her back and put his hand on her breast. He thought he felt her recoil but he wasn't sure. He wanted the faith and the trust to expand into passion. His hand moved from one breast to the other.

'John,' she said softly. 'The ayah. She will be coming in from the garden in a moment.'

'Let's go upstairs,' he said.

'All right.' She moved his hand from her breast.

They went upstairs and she began to undress. As he watched her he remembered Neville Spenser and Charlotte and how it must have been with them. Surely not with us, he thought—it can't be like that with us. She was naked now, breasts ripe and heavy and dark-nippled where once they had been firm and tipped with little nipples that had reminded him of the pink sugar buds they put on iced cakes. Her belly had a crease running across the middle where she was trying to pull it in, conscious of his gaze. He took off his clothes and lay on the bed and she came to him, offering herself rather than joining him in the act of love. He kissed the heavy warm breasts, heard her heart beating. Still it surprised him that he who saw female nakedness every day could be so moved by the sight of one nude woman. The love and affection swelled into passion. 'I love you,' he said.

She didn't reply. Instead she stroked his hair.

He said: 'There has only ever been you. There only could ever be you.'

'I know, my love,' she said. 'I know.'

'Is it the same with you?'

'Yes,' she said. 'It's the same.'

'But you don't feel as you once did.'

She raised his head and pulled his body over her. She murmured small endearments, felt him with her hands, moved her body with his.

Then John Couldridge glanced down at her face and saw that the passion was a fake. She was staring at the ceiling waiting for him to finish. His passion withered. 'I'm sorry,' he said.

'John.' She reached out to him but he was off the bed dressing. 'John, I love you.'

'I'm sorry,' he said. 'I didn't realise.'

'Soon it will be all right. I know it.'

But he had closed the door and thus he didn't hear her crying.

6

On the morning of the operation Couldridge re-read the principles of kerotaplasty laid down at the meeting of the Ophthalmic Society of the United Kingdom in London in 1930. In particular he noted their recommendation that the graft should be cut with a trephine smaller than the one used on the recipient cornea. He selected a trephine .38 mm. smaller. He had also noted Filatov's suggestion that egg membrane should be used to protect the graft.

The boy lay on the operating table, cloudy eyes staring at the ceiling, the mixture of arrogance and fear on his face making him look peculiarly vulnerable. Bose prepared him for the operation with his usual efficiency—and an extra measure of solicitude. Outside the rain fell steadily and occasional flashes of lightning showed above the white glare of the surgery lamps.

Couldridge nodded to Bose to administer the general anaesthetic. Miss Benson hovered happily and eagerly behind the trays of instruments. The donor material from the boy who had died the day before lay in liquid paraffin.

Couldridge said: 'I hope to God everything goes as smoothly as it did with the girl.'

'I'm sure it will,' Miss Benson said.

Bose said: 'If you have any doubts now is the time to call it off.'

'Who said I had any doubts?'

'I know you have doubts.' Bose's strong hands looked very

brown against his gown. 'I have worked with you for a long time and I know that you have doubts. Now is the time to call it off if those doubts are stronger than your belief.'

'Every surgeon has doubts.' But it seemed to Couldridge that Bose was trying to warn him of some additional peril. 'What is it, Bose? What are you trying to say?'

Bose hesitated. Then he said: 'Nothing. I am merely trying to ascertain whether you are quite sure that what you are setting out to do is the right thing.' When Bose was perturbed his speech became tortuous: it was the only clue he ever gave to his emotions.

'But if doctors had abandoned their experiments in the past because they were beset by a few doubts then we'd still be sawing off limbs without anaesthetic or antiseptic,' Couldridge said.

'It is not quite the same when a boy's eyes are involved.'

Couldridge said: 'You've left it a little late to issue your warnings. What exactly are you trying to warn me about, Bose? I don't recall such concern before I operated on the girl.' He remembered the expression on the face of the girl when she had looked at the rose: confidence returned.

Bose said: 'If you are determined there is nothing more I can say.'

The lights flickered as the storm gathered power and rain streamed down the windows.

Couldridge said: 'I am determined. I have doubts. Of course I have doubts. But I mustn't let those deter me. The operation may fail. But I will still have done right. If it does fail then the one after will succeed. And the one after that. There may be more failures. But the work has to start somewhere.'

Miss Benson said: 'Of course it does, Dr Couldridge.'

'Whatever the sacrifice?' Bose said.

'Not necessarily. This boy will go blind if I don't operate. He is suffering from keratitis—I haven't any doubt about that now. And it's particularly bad.'

'You mean his father did suffer from venereal disease?' A

fleeting expression of disgust crossed Bose's unemotional face.

'Either the father or the mother. Possibly both. It's not such a stigma, Bose. Why *should* disease caught from sexual intercourse be any more repugnant than many other diseases?'

'I find it disgusting. In the case of this boy's father I'm afraid I can't accept your diagnosis.'

Couldridge shrugged. 'All right, don't accept it. How's the anaesthetic?'

'He's almost ready for you to begin.'

Couldridge lifted the boy's eyelid. The eserine drops had contracted the pupil and the general anaesthetic had been supplemented by a relaxant to lower the intra-ocular pressure. The milky depths of the cornea damaged by parental folly were bared for the trephine.

He called for a suture needle and stitched the eyelids. Then inserted the tiny sutures under the recti muscles. Sweat was already gathering on his forehead and he told Miss Benson to wipe it away. He prepared the silk mattress sutures with 10 mm. needles.

The storm moved nearer. Lightning flashed brilliantly and the crack of thunder almost synchronised with it.

'A thunderbolt is all we need,' Couldridge said.

Miss Benson made small noises of sympathy under her mask. Bose's face above his mask was expressionless. But it was expressionless *without* a mask, Couldridge thought.

He washed the donor cornea in saline, placed it on its bed of paraffin wax and removed the graft with the .38 trephine. Then, as lightning and thunder exploded together above the clinic, he cut into the boy's cornea with the minimally larger trephine. All decision was now irrevocable.

Vaguely he heard the rain hammering on the roof, vaguely he noticed the bright coughs of light and the detonations of thunder. The diseased tissue was removed, then the muscle sutures. Couldridge slipped the graft into the cavity and tied the sutures. He straightened up and felt the sweat streaming down his body under the gown. Outside the thunder and lightning faded and the rain patted apologetically against the windows. Couldridge imagined that he could smell the fertile scent of wet earth.

He said: 'Put the dressings on Bose, my bloody back's aching. How do you think it went?'

'It looked very good,' Bose said. He placed tulle gras dressing and pads over both eyes.

'Only looked?'

'Neither of us can tell how the body will react to foreign material.'

'For Christ's sake,' Couldridge said. 'Where would medicine be if all doctors were bloody pessimists like you?'

Miss Benson said: 'I'm sure everything will be all right.'

'Thank you,' Couldridge said. 'I'm glad to hear that someone has some confidence in my ability.'

'You must never be over-confident in medicine,' Bose said.

Couldridge went slowly into the consulting room and sat down. In the surgery the boy was just beginning to regain consciousness.

Couldridge left him with Bose and went into the house where Pandit Chet Ram sat with Joanne. They were playing chess— Pandit Chet Ram with accomplishment, Joanne with enthusiasm.

Pandit Chet Ram moved his knight towards Joanne's fleeing king and stood up. 'Well, doctor,' he said, 'how did it go?'

'Fine. Your son is a very good patient.'

'I have no doubt about that, doctor. I was more concerned about the success or otherwise of the operation.'

'The operation was quite successful. We shan't know for quite some time whether the outcome will be completely successful.'

Pandit Chet Ram nodded, moved his bishop with swift triumph, called 'Check' and said: 'I have every faith in your work, Dr Couldridge. You did, after all, say that there was a seventy per cent chance of success.'

Joanne moved her beleaguered king.

Pandit Chet Ram said: 'You are still in check, Mrs Couldridge.'

Joanne moved it again. 'I didn't know you had forecast a seventy per cent likelihood of success,' she said.

'The chances of success are good,' Couldridge said.

Pandit Chet Ram stared at the board. 'I hope so,' he said. 'I hope so—for everyone's sake.' He moved his rook one square and called check again.

Joanne regarded her lonely king with sorrow. 'I suppose I should have resigned ages ago,' she said.

'No,' Pandit Chet Ram said. 'Always make a fight of it, Mrs Couldridge. Never give in. There's always a chance that I might make a mistake.' He implied that there was no chance whatsoever.

Couldridge went to the sideboard and picked up the decanter of whisky. 'Can I get anyone a drink?'

They shook their heads. Pandit Chet Ram said: 'But please pour yourself a whisky, Dr Couldridge. A chota peg I believe you British call it. And I know you like a drink.'

He seemed unable, Couldridge thought, to make any statement without a secondary implication. Now the inference was that he drank more than a doctor should. 'What did you mean just now about hoping for everyone's sake that the operation was successful?'

'Just that.' Pandit Chet Ram looked hungrily at Joanne's king. 'It is still your move, Mrs Couldridge.' Joanne moved her king again. 'It would be eminently sad for my boy to lose the sight of one eye. It would be equally sad for me, his father. And' —his hand hung over the board, a thin brown claw—'it would be a most unwelcome development for you.'

Joanne said: 'No one likes to see an operation go wrong. Why would it be so special for John if the operation on your son wasn't successful?'

Pandit Chet Ram's skeletal fingers descended on the black horse's head of his knight. 'Because, Mrs Couldridge, as I understand it, your husband is something of a pioneer in his field. And, as I understand it, his profession is notoriously wary about practices which they consider to be experimental such as the use of tissue from the dead. In fact you might say, Mrs Couldridge, that they are waiting for him to make a mistake. It might just be that my son could be the mistake that they are waiting for.'

Joanne said: 'You didn't call check.'

Pandit Chet Ram said: 'You aren't in check.'

'Ah,' said Joanne. She peered keenly at the board, at her lonely king and her one pawn that was unable to move.

Couldridge made his whisky stronger than usual. Pandit Chet Ram, he felt sure, would notice how strong it was. He said: 'You sound almost threatening.'

Pandit Chet Ram looked surprised. 'My dear doctor I didn't mean to be. Please let me apologise.' He prayed above the chess board. 'I was merely stating the facts as I understood them.'

'I think,' said Couldridge, 'that our first concern should be the well-being of your son.'

'I agree, Dr Couldridge.' He cocked his head in a bird-like gesture as Joanne raised her hand to move her king; then relaxed when she didn't. 'But tell me—is that *your* principal concern?'

'Of course it's my principal concern.' Couldridge swallowed a mouthful of whisky and hoped he wasn't lying to himself. 'A doctor's principal concern is always his patient.'

'That is nearly always true, Dr Couldridge. But there are exceptions. And surely one of the exceptions is when the doctor concerned is by way of being a pioneer. A man more concerned with the evolution of medicine than with the welfare of a single patient.' He smiled apologetically. 'A man perhaps who is also concerned with the furtherance of his own reputation. Although of course I do not suggest that this is so in your case.'

'That is very charitable of you,' Couldridge said. But if there hadn't been an element of truth in the suggestions then he would have been more angry. 'Surely,' he said, 'pioneering and humanitarian aims can be combined without being detrimental to each other.'

Pandit Chet Ram shrugged: he had made his point. 'I hope so,' he said. He returned to the chess board. 'It is, I believe, your move Mrs Couldridge.'

'I know,' she said. 'It's funny but I don't seem to be able to move without becoming check.'

Pandit Chet Ram leaned forward. Couldridge noticed that his hands, now on his knees, were taut and that the furrow from nose to mouth had deepened. Pandit Chet Ram was angry.

Couldridge said: 'It looks very much like stale-mate to me. A draw I believe.'

Pandit Chet Ram stared hard at the board. Then he straightened up and managed a smile. 'A draw indeed, Mrs Couldridge. Exceedingly well played. I must congratulate you.' He stood up. 'Perhaps I could see my son now.'

'By all means,' Couldridge said.

Pandit Chet Ram said: 'Do you know what game I played then?'

Couldridge shook his head.

'The King's Indian. An out-moded defence I feel.'

7

COULDRIDGE again applied the first dressing forty-eight hours after the operation. The graft looked clear and healthy. He took cultures from the conjunctival sac and removed traces of mucus.

'How is it?' said the boy.

'It's fine,' Couldridge said.

'You mean I'll be able to see properly again?'

'I hope so.'

'I know you hope so. But will I?'

'You stand a good chance of being able to see again. I can't be any more definite than that.'

'I hope it's successful—for your sake.'

'Don't recite what you've heard your father say. You're not a parrot.' Couldridge examined the cobweb sutures across the graft. He found that he regarded both the graft *and* the eye as separate entities from the spoilt boy lying in the spare-room of his house.

The boy said: 'My father could ruin you.' His hand strayed towards his eye.

Couldridge slapped the hand away. 'I doubt that very much. But if you touch your eye you'll ruin any chance you have of regaining your eyesight.'

'You wouldn't like that, would you?'

Couldridge replaced the tulle gras and the eyepad and left the room without replying.

He was more aware after this operation of the hostile expectancy of the other doctors. To counter them he behaved with almost boisterous self-confidence. When he called at the hospital to collect snake serum and other supplies he put on a display of controlled zest that infuriated everyone except Miss Benson. But when he was alone the exuberance evaporated. His surgery was crude and the success with the girl had probably been luck.

Every day he examined the boy's eye looking for known complications. Once he thought he noticed a membrane beginning to grow across the graft; but nothing developed and he attributed it to his own nerves and imagination. What perturbed him most was the dormancy of the graft. He sensed it rather than saw it. The sutured plug remained exactly in place, clear and glistening, but it didn't seem to Couldridge as if it were being accepted.

He said nothing and continued to look optimistic. But he noted the mounting suspicion in Pandit Chet Ram's attitude and he wondered if he had been conferring with Bose. In the evening, when the boy was asleep, he read once again the authorities on keratoplasty. As far as he could see his techniques followed the accepted teachings. So he examined the six reasons for failure itemised by Zirm after his homograft in 1905. Only two, he decided, could be applicable—infection of graft or poor selection and judgement. He recalled that Zirm's first operation on the eye of the patient, Alois Glogan, blinded by lime, at his clinic in Moravia had not been successful. Zirm had then successfully operated on the other eye. But Coulridge knew that if his first attempt failed there would be no second chance: Pandit Chet Ram and his own colleagues would see to that.

He took down the rest of his beloved books from the shelf and looked at the pictures of fierce-bearded surgeons, photographs of diseased and repaired eyes. Once again he pondered on the slow progress of an idea put into practice as long ago as 1789 when the Frenchman Pellier de Quengsy first tried to cure corneal opacity with a piece of convex glass fixed to a circlet of silver and stitched to the cornea with cotton. He lingered at the name Henry Power because Power was his mentor and his example was to be recalled in times of adversity. Like Vincent Nesfield in his own field, Power had resisted antipathy to the theory of grafting. In 1872 he had reported successes with grafts on rabbits' eyes and interest in keratoplasty had been revived. It was, Couldridge thought, a fair reflection on the British attitude to corneal grafting that in the fifty years following Power's work not one article on the subject had appeared in the British literature on ophthalmology. During that time Von Hippel had produced his clockwork trephine, Zirm had carried out what was probably the first clear penetrating graft and Magitot had shown that a successful graft could be taken from a donor eye stored for eight days. . . .

Sitting in his consulting room, fifty yards from a boy sleeping with the tissue of a dead boy in his eye, Couldridge felt the hostility of the orthodox, the reactionary, the hypocritical and the jealous, breathing from the pages of the text books. Now that tissue from the dead was being used they had fresh ammunition —aesthetic, spiritual, religious, moral. The dead were dead and thus they should stay. Bury them, burn them, let them be devoured by vultures but don't let the dead help the quick.

Although Couldridge sometimes had doubts about his own motives he had no doubts at all about the rights of taking flesh and blood from the dead to sustain the living. To him the critics were the enemy, as virulent as bacteria, dedicated to stemming the currents of progress.

366

He picked up a recent magazine and read the pronouncement of Vladimir Filatov from his clinic at Odessa. 'I can say with perfect assurance that corneas taken from the eyes of cadavers, even those which had been conserved for a long time, proved to be just as good as those taken from living persons.'

Couldridge applauded mentally. He had once hoped that his work would find a place beside the achievement of the brilliant Russian who, like himself, had elaborated Magitot's research. There was, he supposed, still a chance. But not if orthodoxy had its way.

To hell with orthodoxy. Couldridge stood up and stretched, the spirit of Henry Power strong within him. It wouldn't be the first unsuccessful operation in the history of keratoplasty. In any case it wasn't the one success or failure that mattered: it was the thread of endeavour of which he was a segment. Whatever happened he would operate again, so would his successors. He closed the books and went up to the bedroom where Joanne was sitting up in bed reading a novel by Sinclair Lewis. 'How was he?' she said.

'He's all right.'

She looked at him sceptically. 'Are you telling the truth?'

'Of course I am.' He wondered if Power and Sellenbeck and Magitot had ever been cross-examined with an enquiring wife at times of crisis.

'The whole truth and nothing but the truth?'

'I think he's doing all right,' Couldridge said. 'It's difficult to say. The homograft looks healthy enough.'

She put her book down. 'You sound as if you're qualifying it a bit. That damned Indian will be after your blood if it fails.'

Couldridge began to undress. 'That's the least of our worries.'

'He's a pretty powerful guy. And a nasty bit of work into the bargain.'

Couldridge slipped into bed beside her. 'He's not powerful. He's just a trouble-maker.'

'Be warned,' she said. 'He's powerful. Haven't you seen the way Bose bows and scrapes to him.'

367

'That doesn't make him powerful.'

She shrugged, plumply pretty in a pink bed-jacket. 'You seem in a very confident mood all of a sudden, Dr Couldridge.'

He closed his eyes and awaited sleep. 'I just know that what I'm doing is right.'

She stroked his hair. 'You've been reading your books again. Getting Dutch courage from the past.'

He smiled as sleep embraced him. 'You could put it that way. I need fortifying occasionally.' His words trailed and he slept.

Next morning he considered some of the possible complications that could follow the graft. Vascularisation was the biggest threat, but there was no evidence of that. There was always the danger of general infection, particularly if there was the slightest injury to the surface of the graft. There was also the possibility of anterior synechias which could cause glaucoma and clouding of the graft. The most unfortunate complication was a cataract caused by damage to the lens. The most puzzling were the grafts which clouded for no obvious reason; none of the experts seemed to be able to agree about the cause of these failures; but they all agreed that the only remedy was another graft.

He went to the boy's bedroom to examine the eye again. But the lid was gummed down. Fear moved inside him.

'Is anything wrong?' the boy asked.

'Nothing. Just hold the dressing against your eye while I fetch some warm water to bathe it with.'

'You've never bathed the outside before.'

'Then it's about time I did.'

He bathed away the slight crust and raised the eyelid. There was no sign of any serious infection. The graft was still neatly fixed with the silk mattress sutures. And it was still clear—although perhaps not quite as clear as it had been. Or was it his imagination?

Next day the infection appeared to have cleared up. Hope returned—but only briefly. Within a week he knew that, although adhesion had taken place, the graft was clouding. The operation had failed.

He said to the boy: 'Have you been touching your eye at all?'
The boy shook his head and Couldridge believed him.

'I just wondered,' Couldridge said.

'Why, what's the matter?'

'Nothing,' Couldridge said.

'Has it gone wrong?'

'Don't worry,' Couldridge said. He put his hand on the boy's shoulder.

'It has, hasn't it?' The boy's voice quavered. 'You've made me blind in that eye, haven't you?'

Couldridge didn't reply.

The arrogance almost mastered the tears. 'You will pay for this. My father will see that you pay for it.' Then suddenly he turned his face away from Couldridge and sobbed.

Couldridge left him and walked to his consulting room, to his books. His grief for the boy was sharp. But such grief would never deflect his purpose. All the ophthalmic surgeons since de Quengsy had experienced it; but they had continued to experiment and operate. He told Bose to go to the boy.

Then he sat down and looked at the beautiful blue eye on the wall of his surgery. After a few moments he opened his books to look for a reason for the clouding. But they didn't help.

After reading for an hour he went outside to his car to drive to the hotel where Pandit Chet Ram was staying to tell him that the operation had failed.

8

THE Secretary of State for India's representative, Mr Ramsey Crockford, was in a state of controlled fury. But he concealed his anger with debonair attitudes and dusty humour, and the only clue to his true state of mind was the savagery with which he clouted the croquet balls with his mallet. The wooden balls, blue, black, red and yellow, cannoned around the watered lawn in Delhi with satisfying cracks and clicks.

The basis of the anger of the Indian expert was his dislike of India. He was a Socialist and therefore all his early learning had led him to the belief that all men should be independent and equal. During his green days in Whitehall he had presumed that such teaching applied as much to India as any other part of the world. He believed—privately and cautiously during Baldwin's premiership—that the Socialists should be more active in pressing for the lifting of 'the Colonial yoke'. But there was, of course, the possibility that if ever the yoke were lifted he as a professional diplomat would be out of a job; so he confined his aspirations on behalf of His Majesty's underprivileged subjects to papers which he wrote in the study of his big morose house in Dulwich on Sunday afternoons.

His wife, a caricature of Tory womanhood complete with straw bonnet bountiful with cherries and a way with servants—they had *one*—mocked his efforts and he kept his theses locked in a drawer in the escritoire. He had only married his wife to further his professional advancement and had never ceased to wonder whether the sacrifice had been worth it.

But the greatest blow to his private ideals had come with his appointment as one of the representatives of the Secretary of State for India. He had hastened to India by sea longing to meet the underprivileged masses crushed under the heel of the Imperialist regime which he represented. But at Bombay an Indian porter stole his suitcase containing his theses and most of his lightweight clothing.

Since then each visit to India had contributed to the deterioration of his ideals. In the caste system he had come across privilege that could never be equalled by Imperialism in its most extreme form; in the Princes' States he had come across arrogance and indulgence in luxury that made the excesses of British aristocracy seem as orgiastic as a church fête; among the merchants and businessmen he had discovered corruption that would have put all of them in the dock at the Old Bailey had they lived in Britain; among the lower castes and the Untouchables he came across a bland fatalism that had no part in any political fervour for equality; among the Nationalist leaders—with the exception of Gandhi—he found that personal ambition powered by chicanery and dedicated distortion of fact was a stronger phenomena than compassion for the underprivileged. In short Ramsey Crockford didn't understand India.

Worse still he found himself acting like the people whom he had been taught to detest. He went shooting with a party from the Viceregal lodge; he applauded the champion pig-sticker when he received the Kadir Cup; he sympathised over tea and cucumber sandwiches with the memsahibs over the stupidity of the servants; he played bridge, drank too much whisky, agreed to take part in a tiger hunt in which he knew that the tiger was virtually trapped before the hunt began; he agreed that he didn't know what the country was coming to and he called letters chits and rupees chips.

Thus Ramsey Crockford, aged forty-five, with the countenance of a village grocer and the airs of an ambassador, was the victim of one of the most vicious furies of all—anger at his own treachery. And as he couldn't castigate himself he looked for other prey. Recently they had not been difficult to find. First there had been the crazy officer who had nearly caused another Indian Mutiny by massacring 149 Indians at Baipur. The feeling of both Congress and the Moslems had to be appeased and the officer had been publicly disgraced. The procedure had afforded Crockford some quiet pleasure. Now there was this bloody doctor who had blinded the son of one of the most virulent of the Nationalist leaders. He gave his croquet ball a savage crack and aimed his spite at the doctor.

He said: 'The Secretary of State is very perturbed about this affair, Couldridge. So, of course, is the Earl of Willingdon. And I understand from the latest cable I have received that Ramsay Mac himself has expressed concern.'

371

'You mean the Prime Minister, I presume?'

'Who else, for God's sake?'

'I didn't realise you were on such intimate terms with him. Quite a coincidence—your Christian name.'

'Different spelling,' Crockford said.

Couldridge cracked his blue ball against Crockford's red one and sent it twenty yards away from a hoop. 'I should have thought the Viceroy would have had more sense,' he said. 'He's got rid of a lot of our snobbery—and he's always refused to discuss civil disobedience with trouble-makers.'

'Just how does that preclude the Earl of Willingdon from expressing disquiet at your actions?'

'Because Pandit Chet Ram is a trouble-maker intent on provoking trouble and I shouldn't have thought he would have listened to him.'

Crockford sensed that the initiative was slipping away from him. He was also hampered by the awe with which he regarded doctors. He took his spite out on a croquet ball; but it missed all the others and churned through a bed of red lilies. 'Blast,' he said with quiet ferocity.

Couldridge sent a ball rolling through a hoop. 'What exactly are you trying to tell me, Crockford? There's been enough fuss already. It isn't the first recorded failure of a corneal transplant. I've offered to carry out another on the boy but the father won't allow it.'

'I can't say that I blame him,' Crockford said. 'The miracle is that he allowed the first one.' He retrieved the ball from the lilies.

They were playing on the lawn of the villa belonging to a senior member of the Viceroy's staff. The owner had gathered the rest of the guests on to the verandah for tea because Crockford had said he wanted a private word with Couldridge.

'I'm not really interested in your opinions,' Couldridge said. 'I came to Delhi because you asked me to. I didn't have to come but I foolishly thought that you might be offering me some help. Now you've got me to yourself on the croquet lawn please tell

372

me what it's all about.'

Crockford cracked his ball back into play. Sweat stained the armpits of the ill-fitting alpaca jacket that had been made for him in Calcutta in one day. On the verandah he could hear his wife's patronising laugh. He detested India, Couldridge and his wife in that order. 'The situation,' he said, 'is extremely delicate. As you probably know the Indians—or Congress at least—are already saying that you used Pandit Chet Ram's boy as a guinea pig because he was an Indian and Indians are expendable.'

'It wouldn't be the first time Indian politicians have distorted the truth for their own ends.'

Crockford said: 'Agreed—but the timing is rather awkward. First of all both Congress and the Moslems are kicking up stink because they feel that the Princes are getting too big a representation in the Central Legislature. Then there's this bloody mess caused by Colonel Spenser.' He paused and looked shrewdly at Couldridge. 'A friend of yours, I believe.'

'He was a friend,' Couldridge said. 'But the fact seems quite irrelevant.'

'It merely seems such a coincidence that you should both be causing His Majesty's Government such a lot of trouble at the same time.'

'What do you want me to do about it? I've already explained my actions. I am sorry about the boy but I would have no compunction about performing a similar operation again. In fact I'm looking for another donor right now.'

Crockford said: 'Coming on top of the Spenser affair your unsuccessful operation has caused quite a lot of damage to British prestige. As you know Pandit Chet Ram is making political capital out of his son's plight.' He paused and concentrated on his shot; the balls clicked with woody resonance. 'Did it ever occur to you, Couldridge, that Pandit Chet Ram authorised the operation on the presumption that it would fail?'

Couldridge shook his head 'No,' he said, 'it didn't. And what's more, evil old bastard though he is, I don't believe he is as devious as that.'

'Perhaps not. The fact remains that the other evening he had his son out on a platform with him. I quote, "He is the victim of white man's medicine. Would a British doctor have carried out such an operation on one of his own kind?" I don't need to tell you, Couldridge, that the crowd went hysterical.'

Couldridge struck a ball towards the winning peg. 'The boy was going blind anyway.'

'You know that. And I suppose I know it. But a few million Indians don't.'

'Very well,' Couldridge said. 'You've made your point. Now what do you want me to do about it?'

Crockford saw his wife coming towards them. Roses on her bonnet for once instead of cherries. As always he looked with awe at her magnificent bosom; she needed a title, he thought, to support such a bust. And she expected him to get it for her. 'Let's have another chat after dinner,' he said. 'A cigar on the verandah perhaps.'

'As you wish,' Couldridge said. 'It's my shot by the way.' The ball hit the peg with a dull thud.

Crockford hit his ball viciously, more in the direction of his wife than the peg. She and her bosom stepped aside graciously.

At dinner Couldridge was privileged to see almost as much of her bosom as he would have in a professional capacity. It was not that the decolletage was particularly revealing: it was merely that the size and thrust of her bust would have stretched the modesty of any evening gown.

Whereas her husband hated India Mrs Crockford loved it. It showed the British at their best, she thought. Like the dinner this evening. The dignity and elegance of the white dinner jackets and rustling gowns, the candelabra and the silverware and the cut glass. All so controlled and refined despite the droughts, famines, plagues and massacres; despite the agitation and ingratitude of the Indians to whom Britain had brought the benefits of civilisation. India really did show the world how well the British ruled.

She finished the cold consommé and turned her bosoms towards

Couldridge, unaware that he had diagnosed that she might have difficulty in breast feeding with the qualification that she probably wouldn't want to anyway.

'I hear, doctor, that you are in a spot of trouble,' she said.

'I carried out an operation that was unsuccessful. It happens to all surgeons.'

The bosoms nodded sympathetically. 'But this was rather a different sort of operation, was it not?'

'It was a corneal transplant if that's what you mean. They started this sort of thing in 1789 so it wasn't all that different.'

'I understood that the method of transplant was a little unusual?'

'You mean because the graft came from a dead body?'

The bosoms shivered. 'Yes. What a dreadful topic to discuss over a meal.'

'Not at all, Mrs Crockford. I see nothing distasteful in it at all. We all die. Why shouldn't our bodies be used to help the living.'

She dropped her lace handkerchief on the floor, bent to pick it up and glanced at Couldridge to see if he was looking at the nipples which must surely be showing. He was drinking a glass of water.

'But dead bodies,' she said. 'It's a bit ghoulish.'

'Call them cadavers if you like,' he said.

'Oh,' she said.

Across the table Ramsey Crockford listened with cultivated attention veiling utter boredom to a civil servant's views on the muted Hindu Woman's Right to Property Act.

The civil servant sensed the boredom and tried to shock. 'They still practise suttee, you know,' he said. And in case the British Government's current expert on Indian affairs didn't understand he added: 'That means they burn themselves alive when their husbands die.'

'I was aware of that,' Crockford said.

'Don't you feel we should do something about it?'

'We've done our best,' Crockford said. 'But you can't end

barbarism with a single act of legislation.' He looked apprehensively at his wife who tended to be indiscreet.

'I wish,' Couldridge said, 'that your husband would forget he's a diplomat for once and tell me what he wants me to do.'

Mrs Crockford said: 'It's not what he wants you to do it's what *they* want you to do. The Prime Minister, the Secretary for State and the Viceroy.'

'I can hardly believe that one unsuccessful operation would provoke discussion at quite such a high level.'

'Oh but it has.' The firm plump mounds moved closer. 'You see it happened so soon after the Spenser affair.' She glanced from side to side and added conspiratorially: 'Frankly I was on the side of Colonel Spenser. It was time the Indians were taught another lesson. But I suppose he shouldn't have shot quite so many ...'

Couldridge applied himself to his cutlets. 'You're entitled to your opinion,' he said.

'But don't you agree?—up to a point.'

Couldridge shook his head. 'What's more I can't see the connection between the massacre and the corneal graft.'

Mrs Crockford glanced around, conscious that neither her bust nor her conversation was impressing Couldridge. 'Of course I shouldn't be discussing this ...'

'No,' Couldridge said.

'But, as I understand it, the British not only want to appease Indian opinion but they want to make a definite gesture of friendship.'

'Oh yes,' Couldridge said.

'That Ramsay Macdonald, of course. But my husband doesn't think he will be in power much longer. Baldwin will be back, thank heavens.'

'I'm afraid I'm not the slightest bit interested in politics. I can't see that it's going to make much difference to me whether Ramsay Macdonald or Baldwin is in power.'

'I'm afraid it won't,' Mrs Crockford said. 'Once the British Government is committed to a line of action they won't be able to change it. And this Pandit Chet Ram is kicking up such an awful stink. He's accusing you of the most dreadful things.' She paused. 'There is one thing that I think you should know about.'

'Are you sure you should tell me?'

Mrs Crockford almost winked. 'I'm sure I shouldn't.'

'In fact,' Couldridge said, 'you're not going to have a chance to. Here's your husband.'

The dinner was over, the cigars were smouldering. Ramsey Crockford walked rapidly around the table and stood behind his wife, looking down at the bosom which his wife seemed more willing to exhibit to other men than himself. 'If you will excuse me, my dear,' he said, 'Dr Couldridge and I have some unfinished business to discuss.'

'Of course, dear.' She stood up, drawing a shawl of blue silk embroidered with gold thread around her broad white shoulders. 'Perhaps we can continue our little chat later, doctor.'

On the verandah Crockford produced his cigar case and offered it to Couldridge.

'No thanks,' Couldridge said. 'I'll smoke my pipe if you don't mind.'

Crockford made a business of his cigar. He removed the band from it, snipped it with a gold cutter, glued down a flake of leaf with spittle, warmed the end and finally lit it. Couldridge lit his scarred old pipe, and waited. The sky was deep with stars and moonlight glowed remotely on the roofs and cupolas of the city: the leaves of palm trees rasped with lonely sounds and crickets called with timeless monotony.

'The best time of the day in India,' Crockford said. Because, he thought, you couldn't see the bloody place.

Couldridge sucked the burning tobacco into incandescence. 'What do you want to tell me, Crockford?'

Crockford sighed. The village grocer in him applauded forthright talk: the diplomat detested it. 'This fellow Pandit Chet Ram,' he said. 'He certainly seems to have developed a healthy dislike for you.'

377

'I once implied that he must have suffered from venereal disease at some time in his life. That never endears you to people. But it was the only explanation of his son's condition.'

Crockford's cigar glowed brightly as he selected his words. 'Of course,' he said casually, 'the question of grafting tissue from a dead man is very controversial.'

'Of course,' Couldridge said.

'Mmm.' He examined his cigar with intense interest. 'It's not likely to help your case, is it?'

'What case?'

'Any case that might be brought against you. Feeling is running pretty high, you know.'

'I can hardly be involved in any criminal proceedings because a single operation failed.'

'The feeling isn't just confined to Indians,' Crockford said.

'In thirty years' time people will still be objecting to the grafting of organs from the dead to the living. It's only natural. Just as anti-vivisection is a natural reaction. Natural but wrong. The good sense of the majority will prevail in the end.'

'Nor is the feeling confined to laymen,' Crockford said. He was rather pleased with the way in which he was working his way around to the point. If he concluded this exercise in the appeasement of Indian hostility successfully he might well be promoted. In fact with his enhanced reputation he might even quit his job and stand for Parliament. With his expert knowledge he might one day become Secretary of State for India. Even if he did loathe the place.

'What do you mean?'

'You seem to have made a lot of enemies in your profession. Both in the Army and in civilian life.'

'You mean people like Buckingham and Emmerson?'

'And a few others.' White dinner jackets and silk shawls appeared on the verandah. 'Shall we take a stroll round the garden?'

Couldridge shrugged. 'If you like.' He knocked out his pipe. 'As long as you're not frightened of the snakes.'

Crockford paused. 'There aren't any out there, are there?' He envisaged the ridicule. Bitten by a snake and saved from death by the man he had been sent to deal with.

Couldridge laughed. 'Come on,' he said, 'we'll risk it.'

'Are you sure?'

'Probably only kraits,' Couldridge said.

'Are they quite harmless?'

'If one bites you in the ankle you're dead in a few minutes.'

The oiled flow of diplomacy faltered: the anger returned. 'I'm beginning to think that your reputation for irresponsibility is well justified.'

'Is that what my colleagues are saying about me?'

'Exactly that,' Crockford said.

'Then you're in a bit of a dilemma, aren't you? Because I'm going into the garden now and I'm leaving Delhi tomorrow. If there's something more you've got to tell me you'll have to come with me.' Couldridge walked down the wooden steps on to the lawn smelling the jasmine and listening to the swoop of the big bats in the moist air. Crockford followed cautiously. He didn't believe there were any kraits in the garden; but he stamped on the turf and whistled casually to warn any reptilian life of his approach.

Couldridge said: 'Now for the last time—just what have you got to tell me, Crockford?'

Crockford relit his cigar. 'It's quite simple really. Public opinion is against this business of using tissue from dead bodies.' A few sparks flew from the glowing tip of his cigar. 'A lot of people are sceptical about the precautions which surgeons take to ensure that the donors are in fact dead. And in any case who is to say that a man is dead just because his heart has stopped beating?'

'There are certain accepted conditions which all physicians will agree signifies that life as we know it has become extinct.'

'Perhaps.' Crockford drew more steadily on his cigar: no snakes had attacked him and the conversation was once again approaching its climax. 'But were those conditions present when this other unfortunate boy died?'

379

'Of course they were,' Couldridge said.

'That's something anyway.'

'What the hell are you getting at, Crockford?'

'Did you get written permission from the boy's parents to take a graft from his eye after his death?'

'Of course I did,' Couldridge said.

Crockford flicked the butt of his cigar away. It fell with a hiss in the lilies. 'Strange,' he said.

'Strange? I see nothing strange about it.'

Crockford paused and steadied himself to enjoy his revenge for the croquet and the snakes. 'It's strange,' he said, 'because Pandit Chet Ram says that no such permission was obtained.'

9

AT first Couldridge didn't believe him. But when Crockford elaborated he realised he was telling the truth. It was not only Pandit Chet Ram who claimed that no permission had been obtained: the dead boy's parents said that no authority had been given for the 'mutilation' of their son's body. And, said Crockford, several doctors were only too willing to testify to Couldridge's general irresponsibility.

Crockford then recited his rehearsed piece. The Government wanted to appease Indian opinion: the doctors wanted to preserve the ethics of their profession. In short both politicians and doctors thought it would be in their interests if Couldridge appeared before the disciplinary committee of the General Medical Council.

Crockford added that the Government would have been dubious about encouraging such a measure if it had not been for unexpectedly enthusiastic support of the doctors. And he confided—off the record—that he suspected that their motives were not quite as righteous as they seemed. It was his only departure from protocol; he appeared to enjoy delivering the rest of the indictment.

As they walked back across the lawn Couldridge told Crockford that he thought he could hear a snake. Crockford ran into the house with a whimper of fear.

Next morning Couldridge said goodbye to Crockford and his wife, who had replaced the roses on her bonnet with cherries once more. Her bosom was flattened beneath a linen dress as if it had been snubbed. Her voice was polite, diffident.

In the train taking him to Lahore awareness of what was being done to him finally settled on Couldridge. He acknowledged that he had been a bloody fool. Pandit Chet Ram had shown him a document which he said was the declaration signed by the parents giving permission for a graft to be taken from their son's eye after death. But he hadn't examined the document; nor had he asked for a copy.

But although Couldridge was appalled by the knowledge that he would have to appear in a court of ethics before his elders he had no doubt that he would be vindicated. He was merely experiencing the sort of setback experienced by pioneering doctors since research began. His reasoning tactfully excluded the case of Dr Nesfield who had been struck off the register a few years before.

He looked out of the window and found that the train had stopped in a village complete with banyan tree and stone image of a bull. Idleness and idolatry shared the village's confines. Along the single baked road came two figures—a tall, cadaverous man and a small boy. The boy was leading the man on a short length of rope; the boy's face didn't question his lot. The man was blind and from the train Couldridge could see the milky cornea, vague and incongruous in his sunken brown face. The boy led the man to the shade under the banyan tree and they sat down. They stared at the train and Couldridge could see the boy telling the blind man what was happening. As the train moved off Couldridge felt moisture stinging his eyes. He swore deliberately and viciously to himself invoking the names of Buckingham, Emmerson, Little and finally Crockford. But he and the cause of progress would beat them.

'I still find it hard to believe that I've got so many enemies,' he said to Joanne that evening.

'I don't,' she said. 'You were born to have enemies. You could have had friends, too. Many people wanted to be friends with you. They were drawn to you by your independence. But you never had time for them—there was always your work. So you were left with your enemies.'

'I suppose you're right. I could do with some friends now.'

'You've got me,' she said.

'Yes,' he said, 'I've got you.' He took one hand from the steering wheel of the car which she had brought to the station. 'Poor old Spenser had no one. Not even his wife.'

'That was his fault,' she said.

'Not really. He needed help a long time ago. I should have done something to help him.'

'You were the last person he would have accepted help from.' She redirected his hand back to the steering wheel. 'In any case I should concentrate on your own troubles now.'

In front of the car the crowd thickened. Couldridge sounded the horn but they didn't disperse. Some were shaking their fists, others were pointing and shouting.

Joanne said: 'I should have warned you. They recognised the car when I was driving to the station. I'm afraid the feeling is running pretty high.'

'Ungrateful bastards,' Couldridge said. He drove slowly and steadily forward. 'There's a Hindu over there that I treated for cholera. He should be dead by rights.' He wound down the window and shouted at them. Their anger was uncertain.

'I shouldn't upset them any more,' Joanne said. But she was too late.

A stone splintered the windscreen. When Couldridge glanced at her he saw blood trickling down her cheek. 'Are you hurt badly?'

'No,' she said. 'Just a scratch.'

The crowd was snarling now. The white man had blinded an Indian boy. Because the boy was Indian, because he was destined to become a great Nationalist leader. Reason, loyalty, gratitude, evaporated to be replaced by hysteria and hatred. As he gazed at the wild sweating faces, at the balled fists and shouting mouths, Couldridge knew that the hatred wasn't genuine: it was incited but it was just as dangerous.

He reached for the pistol under the dashboard. 'I'll try and drive through them,' he said. 'If I can't get through I'll use this.'

A stone bounced on the windscreen and a young Indian, fear swamped by hysteria, ran up to the car and screamed incoherently at them through the open side-window. Couldridge's fist caught him on his nose; there was a tiny crack like the snapping of a green stick and blood spurted thickly down his white shirt. He sat on the ground with his hand to his face looking at Couldridge with astonishment.

The growling stopped because retaliation was not expected on such occasions. All movement was frozen for a moment.

Couldridge said: 'This is it.' He glanced at Joanne. There was no fear in her face, just anger. Glass lay scattered in her lap and the trickle of blood had reached her neck. He laid the pistol beside him on the seat. Then he let out the clutch, pressed the accelerator hard down and drove straight into the mob. They shouted and jumped out of the way; he felt the wing brush against a body; then he was through. A boy tried to jump on the running-board but he fell off. A few stones bounced on the roof and a few youths gave chase. But they soon gave up.

When they arrived home Couldridge phoned for police protection. Then he bathed Joanne's face in the surgery.

'What are you going to do?' she said.

'Go and face the music of course.'

She nodded as if she had known the answer. 'Why does it have to be London?'

'Because they want it that way. The full ceremony of disgrace as administered by the most august body in the medical

383

world—the GMC. And because I qualified in Britain.'

'But supposing they do strike you off the register?'

Couldridge lit his pipe and blew out clouds of confidence. 'Not a chance. You can't be struck off just because an operation wasn't successful. There's absolutely no proof of carelessness or dereliction of duty.'

She looked at him wisely, feeling the strip of plaster on her cheek with one finger. 'I guess you know what you're doing. But I wouldn't trust anyone in your profession—I've seen too many of them at work.'

'You've only seen the worst kind,' Couldridge said.

'But what about this accusation that the dead boy's parents didn't give permission for the graft to be taken?'

Couldridge picked up a trephine and examined it with affection. 'That's only a technicality. Can you imagine what sort of a witness Pandit Chet Ram will make? A good counsel will tear him to bits in a few minutes.' He put down the trephine. 'No, the only thing worrying me is why the operation didn't succeed.'

'You don't think that Pandit Chet Ram told his son to interfere with the graft?'

Couldridge shook his head. 'I don't think even Pandit Chet Ram would go to those lengths.' He paused. 'You know what I'd like to do more than anything once this bloody thing is over?'

'I've no idea,' Joanne said.

'I'd like to go to Odessa to this clinic run by Filatov and see some of his work. There was a time when I thought my research was keeping up with his—even though I was working by myself. Now I might just as well become one of his disciples.'

Joanne smiled at him. 'Then we shall go,' she said. 'After we've been to London.'

'You mean you'll come with me to London?'

'Of course. I'll make arrangements for the children to be looked after.'

'You don't have to,' he said.

'Try and stop me,' she said.

He kissed her on the forehead and watched with love as she walked out of the surgery, one finger still fidgeting with the plaster on her cheek. She hadn't once reminded him that she had advised him not to carry out the graft. Now she was coming with him because of everything they had shared and because of the loyalty that was part of her character. There was nothing more. Not now. One day perhaps.

He opened the window and smelled the night air. Jasmine and curry and dew. Then he sat down and opened his text books.

BOOK SIX

1

JOHN COULDRIDGE walked from the small hotel near St Pancras Station to his counsel's chambers in The Temple. He walked briskly and confidently enjoying the heatwave in which London revelled and grumbled. The temperature was eighty degrees: the frosted glass doors of the pubs were wide open, men wore shirt-sleeves, girls with pale faces wore long-sleeved silk dresses and neckscarves, petrol fumes and the rusty smells of underground railway stations hung in the air. But to Couldridge the sunshine was as soft as the sunshine of a spring day in Lahore or Bombay and the warm odours as inoffensive as catmint compared with the stench of a Calcutta sewer.

He enjoyed London again as he had enjoyed it as a student. The busy, uncommitted people, the stained and friendly build-ings, the red buses and patient policemen and old women chatting to themselves, the humour and the ordinariness and the indiffer-ence to the rest of the world. He embraced it all; but he knew that the enjoyment would not last because its essence was novelty. Soon he would be wanting the hot and helpless muddles and ancient graces of India.

He stood and looked at St Pancras Station. It reminded him of the Victoria Railway Terminus at Bombay. But instead of beggars there was an old woman selling sleek unfurled roses and blue irises and a newspaper vendor selling the racing editions of the three London evening papers. Couldridge bought a paper and read that the Derby had been won by two lengths by a colt called Bahram ridden by Fox. The owner—the Aga Khan. Couldridge smiled because it was the only reference to anyone or anything Indian in the paper. The editors were more interested in the return of Baldwin to the premiership, Italy's threatened invasion of Ethiopia and the forthcoming attempt by the Russians to make a record ascent into the stratosphere with a balloon.

He walked down Gray's Inn Road, past the Royal Free Hospital, to the Tudor façade of Holborn. On the corner stood a blind man selling matches and bootlaces. Couldridge looked at the old man's eyes. They looked as if they had been damaged by injury, by lime burns, perhaps. He gave the man half-a-crown, decided that he would attempt another corneal graft as soon as the disciplinary proceedings were over, and strode on through the mid-day sunshine along Holborn and down Chancery Lane.

His counsel, who explained that the solicitor was sick, was waiting for him. He was a big Welshman with silver hair and an expansive belly taut behind his striped trousers whose court-room manners stayed with him after he had left the Law Courts or the Old Bailey; in his old and leathery chambers he continued to prosecute, cross-examine and mitigate before an invisible jury. Any statement about the weather, the Government or gardening was arguable. His thumbs slipped inside his waistcoat, he toyed with an imaginary wig. In court Henry Lloyd-Williams was still considered to be brilliant although a little old-fashioned : juries were not so influenced these days by the impassioned Welsh rhetoric of his final speeches. But his main fault was his tenacity which, in cross-examination, made him pursue a point until a witness gave an answer that was damaging to his client.

'Ah, Dr Couldridge,' he said. Hand straying to the invisible wig, he put Couldridge into the witness box on the other side of the mahogany desk with the green leather top. 'An unusual case,' he said. 'And a very interesting one. The powers that be in the medical profession seem to have moved with almost unseemly haste to get your case heard.' He waited a moment while the non-existent jury assimilated the point.

'And the politicians,' Couldridge said.

'Do you really believe that there is any political motivation behind these proceedings?'

'I was virtually told so.'

'By whom?'

'By the representative of the Secretary of State for India. A man called Crockford. The Government is very anxious that Indian hostility to the British should be appeased and that the India Act should go through smoothly. I am to be the scapegoat.'

'Interesting.' Lloyd-Williams made some notes with a gold pencil. 'We might very well call the Secretary of State's representative to give evidence.' He stared through the window at an old and mossy rooftop. 'Unfortunately political motive doesn't alter any of the facts. It is a great pity that you have alienated so many of your colleagues. There seems to be as much jealousy among doctors as there is among lawyers.'

'I don't know about jealousy. There's certainly great antipathy towards progress.'

'I am sure there is.' Lloyd-Williams lulled his witness into a false state of security. 'But do you not think that what you consider to be a reactionary attitude is merely necessary caution in a profession dealing with life and death?'

A small shy girl came in with coffee. Lloyd-Williams looked at her as if she were counsel objecting to his question. The girl gave them each a cup, put the sugar between them and disappeared without speaking.

Couldridge said: 'Of course I recognise the necessity for safeguarding the public from irresponsible practices. But, dammit, do you know when the first attempt to cure blindness by replacing corneal tissue was carried out?'

Witnesses were not supposed to question counsel. 'No,' Lloyd-Williams said, 'I don't.'

'In 1789. With a piece of glass. That's nearly one hundred and fifty years ago. You can hardly call that incautious.'

Lloyd-Williams shuffled the papers on his desk and lit a cigarette. Within seconds ash had settled on the lapels of his black jacket and the fly of his tight trousers. Finally he said: 'Unfortunately, Dr Couldridge, we are not today concerned with a piece of glass. We are concerned with the transplanting of tissues from one human body to another. To many people this is repugnant.'

'Is it repugnant to you?'

'Not at all, Dr Couldridge. Not at all. But we must face the fact that this repugnance does exist and it will be one of the factors against us.'

'In the minds of many laymen, perhaps. But not in the minds of doctors and surgeons'

Lloyd-Williams shook his head sadly. 'There is abundant evidence of such feeling among members of your profession. Although I will agree that its sincerity is open to doubt.'

'There must be many medical men who agree with transplants from dead bodies.'

'Indeed there are. But there is not an abundance of such people willing to involve themselves in a case that is going to attract an immense amount of publicity.' He paused. 'However we have managed to get hold of one or two surgeons of some standing who are willing to testify to the efficacy of transplants.'

'Then I don't really see how I can be found guilty if it's merely a question of divergent medical opinions.'

'It's a little more than that, I fear,' Lloyd-Williams said patiently. 'For one thing there are more doctors against you than for you. For another the members of the committee are not noted for their revolutionary approach to medicine. For another' —he replaced his thumbs behind his waistcoat—'there is a question of ethics involved.'

'You mean the question of the parents' approval?'

'Precisely.' Lloyd-Williams looked meaningfully at the twelve phantom citizens in the jury-box. 'Both this fellow Pandit Chet Ram and the boy's parents are going to swear that approval was never given.'

'Then they're bloody liars,' Couldridge said.

'Perhaps. Perhaps, Dr Couldridge. The fact remains that they will testify to that effect. How are we going to refute that testimony?'

'God knows.' Couldridge stared antagonistically at his barri-

391

ster. It's just my word against theirs.'

'Not good enough, Dr Couldridge, I'm afraid. Not good enough at all. Besides that's three against one. Plus the boy of course.'

'They're not going to call him surely?'

'It's difficult to say. Everyone seems very determined to bring about your downfall. More determined than I've ever known them in a GMC case. It wouldn't surprise me to see that boy being led to the witness box feeling his way with a white stick. You have collected your enemies from two extremely powerful, influential and sensitive classes—doctors and politicians.'

'It's monstrous,' Couldridge said.

'I agree. On the other hand you should have taken more positive steps to ensure that you had proof of parental consent from the donor.'

Couldridge stood up and paced the room. 'I was more concerned with saving a boy's sight,' he said.

'They will say that the boy might still be able to see in that eye if you had not undertaken the graft.' He gestured towards the chair. 'Please sit down, Dr Couldridge, and do not agitate yourself. I am merely trying to establish all the facts so that I may be able to defend you adequately.'

Couldridge sat down and said: 'The boy could hardly see out of that eye before the operation. In any case it isn't the failure of the operation that I'm being tried for. If every surgeon who performed an unsuccessful operation were hauled in front of the disciplinary committee of the GMC there wouldn't be any surgeons practising today.'

Lloyd-Williams stood up and took over the pacing, puffing rapidly at his cigarette. 'You are right, of course. The fact remains that here we have the combination of two evils—the lack of evidence that you obtained parental permission *and* the failure of the operation.' He pushed the invisible wig down on his forehead. 'Is there no way, Dr Couldridge, in which you can prove that a document authorising you to carry out the operation existed?'

Couldridge gestured helplessly; the confidence of the sunlit morning was evaporating. 'I only saw the paper in Pandit Chet Ram's hand. It didn't occur to me that he would ever deny its existence.'

'Mmmm.' Lloyd-Williams began to gather up the papers on his desk indicating that the interview was nearing its end. He ground out his cigarette end with a flourish and sat down again. Couldridge felt that Lloyd-Williams should have said, 'No more questions, m'lud.' Instead, he said: 'It's a great pity. It would considerably strengthen our case.'

'I can't help it.'

Lloyd-Williams tied up the papers with pink silk. 'Well, Dr Couldridge, I won't keep you any longer. We must have another chat before the case comes up.' He glanced at the calendar on the wall. 'And that's not very far ahead. There does seem to me to have been most unseemly haste in this matter.' He made a note on a pad. 'I shall make a point of that. Meanwhile if you can think of any way in which you can prove that the parents did give authorisation . . . or if you have a witness present when you saw the document.'

Then Couldridge remembered. 'Wait,' he said. 'There was a witness.'

'Really?' Lloyd-Williams smiled apologetically at an imaginary judge and undid the pink silk. 'Someone who actually saw the document?'

'He didn't read it. But he certainly saw Pandit Chet Ram show it to me.'

Lloyd-Williams sighed. 'I suppose that's better than nothing. Could I have the name of the witness?'

'Bose,' Couldridge said. 'Dr Bose. He came into my consulting rooms when Pandit Chet Ram was showing me the document.'

Lloyd-Williams rustled through the papers again and sighed even more soulfully. 'Do you mean Dr Bose your assistant?'

'Yes,' Couldridge said. 'He helped at the operation. In fact he was the anaesthetist.'

'A pity,' Lloyd Williams said, 'because he is giving evidence against you.'

2

JOHN COULDRIDGE sat in the rose gardens in Regent's Park for most of the afternoon. Nannies in schoolgirls' hats pushed prams covered with tasselled canopies past his seat, lovers smelled the perfume of the roses and planned love, old couples remembered other rose arbours and summers past, a gardener hoed the soil as dry as shale. There were no clouds in the soft blue sky.

Couldridge thought: Bose. It can't be—there must be some mistake. But he knew there wasn't. Who next? Joanne? His children? Self-pity formed a single teardrop in his mind. He patrolled the rose gardens, then walked down Baker Street and turned left along Oxford Street. Shoppers glanced at the tall, sunburned man and stepped aside in the face of such preoccupation.

At Oxford Circus he bought a late evening newspaper. He glanced at his wristwatch. In five minutes the pubs would be opened. He walked slowly down Regent Street and turned into a bar just as they were opening the doors. He ordered a large Scotch and soda. He drank it swiftly and determinedly and then ordered another.

The barman said: 'A large one, sir?'

'A large one,' Couldridge said.

The barman looked at him speculatively because that was four normal whiskies in five minutes and Couldridge did not look the hard liquor sort. Couldridge took the second Scotch slower. Ten minutes later he ordered another.

'A large one, sir? Or a small one.'

'A large one,' Couldridge said.

'Thank you, sir.'

'And some ice, please.'

'Certainly, sir.'

Couldridge tinkled the ice around in his glass. There was, he knew, nothing quite as disgraceful in the public's mind as the spectacle of a drunken doctor. Lawyers, architects, bankers and accountants were permitted to get drunk occasionally: doctors never. Nevertheless John Couldridge drank on.

A plump sighing man sat down beside Couldridge at the bar. 'What a scorcher,' he said. He glanced at Couldridge. 'But you look as if you're used to the sun.'

'India,' Couldridge said. 'I live in India. I've just arrived.'

'Then you missed the Silver Jubilee?' He spoke with a slight North Country accent.

'I'm afraid so.'

'It was wonderful. Bloody wonderful. Would you like another drink?'

'Thanks,' Couldridge said. 'I'll have a Scotch.'

The barman said: 'A small one, sir?'

And because it was someone else's round Couldridge said: 'Yes, a small one, please.'

'I read something about India during the Jubilee,' the North Countryman said.

'Really?'

'I remember what it was. Stuck in my mind because it seemed so daft.'

'What was so daft?' Couldridge asked obligingly.

'This tribe. Somewhere near Bombay I think it was. They decided to give up wife-beating for six months to mark the Jubilee.' He laughed. 'Of all the bloody silly things to give up.' He drank his whisky in one quick movement. 'My name's Bowman. Bill Bowman. I'm in textiles.' He waited for Couldridge to identify himself.

Couldridge said: 'My name's Hatherley. I'm in the Indian Civil Service.'

'I thought as much,' Bowman said. 'Looking for a good night-out in London, I suppose. As it happens I'm not going back

395

to Manchester until tomorrow and I'm at a loose end tonight. Why don't we have a few drinks together and then move on to a club I know of in Soho?'

'I don't mind having a few drinks,' Couldridge said. 'I don't think I'll bother with the club.'

'We'll see how it goes,' Bowman said. 'You must be pretty tired of native tarts. There's one or two French girls at this club. Quite accommodating, too, after you've bought them a couple of bottles of champagne.'

'I wouldn't mind having a few drinks in a pub,' Couldridge said. 'That's what you miss in India—an English pub.' It was, he knew, the sort of remark that Englishmen liked to hear.

'And English beer, I've no doubt. I haven't been abroad very much. Le Havre, Ostend and Amsterdam. But I always say that coming back to Britain is the best part of going abroad.' He laughed and his flesh shook beneath his moist shirt and his thick, badly-fitting suit. 'All right, then, let's go to a pub and have a few pints.'

They walked across Regent Street in which there were now signs of evening leisure and elegance after the hot shopping day. They went into a pub near the Palladium called the Argyll —a dark and comfortable place cool with panels of ornate frosted glass and moistened with the froth of Guinness and beer.

They drank a pint of beer apiece and Couldridge thought: To hell with Bose. To hell with all the timid jealous bastards who want to finish me. Silently he toasted Koch and Nesfield, Zirm and Power and Magitot.

Bowman said: 'You look very thoughtful. Are you dreaming about all those native birds of yours? Having it off in the moon-light at the Taj Mahal and all that?' He had acquired a moustache of foam, from his beer.

'I'm sorry. It's a bit strange at first being back in London.' He called over the barmaid with a deep and freckled bosom and ordered two more pints of beer. He knew he was getting drunk and he didn't care.

'What's your first name?' Bowman said.

'Neville,' Couldridge said. 'Neville Hatherley. Colonialist, bureaucrat and prize pig-sticker.' He saw himself in a patterned mirror. Greying hair, brown face, still slim. He lit a cigarette because a pipe did not seem to be a part of a night-out in the West End and thought of Joanne. For the first time the sadness at her lack of physical affection was replaced by sullen anger. So he had wrongly diagnosed his son's illness; but he had nursed the boy back to health. She had, he supposed, welcomed the opportunity to give an excuse for her distaste for the act of love. He stared into the winking bubbles of his beer with burgeoning and alcoholic wisdom. Since his marriage he had never been unfaithful: but that was no cause for self-satisfaction because fidelity had never been any strain. Now, perhaps, the time had come to perform the single act of adultery without which so many men did not seem to consider their lives complete. He remembered the Indian girl in Bombay, now middle-aged or dead, and smelled again her spiced and musky scents. He finished the beer.

Bowman said: 'What about a short? The old bladder's not what it used to be.'

'All right,' Couldridge said.

'You've got quite a capacity, haven't you? I suppose you booze a lot in India.'

Couldridge nodded. 'Quite a bit.'

'How do you get on with the natives? Ungrateful bloody lot, aren't they, after all we've done for them. I reckon that bloke Spenser knew what he was doing.'

'He thought he knew what he was doing.'

'Ah. You knew him then?'

'Very well,' Couldridge said. 'He wasn't well at the time of the massacre.'

Bowman stared down the barmaid's blouse as she picked up a bottle from the bottom shelf. 'Just the same I think he was dead right. I reckon India could do with a few more men like Spenser. It's the only way to keep the natives down.'

'Let's go on somewhere else,' Couldridge said.

They walked along Oxford Street. Past a hoarding advertising the film *The Lives of a Bengal Lancer* and Ivor Novello's *Glamorous Night* at Drury Lane. Couldridge had promised to take Joanne to the theatre before the disciplinary committee proceedings.

They turned into a big bare pub with a veined marble bar, half a dozen muscular Irish barmen with clean scrubbed faces and a glass case containing slabs of dry veal and ham pie.

'I don't think we'll stay here long,' Bowman said. 'It looks a bit bloody rough. I don't mind for myself but you ...'

'I like it,' Couldridge said. 'It's the sort of place where you find the real Londoners.'

'It's the sort of place where you get a thick ear.'

Couldridge beamed at the thirsty men gathered at the bar. They seemed to him to be the embodiment of honesty and plain-speaking. Not a hypocrite nor a traitor nor a jealous man among them. He felt like ordering drinks all round.

Bowman handed him a half of bitter. 'I think we'd better go a bit easy,' he said. 'The night is young.' He grimaced slyly. 'And don't forget we've got to be fit when we get to the club.'

The beer was warm and tasted of rust. 'It's flat,' Couldridge said. 'Shall I ask the barman to change it?'

'It's not the sort of pub where they change beer,' Bowman said uneasily.

'Nonsense. It's just the sort of place where they appreciate good beer.'

'I wouldn't if I were you.'

But Couldridge was at the bar smiling at a barman and pointing at his glass of beer.

The barman said: 'It looks all right to me.'

Couldridge said: 'But it doesn't taste all right.'

The barman sipped the beer. 'Tastes all right, too,' he said. He put the glass back on the marble-topped bar and went to serve another customer.

The smile left Couldridge's voice. 'I'm asking you to change

398

it,' he said. The barman ignored him. Couldridge leaned over the bar and grasped the top of his stained white apron. 'Didn't you hear me?'

The barman relaxed the grip of his sausage fingers on the beer-pull and addressed the customers standing around Couldridge. 'This gentleman'—he emphasised the word—'is complaining about the beer. I don't recall any of youse complaining about it.' He ran his fingers through his greased curls.

'Nothing wrong with it at all,' said a little man with a face like a jockey's. 'It's a good drop. Perhaps it's just not the right drop for a gentleman like this.'

'It might stain his fine suit,' said another customer with a flushed and battered face.

Couldridge realised that he was surrounded by belligerent Irishmen. The flame of anger inside him flickered and gained strength. He remembered the fight in Calcutta with Spenser. He clenched his fists. 'No one asked you for your opinion,' he said to the Irishman with the punched-up face.

'But I'm giving it to youse whether you asked for it or not.' He peered closely at Couldridge. 'Where did you get that fine tan from? On the French Riviera, I suppose it would be, with all the other pansies.'

Couldridge looked round for Bowman but he had disappeared. 'No,' he said, 'in India as a matter of fact.'

The Irishman with the jockey's face said: 'Twould be Poona and all that, I suppose.' He turned to his friends and said: 'I'm thinking this fellow is a pukka sahib.'

'A fucking sahib,' said the big man.

Couldridge tossed his beer in the big Irishman's face with one neat movement. The beer streamed down his face and into the hairs protruding from the neck of his striped collarless shirt. Couldridge felt rather pleased with the effect. He knew he was drunk but that his reflexes were still quick. He waited.

The bar was silent. The big Irishman stood paralysed with surprise. Then he picked up his fist from the bar. 'You bastard,' he said. 'You fucking bastard.'

The man with the jockey's face said: 'Sweet Mother of God.' And edged his way towards the bar.

Couldridge saw the big fist, knuckles small and white in the flesh, coming at him very slowly. He ducked and the fist passed over his head; still very slowly it seemed. He sunk his left into the big Irishman's belly and then, as the Irishman jerked down sighing, brought up his right. It was aimed at the jaw but it went high squashing his nose and bending a tooth back in its socket. 'What was that about pansies?' he said.

The Irishman stood up and looked at him ruminatively. Then he put his hand to his mouth and removed the tooth. He spat blood in Couldridge's direction. 'I'll kill you for that,' he said. 'I'll bloody well kill you.'

The barman vaulted the bar and said: 'Control yourself, paddy.'

The Irishman pushed him aside with his left hand. The barman fell against another customer knocking his beer out of his hand, and another fight started. But the centre of the arena belonged to Couldridge and his opponent.

Couldridge didn't wait for the Irishman to launch his revenge because he knew that in the crowd he wouldn't be able to dodge the huge meaty punches for long. He punched straight and hard with his left at the bleeding face. He punched at injustice, misunderstanding, hypocrisy and jealousy. He punched at Buckingham and Emmerson and Little. As he punched the incongruity of the situation occurred to him briefly and he saw the headline, 'Doctor in drunken brawl on eve of disciplinary proceedings.' He felt another of the Irishman's teeth bite into his knuckle and break. At least, he thought, he was giving some other doctor—and a dentist—some work. He grinned fiercely, moved nearer and followed the left with a right to the cheek-bone.

He became aware that fighting was going on elsewhere in the bar; that another barman was phoning the police; that there was a lot of broken glass on the floor; that he should escape before the police arrived.

The Irishman was shaking his head, frowning and mouthing red bubbles of obscenity like an actor playing a stunned Irish thug. He put up his fists again and moved closer to Couldridge. Couldridge realised for the first time that the Irishman was very drunk; but then so was he. The Irishman's knee came up comparatively quickly. Couldridge stepped back, dropped his hands and caught hold of the Irishman's thigh. He jerked upwards and the Irishman fell on his back and lay there like a beetle.

'He'll kill you now,' one of the customers said.

'When he gets up,' Couldridge said.

A bottle sailed past his head and crashed into the bottles behind the bar. Two of the barmen stared sadly at the gin and brandy flowing on to the floor. Two other fights were in progress and a woman who had been waiting outside with a port and lemon was swiping with her handbag at a big man kicking a small man on the ground.

Couldridge's opponent was trying to get up. But he was making a business of it. He was breathing noisily, feeling the raw gaps in his teeth with his tongue.

Down the bar another Irishman swung a punch, missed his opponent and knocked the case of veal and ham on to the floor. Four of the barmen were fighting, the others were watching with mild interest as if it were a nightly occurrence.

Couldridge's opponent finally climbed to his feet and stood in front of Couldridge swaying slightly. Couldridge knew that he shouldn't hit him; it was too easy. He said again: 'What was that about pansies?'

The Irishman swore and spat blood.

'Apologise for what you said,' Couldridge said. His own breath was coming with difficulty.

'Go fuck yourself,' said the Irishman.

Couldridge hit him once more. Not too hard, in the chest. I'm the son of a missionary, he thought. Fellow of the Royal College of Surgeons. Sweet Mother of God. He turned and plunged into the crowd. They parted before him.

At the door one of the fighting barmen paused from combat and said: 'If you ever want a job as a bouncer ...'

Couldridge grinned. 'Thanks,' he said. He would have liked to say more but he found he couldn't talk. As he slipped out into the evening sunshine someone hit the barman in the eye.

Outside policemen were piling out of a van. A middle-aged man inflated with outrage caught one the policemen's arms and pointed at Couldridge. 'He's just run out of the bar,' he said. 'He must have been fighting. Go and arrest him, officer.'

The policeman appraised Couldridge's expensive fawn suit. 'What's it like in there, sir?' he asked.

'Pretty rough,' Couldridge said.

The policeman grinned. 'I think we'll give them a few more moments to knock the stuffing out of each other,' he said. He looked at Couldridge's ruffled hair, at his wandering tie, and looked the other way. 'I should hurry on if I were you, sir.'

Couldridge said: 'Thanks.' He paused and inhaled some more air. 'Thanks a lot.'

'Aren't you going to do anything?' said the outraged informant.

The policeman put his arm around the man's shoulders. 'Move along there, sir. We can't have you obstructing the pavement, you know.'

A bottle came through the window showering glass on the pavement. A sergeant with a muscular stomach said: 'Come on lads—we'd better go in now.' They drew their truncheons.

On the edge of the crowd Couldridge found Bowman. 'You were a tower of bloody strength,' he said.

'I can't afford to get into trouble,' Bowman said. 'I've got my position to think of.'

Couldridge straightened his tie. 'I don't blame you,' he said. 'Now let's go to this club of yours.' He felt exhilarated, as if he had just beaten all his enemies instead of one sodden Irishman.

'It's a bit early.'

Couldridge glanced at his watch. 'It's nine o'clock.'

'Too early.' He looked apprehensively at Couldridge. 'I don't fancy it at the club if there's going to be any trouble. I didn't realise you were a scrapper.'

'Don't worry,' Couldridge said. 'I'm finished for the night.'

They had a couple more beers in a Soho pub where most of the customers were drinking Pernod. Then they headed for Bowman's club. Everyone out walking seemed to be foreigners or visitors from the provinces. A few prostitutes stationed themselves in doorways and stared at passing men seductively and belligerently.

One stopped Couldridge and asked for a light. 'Would you like to come and have some fun?' she said.

Couldridge said: 'No, thanks.' He smiled at her.

'Half price for you,' she said. 'Where did you get that tan.'

'India,' he said.

Bowman said: 'Come on for Christ's sake—she's only a tart.'

'I think she's nice,' Couldridge said.

'Why not give me a try?' the prostitute said.

Couldridge shook his head. 'Sorry, some other time.'

'Any time as far as I'm concerned.' She smiled—a little sadly, he thought—hitched up her fur and returned to her doorway.

The club was a small, melancholy place. A few girls sat at a bar smoking cigarettes in holders and a three-piece band played sad tunes. Two men at the door acted like polite warders, the waiters were servile. A large ball studded with pieces of mirror rotated above a dance-floor the size of a boxing ring sending fragments of light spinning around the walls.

A waiter bowed them to a table and Bowman said: 'The girls will be over in a minute.' Some of the spirit that had left him since the fight returned. 'But we'll have to buy a bottle of champagne.' He paused. 'Have you got a few quid on you?'

'A few,' Couldridge said.

'That's all right then.' He turned and stared at the girls at the bar.

There were about a dozen other men in the club, most of them paired off with the hostesses. The band switched from Cole Porter to George Gershwin. Two girls crossed the floor with elaborate nonchalance to talk to Bowman.

Bowman said: 'These two girls wondered if we would like to buy them a drink. What about it, Neville?'

Couldridge shrugged. 'I don't mind.'

The younger and prettier of the two who was apparently to be his partner said: 'Don't strain yourself, mister.' Couldridge suspected that it was a line from the latest James Cagney picture. She was about twenty-five, blonde and tired; as if she had recently had a baby, Couldridge thought.

Bowman said: 'What's it going to be, girls? A drop of bubbly?'

Bowman's girl who was about thirty, dark with a thickly-powdered face, thanked him enthusiastically. Before anyone could change their minds the waiter fired a bottle and filled their glasses.

Couldridge said: 'It doesn't taste much like champagne.'

Bowman looked alarmed. 'Now don't start any trouble,' he said. 'You promised you wouldn't, remember?'

The tired blonde looked at Couldridge with new interest. 'Do you cause trouble? She peered at his face. 'Yes, I guess you do.' She picked up his hand and examined his blood-crusted knuckles. 'Who did you hit?'

'No one. I fell over.'

'Tell that to the marines.' She appraised him and cast him for her next picture. 'You don't live in London, do you? Where do you come from?'

Couldridge wanted to tell her Hollywood to please her. Instead he said: 'India.'

'India. Jeepers.' Suddenly he was Ronald Colman in *Clive of India.*

'Would you like to dance?' he said.

'Sure thing.' From habit she danced very close to him, head against his shoulder. 'We don't get many people in here like you. They're mostly like ...' She stopped. 'Is he a friend of yours?' She pointed at Bowman.

'Not really. I only met him tonight.'

'That's okay then. They're mostly like him.' She giggled conspiratorially and snuggled closer to him. 'Now tell me who you hit?'

'I told you I fell over.'

'I wasn't born yesterday.'

'All right, then, I hit a drunken Irishman. Not very romantic, is it?'

'Not very,' she said. 'But you look sort of romantic. Would you like to come home with me after I've finished here? I don't mean in the normal way. You know—it wouldn't cost you anything. But I have to stay here until about four o'clock.'

'That's five hours time. Five hours and ten bottles of champagne.'

'No, it needn't be. I'll tell them that you're a special friend of mine. You can stay here while I do a bit more work. Or'— she looked up at him, pale blue eyes blinking from her mascara—'you can pick me up when the club closes.'

'Perhaps. Let's go back and finish the champagne before the other two drink it all.' He led her back to the table.

'You two are well away,' Bowman said. There was a rasp of envy in his voice.

'I wish you'd bring more friends like this,' the girl said.

'Bit old for you, isn't he?' Bowman said.

'I like older men,' she said. And to Couldridge she said: 'How old are you?'

'Eighty-two,' Couldridge said. The band changed to Irving Berlin; the spots of light accelerated; Couldridge was suddenly bored. He felt sad for the girl, even affectionate in a remote sort of way. But the brief rebellion was over: he wanted Joanne and her loyalty and all that they had shared. 'I have to go now,' he said.

Bowman said: 'Hey, wait a minute. We've only just arrived.'

The girl said 'Don't go. Not yet.'

He put his hand over hers and realised that he didn't know her name. 'What's your name?' he said.

'Grace. You are going, aren't you? I know because you're the sort of person who always does what he says he's going to.'

'Yes, I'm going,' he said.

'Will you come back afterwards to pick me up?'

'Maybe,' he said.

'You won't,' she said. 'All the others would. But not you.'

Couldridge stood up. 'Cheerio,' he said. 'I've enjoyed myself.'

'Hey,' Bowman said, 'what about some cash?'

Couldridge put a five pound note on the table. 'That should cover it,' he said. He walked towards the door. The doorman looked questioningly at the waiter. The waiter whispered to Bowman who nodded. The waiter nodded to the doormen and they let Couldridge through. As he left he saw Grace walking back towards the bar, slotting a cigarette into her holder.

The light was on in their bedroom when he got back to the hotel. Joanne had fallen asleep reading a book. Couldridge picked it up. *The Daring Young Man on the Flying Trapeze,* by William Saroyan. He undressed, switched off the light and slid carefully into the bed. Once in the night he awoke and called out Bose's name. Then he slept more peacefully with his arm around Joanne's waist.

3

WHEN Couldridge awoke Joanne was up, sitting at the dressing table brushing her hair. She had never employed subtlety in their quarrels. This morning she said: 'Where were you?'

Couldridge said: 'Could you please pass me the aspirins.'

Joanne said: 'Physician heal thyself.'

'Don't try and be funny,' he said. 'Pass me the bloody aspirins and a glass of water.'

He swallowed two, heaved himself up on one elbow and stared out of the window. There was the hush of latent heat in the atmosphere. 'I'm sorry,' he said. He diagnosed his condition: acute frontal headache, mild dehydration—normal aftermath of an overdose of alcohol.

'Where were you?'

'I met some fellow in a bar in Regent Street. 'We had a few drinks and went on to a club.'

'You realise,' she said, 'that I was waiting all day to hear the result of your consultation with your lawyer.'

'I've said I'm sorry.'

'And what happened to your knuckles?'

He looked at them with interest. 'I hit an Irishman.'

Joanne put down her hairbrush and turned around. 'Just what was all this in aid of?'

Couldridge lay back on the pillows. 'Bose is giving evidence against me,' he said.

'Does that surprise you?'

'Yes,' he said, 'it does.'

'It doesn't surprise me.'

'Then you're a better judge of character than I am.'

Joanne said: 'He's an Indian Nationalist for heaven's sake. A future leader of the Congress Party. Pandit Chet Ram is one of his heroes. He'd do anything for him because he reckons he's doing it for India.'

'I didn't think he'd lie.'

'Bose believes that the means justifies the end.'

'Bose was an explorer once like myself.'

'That,' Joanne said, 'seems to be totally irrelevant.'

There was a knock on the door and a waiter came in carrying a tray. Couldridge smelled coffee and bacon, envisaged the accompanying egg and felt sick. 'That's not for me, is it?'

'No,' Joanne said. 'It's for me. I thought I'd leave you to order your own breakfast. The bedroom stank like a brewery this morning.'

'Coffee,' Couldridge said. 'Black coffee.'

Joanne ate hungrily. As she was moving on to the toast and marmalade she said: 'Who is Grace Bates?'

'Who?'

'Grace Bates.' She showed him a scrap of paper. 'This was on the floor beside the bed. Grace Bates. An address in Frith Street and a telephone number.'

Couldridge sipped his coffee thoughtfully. 'She was a girl at this club last night,' he said. 'A hostess. I didn't ...'

'I know you didn't,' she said. She picked up a morning newspaper and began to read.

Couldridge admired her from his pillows. The strong neck, the thick shining hair, the face that had once been sharply pretty now fuller and calmer, just the slightest droop of flesh beneath her chin. Despite his hangover he *wanted* to make love to her. But he knew it was futile. 'You might at least have suspected me of committing adultery,' he said.

'Not you,' she said.

'I don't think that's very complimentary.'

'On the contrary,' she said, 'it's very complimentary.' She turned over a page of the newspaper and buttered herself another wafer of toast. 'Does your lawyer sound hopeful?'

'I didn't really ask him. He kept asking me if I could prove that I had seen the document authorising me to take the graft. I said Bose had seen Pandit Chet Ram hand it to me. That's when I discovered that Bose was going to give evidence against me.'

'But he might still say he saw the document.'

'Hardly—if he's giving evidence against me.'

'But he might.'

'Yes,' Couldridge said. 'He might.'

Through the half-open window he heard the sounds of London. The noise of traffic, the hooting of taxis, a train steaming away from a station, a clock chiming, a pigeon calling.

'Good God.' Joanne put down the newspaper.

'What's the matter?'

She didn't reply. Instead she picked up the newspaper and began to read again. She shook her head slowly and said again: 'Good God.'

408

Couldridge said irritably: 'What is it for heaven's sake?'

Joanne handed him the newspaper and sat on the bed beside him. He read the headline—'British Army Officer involved in Baipur "Massacre" Shot dead'. The dateline was Delhi. He read on:

'Lieutenant Colonel Neville Spenser, aged forty-eight, the British officer who retired from the Army on half pay after the inquiry at the beginning of this year into the "Baipur Massacre" was found dead in his quarters at Jinjabad on the North West Frontier yesterday.

'A pistol lay near the body. According to a spokesman of the military police foul play is not suspected.

'Colonel Spenser's body was found by his widow. He also leaves one son.

'Colonel Spenser, from Leigham Court Road, Streatham, was the officer commanding the military aspect of famine relief at Baipur in the Punjab at a time when Indian hostility towards Britain was once again being incited by extremist elements. When agitators refused to disperse from the bazaar area of Baipur Colonel Spenser ordered his troops to fire at them. In the shooting 149 Indians were killed.

'Two features of the inquiry were Colonel Spenser's unshakable belief in the rectitude of his action and the forthright manner of his evidence. Many observers believed that it was the military brusqueness of his evidence combined with an apparent lack of compassion for the dead and the wounded that contributed to the stern condemnation of his behaviour in the findings of the committee.

'Colonel Spenser maintained that his prompt action probably prevented a slaughter of Europeans on the same scale as the Mutiny of 1857. Indian Nationalist leaders, on the other hand, claimed that Colonel Spenser considerably worsened relations with Europeans.'

The report recalled the flogging of the three Indians and the salaaming order and traced Spenser's military career back to Sandhurst.

Couldridge sank back in the pillows. He saw the body of a young Parsee teacher being laid on a grill. He saw the vultures, circling, waiting; he felt the thud of horses' hooves on the journey back to Bombay.

He turned his head into the pillows.

4

BEFORE Couldridge's case was called the disciplinary committee of the General Medical Council passed judgement on a syndicate of fashionable abortionists—gynaecologist, psychiatrist and anaesthetist—a back-street abortionist from the East End of London one of whose patients had died from a perforated uterus, a physician accused of advertising because he had been quoted extensively in a French magazine on the subject of a new 'cure' for cancer, an anaesthetist addicted to his own anaesthetics, a general practitioner twice convicted for driving while under the influence of drink and a doctor who had seduced—or been seduced by—the wife of a well-known financier while attending her professionally.

The case against the syndicate was dismissed because in each abortion unshakable medical and psychiatric evidence was given that the woman's health would have been impaired if her pregnancy had not been terminated. Cynics calculated that it would take the syndicate a week to reimburse themselves for the costs of their defence. The doctor convicted on the driving charges was put on probation; all the others were struck off the register for 'infamous conduct in a professional respect'.

Couldridge listened to the evidence from one of the two

galleries in the Council's chamber in Hallam Street. In the public gallery across the chamber elegant women in floppy hats listened hungrily to the copulative details in the case involving the financier's wife who had told her husband about the doctor's attentions when he refused to see her any more. Outside newspaper photographers waited in the sunshine.

From the book-lined gallery Couldridge looked down on the heads of the arbiters of ethics and morals listening, analysing, questioning, writing, deliberating, ruining. All but one were old or middle-aged, all but one wore glasses. Couldridge wondered if any of them remembered the occasions when they had erred. Because at some time or another every doctor erred. A hasty diagnosis committing a patient to unnecessary suffering, a sleepy refusal to answer a late-night call resulting in death, over-prescription of drugs, a careless incision. Mistakes of judgement that were not necessarily indictable. But surely just as serious as the lapse of a young doctor who succumbed to the advances of a promiscuous patient.

The committee sat in the well of the chamber beneath a platform on which the chairman sat with the law assessor and the registrar on either side of him. Opposite the chairman, across the chamber, sat the accused doctor denuded of the dignity and absolute authority accorded him by the public. In front of each member of the committee nominated by the King on the advice of the Privy Council, appointed by universities and colleges or elected by the registered medical practitioners of Britain, were copies of the Medical Register. Marble busts and oil paintings of eminent physicians who looked as if they had posed under general anaesthetic, oak-panelling and a stained-glass window—all contributed to the somnolent dignity of the proceedings. A dignity that was occasionally fractured by acoustics that tended to numb sound so that the chairman couldn't hear the defendant or the barristers.

Couldridge scanned the faces of the committee. Grave, decent, bored. Not self-righteous, perhaps, but out of touch with human frailty; passing judgement on colleagues exposed to temptations that they had never experienced, or temptations that they had been strong enough to resist. One member of the committee was younger than the rest of them. Fortyish, sleek hair greying at the temples, elegant brown suit, polished collar, Old Epsomian tie; sharing a Harley Street practice, owning a Rolls-Royce and a chauffeur and a house in The Bishops Avenue, Hampstead. It was difficult to believe that his career had been dedicated to the alleviation of suffering or the advancement of medicine: it was difficult to accept that he was qualified to pass judgement on a doctor working in a slum who had agreed to terminate the pregnancy of a desperate mother of eight children.

Couldridge read the programme of business. He was item No. 7. Couldridge, John Edward. Inquiry on Monday, July 20, 1935, into the following charge ...

Joanne joined him in the gallery, beautiful and summery in a long green silk dress. 'Those photographers outside,' she said. 'They took my picture.'

He grinned at her. 'I don't blame them.'

'But why, John?'

'Because I'm the star defendant. There has never been a case like mine before. And you're my beautiful wife. They'll use the picture when my hearing has started.'

In the witness box at the end of the chairman's bench the financier's wife was telling the committee how the defendant had taken advantage of her while examining her for a female complaint. The women in the public gallery leaned forward, the committee made notes, sipped glasses of water and regarded the witness with morose interest.

Counsel for the G.M.C., Mr Leslie Maitland, an astute and sharp man, said: 'Was there a nurse or any other woman present during the examination?'

'No there wasn't.' She spoke softly, exuding shame and penitence.

'Why was that?'

'Because Dr Evans said it wouldn't be necessary.'

In the public gallery the women sighed with disgust because

of the perfidy of men and with envy because Dr Evans was tall and curly-haired and had beautiful hands.

Counsel nodded gravely. 'Could you please tell us in your own words what happened then, Mrs Bathurst. I know it will be a painful and embarrassing experience for you but we must know all the facts.' Mr Maitland paused, looked up at the public gallery and said: 'I should like to warn the ladies present that the evidence we are about to hear is of an extremely intimate nature. If any of them feel that their sensibilities might be offended I suggest that they leave the gallery for ten minutes or so.'

The ladies looked at one another with alarm and then tacitly decided that they should stay to lend the support of their sex to Mrs Bathurst in such overwhelmingly male company.

Mrs Bathurst said: 'I would rather not go into details.' She was plump, pretty, peering into middle-age, and despite her shame, despite the sobriety of her grey gown, could not wholly conceal her repressed enthusiasm for her role.

'I'm afraid you must, Mrs Bathurst, in the interests of justice.'

'Must I really?'

'I'm afraid so.'

And in detail which surprised even Mr Maitland she described what the doctor had done with his beautiful hands.

Up in the gallery the women shifted happily in their seats and reporters pondered over shorthand outlines for some of the anatomical words used by Mrs Bathurst; downstairs the committee made more notes and drank more water.

Mr Maitland said: 'Thank you, Mrs Bathurst.' And with some trepidation asked: 'What happened then?'

Mrs Bathurst told him how the doctor had not confined his activities to his beautiful hands. But the chairman, an astute and forthright man of medicine, interrupted her. 'I don't think you need elaborate any more, madam,' he said. 'I think most of us in this chamber know how the sexual act is performed.'

'I was only ...'

'Pray proceed, Mr Maitland.'

413

Couldridge whispered to Joanne: 'Why didn't you leave the chamber?'

'Because I wanted to hear the dirt.'

'Come on,' he said, 'the dirt's over. Let's get some lunch.'

They had lunch in a pub round the corner. Then went shopping in the West End. Then, because *Glamorous Night* was booked up, Couldridge took Joanne to see Emlyn Williams in *Night Must Fall*.

Next morning they returned to Hallam Street. Up in the gallery, above the fifteen or so elders of medicine nominated, appointed and elected to clear or crucify their colleagues, Couldridge listened to the chairman addressing the doctor who had examined Mrs Bathurst.

'I have to announce that you have been found guilty of infamous conduct in a professional respect in relation to the facts alleged against you in the charge and we have directed the registrar to erase your name from the register. Case number seven please.'

The young doctor sat for a moment staring at his beautiful hands. He glanced at the women in the public gallery and each believed that he was looking at them. He stood up and walked slowly out into the sunlight carrying his briefcase with him.

The chairman said again: 'Case number seven please.'

Couldridge stood up. Joanne said: 'Good luck.' Couldridge nodded. He walked down the stairs into the chamber. It smelled, he thought, of Mansion Polish and ether.

He sat down in the 'dock' opposite the chairman and waited for his infamy to be explained to the committee.

5

Mr Leslie Maitland was a small, sharp, brilliant lawyer with a sharp, sour wit that did not endear him to juries. He was as dapper as a chaffinch, his hair was clipped and glossy grey, he took snuff during court adjournments and throughout his career he had harboured an intense hatred for Mr Henry Lloyd-Williams, K.C., who now sat opposite him on the long table dividing the ranks of the committee.

He stood to the right of Couldridge addressing the chairman on the panelled bench. Up in the gallery to his left Couldridge could see Joanne; in the gallery to the right he could see the reporters. On the left of the long table in front of him Mr Lloyd-Williams made notes, his hands occasionally searching for the wig and gown that he only wore in criminal and law courts. Couldridge perused the faces of the committee on either side of him; they looked unusually intent, alerted by the novelty of the evidence and the cutting edge of Mr Maitland's voice. Mr Maitland opened the case comprehensively and waited fatalistically for a flambuoyant interruption from Mr Lloyd-Williams.

'... as members of the committee will be aware the phrase "infamous conduct in a professional respect" was first coined in the Medical Act of 1858 and was defined by Lord Justice Lopes in 1894 as follows:

' "If a medical man in the pursuit of his profession has done something with regard to it which will be reasonably regarded as disgraceful or dishonourable by his professional brethren of good repute and competency, then it is open to the General Medical Council, if that be shown, to say that he has been guilty of infamous conduct in a professional respect."

'This case is unique in the annals of medical jurisprudence because it concerns surgical techniques still in their infancy. It might well be contended that it must necessarily be unique because in fact it concerns a landmark in medical progress not hitherto attained. I for one would not dispute this contention.'

Mr Maitland paused to give dramatic emphasis to his fair-mindedness. Mr Lloyd-Williams sighed. 'Furthermore I wish to make it clear that this inquiry has not in any way been instigated with the object of detracting from Dr Couldridge's contributions to the development of ophthalmic practice or with the object of dissuading other such pioneers from their endeavours. I am sure that no one here today wishes in any way to retard the evolution of medicine. I am equally convinced of the futility of any such wish should it be harboured: the progress of all the sciences is an inexorable process that cannot and will not be stopped.'

Lloyd-Williams scribbled on a piece of paper and handed it to Couldridge. The note said, 'Methinks he doth protest too much.'

Mr Maitland paused again to refurbish his voice with challenge. 'However it does not follow that the purveyors of progress can have licence exceeding that of other physicians and surgeons to accomplish their mission. They must never be allowed to presume that the means can justify the end, they must never stray from the ethical and moral standards which the public they serve expects of them.'

Mr Maitland turned slightly towards Couldridge. 'In this case it is alleged that Dr Couldridge did presume that the means could justify the end. As I have said the evidence against him does not fall into any category hitherto considered by the committee. But I would invite the members present today to conclude, after they have heard the evidence of witnesses and, perhaps, the evidence of Dr Couldridge himself, that in implementing the means to the end—however admirable that end might have been—his conduct was such that it could reasonably

416

be regarded as disgraceful or dishonourable. In other words that Dr Couldridge was guilty of infamous conduct in a professional respect.'

'Phew,' said Lloyd-Williams.

The chairman said: 'Thank you, Mr Maitland. Perhaps we could have some of the facts now.'

Maitland, grey hair gleaming in the electric light which blended uneasily with the sunlight from outside, described the events leading up to the corneal graft on Pandit Chet Ram's son. Pandit Chet Ram, he said, had indicated that the parents of the dying boy might be willing to sign papers donating the eyes of their son to medical research in the event of his death. But Pandit Chet Ram's enlightened outlook had not extended to the boy's parents. They had insisted that if he died then his body should be burned in its entirety.

Mr Maitland sipped precisely at a glass of water as if he were tasting it. 'Members of the committee,' he said, 'might well hold the view that any parents, whatever their creed, religion or race, would view with equal horror and repugnance the mutilation of the body of their child immediately after death. In fact, in similar circumstances, many parents might well wonder if death had, in fact, taken place at the time the graft was taken.'

Lloyd-Williams rose and addressed the chairman. 'My learned friend,' he said, 'is exceeding the limits of his opening address in relation to the facts alleged'—he emphasised the alleged—'against Dr Couldridge. At no time has it been suggested that the unfortunate boy was not dead at the time the graft was taken and accordingly I take the strongest objections to such imputations. Furthermore it occurs to me that the opinions which seem to be replacing facts—or alleged facts—in Mr Maitland's address are hardly in accordance with his assurance of—and I quote—that the inquiry "has not been instigated with the object of detracting from Dr Couldridge's contributions to the development of ophthalmic practice."'

Maitland gave the chairman a neat smile indicating that he was grateful for the opportunity to elaborate. 'I was not necessarily referring to physical death,' he said. 'There is the delicate question of spiritual death.'

The chairman said: 'We are doctors, Mr Maitland, not spiritualists. Please confine yourself to the facts.'

Lloyd-Williams winked at Couldridge.

Maitland told the committee that, despite the absence of any authority from the parents, Couldridge had removed one of the dead boy's eyes after he had certified death. His action had caused the parents suffering in excess of the grief that a bereaved couple might normally expect. They had subsequently agreed to delay any formal complaint until the success or failure of the operation on Pandit Chet Ram's son had been ascertained. Regrettably, said Maitland, the operation had failed.

Maitland then called the dead boy's father who gave evidence through an interpreter. He was a thin, frightened man dressed uneasily in a blue chalk-stripe suit two sizes too big for him. His son had died, he said, while Couldridge was attending him. When he was allowed to look at the body he saw that one eye was covered by a dressing. When he asked Couldridge to remove the dressing he was told that his son's eye had been removed. He was horrified because he had asked Couldridge not to interfere with his son's body after death.

Maitland said: 'You are satisfied that your son was in fact dead when Dr Couldridge removed the eye?'

As the interpreter began to translate Lloyd-Williams jumped up. 'Really,' he said, 'I must call my learned friend to order. The question is both irrelevant and offensive. Mr Maitland is fully aware of this. But he is intent upon sowing a seed in your minds which he hopes will lodge there, like repetitive advertising, even though the learned assessor may instruct you to disregard it.'

Maitland took a silver snuff-box from his trouser pocket and fondled it. 'On the contrary,' he said, 'it is my intention to remove from the minds of members of the committee any doubts about an aspect of the case that can only complicate their deliberations. My learned friend seems particularly sensitive on this point.'

Lloyd-Williams said: 'I am particularly sensitive to the tactics of counsel for the prosecution.'

The chairman interrupted. 'This is not a prosecution, Mr Lloyd-Williams.'

'My apologies, sir. I feel I must however object to the question.'

The chairman conferred with the legal assessor and nodded. 'Mr Maitland,' he said, 'I should be grateful if you would discontinue this line of questioning.'

'I am much obliged,' Maitland said. 'I have one last question for the witness.' He turned to the unhappy Indian. 'Did you at any time sign any document or piece of paper that might be construed as your authority for research of any kind to be carried out upon your son's body after death?'

The interpreter translated and the witness shook his head vigorously.

Maitland sat down and the Indian stood down from the witness box with a look of relief on his face.

Lloyd-Williams stopped him. 'Just a minute,' he said. 'There are one or two points I wish to clear up before you leave.' He looked at the notes he had made. 'Could you please tell the chairman and members of the committee why you permitted your son to stay in Dr Coulridge's care when you knew he wanted to operate on the body after death?'

The worry returned to the Indian's face as the interpreter spoke to him. Then he said: 'Because Dr Couldridge had promised to do his best for him.'

'But surely your son would have been better off in hospital under the care of other doctors? Was there perhaps some special relationship between yourself and Dr Couldridge? Some sort of agreement, maybe?'

The Indian spoke excitedly in Hindi and the interpreter said: 'He says that Dr Couldridge promised to give him special treatment. It was only afterwards, when it was too late, that he realised Dr Couldridge's real purpose.'

'Did it not strike you as strange that Dr Couldridge still

wanted to keep your son at the clinic although you had refused his request to take a graft?'

The boy's father said through the interpreter: 'No, I believed Sahib Couldridge.'

Pandit Chet Ram gave evidence next. He wore a brown suit, a white shirt and a very-British striped tie. The deep eyes in the fragile face stared at Couldridge and a little smile creased the side of his mouth.

He told the committee that he had been told about Couldridge's work on eye grafts by a Mrs Charlotte Spenser.

Maitland said: 'The wife, I believe, of the late Colonel Neville Spenser who gave evidence at the inquiry into the Baipur Massacre.'

Pandit Chet Ram said: 'That is correct.'

Lloyd-Williams moved as if to object. But the question was posed and answered so quickly that there was no point.

Pandit Chet Ram said that Couldridge had shown interest in his son's condition and had indicated that he thought that the defective vision in at least one eye could be cured by a corneal eye graft. He told Dr Couldridge that he knew of a youth, obviously dying, whose parents might permit such a graft to be taken from their son in the event of his death.

Maitland: 'And was that permission given?'

Pandit Chet Ram: 'No, sir.'

'Did you try several times to persuade these unfortunate people to change their minds?'

'I did, sir, but without success. I was upset at the time but as it has turned out it would not have mattered one way or the other because the operation failed.'

'Were you aware that the dying boy was admitted to Dr Couldridge's premises?'

'I was, sir.'

'And for what purpose did you understand that he was being treated there?'

'I understood that it was purely because of Dr Couldridge's promise to the parents to do his best for their son.'

420

Couldridge stared at Pandit Chet Ram searching his face for any flicker of shame or guilt. But there was none. The only change in the man was in his manner. The elaborate politeness and touches of servility remained—but they were no longer the trappings of mockery.

Maitland said: 'Did you at any time show Dr Couldridge a document purporting to be authorisation from the dying boy's parents for the graft to be taken?'

'I did not, sir.'

Couldridge looked at him with hatred. He imagined his fist smashing into the bland face. He looked down at his hands and saw that they were clenched. He hoped that his feelings had not shown on his face.

Lloyd-Williams stood up to cross-examine. He had the air of a man anticipating his task with pleasure. 'It is true, is it not,' he said, 'that on at least two occasions you have been imprisoned in India?'

'That is true.'

'Once for taking part in an illegal demonstration and once for inciting riots?'

'Those were the charges,' Pandit Chet Ram said.

Lloyd-Williams looked theatrically surprised. 'Are you suggesting that the charges were ill-founded?'

Couldridge listened with pleasure because Pandit Chet Ram was in a quandary. If he indulged in any of the anti-British propaganda on which his reputation was founded in India then he might antagonise the committee.

Pandit Chet Ram said: 'No, sir, I am merely confirming that those were the charges against me.'

'I see. That was very thoughtful of you.' Lloyd-Williams picked a transcript of one of the trials. 'I believe that when you were accused of inciting a riot evidence was given that you had told a crowd that the British had deliberately spread cholera in areas where the Nationalistic spirit was at its most fervent.'

Maitland rose busily and said: 'Mr Chairman I must protest.

421

I cannot see that this attempt to blacken the character of my witness can in any way assist the committee in considering the allegations against the defendant.'

Lloyd-Williams searched for his non-existent wig. 'I wish,' he said, 'to prove that the witness is a liar.'

The chairman said: 'Please continue, Mr Lloyd-Williams.'

Lloyd-Williams turned again to Pandit Chet Ram. 'That was a very malicious allegation to make.'

Pandit Chet Ram shrugged.

'I put it to you that it was not only malicious but it was a deliberate untruth.'

'I do not think so.'

Lloyd-Williams read aloud Pandit Chet Ram's evidence under cross-examination at the trial. 'I agree now that I must have been mistaken about the British deliberately spreading cholera.' Lloyd-Williams put down the transcript. 'This was your final admission after exhaustive cross-examination. You do not, I suppose, deny that you did refute your allegations at your trial?'

'No, sir, I do not.' He stared malevolently at Lloyd-Williams.

'And in that case your original assertion was a malicious and deliberate lie?'

'I was mistaken.'

'I put it to you that you are mistaken in this instance.'

'No, sir, I am not.'

'I put it to you that your evidence is a pack of malicious lies concocted to bring attention to yourself and the anti-British campaign to which your life has been dedicated.'

'No, sir, I would not use the suffering of my son to further my political aims.'

'Then why, sir, did you suggest that your son should give evidence here to support the charges against Dr Couldridge?'

Pandit Chet Ram placed his hands in their praying position. 'My son is not giving evidence.'

'I am fully aware of that,' Lloyd-Williams said. He was, Couldridge thought, enjoying himself a little too transparently. 'But you did, did you not, suggest that it might assist the case

422

against Dr Couldridge?'

'I gave permission for my son to give evidence.'

Lloyd-Williams sighed. 'Please do not waste the time of members of the committee by pedantic evasion.' He picked up the transcript of the other trial. 'When you were accused with other defendants of taking part in an illegal demonstration you gave evidence to the effect that you had not been in the district of Delhi where the demonstration took place at the time in question.'

'I may have,' Pandit Chet Ram said.

'Take my word for it, sir, you did. And subsequently two witnesses were produced who said that they had seen you at the demonstration.'

Pandit Chet Ram smiled as if he were humouring Lloyd-Williams. 'They were members of the Moslem League.'

'Members of the Moslem League or not the learned judge appears to have believed them because you were found guilty and sentenced to two years in prison.'

'I am afraid I do not appreciate the relevance of all this,' Pandit Chet Ram said.

'I have already explained the relevance to your learned counsel—it is to prove that you are a liar, sir.'

Pandit Chet Ram appealed to the chairman. 'I am asking you, sir, if I have to suffer these insults from this gentleman?'

The chairman said: 'Mr Lloyd-Williams is entitled to question the veracity of your evidence. Pray continue, Mr Lloyd-Williams.'

Lloyd-Williams bowed graciously and turned to Pandit Chet Ram again. 'Did you on one occasion before the operation on your son's eye call at Dr Couldridge's surgery carrying a document?'

Pandit Chet Ram relaxed a little. 'I did, sir.'

'Could you please tell the chairman and members of the committee what that document was?'

Pandit Chet Ram parted his praying hands. 'It was merely my own authority for Dr Couldridge to carry out the operation on my son.'

'I put it to you that the document that you brought to Dr Couldridge's consulting rooms was a written authorisation from the dying boy's parents for a homograft to be taken from the boy's eye in the event of his death.'

Pandit Chet Ram said: 'It was not, sir.'

'I shall be bringing evidence to the effect that it was.'

Pandit Chet Ram inclined his head.

'It will not be your first experience of having your lies exposed in court.'

Maitland snapped to his feet. 'I must object to that last offensive comment,' he said.

The chairman nodded. 'Please tone down your remarks, Mr Lloyd-Williams. And I must remind you that this is not a court of law.'

'I'm much obliged,' Lloyd-Williams said. He sat down and leaned back, thumbs in his waistcoat.

Over lunch at a pub not frequented by journalists and spectators he gave his opinion on the morning's evidence. 'I think we did pretty well,' he said. 'Better than I expected. I don't think anyone believed either of those bloody Indians.' He filled his mouth with cold, bloody beef and potato salad and washed it down with a great suck of draught bitter.

Joanne pointed at the front page of the early edition of one of the evening papers. 'Look at this,' she said. They had printed one of the photographs of her taken the previous day. There was also a photograph of Couldridge looking with surprise into the lens of a camera. The headline read: 'Doctor accused in Human Transplant Case.' And underneath in smaller type: 'Wife of Baipur Massacre Officer Named.'

Lloyd-Williams nodded. 'This is going to attract a lot of publicity. It's a pity that snide little bastard Maitland got that in about Spenser.'

Couldridge said: 'What do you think of our chances now?'

Lloyd-Williams said: 'Excellent. I don't think they'll take too much notice of what the Indians had to say.' He produced an

ivory tooth pick and began to excavate. 'But they will take notice
of the other doctors. It's a pity they're so against you. But I
think I'll be able to stop a lot of their evidence on the grounds
of malice and irrelevancy.'

'Bose should be able to help,' Couldridge said.

'I know. I'm pinning a lot of hope on him. If you say he saw
the authorisation from the dead boy's parents then that's really
the crux of the whole thing—even if he is giving evidence against
you.' He inspected his catch on the end of the toothpick. 'You
say he's an honest man?'

Couldridge nodded.

Joanne said: 'When does he give evidence?'

Lloyd-Williams said: 'This afternoon or tomorrow morning.'

A photographer came up to their table and said: 'Do you
mind if I take a picture of you having lunch?'

Couldridge said: 'I don't mind. You'd probably take one
even if we did mind.'

The photographer smiled. 'Probably, sir.'

'How did you find us here?'

The photographer said: 'All witnesses who don't want to have
their pictures taken come here.'

He took his picture and departed.

Couldridge said: 'So you really think Bose can sway this in
my favour?'

Lloyd-Williams nodded. 'Particularly as he's a doctor.' He
put away his toothpick. 'The trouble is he's also an Indian.'

6

BUT two other doctors were called to give evidence before Bose.
Colonel Randolph Buckingham and Dr Benjamin Emmerson.

Buckingham, Couldridge thought, had not changed much

425

over the years. His greyness was lost in his sandiness and his arrogance diverted attention from his stoop. He was on the point of retirement, a mature master of the art of masking ineptitude. But he was a doctor, one of the committee's own kind and his evidence would be considered with respect. Couldridge searched the chamber for any sign of a revolutionary spirit but he could see none: they conformed in dress, age— with the exception of the young Harley Street man—posture and, Couldridge suspected, in their attitude to unorthodoxy.

Buckingham told the committee that he held an executive position in the Indian Medical Service, that he had known Couldridge since his first appointment as a medical officer on the North West Frontier.

Maitland said: 'Were you in fact on the headquarters staff of the Indian Medical Service when Dr Couldridge was working at a hospital under the jurisdiction of the I.M.S. in Calcutta?'

'I was, sir.'

'Did you form any opinion about his attitude towards medicine in those days?'

'I did, sir. I had occasion to see certain reports from Colonel Little who was then in charge of the hospital. It seemed to me that Lieutenant Couldridge as he was then was acting in a highly irresponsible manner.'

'In what way, Colonel Buckingham?'

'He was using the hospital laboratories for his own experiments. On one occasion he attempted to purify drinking water by chemical application when the accepted method in those days was boiling.'

'Anything else, Colonel Buckingham?'

'Throughout my service on the headquarter staff of the Indian Medical Service I received from time to time reports indicating lack of both military and medical discipline.'

A well-rehearsed phrase, Couldridge thought. He wondered why Lloyd-Williams had not objected to any of Buckingham's evidence.

Maitland said: 'Anything else?'

Buckingham smiled slightly and Couldridge guessed instinctively that an anecdote, also well-rehearsed, was about to be related. 'There was one occasion,' Buckingham said, 'when I first met Second Lieutenant Couldridge as he was then. He diagnosed glaucoma in a Gurkha who had reported sick. It turned out to be a hangover.' There was some laughter in the two galleries and one or two doctors smiled.

When Lloyd-Williams rose to cross-examine he said: 'I gather that you are something of a comedian, Colonel Buckingham?'

'I do not consider myself to be one, sir.'

'But you just made people laugh, Colonel Buckingham. You have an enviable talent and an unusual one in an officer and physician of your standing.'

'I rather thought that it was Dr Couldridge's actions that made people laugh.'

'On the contrary, Colonel Buckingham, it was your sense of timing. You had in fact determined to extract a cheap laugh from the inexperience of a young doctor, had you not?'

'No, sir. It just occurred to me.'

'Really?' Lloyd-Williams paused to consider his next question. Couldridge realised that he was about to score a point and wished that he would not gloat. 'It had only just occurred to you, had it Colonel Buckingham?'

'Yes, sir.'

'Then do you mind showing members of the committee what was written on that piece of paper that you screwed up and put in your pocket at the conclusion of your evidence in chief?'

'What piece of paper?'

Lloyd-Williams growled. 'You know what piece of paper, sir. Please do not prevaricate.'

Buckingham looked appealingly at Maitland. But his counsel declined to look in his direction.

Lloyd-Williams said: 'The piece of paper, please, Colonel Buckingham.

Buckingham's hand went slowly to the pocket of his khaki

trousers and emerged holding a scrap of paper.

Lloyd-Williams said: 'Now read out what is written on it if you please.'

There was a pause and Buckingham's stoop was suddenly noticeable. His voice was hardly audible as he read out the words: 'Memo—don't forget story about C and glaucoma.'

Lloyd-Williams said: 'Do you still maintain that the anecdote just occurred to you?'

'I remembered it last night. I made a note of it in case it would help.'

'Answer the question, Colonel Buckingham. Do you still maintain that the question just occurred to you?'

'No sir.'

'Then you lied, did you not, Colonel Buckingham? Hardly the behaviour one expects from an officer and a gentleman—and a doctor.'

'Not a lie, sir. An oversight.'

The committee, Couldridge noticed, looked uneasy. They were not accustomed to seeing one of their kind exposed. The trouble was that their displeasure might be redirected against him because he was the catalyst.

Lloyd-Williams said: 'I have one more question to put to you, Colonel Buckingham. Do please try to answer it truthfully.'

'I am not a liar, sir.'

Lloyd-Williams oiled his voice. 'That is for the members of the committee to decide, Colonel Buckingham.'

The members stared at their blotting paper, consulted their copies of the Medical Register and polished their glasses.

Lloyd-Williams said: 'You gave evidence that Dr Couldridge carried out experiments in the purification of water in the hospital in Calcutta.'

'I did.'

'Are you aware that he was employing a technique employing a substance now known as chlorogen that helped to save the lives of thousands of British soldiers in the Great War and that this method of purification is now accepted practice?'

Buckingham said: 'I believe that is so. The fact remains that it was not accepted practice when Lieutenant Couldridge was experimenting with it.'

Lloyd-Williams nodded as if it were the answer that he had expected. 'May I suggest, Colonel Buckingham, there is one medicine that you have never prescribed in your life and that is the milk of human kindness?'

Buckingham started to reply but Lloyd-Williams was already sitting down searching through the papers on the table in front of him.

Maitland told the committee that Little who was now retired was too ill to give evidence. But it would merely have corroborated what Buckingham had said. He called Dr Benjamin Emmerson.

Emmerson had aged dramatically since Couldridge first met him. He was almost bald and the flesh on his face was pouchy. And he peered around him as if his pale eyes were prematurely afflicted with presbyopia. Only his sartorial sense had retained its youth. His old flesh was clothed in crisp fawn shirt, plum-coloured tie and a lightweight beige suit that must have been pressed that morning. His hands shook and Couldridge guessed that he was probably an alcoholic.

In a weak squashy voice he told the committee that he and other doctors had warned Couldridge that experimental surgery had no place in the rounds of a Lahore general practitioner. They had warned him, he said, for his own sake. But Couldridge had ignored their advice and had been arrogant and rude in his behaviour towards them. Emmerson glanced up at the book-lined gallery and Couldridge followed the direction of his glance. There he saw the immense figure of a woman beneath a fashionable floppy hat. Bovine arms were attached to a bulk of body on which the flesh of the neck and belly had expanded to smooth away the contours of the bosom. Between the neck and under the hat Couldridge recognised the face of Mollie Emmerson.

Emmerson said that, for the sake of the profession, he and

429

other doctors had paid close attention to the first corneal transplant attempted by Couldridge. In particular they had investigated the willingness of the donor's next-of-kin to allow the body to be 'mutilated' after death.

Maitland: 'And did you find in this instance that permission had been given?'

Emmerson: 'I did, sir. Although I was still not convinced that it was morally right to take tissue from a cadaver.' His weak, wet voice touched the word with obscenity.

Maitland: 'You were entitled to your opinion, Dr Emmerson. But that has no bearing on these proceedings. Did you pay equally close attention to the subsequent corneal graft carried out by Dr Couldridge?'

Emmerson: 'I did, sir. I had formed the opinion that there was a strong element of luck in Dr Couldridge's first operation.'

Lloyd-Williams rose and said: 'I should be extremely obliged if Dr Emmerson would confine himself to alleged facts in preference to opinions apparently motivated by jealousy.'

Maitland nodded as if he agreed with Lloyd-Williams' view of the witness. 'Facts, please, Dr Emmerson, not opinions.' He consulted his brief. 'What did you find on the second occasion?'

'That the operation had failed and that permission had not been granted by the dead boy's parents for Dr Couldridge to interfere with their son's body.'

'So what did you do?'

'I and two other doctors laid a complaint in deference to the parents' feelings and to uphold the ethical traditions of our profession.'

After a few more questions Maitland sat down. With relief, it seemed, as if he had little sympathy with his witness.

Emmerson asked for a glass of water and drank it quickly in the way that alcoholics drink liquor. Outside Couldridge could hear the sound of traffic. He looked up, saw Joanne and smiled at her. Then Lloyd-Williams stood up and delivered a barrage of short tight questions.

'Did anyone visit you before you decided to lay the complaint?'

430

'Visit me? What do you mean?'

'Did anyone visit you and suggest that you lay a complaint?'

'Not that I can remember.'

'Then think, Dr Emmerson.'

'Do you mean another doctor?'

'I am asking you, Dr Emmerson.

'I discussed the matter with several doctors and we all came to the ...'

'Did any layman approach you?'

'No, sir.'

'Did not a Mr Ramsey Crockford approach you?'

'I can't ...'

'Did he or did he not approach you, Dr Emmerson?'

'I did speak to a Mr Crockford about the operation.'

'That's better, Dr Emmerson. Your memory is flooding back to you is it not? Would you perhaps like another drink of water?'

Emmerson shook his head. There were scarlet patches on the slack pouches of his cheeks and his forehead was moist with sweat. 'No thank you,' he said. His hands strayed to the crease of his trousers.

Lloyd-Williams glanced up at the gallery where the Press were taking notes and said: 'Were you aware, Dr Emmerson, that Mr Ramsey Crockford was a representative of His Majesty's Government in that he was employed by the India Office.' He was rewarded by a flurry of note-taking by the reporters.

'I knew that he was some sort of diplomat.'

'Diplomats are, I believe, usually employed by the Government.' He waited for the reporters to catch up. 'Perhaps it was the Christian name Ramsey which gave you the hint.' He was rewarded by some laughter from the two galleries. 'Now that we have refreshed your memory and ascertained that you were in fact visited by a Mr Ramsey Crockford who was representing His Majesty's Government I should like to return to the original point of this line of questioning. 'Did Mr Crockford suggest at any time that you should lay this complaint?'

'I was quite prepared to lay the complaint without the intervention of Mr Crockford.'

Lloyd-Williams sighed deeply. 'Please answer the question,
Dr Emmerson. Did Mr Crockford suggest that you should lay
the complaint?'

'We did discuss it.'

'Ah.'

'He happened to be in Lahore and we met at a dinner.'

'Ah. Why did he just *happen* to be in Lahore, Dr Emmerson?'

'I have no idea. Travelling around India was part of his job.'

'So he just happened to be in Lahore, he just happened to
be at the same dinner as yourself, he just happened to sit next
to you and he just happened to mention Dr Couldridge's corneal
graft. Is that how it happened, Dr Emmerson?'

Maitland started to stand up but Lloyd-Williams held up one
imperious hand. 'I quite agree—Dr Emmerson is not qualified
to express an opinion about Mr Crockford's motives. However
he can answer with a single Yes or No the simple question, "Did
Mr Crockford suggest that he lay the complaint?" '

Emmerson said: 'He did agree with me that the bad publicity
already caused by the failure of the graft might be injurious to
the medical profession as a whole.'

'But who raised the question first, Dr Emmerson?'

'I raised the question of the homograft. After all it is one
of the current talking points in India.'

'But who raised the question of a complaint being laid?'

'I can't remember.'

'Think, Dr Emmerson. We have already been able to refresh
your memory once.'

'Could I have another drink of water, please?'

'By all means.'

The chairman, the committee, the Press, the public and the
lawyers waited while Emmerson drank noisily from his glass.
An aircraft droned overhead and the curtains in a block of
flats opposite billowed in the warm breeze.

Emmerson handed back his empty glass and Lloyd-Williams
said: 'Well, Dr Emmerson—has the water helped you to recall

who mentioned the complaint first?'

Emmerson looked up into the gallery for strength. But his wife had left. She was probably upset, Couldridge thought, because someone other than herself was bullying her husband.

Emmerson said: 'You may be right—it may have been Mr Crockford who suggested it.'

'It is not a question of whether I was right. Did Mr Crockford suggest to you that you should lay the complaint?'

Emmerson looked away from the public gallery. 'Yes, I rather think he did.'

'Thank you, Dr Emmerson. I am glad you have remembered that because I shall be calling Mr Crockford to give evidence on subpoena.' He sat down and adjusted his invisible wig.

The chairman said: 'I rather feel that it would be an opportune moment for a brief adjournment.'

On the landing outside the chamber Couldridge congratulated Lloyd-Williams. 'How the hell did you know that Buckingham had written that note?'

'I saw it in his hand. I also knew that Buckingham was a man devoid of humour. So I presumed—somewhat rashly I must agree—that the note was reminding him to make his little sally. Did you really mistake a hangover for glaucoma—whatever that is?'

'I'm afraid so,' Couldridge said.

'Remind me to consult another doctor if I should ever come to India.'

'You may not be able to consult me anyway if I'm struck off. How do you think it's going now?'

'Very well. These doctors are such appalling witnesses.'

'How did you know that it was Crockford who had suggested that Emmerson lay a complaint?'

'I didn't know. I guessed. After all, if both the doctors *and* the politicians are out to get you it's a fairly safe bet that they would collaborate.'

'Who's the next witness?' Couldridge said.

'Your friend Bose,' Lloyd-Williams said.

7

BOSE, Couldridge thought, had aged least of anyone. There hadn't been enough laughter to crease the skin at the corners of his eyes and the scowl in his soul had remained unrecorded except for one line from nose to mouth. The unpigmented patch of white in his hair had perhaps spread a little but it only emphasised the virility of the rest of the blue-black cap. He wore a fawn linen jacket and charcoal grey slacks. He looked composed and responsible, the personification of a reliable witness. He didn't avoid looking at Couldridge but he didn't acknowledge him.

The voice of Maitland broke the silence, as sharp as the cracking of a twig. 'You have, I believe, known Dr Couldridge for a long time and have in fact acted as his assistant for many years.'

'That is correct.'

'What has been the tenor of your relationship during that period?'

'It has been a professional relationship,' Bose said.

'Nothing more?'

'Nothing more, sir.'

But it could have been, Couldridge thought. If he had listened to Bose many years ago. It could have been a friendship, a partnership closer than anything that man can normally expect. It had been there waiting to burgeon beside the banks of the Hooghly. If he had bothered to raise his head from his work and look at the world around him.

'Then you must have had ample time in which to form an opinion about Dr Couldridge's capabilities.'

'I have, sir.'

'And what are those opinions, Dr Bose?'

'He is a doctor of outstanding ability.' He looked across the doctors at Couldridge, but still there was no recognition on his face.

'What were your views on his work on corneal grafting?'

'I was more interested in his earlier research into the endemic diseases of India. Cholera, typhoid, plague.'

'Do I take it that you disapproved of his subsequent work?'

'I didn't disapprove, sir. But it was not the sort of work that attracted me. In any case Dr Couldridge was not the only doctor engaged on such work. . . .'

'I am fully aware of that, Dr Bose.' Maitland's dry voice cut him short. 'Did you approve of the removal of tissues from cadavers for the furtherance of Dr Couldridge's research?'

'I would not have undertaken such an excision. But I do not condemn the practice in other men. As I have said Dr Couldridge is not the only one engaged on this type of pioneering surgery.'

Maitland's voice crisped from dry to brittle. 'I must remind you, Dr Bose, that you should not allow loyalty to interfere with the veracity of your evidence.'

'I am aware of that, sir.'

'Very well. Please cast your mind back to day earlier this year, shortly before Dr Couldridge performed the operation on Pandit Chet Ram's son. Did Pandit Chet Ram himself call at the surgery?'

'He did, sir.'

Couldridge leaned forward because his future depended on Bose's answers to the next few questions.

'Did he have with him a certain document?'

'He did, sir.'

'Have you an idea what that document was?'

Couldridge stared at Bose. Bose stared back and through him. It was very quiet and everyone was looking at Bose. Outside Couldridge heard a newspaper seller shouting about a murder.

Maitland said again: 'Have you any idea what that document was?'

Bose paused. Then he said: 'No, sir.'

435

In the two galleries men and women sighed. The doctors rustled their papers. Lloyd-Williams sat back in his chair. Inside his trouser pocket Couldridge clenched his hand around his pipe and snapped the stem.

Maitland said: 'Thank you, Dr Bose. I have no further questions.'

Lloyd-Williams cross-examined Bose. But Bose didn't waver. He had seen a document: he had no idea what it was.

During the lunch adjournment Couldridge stopped Bose in the street outside. 'Why, Bose?' he said. 'Why?'

Bose said: 'I do not think it is proper for us to discuss the case before it has finished.'

Couldridge caught his arm. 'Why? Just tell me why you lied?'

Bose looked surprised. 'I did not lie,' he said. 'You should not say that.'

'But you knew what that document was.'

Bose shook his head. 'I did not,' he said. 'I knew what you claimed it was. But I never examined it.' His face was expressionless, but his voice was suddenly thick with emotion, 'Years ago I asked you why you had not done more to save me in court.'

'I did all I could but I had to tell the truth. I couldn't lie.'

'I told the truth,' Bose said. 'Just like you I couldn't lie. Perhaps now you know how I felt.'

He turned and walked down Hallam Street staring straight ahead of him, not smiling at the cameramen as they photographed him walking out of the partnership for ever.

8

THEY dined in their small hotel off Gray's Inn Road and through the lattice windows watched the bruised storm clouds gather-

ing. As the first fat blobs of rain fell they fancied they could
smell the thirsty scents of India preparing for the monsoon.
Tyres hissed on the wet road and lightning lit the dying evening. They drank brandy with their coffee and Couldridge lit
his pipe in defiance of the waiter who offered him cigars.

He smiled at Joanne through the smoke. 'At least you won't
find a Russell Viper in your bed.'

'I can't wait to get back,' she said. 'I never was a city girl.'

The waiter lit candles on the tables. The rain rushed down
the street outside and hurled itself against the windows deepen-
ing the cosiness of the dining room.

He stared out at the shining street and said: 'It hasn't been
too bad, has it, Joanne?'

'What?' she said softly.

'Our time together.'

'It's been wonderful,' she said. She picked up the big brandy
glass and cradled it in her hands.

'You've put up with a lot, I suppose.'

She smiled over the rim of the glass. 'I have,' she said.

A bus sailed past on the glistening river, red and exciting
in the streaming evening. The reflections of street lamps were
pulled out on the road like harbour lights.

'I wonder what's happened to Charlotte,' he said. 'Poor Charlotte.'

'She won't grieve,' Joanne said.

'You sound very hard.'

'Not hard, just realistic. She had no feeling for Neville in the
end. She's got her child and her pension and her theosophy. She'll
probably come back and live quite happily in Streatham.'

'She should never have left,' Couldridge said. 'More brandy?'
She nodded.

'We seem to be avoiding the principle issue,' he said.

'I know. It's tomorrow, isn't it. We'll know tomorrow.'

'We'll know tomorrow,' he said. 'After I've given evidence.'

'You'll win,' she said.

'I shan't beg forgiveness. I must stand by my principles. I

represent progress, they represent complacency.'

'Lloyd-Williams is becoming more and more confident,' she said.

'I know,' he said.

Thunder cracked overhead and lightning ran across the sky. The rain bounced high on the black and silver road. There were two other couples in the dining room; they went on eating as if acknowledgement of the storm showed weakness. Couldridge called for more brandy.

'You'll get me drunk,' Joanne said. 'And you shouldn't be drinking so much the night before you're due to give evidence.'

'To hell with it,' he said.

'It's Bose who really upset you, isn't it?'

He nodded. 'But it was my own bloody fault. I patronised him many years ago. Like Britain patronised India.'

Joanne stared out of the window. 'It's exciting, isn't it? It's not the sort of weather you expect in London.'

But Couldridge knew that Joanne was more worried than excited. He looked at her and loved her for her worry. 'No,' he said, 'it's more like the start of the rains at home.'

'What are you really thinking about?' she said.

'You know,' he said.

'I was thinking about that day at the ruins on the way to Delhi. The moss was so thick on the stones it was like green plush.'

The rain was weaker now and there were wounds of starlit sky in the smoking clouds.

'And we could smell the smoke from the fire they had lit by the train. I remember the train making exhausted sounds as we walked past it.'

'And the owls were hooting,' she said.

In the strip of sky above the street he saw a scimitar of moon between the clouds.

Joanne said: 'I think I'll go up now.'

'I'll come with you,' he said.

'No,' she said, 'come up in about ten minutes.'

438

He drank another brandy and felt the excitement expand inside him as it had done the day at the ruins. He lit his pipe but the smoke was ash on his tongue. He found that he was trembling. After eight minutes he went upstairs.

The bedside lamp was on. She was lying in bed and he noticed that her nightdress was still on the chair. She smiled at him hesitantly.

'Hallo,' he said. He stood beside the bed without moving.

'Are you coming to bed then?'

He glanced at his watch.

Joanne said: 'I know it's only nine. Don't make me feel more embarrassed than I am already.'

He began to undo his tie. He could smell her perfume.

She said: 'I expect you're wondering what's happened.'

'Wondering perhaps. Certainly not questioning.'

'It was up in the gallery today,' she said. 'When Bose was giving evidence. I looked down at you and saw you just sitting there kind of trusting him. And I knew how much I loved you.'

'Or felt sorry for me, perhaps.'

She shook her head. 'No, loved you. And knowing that I always have done.' She frowned. 'You don't think I'm too old for this sort of thing, do you?'

He shook his head because he didn't want to speak.

'Not too old and fat and sentimental?'

'I think you're beautiful.'

'Come here then,' she said as he took off the last of his clothes.

'You know,' he said, 'I don't give a damn whether you are feeling sorry for me.'

'I'm not,' she said. 'You're not the sort of person one can ever feel sorry for.'

'Good,' he said, 'because I'm going to win this case.'

'Be quiet,' she said. And as they joined each other he imagined that he could smell the autumn scent of moss.

439

9

DR JOHN COULDRIDGE faced the committee at 10.35 next morning. To his left, just above him, sat the chairman. In front of him the 'jurors' divided in the middle by the lawyers' table. The Press and public gallery was packed because of the publicity the case had already received. Couldridge found that he kept wanting to swallow and that his hands were searching his pockets for the pipe he couldn't smoke. Among the legal papers in front of one of the solicitors was the racing edition of an evening newspaper. The front-page headline said: 'Transplant Doctor Gives Evidence Today'. Beside it was a report about the record ascent of the Russian balloon nine miles into the stratosphere. Couldridge hadn't read any papers that morning: instead he had started to read Willmer's 'Tissue Culture' on the optimistic premise that he would soon be able to implement some of Willmer's research.

The doctors in the well of the chamber regarded him thoughtfully. Wondering, Couldridge imagined, why any doctor should forsake the aseptic seats of medicine in Britain for the buoyant sepsis of India; wondering why he had defected from conventional research for surgical experiment involving ethics and morals. Such men, he thought would have gladly accepted Dieffenbach's view in 1831 that the theory of corneal grafting was an 'audacious phantasy'. The fact that Filatov was successfully taking homografts from the dead would not surprise them: it was the sort of barbarism that they expected from the Russians. Only that year Filatov had stated: 'I can say with perfect assurance that corneas taken from the eye of cadavers, even those which had been conserved for a long time, proved to be just as good as those taken from living persons.' Unorthodox, barbaric—and boastful.

These were the men, Couldridge thought, who had struck Nesfield off the Register. Nesfield who had discovered chlorogen, the man whose principal crime had been versatility. What chance did he stand? He looked at their obedient faces and wondered how big a part jealousy played in their deliberations? In the case of Nesfield, for instance, where the charge seemed of such little consequence beside the achievements.

Couldridge looked up at the galleries and saw Joanne looking down at him. She waved hesitantly with a white-gloved hand. He thought about the previous evening in the hotel and relaxed a little.

Lloyd-Williams stood up and asked him to confirm his name, age and qualifications; his experience and his research and the details of his successful corneal graft. Maitland made cramped notes, occasionally holding the bridge of his sharp nose as if he were wearing pince-nez.

'And now, Dr Couldridge,' Lloyd-Williams said, thumbs in his waistcoat, 'could you please tell the eminent gentlemen of medicine here today exactly what you hoped to achieve by transplanting corneal tissue to this boy's eye?'

'I formed the opinion that he was suffering from interstitial keratitis and I hoped to restore adequate vision to one eye.'

'Could you please describe to members of the committee your techniques from the pre-operative to the post-operative stages.'

Couldridge related the treatment from the first precautions to ensure that there were no pathogenic organisms on the conjunctiva to the last dressing when he realised that the operation had failed.

'In what respect had it failed?'

'The graft had clouded,' Couldridge said.

'Obviously this is one of the complications that ophthalmologists most dread?'

Couldridge said: 'The most common threat to a clear graft is vascularization. But obviously clouding is the complication which surgeons dread most because it really means that the operation has failed.'

Lloyd-Williams paused and perused his brief. 'I believe that clouding can occur despite the most favourable conditions—optimal quality of the tissue, skilful surgery etcetera—and that expert opinion is divided as to the cause of the clouding under such favourable conditions.'

'That is correct.' Couldridge noticed Maitland consulting a medical text book.

'So you don't know the cause of the clouding and therefore you don't know the cause of the failure of the operation?'

'I have no idea,' Couldridge said. He turned towards the chairman. 'I have studied every possibility. I can only place my failure in the category to which Mr Lloyd-Williams has referred —those which occur for no definable reason.'

'Ah.' Lloyd-Williams studied his brief again. 'Am I right in presuming that the only possible cure lies in further kerato-plasty?'

'That is the only possible answer,' Couldridge said.

'Dr Couldridge.' Lloyd-Williams laid down his typescript. 'Have you offered to perform this operation on this unfortunate boy?'

'I have.'

'And has permission been granted?'

'It has not.'

'If such an operation were successful the boy's father would not be in a position to use the condition of his son for political agitation?'

Before Couldridge could reply Maitland was on his feet. 'The question,' he said, 'is both offensive and improper as my learned friend well knows ...'

The Chairman nodded. 'I wholly agree,' he said.

Lloyd-Williams said: 'I apologise and unreservedly withdraw the question.'

But Couldridge knew that the idea had been planted and would grow. Pandit Chet Ram *was* currently using his son's plight for political motives. Therefore it was conceivable that it would further his interests if the boy's eyes were left untreated. Therefore was it not possible that he had faked the whole case against Couldridge for political motives? Couldridge was not sure that he approved of Lloyd-Williams' methods: but they *were* fighting a conspiracy founded on dishonesty.

'Now,' Lloyd-Williams said, 'let us move retrogressively to the operation performed on the dead boy. Or more precisely to the parents' attitude to the role of their son as a donor. Did you personally obtain permission from the parents?'

'I did not.'

'You relied on the word of Pandit Chet Ram by whom the parents were employed?'

'I did. He showed me a document signed by the boys' parents giving me permission to treat their son as a donor.'

'Had the boy himself been consulted?'

'I don't think so—he didn't know he was dying.'

'Can you conceive of any reason why Pandit Chet Ram should now deny the existence of this document signed by the dead boy's parents?'

Couldridge decided that it would reflect unfavourably on him if he suggested political motive. 'I cannot,' he said.

'But you swear that such a document did exist?'

'I swear it.'

'Earlier,' Lloyd-Williams said, 'I asked you what you hoped to achieve from this graft. You answered that you wanted to restore vision in one of the boy's eyes. Am I right, Dr Couldridge, in supposing that there was a wider and more ambitious motive in addition to the immediate curative possibilities?'

Couldridge said: 'If you mean making a contribution towards the progress of medicine then the answer is yes.' He glanced around the intent faces in front of him. 'I believe that it is the calling of most doctors to heal, but it is the calling of a few to experiment. Those who experiment should in no way be disdainful of those who heal: it is merely that they are afflicted with an incurable compulsion. But equally those who are content to heal should in no way resent those compelled to experiment: they should in fact implement the successful experiments. In this way both contribute to the advance of medicine and ultimately perhaps the alleviation of all suffering.'

'And you feel that you were one of those called upon to experiment?'

Couldridge knew that his words sounded pompous and that he might be antagonising the committee. But the desire to explain was strong upon him. 'Yes,' he said, 'I do. In this particular ophthalmic field, I envisage a day when grafting using tissue from dead persons will be an everyday occurrence and sight will be restored to countless numbers of people going blind. As you know gentlemen, I am not alone in this view.'

Lloyd-Williams began to sit down then straightened up again. 'You use the word experiment, Dr Couldridge. You do not, I presume, mean experimentation on a living person? Trial and error as it were?'

'No, sir. The experimental stage precedes the implementation. But there are, of course, instances of failure in any new technique. As in fact there are with proven techniques.'

'Thank you, Dr Couldridge.' Lloyd-Williams sat down.

Maitland stood up holding the notes he had made during Couldridge's evidence-in-chief. 'I shall not keep you long, Dr Couldridge,' he said. 'In fact I have very few questions to put to you. They concern the pertinent issues and not your compulsions however commendable those may have been.' He coughed and sharpened his voice. 'Do you not think that you would have been less vulnerable to a charge of irresponsibility if you had personally sought the permission of the parents to remove tissue from their son's body?'

Couldridge said: 'I realise now that it was foolhardy not to have asked them myself. But my first concern was to treat the living. And, of course, I had no idea at the time that a conspiracy was going to be hatched against me.'

'I see.' The dry voice implied that Maitland did not see at all. 'Did Pandit Chet Ram in fact give you written permission to perform an operation on his son's eye?'

'He did.'

'But that wasn't the document that he produced in your surgery—the document seen by Dr Bose?'

'It was not. I have already testified to that effect.'

'I see.' Maitland paused and stared at his notes. 'Dr Couldridge I am going to suggest to you that this story of Pandit Chet Ram producing a signed authorisation from the parents is a pure fabrication invented when you discovered that the ethics of your conduct were being challenged.'

Couldridge contained his temper. 'No, sir. I saw the authorisation.'

'And that you have perpetuated this story to save your professional skin.'

'No, sir.'

'You maintain that even though there is not a shred of evidence to support your story?'

'Yes, sir.'

'Very well. One last question, Dr Couldridge, on a broader basis. Which do you believe is medically the more important in the public interest—caution or ingenuity?'

'Neither,' Couldridge said. 'They complement each other.' He refrained from adding that he didn't condone caution when it involved the exclusion of all articles on corneal grafts from the literature of British ophthalmology for fifty years.

'Thank you, Dr Couldridge.' He sat down quickly and neatly.

Lloyd-Williams said: 'No further questions.'

Couldridge moved to leave the witness box but the chairman stopped him. 'Dr Couldridge,' he said, 'I have a couple of questions that I should like to ask you.'

Couldridge stepped back into the witness stand.

The chairman leaned forward. 'Dr Couldridge,' he said, 'has it occurred to you that the clouding of the cornea could have been caused by an injury during surgery to the lens? And furthermore that such injury can only occur when instrumentation is not fully controlled?'

445

'It did occur to me, sir.'

'And what conclusion did you reach?'

'I rejected the possibility because the complication caused by injury to the lens is a cataract. This clouding occurred too soon after the operation and in any case it was not a cataract.' Anger spurted briefly. 'But in any case—presuming for one second that I did injure the lens—I doubt if there is one surgeon or one physician present here today who has not at some time or another made a mistake.'

The chairman said: 'And I for my part doubt whether any of us present today would dispute that last observation, Dr Couldridge.' He smiled and the smile was not unkindly. Then he said: 'I am interested, Dr Couldridge, in your philosophy regarding medicine. You referred at one time in your evidence to the ultimate alleviation of all suffering. Do you really believe evolution will culminate in heaven here on earth?'

'There's no harm in hoping so,' Couldridge said.

'One last question, Dr Couldridge. And I should like you to think hard before answering it. Your motives in contributing to the advancement of medicine are very praiseworthy. Is there not perhaps an element of personal ambition in your endeavours?'

All the doubts about his motives broke loose from the past. He looked at the chairman, at the doctors in their spectacles, at the intent and hungry faces in the two galleries. But there was only one answer. 'There is,' he said. 'Few men are without it.'

The chairman nodded. 'I am afraid you are right, Dr Couldridge.'

After Couldridge had left the stand Lloyd-Williams called Ramsey Crockford on subpoena. He tried to force an admission that there had been a political motive in the arraignment of Couldridge. But he failed. And Crockford's evidence about his meeting with Emmerson was too hazy to be of any value.

After a precise and analytical speech by Maitland and some impassioned oratory from Lloyd-Williams the chairman cleared the chamber for the committee's deliberations

On the landing outside Couldridge said: 'What do you think?' His hands were greased with sweat and his head ached.

Lloyd-Williams said: 'You did quite well—except for that remark about every doctor in the room having been guilty of making a mistake at some time or another. They don't like to be reminded about that sort of thing, you know. No one does.'

'Do you think I stand a chance?'

'I think you're home and dry,' Lloyd-Williams said.

Couldridge looked at his watch. It was 12.10 p.m. He shook his head at the reporters who approached him. He went into the washroom, straightened his tie and came out again. He looked at his watch again. It was 12.15.

At 12.20 they were summoned back into the chamber and at 12.23 the chairman announced that John Couldridge had been found guilty of infamous conduct in a professional respect.

At 12.50, after a plea of mitigation from Lloyd-Williams and another recess, the chairman announced that the registrar had been instructed to erase the name of John Couldridge from the Medical Register.

At 12.55 the Disciplinary Committee of the General Medical Council was already hearing evidence against a doctor accused of improperly prescribing drugs in which he had a financial interest.

10

He walked briskly along the crowded pavements. Down Regent Street, across Piccadilly, through Leicester Square, down Charing Cross Road. Walking, without realising it, towards the river.

Beside him walked Joanne. 'Are you going to appeal to the Privy Council?' she said

'No,' he said. 'There wouldn't be any point.'

'But it's so terribly unfair.'

'I know,' he said. He glanced at her and saw that she was crying. He held her up for a moment. 'Don't cry,' he said. 'It will be all right.'

'My love,' she said.

Soon they came to the river, swift and muddy beneath a dead sky. They leaned on the wall of the Embankment and watched the driftwood racing towards the sea.

Joanne said: 'In a little while you can apply for re-instatement.'

'I know,' he said.

'And will you?'

'Perhaps.' And then because of her grief he said: 'Yes, I will. It's only right that I should.'

Behind them, outside Charing Cross Underground Station, a newsboy shouted: 'All the latest—Transplant Doctor Verdict.'

'That was quick,' he said.

He stared at the fast water plucked now with raindrops. He could smell mud and paint and ships. The smell of the Hooghly, the smell of all rivers.

'What are you thinking?' she said.

He turned and smiled at her because she always wanted to know beyond his words. 'I was thinking about a girl who can see because of what I did.' He lit his pipe and flicked the smoking match into the water. 'I don't suppose anyone can stop me studying and experimenting in the clinic and perhaps dispensing castor oil and aspirins in the villages.'

She tried to smile. 'I don't suppose they can,' she said.

'Then let's go back to the hotel and book a passage,' he said.

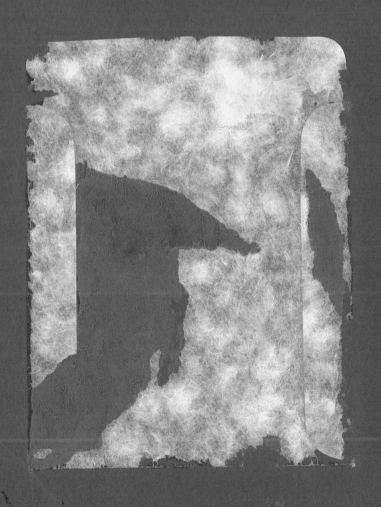